VIOLEN

Duncan Lord has everything to live for — a prestigious college, the prospect of a top government job, an apparently happy marriage. Yet Chester Drum, hired to find out who the professor is sleeping with, penetrates a police cordon just in time to see Lord jump to his death from a fourth-floor ledge in the midst of Homecoming festivities. When Drum is accused of using his knowledge to blackmail the professor, his private investigator's license is revoked. The only way he can get it back is to learn what drove Lord to suicide. Was it an obsession with the call girl Bobby Hayst? Or was there something far more sinister? To find the truth, Drum must dodge a sadistic sheriff, a vengeful fellow professor, and a crooked investigator with the highest Washington connections—all conspiring to make Drum's exit from his line of work a permanent one!

TURN LEFT FOR MURDER

As a teenager on the mean streets of Brooklyn, Norm Fisher had found himself in the wrong place at the wrong time. He'd witnessed a gangland killing. Worse, he'd driven the getaway car for Big Danny Cooper and Buggsy. They wanted him in the gang, but Fisher joined the Army instead. Now he's out, married with one kid and another on the way, and Buggsy wants him back. Buggsy has a particular hit in mind—the special prosecutor for gangbusting!—and he'll do whatever it takes to bring Fisher into it. Big Danny, execution expert for the mob's Brooklyn branch, has plans for Fisher too, and between them they give him no choice. The lives of his wife and child hang in the balance, and no matter which way he turns, the road leads to murder.

STEPHEN MARLOWE BIBLIOGRAPHY

Catch the Brass Ring (1954)
Model for Murder (1955)
Turn Left for Murder (1955)
The Second Longest Night (1955)*
Dead on Arrival (1956)
Mecca for Murder (1956)*
Trouble is My Name (1957)*
Killers are My Meat (1957)*
Murder is My Dish (1957)*
Terror is My Trade (1958)*
Violence is My Business (1958)*
Blonde Bait (1959)
Passport to Peril (1959)
Homicide is My Game (1959)*
Double in Trouble
  [w/Richard Prather] (1959)*
Peril is My Pay (1960)*
Death is My Comrade (1960)*
Danger is My Line (1960)*
Manhunt is My Mission (1961)*
Jeopardy is My Job (1962)*
Francesca (1963)*
Drum Beat—Berlin (1964)*
Drum Beat—Dominique (1965)*
Drum Beat—Madrid (1966)*
The Search for Bruno Heidler (1966)
Drum Beat—Erica (1967)*
Drum Beat—Marianne (1968)*
Come Over, Red Rover (1968)
The Summit (1970)
Colossus (1972)
The Man With No Shadow (1974)
The Cawthorn Journals
  [aka Too Many Chiefs] (1975)
Translation (1976)
The Valkyrie Encounter (1978)
1956 [aka Deborah's Legacy] (1981)
The Memoirs of Christopher
  Columbus (1987)
The Lighthouse at the End
  of the World (1995)

The Death and Life of
  Miguel de Cervantes (1996)
Drum Beat: The Chester Drum
  Casebook (2003)*

  *Chester Drum series

**As Adam Chase
  (with Paul A. Fairman)**
The Golden Ape (1959)

As Andrew Frazer
Find Eileen Hardin—Alive! (1959)
The Fall of Marty Moon (1960)

As Darius John Granger
[various sf stories, 1955-1959]

As Milton Lesser
Earthbound (1952)
The Star Seekers (1953)
Looking Forward [editor] (1953)
Recruit for Andromeda (1959)
Stadium Beyond the Stars (1960)
Spacemen, Go Home (1961)
Secret of the Black Planet (1969)

As Jason Ridgway
West Side Jungle (1958)
Adam's Fall (1960)
People in Glass Houses (1961)
Hardly a Man is Now Alive (1962)
The Treasure of the Cosa Nostra
  (1966)

As S. M. Tenneshaw
[various sf stories, 1948-1957]

As C. H. Thames
Violence is Golden (1956)
Blood of My Brother (1963)

VIOLENCE
is My Business

Turn Left for
MURDER

Two thrillers by
STEPHEN MARLOWE

STARK
HOUSE

Stark House Press • Eureka California

VIOLENCE IS MY BUSINESS / TURN LEFT FOR MURDER

Published by Stark House Press
2200 O Street
Eureka, CA 95501
griffinskye@cox.net
www.starkhousepress.com

ISBN: 1-933586-02-8

Text set in Dante. Heads set in Metamorph and Gill Sans.
Cover design and book layout by Mark Shepard, shepardesign.home.comcast.net

First Stark House Press Edition: February 2006

0 9 8 7 6 5 4 3 2 1

TABLE OF CONTENTS

to
Doris Gwaltney and *Madaline Herlong*
and, as always, for
Ann

STEPHEN MARLOWE ON STEPHEN MARLOWE

I

S ome weeks before bringing out the double volume now in your hands, the publisher of Stark Books e-mailed to ask me to check the accuracy of the bibliography of my work that he'd compiled, to supply an author photo, and to write an introduction.

Only the second of these three seemingly simple tasks was easy for me. Spouses take pictures. Friends do. Sometimes even professional photographers. Or, if all else fails, there are those ID photo booths that make you look like someone trapped in front of a trick mirror at a fun fair.

Writing about yourself and your work is trickier. Should you be modest, self-effacing? Or right out front with the observation, possibly shared by no one, that you are an unsual sort of guy and one hell of a writer? My first inclination was to ask that someone else write the intro.

Then I looked at the bibliography so assiduously and, as far as I could tell, so accurately compiled.

Why only "as far as I could tell"? Because a long time ago, on the eve of my first really extended (we are talking years) sojourn overseas, I left the manuscripts and bound copies of most of my work in my stepmother's attic. And she moved. And the contents of her attic vanished.

So my Marlowe collection consisted mostly of holes until, a quarter of a century later, the Private Eye Writers of America gave me their Life Achievement Award. At Monterey, where the Bouchercon convened that year, word soon got around, in the mysterious way word spreads at a convention, of an honoree who had led a more or less gypsy existence and actually lacked copies of most of his early works. And how wonderfully kind the conventioneers were! Pretty soon I had an almost complete collection for the first time in twenty-five years.

The bibliography reminded me that my career as a writer has so far

spanned—good Lord!—more than half a century and that I've written close
to sixty novels, most of them even under my own name, plus I don't know
how many short stories. I couldn't help thinking: well, it sure beats working.
It reminded me, too, that most though not all of these novels were set abroad
and that most though not all of them were suspense stories in varying
degrees noir.

That bibliography also made me reminisce. It made me ask myself questions I hadn't bothered to ask in years, or maybe ever. Why, for example, was
so much of my work set in foreign locations? Why did I write twenty novels
about a globe-trotting private eye who hung his hat in an F Street office in
Washington when he absolutely had to hang it somewhere, or else in an
office on rue du Rhône in Geneva, Switzerland? Are there such things as real-
life, full-time globe-trotting shamuses? Probably not. But there aren't many
almost constantly peripatetic novelists either. And traveling is not just a way
of life to me, it's lifeblood and mother's milk and—well, why couldn't Chet
Drum feel that way too? And if he really worked at it, as I had, he could—
clients available—build his career around his wandering. It was my job to
keep those clients knocking at his movable door.

I like to travel. I like to wake up mornings in strange beds (with or without
company) in unfamiliar cities in distant countries where I don't speak the language—Serbo-Croatian, Icelandic, Arabic, you name it. There is an excitement in everything you do, all the little routines that make up your day and
your night (leave us not forget the night) in a foreign land. And, if what you
are doing is not routine, if there is a tension in your day, it mounts in direct
proportion to the unfamiliarity of your environment. How do you dial 911
in Katmandu or Kandahar, in Tashkent or Timbucktoo? How, in fact, do you
even spell Timbucktoo? I'm a terrible speller, in any language, having long
since persuaded myself that spelling well reveals a woeful lack of imagina-
tion.

2

It's been said that anyone who's spent too long living outside his own country can't write convincingly about it. But it's also been said that there are
two ways a writer can look at the world—as an insider, or as an outsider. Is
either of these statements right? Neither? Both?

I've spent most of my adult life abroad gathering materials for the novels
I've written and, like my alter ego Chet Drum, can sometimes almost see my
own country with foreign eyes, which is to say, with a sense of wonder.

The sense of wonder—this is not one of those it's-been-said's, this is just
me thinking out loud—is crucial to creativity, at least to my creativity. Take
it away and I wouldn't know how to begin a novel, let alone how to finish it.

(Edgar Allan Poe had the latter problem. Endings were very difficult for him, which may be why he never wrote a full-length novel. Some years ago when I was writing my fictional take on Poe, *The Lighthouse at the End of the World*, I told my wife that endings came very hard to my protagonist. She sighed. She was right to sigh. I did finish the book, but it took me two years and I spent the final six months struggling with the last thirty pages. You see, when writing that book, I *was* Poe, just as, when writing a Chet Drum novel, I *am* Drum.)

The same is true of a stand-alone crime novel like *Turn Left for Murder*. Writing it, as insider *or* outsider, I was the hapless protagonist—"hero," in the sense that Chet Drum is a hero, is too dynamic a word for Norm Fisher, though with his back to the wall he shows a surprising, and I hope commendable, strength.

I wrote *Turn Left for Murder* a year or so before I wrote the first book of the Chet Drum series. I'd hardly begun my expatriate wandering by then, and, give or take a wrong turn in his/my youth, Norm Fisher's world was very much my world. Norm was a recent army veteran who lived in a New York suburb; so was I. Norm was about to become a father; so was I. Norm got into the kind of trouble that could get him, or his wife, or his infant child, killed. There, fortunately, we parted company—but my two-year army stint was enough to show me more than a book's worth of trouble, and *Turn Left for Murder* more or less wrote itself, featuring an ordinary guy confronted by terrifying noirish circumstances when The Mob enters his life to demand its pound of flesh at exactly the wrong time.

Chet Drum got his name during that army stint, by the way, when I spent some time at Camp (now Fort) Drum in Northern New York with the 82nd Airborne—which wound up tailgating what was to have been the biggest drop in history because the ground was frozen so solid that the "jump" had to be made from the rear end of trucks. But that's another story. So is the 82nd's press officer demanding to know if the *New York Times's* longtime expert on all things military, Hanson W. Baldwin, who had flown up to cover the jump, had security clearance. You can put a lot in the novels you write, but you can't put everything.

3

Some experts in the suspense field—Ed Gorman in his splendid blog Ed Gorman & Friends, for example—have maintained that the first few novels of the twenty I wrote about Chet Drum were set Stateside, and that I did not decide to take Chet overseas into the flamboyantly romantic world of, say, Ian Fleming or even the pitilessly noir world of early John LeCarre until after they had achieved their deserved fame. This happens not to be the case.

I'd been overseas a lot since writing *Turn Left for Murder* and would frequently wander the world for many years after that. Chet Drum number 1, *The Second Longest Night*, is partially set in South America. Number 2, *Mecca for Murder*, climaxes in that eponymous city, and Chet went on from there.

Violence Is My Business is unusual in that it's the only book in the Drum series—not counting *Double in Trouble*, which I wrote in collaboration with Richard S. Prather—set entirely in North America, most of it here in the Lower Forty-eight and a few chapters in Canada.

But by then I was seeing my country with, almost, foreign eyes, and I think that's one reason for the tension in the opening chapter. In his introduction to a Chet Drum story in *A Century of Noir*, the fine anthology he compiled with Mickey Spillane, Max Allan Collins had this to say about that I-guess-by-now-famous beginning: "The opening chapter of *Violence Is My Business*... should be force-fed to anybody who is even thinking of writing suspense fiction. It's a masterpiece of atmosphere, plot, and genuine anxiety."

I hope the rest of the novel lives up to the apparent promise of its opening chapter, and I'm please to see it in a double volume with *Turn Left for Murder*, for these novels sprang from different parts of my career and attack suspense in different ways. Noir is where you find it—and who you are when it finds you.

Williamsburg, Virginia
October 2005

VIOLENCE
is My Business
by STEPHEN MARLOWE

CHAPTER ONE

W hen I got there the man hadn't yet made up his mind about jumping. I tried to drive through to where the state police were
unloading big floodlights from a truck, but a burly deputy stood in front of
the car with his hands on his hips. I braked and he came around to stick a red
face in through the window.

"End of the line, Mac," he said. He had peered through the dusk at my District of Columbia plates, not liking them. "You can't park around here. Any
place around here. We got enough trouble with the college crowd."

I took out the photostat of my license and showed it to him. He wasn't
impressed. "Now tell me the guy up there is your client."

I shook my head. "No, but he's involved in a case my agency's on."

"Besides, this ain't D.C."

I pointed to the small print at the bottom of the license, where it says I'm
bonded in Virginia too. Before the deputy could make up his mind about
that, one of the floodlights came on. The crowd buzzed and hummed with
excitement as the beam swung and probed up through the gloomy twilight
of the cold autumn sky.

"There he is!" someone shouted.

"Well, park over there anyhow," the deputy said, waving vaguely toward
the fringe of the crowd. He shouldered his way back from the car. I couldn't
move it now: the crowd had closed in on both sides and behind me. I even
had trouble opening the door and getting out.

Shouldering my way through college boys in tuxedos and girls in evening
gowns, I walked across the wet grass toward the floodlights. One of the boys
brought a hip flask down from his lips, breathed raw whisky in my face and
said: "So let the s.o.b. jump if he's gonna. He flunked me in History 202 last
year."

"Harry, honestly," his date said.

"Chrissake, keep back!" the red-faced deputy bawled as the state police
tried to wheel one of the portable floodlights through the crowd. The light
had not been turned on. Only the one mounted on the truck was lit. I lit a
cigarette and followed the beam up with my eyes to where it pinned the small
dark figure of a man against a wall of red Georgian brick. He stood with his
hands flat, palms backward, against the wall. The ledge which supported his
feet probably wasn't more than a foot wide. He was a good fifteen feet from
the nearest window and four stories from the hard cold autumn ground. He
didn't move. He looked as if he had been impaled by the light. Then suddenly

he turned sideways and took two steps along the ledge away from the lighted window. The light lost him. It swung and probed. A sound half collective
sigh and half collective scream rushed like wind through the crowd.

"There he is."

The light caught him again. This time he was standing in a half crouch.
There was nothing stiff about him up there on the ledge which circled the
top floor of the Social Sciences Building of William of Orange College. From
this distance he seemed relaxed and almost nonchalant. He had been on the
ledge for four hours now, and had learned to ignore the people who pleaded
with him from the lighted window. His two steps had taken him quite close
to another, darkened window. In the dusk, and with the light to one side of
the man on the ledge, you could just make out a face in there.

"Holy smoke, that sheriff," one of the deputies near the floodlight truck
said.

"I hope to hell he knows what he's doing," said a state policeman with
sergeant's stripes on his sleeve. "You scare a guy up there like that, he'll
jump."

"You think maybe he's up there for some fresh air?"

"Sometimes they just go through the motions," the state policeman persisted. "They want sympathy. What I mean, if he sees the sheriff in there,
waiting to grab him, he could be scared into jumping." He looked at me.
"What the hell do *you* want?"

"I'm looking for a private detective named Jerry Trowbridge."

"Yeah? What for?"

"He works for me, Sergeant."

"Hey, Bill! You seen that private dick around?"

"Up front with the captain."

The sergeant jerked a thumb toward the front of the truck. He told the
deputy, "All this and Homecoming Weekend too." He looked up at the flood-
lit ledge sixty feet off the ground. It was now too dark up there to see the
sheriff waiting inside the open window. He was just outside the circle of
light, though, doing the only thing he could, which was wait. If the man on
the ledge decided to take another two steps, there was a chance. Not much
of a chance, but a chance. Then maybe the sheriff could grab him and haul
him inside. Balanced against that slim hope high above us was the long, quick
drop to death.

I went around to the front of the truck. The state police captain was drinking coffee from a cardboard container as he leaned against a fender of the
truck. He was a surprisingly small man with dark eyes punched in under a
beetling brow. He was saying: "All right, it's dark enough. You can set up the
fire net under him."

"He threatened to jump if we didn't take the net away this afternoon, Captain."

"It's dark enough, I said."

"Yes, sir." Several figures drifted off into the darkness with the round canvas fire-net. If you could see it through the gloom from the ledge up there, it would look about the size of a half-dollar. You'd have to be very good to hit it. You could be very bad and still miss it.

"Here I am, Chet," Jerry Trowbridge called.

The captain's grin spread over a tired face. "This bucko belong to you?" he asked.

"I'm Chester Drum of the Drum Agency in Washington. He's the rest of the agency."

Jerry Trowbridge was lounging against the radiator of the truck drinking coffee. He was leaning down and over to one side awkwardly, like a ship taking in water. Then I realized his left wrist was handcuffed to the radiator of the truck. He gave me a sheepish smile.

The captain was still grinning, so I said, "What'd he do, try to steal one of your floodlights?"

"I couldn't spare a man to escort him out of here, so I figured the nippers would at least keep him down on the ground where he belonged. We caught him trying to go up there where the sheriff is."

Jerry's sheepish grin became a cocky one. "Well hell, it was my idea."

"For which we're grateful," the captain said. "But that's what the sheriff gets paid for." You could see he wasn't mad at Jerry, but just doing his job as he saw it. Jerry has that effect on people: he's young, clean-cut and crew-cut, and lounging there in front of the truck with his dark hair and pale face he looked more like one of the college boys than a private detective.

"I'll be a good boy now," Jerry promised.

The captain looked at me. I nodded and winked. The captain unlocked the handcuffs and Jerry set the coffee container down on the hood of the truck, massaged his wrist and lit a cigarette. Then he told me: "The poor slob's been up there better than four hours now."

"Where's Mrs. Lord?"

"They had to take her away. She got hysterical."

"And the daughter?"

Jerry brushed off the left sleeve of his tuxedo jacket. "That's how I happened to be down here. I was taking Laurie to the Homecoming dance. The poor kid, it really rocked her. Mrs. Lord suffers from asthma, though, and they thought she was going to get an attack. So Laurie went away with her."

"They hadn't seen your report on Dr. Lord yet?"

"No, of course not. I put it on tape in the office, Chet, but it hasn't been typed yet. That Laurie's a sweet kid."

"You should have brought the report down. Weren't they expecting it?"

"I know, but Laurie..."

"Okay, it doesn't matter now. And whatever happens, I'll take care of delivering the report. It isn't pretty?"

"No, it isn't. And thanks, Chet. Don't think I'm not grateful. Thanks a lot."

It was completely dark now. The spotlight stabbed up at the night, trapping a small segment of it. Dr. Lord hadn't moved. He stood crouching on the ledge sixty feet off the ground and six inches from death. He had the rapt attention of the crowd gathered on the campus of the college for the big weekend of the year. A lecture audience had never been so intent on him. His studious books had never aroused such interest. Even the work he had done and was doing for the government, hard work and important work, had never brought him the headlines he would get if he moved his feet six inches and took the long fall. I wondered if he was thinking any of that now. You never know what goes through a suicide's mind if he's successful. If he fails they give him drugs so he'll forget.

I felt helpless and frustrated. There was very little I could do. The cops must have felt the same. They had pinned what little hope they had on the unseen figure of the sheriff waiting in a dark window. A man was going to die tonight, a healthy man involved in no accident more fatal than the accident of being who he was and involved in the web of life he had spun around himself. I felt small, lonely and insecure. I recognized the feeling for empathy, something a private detective must avoid unless he wants to take down the shingle and sell real estate or shower curtains. In my mood, the ebb and flow of sound from the crowd was the wail of disembodied spirits urging the man sixty feet above us to jump.

"He's going to jump!" someone cried.

The man up there had moved out of the light again. He took another two steps along the ledge, and that brought him in front of the dark window. The beam of the floodlight followed him.

"God damn it," the captain roared, "cut that light!"

But it was too late. The beam swept slowly across the ledge. The outer edge of the circle of light silhouetted the sheriff suddenly. He was almost in position to reach Dr. Lord with his outstretched arms. He froze that way, leaning out the window. Maybe he said something in a soft soothing voice. He must have made that one last desperate try. We didn't hear him. Dr. Lord stood frozen in his tracks too.

Someone near me coughed. After that there wasn't a sound.

Then the light blinked out.

"Not now, you idiot," the state police captain hissed. "He already saw the sheriff."

The light came on again. For another moment the tableau up there remained unchanged.

Then Dr. Lord took a step. He didn't jump. He didn't have to jump. He simply took one step to get off the ledge.

His body falling was seen tumbling slowly head over heels before the light lost it. Tumbling like that during the few instants of life he had left, he was still Dr. Duncan Hadley Lord, historian, teacher, human being. He missed the fire-net. After that he was only a body—a badly broken body—waiting for the death wagon.

CHAPTER TWO

Once the body came down, there wasn't much to keep the crowd. The state police and sheriff's deputies formed an efficient cordon, the floodlight blinked out and the red Georgian brick facade of the building became part of the darkness. Also, it was a moonless night with a stiff wind blowing the first really cold weather of autumn across the tidewater flats.

"That poor slob," Jerry said, calling Dr. Lord that for the second time as we headed for my car. "Why'd he have to go and kill himself? Isn't there enough trouble in the world without a guy taking his own life?"

We got into the car. Jerry had taken the train down to William of Orange College early this afternoon, so he needed a lift. "Where to?" I said. "You want to go over to the Lord house and stay with Laurie, or are you coming back to D.C.?"

"Maybe I better check in at the inn and see Laurie tomorrow."

I kicked the engine over and put the car in reverse. Before I could get her rolling a voice called: "Hey, you guys! Just a minute." The state police captain came over and said, "I think the sheriff will want a word with you."

I looked at Jerry. Jerry looked at me. I turned off the ignition key and said, "It figures." I didn't say it happily. The captain grunted something and we got out of the car.

The sheriff was waiting in the lobby of the Social Sciences Building. He wasn't alone. He sat in a huddle with three of his deputies, including the one who had halted my car. He looked up.

"This them, Matt?"

The captain nodded. No one asked us to sit down, so we remained standing. The sheriff got up and did some pacing. He had a big, powerful torso and the thick, muscular, slightly bowed legs of a dwarf. He was a bitter-faced man with a perpetual squint in one eye, as if there was some damage to the lid. Failure lines had etched themselves deeply into his face between his nostrils and narrow-lipped mouth. He had a weak chin and a heavy beard which he would have to shave twice a day. He had not shaved twice today. There was a small patch on his chin where no beard grew. He kept scratching at it, when he wasn't rubbing his hands together.

"Christ, Matt," he said suddenly, "who was the joker on the floodlight? I'd of had the doc in another minute if he didn't put the freakin' light on me."

"It was a natural mistake, Sheriff. He was trying to follow Dr. Lord with the light. Those were his orders."

The sheriff chewed on that for a minute, dry-washing his hands. Finally he shrugged and nodded, accepting the fact as irrevocable, but not liking it. "Well, thanks for your help out there today, Matt. I reckon an honest mistake's an honest mistake." In almost the same breath he added: "Now about these two."

He waited, but no one spoke. He said, "You're private dicks? From D.C.?"

I said we were.

"Then what the hell you doing in my territory?"

I showed him my photostat, pointing out the bonded-in-the-state-of-Virginia part.

"What about him?"

"He's licensed in D.C. and bonded to me."

"What did you have on Lord?" He looked up and changed that almost immediately to: "What brought you down here today?"

"I had a date with Laurie Lord," Jerry said.

"Business?"

"Pleasure."

"But you were working on Lord?"

Jerry glanced at me. I said, "You better make that clearer, Sheriff. What does working on him mean?"

"George!" the sheriff barked irritably.

One of the deputies got off a bench and came over. He was the deputy who had stopped my car. "Yes, sir, Sheriff Lonegran?"

"Tell them, George."

The red-faced deputy said, "This guy"—indicating Jerry with a jerk of his thumb—"has been staked out on Dr. Lord three weeks now. If you want the detailed report, I can—"

"Later," Lonegran said.

I muttered, *"Quis custodiat..."*

"What was that?" Lonegran snapped.

"Later," I said. Jerry grinned. The state police captain almost let himself grin. Lonegran scowled and made himself look morose and sleepy. He had a way of doing that. It was supposed to get you off your guard. This time when his head snapped up he said:

"Now you gonna come clean?"

"Dr. Lord was the subject of an investigation conducted by our agency," I admitted.

"Aha! Conducted for who?"

I shook my head.

"I said conducted for who, God damn you."

I got a cigarette out and went through the elaborately slow motions of lighting it. There aren't many law officers left like Lonegran, just as there aren't many private detectives left who make law officers like Lonegran a necessity. But both halves of that statement would have been meaningless to

Lonegran. I said slowly, "I don't have to answer that and I'm not going to answer it."

Instead of barking Lonegran purred, "Why not?"

"For one thing it's against the law. That would be violating a client's confidence. I could lose my license."

"Damn it, Drum, a man's been killed."

"Wrong. He killed himself."

"You're quibbling. I want an answer. I want it now."

He came very close to me. His stunted legs made him look up at me and he didn't like it. Blood darkened his face. He was breathing hard. At first I thought he was going to hit me. I tensed myself, ready to move either way. I think the only thing that stopped him was the presence of the state police captain. Sheriff Lonegran flicked imaginary dust off the shoulder of my jacket with a thick forefinger the way you flick a used cigarette butt away.

"What kind of investigation?" he demanded.

"A private investigation."

This time the captain did smile, and Lonegran saw it. A vein stood out on his low forehead under the uncombed, no-particular-color hair. He balled his right fist. The shoulder dropped. I decided to let him hit me once. A law officer can get away with that much, especially with three of his deputies around to say I started it. But only once. If he did it a second time one of us would wind up on the floor. But all he did was say:

"About your license, Drum. You can forget about that. As of now it's all washed up in this state."

Jerry said, "When they give a county sheriff the power to do that, buddy, I'll start selling life insurance."

It was a pretty good line. Lonegran swung around. "You call me sheriff, Johnny," he said. "You call me sheriff with respect."

"Yes, sir, Sheriff Withrespect," Jerry said.

Lonegran hit him.

He had power in his fists. He swung the right once and didn't swing it very far, but Jerry went down. Lonegran lifted a foot to kick him. I bent, and grabbed the foot, and pulled. Lonegran went forward on his face next to Jerry. They both scrambled up, mad. The state police captain moved between them. Two of the deputies were holding me. If you had blinked your eyes you'd have missed all of it.

"Don't make a fool of yourself, Rog," the captain said quietly.

Lonegran spat, "Don't go telling me how to conduct an investigation in my own territory, Captain Masters."

"Well, hell. You've been trying to tell Drum how to conduct one—in his business."

"Yeah? Drum's business is going to be the State Board's business. I'm bringing his license up for review."

Captain Masters nodded. "Yeah, you can do that, Rog."

"But you don't think I ought to?" Lonegran sneered.

"I wouldn't. Not on what you've got. You don't have a thing."

"Listen, a man's been killed."

"Drum told you. He hasn't been killed. He killed himself. If you had a crime on your hands, and if a grand jury met on it and called it a crime, then you could have Drum's records subpoenaed."

Lonegran looked at his deputies for support. They didn't live where he lived. They didn't belong to his personal world of violence. They were citizens of the county on part-time voluntary duty. They wouldn't meet his eyes. Doggedly he persisted:

"The way I see it, Drum or his man found something on the doc. I don't know what. They figured it was worth more to them telling the doc than giving a report to their client. I call that blackmail. They must have tried it and it must have backfired. You saw what the doc did."

Captain Masters' eyes showed a flicker of interest. He looked at me coldly. I gave it back to him that way and he turned to Lonegran. "You have some proof of this?"

"Hell no, but the doc killed himself and they were snooping on him and they're peepers, ain't they?"

"Ah, for crying out loud, Rog," Captain Masters said in exasperation.

That did something to Lonegran's eyes. It made the good one close like the bad one, the one with the squint. It dug the failure-lines around his mouth in deeper. He finally said, "All right, get out of here. All of you. You too, Matt. Just clear out of here."

I left with Jerry and Captain Masters. Outside it was colder than before, but the stars had come out. An ambulance from the local hospital was just taking Duncan Lord's body away. Only a few of the more morbid college kids were still hanging around. From the other side of the campus you could hear music. The big dance in the college gymnasium had been called off, of course, but that didn't stop some of the local combos from playing at the fraternity lodges.

Captain Masters walked us to our car. "Lonegran will follow through on his hunch, you know," he said.

"I kind of thought he would. And I want to thank you, Captain. He could have given us a rough time in there."

"Well," Masters said slowly, as if it was something he had to say, "maybe you won't believe this, but Lonegran's all right. When he gets riled he's unpredictable, but otherwise he's all right. A good peace officer."

"Then he gets riled too easy."

We got into the car for the second time. "Drop you somewhere, Captain?"

"No thanks. I have my own car. But I wouldn't hang around town if I were you, not tonight anyhow. Give him a chance to cool off."

I looked at Jerry. "Suits me, I guess," he said.

"And one more thing, men," Masters said. "I've known Sheriff Lonegran a long time. I got him mad at me by going out on a limb for you."

"It wasn't a limb, Captain," I said.

"Well, good. Let's make damn sure it wasn't, Drum. Because if it was we'll find out, and if we find out I'm going to take that license of yours and tear it into pieces and make you eat them."

He walked off into the darkness. We drove away without speaking. On the long drive back to Washington, Jerry was moodily silent.

CHAPTER THREE

"Phew, what a business!" Jerry said as he came into the office the next morning. He had a purple welt on the side of his jaw and was carrying the portable tape recorder which was part of our office equipment. "A guy has to be crazy."

"So we're crazy. That the Lord report?"

Jerry nodded, putting the tape recorder down on the desk, opening it and plugging it in. He did it very efficiently, setting up the tape reels and getting the recorder ready for play-back. Jerry did everything efficiently: he had a natural economy of motion and effort, handling himself like an athlete. I was proud of the way he had handled himself yesterday, and had told him so on the way back to Washington. He hadn't answered me. I had respected his mood, and dropped the subject. I thought he'd fallen hard for Laurie Lord.

Jerry Trowbridge was the second try I'd made at a two-man agency. The first, a couple of years ago, had ended tragically in the death of my partner and best friend. But some of my cases took me out of Washington and even out of the country, and that meant shutting the office and throwing business to the competition which prowled along F Street like ambulance chasers, so when Jerry had come to me asking to learn the ropes, I took him on on a salary-and-percentage basis. The Lord affair was his third case in two months. He'd come through the first two with an expertness that astonished me.

Jerry was in his early twenties, ten years younger than I am. His father had been my senior partner during my two-year hitch in the FBI, and had been shot to death in a kidnapping case we'd worked out of the Miami office of the Bureau. I'd lost track of the family for a while, but Jerry had come out of the Army where he'd been assigned to the CID, had propositioned me about a job and had come to work for me.

"What I can't figure," Jerry said, "is why a guy like Duncan Lord, a guy with a responsible position and even moderately famous, a guy with a swell family and who had a top-flight government job, why a guy like that still has to play around."

"Oh, then he was?"

"Sure he was. Married twenty-five years and he probably never looked at another woman. Mrs. Lord is still a handsome female, too. Then all of a sudden, the last few months..."

"Playing the field?"

"Not that I could find. It was one girl, Chet. A classy and expensive call-girl named Bobby Hayst. Anyhow, here's a way it went." He switched on the tape recorder.

To a private detective, it was the most familiar of all sordid stories. Only the cast of characters and a jump into the cold autumn night that ended it made it deviate from the norm. Middle-aging man, pillar of the community type. And a girl young enough to be his daughter, a girl who could put the spring back in his legs and the gleam back in his eyes and the maleness back in his loins to make him think the good years were still ahead of him. The odd part of it was, the good years had still been ahead of Duncan Hadley Lord. He was up for a full professorship and would get it even while taking a leave of absence to work for the government. His latest book, on which his government job was based, was a strong candidate for the Pulitzer Prize. He had called it *The Revolution the Russians Really Fear,* and it outlined the movements toward economic equality on behalf of the common man under the democratic process throughout the western world.

But the book hadn't been important enough to Duncan Hadley Lord. Achievement never is, if somehow you have not learned the difficult art of growing old and accepting it. This Duncan Lord had not learned. His own personal revolution had overshadowed the revolution he had written about, and he had started seeing Bobby Hayst three months ago. His wife had suspected something. She had called me, and because I don't handle potential divorce cases I had turned the job down. The next day I got a call from Professor McQuade, who had taught me the law I'd had to learn down at William of Orange ten years ago in order to qualify for the FBI. An old friend of Mrs. Lord's family and of Dr. Lord himself, Professor McQuade had urged me to take on the job as a personal favor to him. I still wasn't happy about it, but then I remembered the way Professor McQuade had patiently drummed torts and criminal law into my skull. Besides, it had seemed the kind of routine, comparatively safe case Jerry could be weaned on, learning investigative technique as he went along, so in the end I'd taken it on and assigned it to Jerry.

Jerry camped unseen on Lord's doorstep for three weeks. Lord and Bobby Hayst got together once a week, Monday nights. It had been Monday nights because Mrs. Lord was helping in the rehearsal of a college play at William of Orange on Monday nights and usually didn't get home until after one in the morning.

Lord would meet Bobby in Richmond and drive with her to a small farm he owned between Richmond and the college. He wasn't working the farm, but it was a retreat where he could get away and do some writing. A farmer named Fuller was working the land for a percentage of the yield, but he had his own place and didn't live in the Lord farmhouse.

His wife was given the excuse that Lord would work late Monday nights

too, supposedly driving up to Washington to meet the people he'd be working with on the pending U.S. Information Agency job. Sometimes he stayed
overnight. This was because sometimes he'd drive Bobby Hayst back to
Washington, and it was a pretty long run. But they never slept together in
Bobby Hayst's apartment. Jerry didn't even know where the apartment was.
Duncan Lord would drop her off on 16th Street, occasionally having breakfast with her in an all-night place. They did their lovemaking only at the farm,
as if it was part of some obscure cabal they alone understood.

Then yesterday, which had been a Friday, Duncan Hadley Lord killed himself.

Jerry removed the reel of tape and lit a cigarette. "Stinking shame, huh?"
he said.

"Yeah, but it doesn't tell us why Lord jumped."

Jerry frowned. "No, it doesn't. That's true."

"You have an address for Bobby Hayst, or a phone number?"

"No, I wasn't able to get one."

"What about Fuller?"

"What *what* about him, Chet?"

"Nothing, I guess. But something made Lord kill himself. He didn't just
decide he'd been living in sin long enough. It doesn't work that way."

"I see what you mean," Jerry said. For some reason he looked uneasy. I
thought his relationship with Laurie Lord would explain that. "You mean
you want to tag that onto the end of the report?"

"Yes and no. I don't even know if there'll be a report. Have you called Laurie yet?"

"No. Jesus, Chet. I just don't know what to say to her." Jerry did a double-
take. "No report?"

"You figure it out," I explained. "The guy's dead. He can't hurt them now.
Maybe they won't even want to see the report. I'll put it to them, and we'll
see. Did you do any kind of a make on Fuller?"

"No."

"He was at the farm plenty. He could have seen them. He might have asked
for money. Hell, he might even have taken pictures. And maybe we're going
to need that information, Jerry."

"Why?"

"Sheriff Lonegran and the State Board, remember?"

"I thought Lonegran was just foaming at the mouth."

"Maybe. But we've got to protect ourselves if we can. There are two angles
we'll have to follow up—Bobby Hayst and this man Fuller. Because if Lonegran gives us trouble with the State Board it would be nice to be able to tell
them why Lord killed himself. If Lonegran raises a stink, it would be our
word against his, not enough to get the license suspended, maybe, but we

could do without that on the records if ever there's some real trouble. See what I mean?"

He frowned and he saw. "So what do we do?"

"Fuller and the Hayst dame. I'll want to see Bobby Hayst Monday night. I have a little idea on that one. It isn't pretty, but neither is what happened to Lord."

Jerry gave me a look. "Monday night, huh?" He made a face. "Ouch!"

"But let's drive down and pay a visit to Mr. Fuller today. Did you ever buy real estate?"

"Real estate? No."

"As of now, we're in the market. But first I have a phone call to make."

The call was to Ike Wilson, who writes the gossip column for the Washington *Star-Courier*. I'd once done some leg work for him and undercharged him enough so he'd owe me a couple of favors.

"A phone number, Ike," I said.

"Anything but my namesake's private line."

"Call-girl name of Bobby Hayst?"

"Stepping out this weekend?" His voice ogled me. "She's expensive."

"Worth it?"

"So they tell me. The wife doesn't let me sample the merchandise I write about." He gave me the number, I thanked him and he said we'd have to have a drink together sometime soon. Bobby Hayst lived in a first-class apartment hotel near Georgetown.

"Chet, I've been thinking," Jerry said as I hung up. "I really ought to go down and see Laurie. If you could handle that Fuller thing yourself—"

"Sure, kid. We could drive down in the same car, though. Fuller's place is on the way, isn't it? I could take the train back from College Station."

"You leaving right away?"

I said I was.

"Then you better go without me. There are a few things I have to do, but thanks anyway. I'll drive down in my own heap."

Three and a half hours of hard driving got me to Lord's farm on the Tidewater Peninsula. It was a bright and crisply cool autumn afternoon and the smell of drying hay was heavy on the air. It would be the last hay of the season.

The farmhouse itself stood between Route 60 and a dry streambed a few hundred feet off the road. It was a white clapboard building slowly succumbing to the damp tidewater weather. The front porch had caved in and loose roof shingles were like scabs on the weedgrown lawn. A big bird flew up and out of the roof as I poked around the porch.

After a while I tromped through weeds toward the hayfield. The dry weeds rustled underfoot. I could see a man who had been turning the drying hay in the hayfield with a pitchfork. There seemed to be about five acres of it. The man wasn't turning hay now because he had stopped to lean on the handle of his pitchfork and watch me.

I went over there. He was a big, rangy fellow in faded and patched overalls. The overall suspenders covered bare, leathery skin. He was old enough for his pectoral muscles to have gone flabby, but his bare arms looked powerful and his shoulders were immense.

"Hello there," I said. "You Mr. Lord?"

His small eyes took in my city duds and he moved a chaw of tobacco around to his left cheek and spat a thick brown stream. "Nope. He owns the place. I share a crop."

"Mrs. Lord sent me down for a look," I said. "I might be interested in the place."

"To farm hit?"

"Why, sure."

He looked me over suspiciously and spat again. He had a wall of reserve which no one dressed the way I was could breach easily.

I looked at the pitchfork fondly. "How's about a whack at it?" I said. "It's been years."

He almost swallowed his tobacco, then his face got suspicious again. "What fer?"

"Oh, just for old times, I guess. Well?"

"Raised on a farm, was you?"

I didn't answer that one. As a young teenager during the tail end of the Depression I had done some farm work, the kind they would entrust to a kid out of the slums of Baltimore, which was mostly pitching hay.

Wordless, he let the handle of the pitchfork fall in my direction. I caught it, leaned it against my leg, took off my jacket and dropped it on the ground. Then I bent my back and went to work. I didn't stop until sweat poured from my face and drenched my shirt. I had turned several hundred square feet of hay.

He reached into his hip pocket. "Want a chaw?" We were friends.

I declined the tobacco and, still breathing hard, lit a cigarette. "Think I could grow tobacco here?" I asked.

"Yep. Right good tobacco land. If you had the time to watch hit."

"How about the house?"

"Well, you'd need to put some money in. Got her inside plumbing though. Roof's shot. So's the porch. Man don't need a porch, though, if he's got the TV."

"Didn't Mr. Lord use the house at all?" I asked casually.

His smile was as fleeting as a debt collector's. "Oh, I reckon he used it once in a while."

"Recently?"

"Why? What difference it make?"

"Just wondering."

"You say Mrs. Lord sent you? His old lady?"

I knew then that had been a mistake. He wouldn't talk freely to anyone Mrs. Lord had sent, and he seemed to know something.

"Not that I know her," I tried.

"Well, she sent somebody else too. Down to look and see about repairing the roof, he said. Roof, my eye! He was a dee-tective."

"I'll be darned," I said.

He stopped chewing. He said, "Mr. Lord's dead. Kilt hisself."

I just stood there looking at him.

"Using the house. I'll say he was using it. Fer a shack job."

I bent over for my jacket. As I picked it up my billfold fell out. He stooped very quickly and got it, letting it fall open as he did so. He slapped it closed against his palm and thrust it at me.

"So that makes two of you," he said, his voice hurt. "I talk too damn much." He lifted the pitchfork. The sun gleamed on the clean, oiled tines. "Get off of this farm, mister, before I throw you off."

He was still watching me, still holding the pitchfork up and ready, when I got into the car and drove away.

On Sunday afternoon I called Bobby Hayst from my apartment.

"Hello?"

"Miss Hayst? This is Chester Drum. A friend gave me your number."

She had a cool, contralto, no-nonsense voice. "What friend would that be, Mr. Drum?"

"Ike Wilson."

"Ike's nice. A little stuffy, but he tries so hard not to show it. I like him."

"That makes two of us."

"You said your name was Chester Drum. That sounds like a real name."

"Sure it is."

"Thank you, Chester Drum."

"I was hoping I could see you."

"When? I have a date next weekend."

"No. I meant sooner than that."

"Thursday night would be all right."

"It would have to be sooner than that." I waited. She didn't say anything. "Tomorrow night?"

"My, you are in a hurry."

"I meant to call you sooner."

"I'm afraid tomorrow night I'm—sitting up with a sick friend."

Monday is the least likely night for a call-girl to be working. I wondered if that meant she was sentimental, having a last drink to the memory of Duncan Hadley Lord or smoking a quiet cigarette and staring across a table set for two at the ghost of him. It didn't figure with a call girl, but there was something about her voice. Cool and yet vibrantly alive and, somehow, wistful.

"You could always send flowers," I suggested.

Her laughter was throaty and easy. It sounded as if she was a girl who liked to laugh but would not laugh unless she meant it. "No, Chester. I think we'll have to make it some other time. I'm really sorry."

"In honor of my real name?" I said.

She laughed again. "The man won't take no for an answer."

"Not unless I have to. How about it—Bobby?"

"Well, then, we'll make it in honor of your telephone manner. You'd be surprised what you could get to know about a person from how he is on the telephone. What will we do?"

"Dinner at the Ante-Bellum Inn, then a drive down into Virginia. How does it sound?"

"It sounds swell. I guess maybe I will send flowers. Pick me up here at eight, Chester, and we'll have cocktails. All right?"

"Fine," I said. I hung up feeling a little like a heel. But then I thought of Duncan Hadley Lord, and the feeling went away.

CHAPTER FOUR

"Here is your party in College Station, Virginia, sir," the long-distance operator told me late Monday afternoon.

I sat in the swivel chair, looking, across the scarred desktop where I do my doodling, at Jerry. He sat on the other side of the desk leaning forward anxiously, so I jerked my head toward the door of the small inner office that acts like a psychiatrist's couch for some of our clients. Jerry got up and went in there. A moment later I heard a click as he picked up the extension phone.

"Hello?"

"Mrs. Lord? This is the Drum Agency calling. Chet Drum speaking. First of all I want to tell you how sorry we are here over what happened. If there's anything..."

"No. No, of course not, Mr. Drum. And thanks for your sympathy." She got the words out well enough, but her voice was held together with wires.

"Our report is ready, Mrs. Lord, but there isn't any law says we have to deliver it. That's up to you."

"I don't understand."

"If you want, we could destroy the report and return your retainer to you."

"Oh, I see. No, Mr. Drum. No, I don't think so. You see, Duncan... Duncan never left a note. At least none that we've found. In the morning I'm going through the papers in his office with Professor McQuade. As you know, he's a very dear friend of the family. But Duncan always kept such a spartan office, I'm sure we won't find anything. I... I think I'd like to see that report, despite everything. In the morning?"

"You name it."

"How's eleven o'clock in my husband's office?"

"Fine with me," I said. "One more thing, Mrs. Lord. You didn't by any chance let your husband find out you had a detective on him, did you?"

There was a silence, then the phone almost crackled with her anger. "What kind of question is that?"

"All right. Sorry. I'll see you at eleven tomorrow."

When he came back into the room Jerry said, grinning: "Heel." After the grin went away, Jerry looked grumpy.

"Someone has to be. Anyhow, at least we're on record saying we're willing to forget about the report, to destroy it and return the client's money. That ought to sit pretty well with you and Laurie."

It's funny how those things can sometimes jump up and bite you. We were on record all right.

It was raining when I picked Bobby Hayst up that night, a steady black autumn rain with almost no wind and a raw dampness in the air.

The apartment hotel was located on one of the newer streets which end at Rock Creek Parkway before the red brick of Georgetown begins. It was called Potomac Apartments and came equipped with a glassed-in lobby, a planter which tried to reproduce a tropical rain forest in sixty square feet of moist soil and a liveried doorman who announced me on the house phone.

The name on the door was Roberta Hayst. Somehow I had expected it to be Barbara. That was the first surprise about Bobby Hayst, a small, neutral surprise. All the others were king-sized and pleasant.

Bobby Hayst was a pretty blonde in an aqua cocktail dress and a mink shrug the color they call champagne. But that's like saying the Lincoln Memorial is a granite monument to a former president. She had warm smiling eyes which mirrored and were cooled slightly by the color of her dress. Her blonde hair was thick and worn long enough to brush her shoulders. Her lips looked eager for laughter or talk. She had an ingenuously curious way of looking at you, as if you were a gift left at her door Christmas Eve. She wasn't stunning. She wasn't as obvious as a ripe peach with a stem about to break. She didn't have any up-from-under looks or coy smiles. She didn't even have a special way of standing to show the firm upward thrust of her good breasts or the lovely curving line of her slim waist and small round hips. One tiny smile was all she needed, or maybe she didn't even need that. As far as I was concerned she didn't need anything. She had it all. She was beautiful.

I grunted something not very world-shattering and held out my boxed orchid. I followed her inside and closed the door. Don't ask me what that apartment looked like. It was probably very nice, but I never saw it.

She turned around with the orchid and said, "Put it on for me, Chet?"

She stared with frank, eager curiosity at my face while I pinned the orchid on for her. She had a way of staring at you; maybe it was the only gimmick in her bag of tricks. She made you feel, before you'd said ten words, that you were the greatest adventure that had ever dropped out of the blue on her sheltered life. Considering her equipment, it was a pretty good trick. Hell, it might have been necessary. Because half her dates, knowing her profession and then seeing her, would have clubbed her and dragged her by that beautiful yellow hair to the nearest bed.

"There we are," she said, tearing her eyes away from mine and looking down at the orchid. "Like a cocktail?"

I said whisky on the rocks would be fine.

"Jack Daniel's all right?"

"It's the only whisky a real drinker will drink."

That's the way it went. She had my favorite whisky. She drank it on the rocks too, with no delicately reluctant sips and no ladylike oh-this-is-so-strong grimaces. But she didn't open up her throat and pour the Jack Daniel's down either. She drank it as I did: she enjoyed it.

Then she went to the window, scowled out at the rain and put her mink shrug to bed. She wore a sensible dark blue plaid raincoat instead, with a matching round hat that turned her hair to gold. From the hall closet she got one of those big hatboxes a model carries, and we were all set.

We drove through the rain across Francis Scott Key Bridge, the tires whispering, the wipers thumping, then down Mount Vernon Memorial Boulevard along the Potomac and south in Virginia on Route 1. She sat sideways looking at me while I drove. We didn't say much. Once on the outskirts of Alexandria a taxi cut us off and I had to throw the wheel hard to the right. Bobby came against me heavily, her hair brushing my cheek. She squeezed my arm and leaned away again. I don't usually have to pay for an evening's entertainment and I was going to pay for this one, but she was electric. Just her touch like that and my throat felt constricted.

A few minutes later we parked in the big lot behind the Ante-Bellum Inn. The rain was coming down harder, so I grabbed her hand and made a run for it.

The Ante-Bellum is one of those big Georgian places in northern Virginia. Good Southern food, candlelight, a big dancefloor and the kind of music you can dance to without bringing home a case of indigestion. We had more Jack Daniel's, clams, Southern fried chicken with good Orvieto wine in a wicker bottle-jacket, deep-dish apple pie with ice cream, and brandy in our coffee.

After that we danced. They played slow foxtrots and some South American numbers and even a few waltzes. Bobby was the best dancer I'd ever had in my arms, and I told her.

She smiled. "You lead beautifully." The music stopped. "I'm glad you got my number from Ike."

"I'm glad you decided not to sit up with your sick friend."

We went back to the table and had one for the road. The candlelight made her eyes dance. Her hand appeared on the table. I covered it with mine.

"What do you do, Chet?"

"Oh, I'm an investigator."

"Like for an insurance company?"

"Something like that. Smoke?"

We smoked, and I paid the check. Then, because the music had started again, we went to the dancefloor before we went to the check room. There was no space between our bodies this time. Bobby danced warmly and supplely against me. The electricity was there, stronger than ever. At the break in the music, Bobby stepped back and looked at me. Her eyes were funny. They looked warm and eager, but confused. She brushed a wisp of hair back from her forehead.

"Wow," she said softly. Her cheeks were flushed. The couples were drifting off the dancefloor, but we just stood there looking at each other, holding hands.

"Yeah," I said. "Me too."

"We hardly even talked. I'm usually pretty good at idle chatter, honestly. That's part of my line of work, or do you mind me putting it like that."

"No. I don't mind."

She actually blushed. "You do funny things to me, Chester Drum. I haven't felt like this since I was a little girl. Or blushed either, darn it."

"Look who's talking. You socked me right between the eyes, Bobby." That was the truth.

"I guess if I knew why, it wouldn't be there. But it's not supposed to happen. So pardon me if I act all mixed up. You, you big lug, you're *supposed* to get socked between the eyes. They—they tell me I'm pretty good. I wouldn't know right now. I feel like a girl on her first heavy date. Well," she added in a barely audible voice, "are you going to keep me here stuffing your ego with compliments all night?"

"No," I said.

"Is it very far, where you're taking me?"

I didn't say anything right away. Route 1 is lined with first-class motels. Bobby had her hatbox and I had an overnighter. And we felt the way we felt. There's never anything permanent in that kind of feeling, it's too sharp and sudden and all-consuming. There is only one answer to such a feeling—jump in head-first and enjoy it while it lasts. If you don't, then you're one of the pale people, the shadows in doorways with life rushing by, too timid to grab at it, too frightened to leap into it, too cautious even to admit it was there.

A night with Bobby, the way we felt? Or a week, or however long it would last? I thought, why not, we're grownups, we know the score, we'd have no regrets. Besides, get right down to it, that's why Bobby thought she was here.

But then I remembered a man falling through space with his whole life suddenly and irrevocably behind him. And I knew I wanted to know why. I had to know why.

"It's pretty far," I said. "It's a long drive. Come on."

We got our coats and ran out through the rain to my car. On the front seat, Bobby came into my arms. She snuggled there with her head against my chest. I smelled the clean fresh smell of her hair. I lifted her head and kissed her on the mouth. It was a long kiss and a good one, but it completed nothing. It was like a promise.

"Hurry, Chet," she said breathlessly. "Drive fast."

I drove fast. I didn't want to think that she was going to hate me before the night ended.

CHAPTER FIVE

The plan had called for telling Bobby Hayst nothing until we drove off the road to Duncan Lord's farmhouse. But the plan had been made when Bobby Hayst was just a name. Now she sat next to me, her head on my shoulder, her eyes shut, a faint smile on her lips, and I knew I couldn't sock her with it like that.

Once she had opened her eyes drowsily and asked, "Where are we, Chet? It seems we've been driving for ages." It was a question that didn't want an answer. She turned her head, still drowsily, and kissed the side of my neck and mumbled against it, "Hurry up, darn you." That made me feel like cock-of-the-walk, but it also made me feel like Bluebeard, if Bluebeard had a conscience after he'd opened his hotel for women.

"Passing through Richmond," I said. "Be there in about twenty minutes."

She straightened up slowly and I felt the warmth of her body leave my side. She was wide awake suddenly. "That's funny," she said.

"No. It isn't funny."

"I don't understand you, Chet."

We stopped for a light. It was near Main Street, the old center of town before Broad Street had been built out to the new railroad station. It was the last traffic light before we hit the open road again. I didn't say anything until we were moving. I didn't want her to run out on me.

"A farmhouse on Route 60," I said when we were rolling. "On the way to College Station. We're going there."

She let out a little gasp. I felt the seat move under me and knew she had changed her position. She way sitting stiffly against the door now. There was a lot of space between us.

Her voice was very cold and distant, but the worst thing about it was the disappointment, like the voice of a small child whose favorite doll had been snatched away. "Duncan Lord's farmhouse?"

I watched the wipers cutting pie wedges through the rain on the windshield. Neon slipped by, glowing wetly like neon does in the rain. A couple of gas stations, an all-night diner, a custard stand. I cut out to pass a Greyhound bus.

"Yeah, baby," I said. "I'm sorry."

She lit a cigarette and smoked for a while. "Who are you?" she asked finally in a defeated little voice. "I mean, besides the name? It *is* your name?"

"I'm a private detective working for Mrs. Lord."

She laughed. A harsh, ripping sound.

"Bobby," I said. "Bobby, I couldn't know it was going to work out like this for us. Bobby."

"Me," she said. "I've been around. I've been through the mill. I'm supposed to know the score. That's pretty funny. To let a thing like this happen. Oh, brother!"

The neon faded behind us. The dark tidewater flats rushed by. An occasional farmhouse loomed and retreated, the lights in the windows like brooding yellow eyes watching us. I said, "We're almost there."

The harsh laugh again. I hardly recognized Bobby's voice. "Are you going to take notes?" Then a new thought entered her mind. "Have you been here before? You seem to know the way. Did you follow us out here? Did you look through a keyhole, peeper? Or maybe you had one of those infra-red camera gadgets?"

"All I want," I said, "is to find out if Duncan Lord had a reason to kill himself."

Silence.

"If you gave him a reason."

When she moved, she moved fast. Her hand stung my face. "Stop the car. Let me out. I'll hitchhike back. I've done it before. Stop the car."

Five minutes later, we reached Duncan Lord's farm and pulled to a stop in front of the dark house with its caved-in porch and battered roof. There was no real reason to go in there now, but I wanted to go through with it.

I opened the door and stepped out on wet gravel. I started going around the car. Then I heard the door on Bobby's side open and slam. Her high heels kicked up gravel as she ran.

"Hey, you little fool!" I shouted. "It's the middle of the night."

She didn't stop. I ran after her. Over gravel at first, then into mud and the hayfield. She was a dark blur racing through the rain. She could really move, or she was desperate. She'd had about fifty feet on me and I was cutting the gap down only slowly. Then suddenly her dim shape wasn't there ahead of me. I heard a whimper.

I almost fell over her. She'd gone down in the mud and she was curled up, holding her ankle with both hands. When she saw me she tried to get away again, first on hands and knees and then hobbling. I grabbed for her and got her coat, slipping in the mud myself. She ran out of her coat, went on a few steps and stumbled again. This time she went out flat, knocking the wind from her lungs. By the time I draped the coat over her and picked her up, she was drenched. She didn't fight me. I carried her back to the farmhouse.

I used one of the keys on a ring of skeletons I carry to open the front door. I went inside with her in my arms. It was dark, cold and damp in there. I couldn't see anything. I heard rain dripping steadily in through the roof.

"Room on the left," she gritted. "Roof's good in there. Candles."

I took her through a dark archway and bumped a bed with my knees. I set her down and groped back across the room. On a dresser I found three candles stuck in their own melted wax in saucers. I lit two of them and brought one over to the bed. There was a night table and I set the candle down. The room was cold but could be cozy, with the big bed, the dresser and a couple of big old-fashioned rockers. There was a fireplace with dead ashes on the hearth.

"Get out of your clothes," I told Bobby. "You'll be chilled to the bone. Let's have a look at that leg."

"Wood in the next room. For the fire." Her teeth were chattering.

I found the wood and brought back two big split logs and some kindling. In five minutes I had a pretty good fire going. When I turned around, Bobby was just slipping sleekly under the covers. Her clothing was in a pile on the bed beside her. She pulled the covers up to her neck.

"Cold," she said. "Can't get warm."

I was cold myself. I hadn't even taken my trenchcoat off, but it had protected me from the freezing rain. I went over to the bed and scooped her up, covers and all, and carried her over to the fire. I set her down, brought a couple of pillows over and made her comfortable right in front of the blazing fire. Then I lit a cigarette and put it between her lips.

"I wish there was something for you to drink."

"In the dresser."

It was a pint of rum, half full.

"Rum was his favorite," she said, slipping one bare arm out of the blanket and taking the uncapped bottle. Gooseflesh covered her arm. She tilted the bottle and drank. The rum gurgled in the bottle. She had plenty of it.

"What did you mean before?" she said at last.

"Hold your horses. Feeling better?"

"Rum really warms you up. I'm all right now."

"The ankle?"

"I just turned it. It only throbs now."

"Let's have a look, huh?"

She stuck it out of the blanket. Her calf was golden in the firelight and beautifully curved.

"Move it," I said.

She did. She had a trim ankle and apparently it wasn't swollen.

"Comfortable, Bobby?" I asked.

"Umm, and drowsy." Things had happened so fast, she hadn't remembered her anger yet. Then it came back to her. She repeated, in a different tone, "What did you mean before, if I gave Duncan Lord a reason to kill himself?"

"You could have decided to blackmail him."

"Oh, sure," she said with bitter sarcasm. "First I let him make love to me, then blackmail him for committing adultery with a call-girl. That's the way I operate."

"I didn't say so. But it's happened before."

"And especially," she said, as if I hadn't spoken, "with Duncan Lord. I—I've been on weekends with men who could buy and sell college professors—and private detectives—fifty times over with their pocket money. So that's why I decided to blackmail a history teacher who half the time couldn't even scrape together the going rates."

"Stop trying to talk tough. You're not tough and you know it."

"No? I suppose you think I'm lily-white? I suppose now you're going to ask me how I got into this sordid business and I'm going to cry on your shoulder and tell all."

"I don't want you to tell me anything, except about Duncan Lord. That's why we're here."

First she glared at me. Then her eyes filled and she swallowed a couple of times before she said: "There isn't much to tell. I don't know why he thought he—needed me. You never know why. You never bother about it, I guess. I met him at a party in Washington. I'd been invited for the usual reasons. He seemed so out of place among all those wheeler-dealers. Did you know him?"

"No."

"He was so alone and shy. We got to talking. Once I got through his shyness, he was the most interesting man I'd ever met. Intellectually interesting, I mean. He knew so much about so many things. But also in a lot of ways he was like a babe in the woods. You know what I mean?"

I said I knew what she meant.

He took me out of the party and we just went for a drive. He said—blushing and very timidly—that he wanted to see me again. He must have been unhappily married. They usually are. I saw him. I—we were together. Here. Six or maybe seven times in all. It really broke him up when he found out I was a call-girl. He wanted to take me out of all this, he said. That's just the way he put it. Said he'd divorce his wife and marry me if I'd have it. I had to explain the facts of life to him, why it couldn't be done and why he shouldn't break up his home. You know. He said he was in love with me." She paused. "Maybe he was. I guess maybe he was. He was at that dangerous age and he must have been missing something at home. Did you ever meet his wife?"

"No, I never met her."

"I thought you said you were working for her?"

"A guy who works for me saw her. Go on."

"There isn't anything else. I said we'd have to stop seeing each other if he couldn't get that idea of marrying me out of his head. I tried to be frank. I told him I didn't love him."

"How'd he take it?"

"Kind of with a sad smile. Then we were together once more. Then he killed himself." Her hand moved to her lips. Her eyes got round. "I never thought of it like that before," she said softly.

"You mean he killed himself because you said no to his proposal?"

She nodded, and sat up. The blanket fell to her shoulders. Firelight danced on them. "I wouldn't want to think it happened that way. I'm going to tell myself it didn't. But it won't work."

"Forget it, then. You can't do anything to change it now. Assuming it did happen that way. Which it probably didn't." I looked at her beautiful blue eyes. They were full of grief and uncertainty. She'd carry the idea with her a long time, unless I could learn the real reason Duncan Lord had jumped. At the moment it didn't seem like a good bet. I thought of how we worked on each other, like electricity, like magic. And we were almost back where we'd been at the Ante-Bellum. Bobby wasn't sore at me now. I weighed that against the grief in her eyes and I knew I had to make her hate me again.

I said off-handedly, "Hell, you don't think a grown man would kill himself over a—" I stopped dramatically, as if I'd caught myself in a blunder.

Her eyes changed, going darker and narrower. "Well, why don't you say it?" she demanded angrily. "Say what you're thinking. A grown man wouldn't kill himself over a whore. Go ahead and say it."

She stood up and took the pint and finished the rest of it. The blanket looked like a tent on her. She lurched over to the dresser and put the bottle down. "Because that's what I am," she said, her voice thick. "Oh, a fancy name goes with it, and the party trimmings, and weekend trips to the country, and a cockeyed surface respectability." The hatred was turning inward again. The rum wasn't helping any. She was in a mood to hate herself and all at once she was more than a little drunk.

"But strip off all the respectability," she said, "and what have you got? I'll tell you what you've got. Strip off..."

She smiled. Or maybe it was a leer. She was going to show me. She was going to show me, all right. She spun around toward me from the dresser and the smile which I had seen in the mirror had fled her face. Whirling like that, she flung the blanket off.

We stood. I heard the rain on the roof. It was dry in there. She tried out a saucy smile and flaunted her body. For a moment it worked. She saw my face and what she saw on it gave her some satisfaction. She had a glorious body. She made a lewd suggestive movement, digging the knife deeper into both of us. Her breasts were firm inverted tawny cups in the fire's glow. The phony smile drained slowly from her face. My arms moved out toward her. I remember it was suddenly hard to breathe.

"Well, it's what I do," she said in a very small voice. A hurt little defensive voice, because everything had failed now, including her play-acting. "I'm free, white and twenty-one," she said defiantly. Then her voice broke. She came rushing over to me with a little whimper. The fire rose, and then magically was gone. The rain drummed on the roof, and was swallowed. I carried her to the bed and her face swam immensely before my eyes.

"Chet," she whispered. "Chet, be good to me. Please be good to me."

CHAPTER SIX

Tuesday morning I really rolled up the mileage on my car. Bobby's breath blowing in my ear woke me. "Hey, sleepyhead, come on."

I rolled over and unglued my eyelids. She was up and dressed, and looked as fresh as a May morning. She was also shy, and it was no act. We kissed, and she waited in the car while I dressed. Then we drove west on Route 60, taking half an hour at a truckstop for breakfast. We didn't talk much. Bobby said she had to find out what really happened to Duncan Lord. I said I would try to find out and that seemed to satisfy her. We didn't talk about ourselves at all. You always have to start from a little way back the morning after.

I drove her to her apartment hotel through the Washington rush-hour traffic.

"Call me soon, Chet."

"I will."

"I'll come running."

She blew me a kiss and went inside.

Then I drove over to the office on F Street and picked up the typed copy of the Lord case report from the public steno who has an office down the hall. Jerry wasn't in yet. The steno, whose name was Sally, did a lot of work for the lawyers in the building, had been bonded by the Lawyers' Association, and could be trusted. We smoked together and made some small talk, and then I took the report in its crisp manila envelope, went down to the car and drove south out of Washington again....

I reached College Station just before eleven o'clock. It was a crisp fall morning which put color in the faces of the co-eds on the old Georgian campus. Groups of students were gathered during the eleven o'clock class break in front of the Social Sciences Building, still talking about it. In the daylight, it was a red-brick five-story building with a Georgian portico out front. I went inside and up three flights of stairs to the fourth floor. His office was the third door on the left up there. It had been the window of that office he had stepped out of to reach the ledge Friday night. The sign on the door said, Duncan Hadley Lord, Ph.D., Chairman, Department of History. They hadn't scraped Professor Lord's name off the door yet. I heard voices inside. They stopped when I knocked.

"Come in."

There were three of them. The man was an old fellow, straight as a mountain ash, with rimless glasses, a brown herringbone suit and a vest. He'd call it a waistcoat. He had very fine white hair through which his pink scalp showed. He was Professor McQuade, and although I'd spoken to him on the phone I hadn't seen him in ten years. He looked mad.

Both the women wore black. The older one would be Mrs. Lord, tall and leaning toward stoutness, with a stern and still handsome New England face which said she'd probably dominated her husband's life, or tried her best to dominate it. She wasn't wearing any makeup, and neither was her daughter. The daughter was a pale brunette, smaller than her mother, and pretty. She had been crying and was holding it back with difficulty now. If Professor McQuade looked mad, Mrs. Lord looked ready to burst a blood vessel, in her stern New England way.

I got out, "How are you, Professor? I have our agency report on your late husband's activities, Mrs. Lord. I'd still like to say that if you don't—"

That was all I got out. Professor McQuade rushed over in front of me and shook his fist in my face. He was so mad, his lips trembled. "If I were a younger man," he said, his voice unsteady with anger, "I would delight in punching you in the nose. How you have the gall to show up here after what we found I don't understand. In my day—they'd have tarred and feathered you!"

Laurie Lord started to cry. Mrs. Lord stood in front of her husband's desk, not saying anything.

"I taught you law," Professor McQuade said. "Apparently I didn't teach you enough of it. If it's the last thing I do I'm going to see that you pay for this." He was getting control of himself now, though a pulse throbbed in his temple and his lips were still trembling. "Duncan Lord was my best friend!" he shouted. "You good-for-nothing scoundrel, you did everything but push him off that ledge!"

"I did what?" I said. Laurie wailed. The report was forgotten in my hand.

"I ought to punch you in the nose," Professor McQuade repeated, jabbing a bony finger at my chest.

"Look here," I said. "I'm getting a little tired of this. I came to deliver a report. Here it is. If you've got some kind of accusation to make, make it." I held out the report. McQuade didn't take it.

"That was very clever of you," McQuade said bitterly. "Offering to destroy your report. We're going to report that part of it to the authorities too."

Mrs. Lord spoke for the first time. "Harold, please. Perhaps it was the girl."

"It wasn't the girl, I tell you. I know how these private detectives operate. I thought Drum was different. They're slippery fellows, Mary. One foot outside the law every Monday, Wednesday and Friday. He's our man all right. Make no mistake about that."

"Come here, Mr. Drum," Mrs. Lord said. I went over to the desk. McQuade followed after me, mumbling. Mrs. Lord picked up an envelope and thrust it at me. The letterhead bore the name of the government agency which employed Duncan Lord. Inside was a covering letter and several sheets of manifold paper covered with typing. The letter said:

Dear Duncan:

As a followup on our phone conversation yesterday, herewith is an extract of the report the agency received. I can only reiterate that I hope the report is a complete fabrication. If it is not, I am sure you can see the embarrassing position in which this places us.

Unless you can refute the report with documented evidence as to your whereabouts on the evenings indicated, we will be unable to reveal the source of this material. However, we can say that it is a source which is usually as reliable as it is infuriating. The writer of the report, with whose views this agency is not in sympathy, would like nothing better than to dictate policy to us. The demand is presented with more subtlety than I have indicated, but morally it is only a shade above blackmail. If the writer of the report were allowed to dictate policy to us, knowing his background, I can safely say that the whole purpose and function of the agency would be undermined. Yet if we refused—assuming the enclosed report is accurate—the writer would be in a position to smear us and possibly have our appropriations cut out from under us. I don't have to tell you that moral indignation in Washington, when stirred, can be a pretty damning thing. Nor do I have to tell you that our current program, so vital to the interests of this country, is based in large measure on your book and your ideas.

I hope and pray you will be able to refute these allegations categorically.

The letter was signed by the chief of the United States Information Agency.

I read through the sheets of manifold paper, and felt my jaw hanging. The facts were incredibly accurate. They even had the location of Lord's farm, and the dates of his meetings with Bobby Hayst jibed perfectly with Jerry's own report.

"Let me get this straight," I said, putting the papers in the envelope and the envelope on the desk. "You found this on Professor Lord's desk? You think I supplied the information?"

"We found it right there where you just put it," Mrs. Lord said. "It must have been there Friday. He must have read it and put it there. As you know, he took his life Friday night. You and your man Trowbridge had access to that information. You were gathering it. You—"

"Jerry had nothing to do with it!" Laurie Lord wailed.

"Please, my dear, keep out of this. Well, Mr. Drum? Can you deny it?" Her composure was amazing. "In my heart, Mr. Drum, I have already forgiven my husband his sins. He was an extremely talented man. A genius, almost. I know God will forgive him too. Like all extremely talented men, he had a flaw. It is the penalty they pay for their genius. In so many ways he was like a little boy. A bewildered little boy. Well, can you deny it?"

Before I could answer, Professor McQuade said, "There are laws in this state. The violation of a client's confidence by a private detective is a crime. You'll pay, Drum. I'll see that you pay!"

"Because if you and your man Trowbridge didn't do it, Mr. Drum, then the girl did. And in her profession that doesn't make sense. Does it?" Mrs. Lord paused only long enough to take a breath. "How much did they pay you, Mr. Drum, for my husband's life?"

I picked up the envelope again and looked at it. Like a leopard, it hadn't changed its spots. Laurie Lord came over to me. She said through her tears, "Please, Mr. Drum. I beg you. If you... if you did this terrible thing, admit it. But don't let them drag Jerry into it too. Because Jerry never..." She was crying so much, she couldn't go on.

Jerry, or Bobby Hayst? It had to be one of them. Except for the dead man, only one of them could have given the as-yet-unidentified informant all the information he had. A weary voice, beyond cynicism, beyond disillusionment, said: "If you haven't reported this to the police, don't. I want to get to the bottom of this myself. But if they get the wrong kind of publicity—if they get any kind of publicity—the agency will clam up. And if the cops see this the way you did, they won't give me the chance to dig into it." The voice was my own; I hardly recognized it.

Mrs. Lord didn't answer me. McQuade shouted, "How dare you make such a proposition, after what you did! The only reason we haven't notified the authorities yet is because Mrs. Lord insisted we give you a chance to explain. Apparently you're not even going to try."

"There's nothing to explain. I didn't do it. But that doesn't matter. You already have me tried and convicted."

"I'm calling the police right now," McQuade said. "And I'm placing you under citizen's arrest until they get here."

He picked up the phone on the desk. He was shaking again. I took a step toward the door. He dropped the phone and ran across the room, barring the door with his frail back.

"You're under arrest! You're under citizen's arrest!"

I looked at him. "Don't be a fool," I said. "You'd need a cannon."

He got out of the way. As I opened the door he was at the phone again, asking for the police.

I stayed in College Station long enough to make a phone call of my own from a pay booth, long distance to Washington.

"Hello?"

"Jerry, this is Chet. We're in trouble."

"Wha—"

"Don't talk, just listen. Close up the office. Don't go back to your apartment. Meet me—make it Hamling's Bar and Grill on Sixteenth Street. I ought to be there in three hours on the nose."

"But what—"

I hung up.

I gave the car a workout on the way north. The manila envelope was on the seat beside me. Jerry, who had compiled it? Or Bobby, who had lived it?

A state cop stopped me for speeding on Route 60. I showed him my buzzer, and for once it worked.

CHAPTER SEVEN

That early in the day, the smell of hamburgers grilling still dominated the smell of beer in Hamling's Bar and Grill. It was a small place on 16th Street a few blocks north of the White House and Lafayette Park and not far from our office on F Street. There was a long bar in front where a couple of lushes were getting an early start and arguing about the Washington Redskins, three of those bowling machines opposite the bar and eight or ten booths in back.

"Hey, Chet. We're back here."

I saw Jerry half stand up in one of the rear booths. I went back there. Another man sat across the table from Jerry, nursing a beer.

"Boy, you can scare the life out of a guy. Trouble, the man says. What kind of trouble?"

"I have to see you alone, Jerry." I was annoyed that Jerry had company.

"Wait a minute, Chet. I want you to meet Ernie Dygert."

The man seated across from Jerry craned his neck to look at me and show me a slow, lazy smile. He had thick, dark hair that came down in a very low hairline, heavy brows on a thick ridge of bone, eyes so deep-set that you only saw the socket shadows in the dim light, a wide nose that had been broken and heavy, sensuous lips. His head was huge. If the rest of him matched it, he would be an enormous man.

"Maybe I can name your trouble, Drum," he said. "Sit down. Sit over there next to your boy."

"Your reputation came in with you, Dygert," I told him. "Take it and get out of here."

Dygert's lazy smile stayed put. Jerry smiled up at me nervously. "Hold your horses," Jerry said uneasily. "Give Ernie a chance to talk, will you, please?"

"No," Dygert said. "I want to hear all about my reputation."

"That's easy. I can give it to you in one word. We're in the same business. You make the business stink, Dygert."

Dygert laughed. The sound was deep in his throat. "I netted a hundred grand last year, big shot. Enough to buy and sell you how many times?"

"Remind me to tell the IRS. Now get lost."

Dygert made circles with the bottom of his beer glass on the table. Jerry lit a cigarette, took two anxious drags and crushed it out. Dygert asked me: "If I named your trouble?"

"Name it."

He laughed again. "I can give it to you in one word too, big shot. Lord."

Jerry must have seen my eyes. "No, wait a minute, Chet. You got it all wrong."

Maybe I did have it all wrong. Maybe this just wasn't my day. I made a move toward Dygert, then stopped. I thought about his reputation. He had made the wire services regularly and *Time* magazine two or three times. He had retired under fire from the D.C. police force, where he'd been number-two man on the vice squad, to set up his own detective agency. That had been less than two years ago. Since then he'd had his fat finger in every dirty pie that the Potomac fog couldn't hide. He used wiretaps and he used infra-red cameras, he used telephoto lenses and cops living off the badge, he used second-rate politicians riding the brittle bright trail to nowhere and he used Washington's morbid fear of the wrong kind of publicity. With all of it he had made a mint of money and the law had not wanted to or had not been able to touch him.

"My rep ain't the only thing that came in with me," he said. "One of my ops came in, too. Nice young guy name of Trowbridge? You see, one of my clients, that pays a thirty-grand retainer for a year's work, has an expense account waiting for smart young cookies like Jerry here. I'll give it to you straight, Drum, so we can stop beating around the bush. Some of that folding green can be yours too if you say the word."

Jerry wouldn't meet my eyes. Up front someone ordered two hamburgers all the way. A kid slammed a loud strike down the miniature alley of one of the bowling machines. I said, because at the moment I had nothing else to say, "You little punk, you told me you came straight out of the Army."

"Leaving out six weeks I worked for Ernie first. Christ, Chet. My old man gave the Bureau fifteen years and got shot to death in an alley behind a Miami luxury hotel he couldn't have afforded a weekend in. When my time comes I don't want to go like that."

"You're working for Dygert?"

"He already told you."

"Spell it out for me, kid."

"I'll spell it out for you," Dygert said. "This country's full of bleeding-heart internationalists who'd turn us into a second-rate power if they had the chance. My client's willing to spend money to stop them. And where I come in is to smear them if smearing them's the only way. There's room for you, Drum, and you get an expense account that would choke a Congressman. This here Lord guy is small-time, but he's a start. Well?"

Eagerly Jerry explained, "It's a chance to make money and do a patriotic service at the same time, don't you see? Ernie says the way to get off the hook on his thing is to set up a phony breaking-and-entering deal in our office. You know, to make it look like the Lord file was stolen? Then—"

"They'll rake you over the coals," Dygert went on for him. "That's where the expense account comes in. We can buy your way out of it, Drum. Then, from now on, you do your digging straight. No clients to squawk, get it?"

I asked Jerry, "Why don't you tell Laurie Lord all about it?"

"That's different, Chet. You don't understand. You don't want to understand. Don't you think it rocked me too when Mr. Lord killed himself? Don't you think I tried to stop him? Besides, no one asked him to take up with that little whore of his." He shook his head, as if I was the young kid who needed straightening out. Then he smiled and asked, "Say, how'd you make out with her, anyway?"

Dygert leered. "Man, I'd like to do some research in that myself. Well, is it a deal, Drum?"

"I'll tell you," I said. He leaned toward me expectantly, one big leg out from under the table. I picked up his half full glass of beer and threw its contents in his face.

He got up, yelling. I heard a funny kind of low growl, an animal sound. It came from my own throat. There are times when the world crowds you and the only release is violence. This was one of those times. I wanted to hurt Ernie Dygert. I had that, and I had my fists, and everything else went away.

He was a big man, bigger than I am, and I pack a hundred and ninety pounds. We squared off and he hit me. It jolted me, but I didn't feel any pain. He might have beat me, but he couldn't have hurt me with a sledge hammer. He hit me again and when I didn't go down it began to worry him. I hooked my left at his face. His right whistled past my ear and we went into a clinch. I pushed him away. We glared at each other and stood two feet apart, slugging. That didn't last long. He went over backward on the table. I stood there for a second breathing through my mouth, then dove after him. The table collapsed under our weight. We didn't try to wrestle on the floor. We got up breathing raggedly through our mouths, and started slugging again.

They would remember that fight in Hamling's. It almost wrecked the place. He drove me toward the front and the bar cleared like magic. For a moment another face intruded on our private world of violence. Next to the face was a sawed-off bat, and it swung. That was the barman. He didn't hit anything. One of us hit him and we were alone again.

Then Dygert had the jagged neck of a broken bottle in his hand. I don't know how he got it. I don't know how I took it away from him, but I did. I threw it away because I wanted to use my fists. We slugged again. I remember picking myself off the floor; I don't remember falling. Then Dygert went down and when he got up he got up slowly. I hit him again. My arms were too heavy to hold up but he didn't counterpunch. I swung slow soggy-sounding blows at his face. Pretty soon I was swinging at air. I leaned against the bar. No one touched me. No one was there for me to hit, not even Jerry. I wanted to hit him too. Everything was blurry.

"That's your answer, you son of a bitch," I said. But by then I was talking to a uniformed cop.

CHAPTER EIGHT

"Maybe we ought to put some novocaine in that before sewing it up, son," the police doctor said.

He was a garrulous old man with small, pink, steady hands, and it probably made no difference to him whether he was sewing up the latest candidate for the police medal or a sex fiend. He plucked at my eyebrow with those small pink fingers, then slipped the novocaine needle in. After that the brow felt like leather, and he put six stitches in it with thick black thread and a curved needle.

Detective Lieutenant Danny Kubisek squirmed his big rump on the edge of his desk and growled, "No charges, Mr. Hamling? You're sure?"

Hamling was a short fat fellow with very little hair. "Naa, no charges, Lootenant. The big guy already give me a check to cover the damages. I won't make a complaint."

Kubisek nodded, neither liking nor disliking it, but probably glad he wouldn't have to appear in court on his own time when the case came up. He could have slapped us with disturbing the peace, but they don't usually when no charges are pressed and what happened happened indoors. He'd sat on the edge of his desk while the old police doctor cleaned us, sewed us and made small talk. During that time I'd begun to ache in places I hadn't know I'd been hit. I felt a little sick to my stomach and wished I could go home for some sleep.

If it was any consolation, Ernie Dygert looked worse than I did, with bruises and contusions all over his face. But that didn't change Dygert and his plans, and it didn't change Jerry and what Jerry had done.

After the doctor went out Kubisek said, "You ought to have more sense than that, Drum."

I didn't say anything. I'd known Lieutenant Danny Kubisek on and off for years. In my business it's not smart giving any cop anywhere a reason to chew you out.

"Well," he said wearily, "I guess all of you can beat it."

Hamling went out first while Dygert and I got dressed. Then I went outside with Jerry and Dygert. The desk sergeant didn't even look up at us.

"They're going to run you guys in," Dygert predicted while we waited for a cab on the street. "Don't forget it and don't try to run away from it. Get it over with. Remember, breaking and entering. Stick to that story and you'll be all right." His face looked puffy and swollen in the glow of light when he lit a cigarette. It was almost dark out. "Listen, Drum," he said. "Okay, you made a mistake. I'm willing to give you a break, and we can still be in business the way I spelled it out for you this afternoon. What do you say?"

Instead of answering, I went to the curb and hailed a cab. But it had a passenger and went cruising by.

"Well, Christ, man, you did a damn stupid thing in there this afternoon. You know that, don't you? I said I was willing to give you a break and forget it. Why don't you give me a break and climb on board?"

"I wouldn't give you a bent match to pick your teeth with," I said.

Jerry looked unhappy. He put a hand on my shoulder and said, "I thought I was setting it up for you, Chet. I thought you'd really go for it."

"Get your hand off me. We're through, Jerry. Go clean your stuff out of the office and beat it. I don't want to look at you."

I started to walk away from them and bumped into a man coming the other way in the steady flow of rush-hour pedestrians. "Why don't you look where—" he started to say. Then he saw my face, shut up and hurried on. When I looked back, Jerry and Dygert were getting into a cab.

I walked three blocks, found a cab for myself and got driven home.

They were waiting for me in the lobby of the apartment house where I live, which is not far from the Uline Ice Arena. One of them wore the uniform of the Virginia State Police, a trim man with dark eyes punched in under a beetling brow. The other was a big fellow in mufti. I had never seen him before.

"Don't bother ringing for the elevator, Drum," the Virginia trooper said. "You're not going up."

"All right, Captain Masters," I said.

The big fellow came over and showed me his buzzer. "Lieutenant Malawister of D.C. Special Forces," he introduced himself. He looked tough and competent, with jug-handle ears, a gaunt face and small steady eyes so dark brown they almost looked black. "They want to ask you a few questions down in Prince Charles County. You'll go?"

I shrugged, and Malawister looked relieved. Captain Masters said, "Then I guess you don't have to drive down with us, Del."

"No, I'll go. The fresh air will do me good."

Captain Masters stared at me. "Fresh air, the man says. Well, come on, Drum."

We went outside with them flanking me. The state police car was parked around the block. No one said anything until we were inside. A uniformed driver sighed when we climbed in and shoved a science-fiction magazine over the sun visor. I had caught a glimpse of its cover, which showed a bug-eyed monster about to ravish a girl with incredible mammalian development, and smiled.

"You think it's funny?" Masters said. "I warned you last Friday, Drum. I made a fool of myself with Sheriff Lonegran because of you. I warned you."

"If you're that mad," I said, "a law professor named McQuade must have called you."

Masters shoved me to the far end of the rear seat. Lieutenant Malawister went in front with the science-fiction fan. "Dr. McQuade called Sheriff Lonegran," Masters said. "Now sit still over there. I don't want to hear the sound of your voice."

We drove like part of a funeral procession across the Memorial Bridge and down Washington Boulevard to Shirley Memorial Highway in Virginia. I wondered if they had picked up Jerry too. It was after ten when we reached College Station.

Sheriff Lonegran was waiting with his morose and sleepy look outside the sheriff's office when we arrived. It was a red brick colonial building in the pattern set by William of Orange College, two stories, with bars on the windows of the second floor. Lonegran and Malawister were introduced and shook hands, but Lonegran couldn't get his eyes off me.

"He put up a fight?"

"Came like a lamb, Sheriff," Malawister said.

"Look at his face."

"He walked in on us with a face like that."

Lonegran nodded, still looking sleepy, still looking morose. It was only when his face changed that you had to worry. His face changed suddenly, one eye opening wide and the other remaining in its perpetual squint. He said, "You want a receipt for the merchandise, Lieutenant?"

"I just want a bus ticket back home, Sheriff."

Lonegran scrawled a note and gave it to him. "Show this to Charlie Roy over at the bus depot, all right?"

Malawister said it was all right, shook hands all around but not with me, and left.

"How's about a cup of coffee, Matt?" Lonegran said.

"Thanks, no. Pinky probably wants to call it a night. So do I."

"Well, thanks for picking him up for me. Man, look at that face, will you? Wouldn't surprise me if he was bruised all over like that."

Masters shrugged.

"No, Matt. I want you to take a good look."

Masters' eyes narrowed, but he looked me over.

"Fists?" Lonegran said.

"Would be my guess, Rog."

"And you had a good look? A real good look?"

For a moment I thought Masters would be annoyed, but then he smiled and said, "Heck, Rog, I could draw a map of his mug."

"Well, I just wouldn't want anyone saying I did anything like that to the overnight guests over here."

"I won't forget how he looked all chewed up, Rog."

"Well, see you."

"Night."

Masters went back to the car, and it drove off.

It was suddenly very quiet outside the sheriff's office. I could smell wood smoke. Far off, a dog yapped. Lonegran's bark almost matched it. "Inside, you!" Then he looked morose and sleepy again. I turned and took a step toward the open doorway. Lonegran shoved me so hard I stumbled over the doorstep. He came in behind me and shut the door. We stood in a wide room with a railing partitioning off three desks on the left side, a corridor and a staircase straight ahead and a locked rifle rack with a dozen greased and polished Winchesters on the righthand wall.

Lonegran leaned against the railing, his barrel-chested, wide-shouldered torso looking huge and his sawed-off slightly bowed legs looking almost withered.

"How much trouble you think you got?" he asked.

"You tell me, Sheriff."

"Don't get snotty."

"I don't know how much trouble."

"That how you're gonna answer all my questions? You don't know?"

That one I didn't answer at all. Lonegran's questions were tough, but he still appeared morose and sleepy. He wanted me to rile him.

"Who beat the crap out of you?"

I didn't answer that one either. If I told the truth, a fight between me and Dygert might make things look bad for Jerry. I had already decided, more or less, to let Dygert and Jerry deal the cards. I owed that much to Jerry Trowbridge, Sr. Because I'd been with him that night in Miami, and one of us had had to lead the way into that alley. Trowbridge was my senior partner, and he'd gone in first. They had been waiting in the dark shadows near the alley's entrance. They let him go in about five yards before shooting him in the back. A half hour later, with the help of the local police, I'd flushed them out. But that hadn't helped the dead man.

"I said, who beat the crap out of you?"

"I cut myself shaving, Sheriff."

He moved fast, even faster than he had when he knocked Jerry down in the lobby of the Social Sciences Building of William of Orange College. He came off the railing and clubbed the side of my neck with his fist. It felt as hard as a rifle stock. I gagged, took two steps back and didn't quite fall down.

"It looks like you hurt your neck, too," he said. Then he raised his voice. "Hey there, George! Look what the cat dragged in."

I heard footsteps coming along the corridor. I had thought we were alone in the building. The red-faced deputy came into the front room, looked at my face and grimaced.

"Hell's bells, George, I didn't do it. Ask him. Better yet, look at his eye. He's got stitches over his eye. Could I of put them there?"

George admitted the impossibility of that.

"We're going in back, George, where it's nice and quiet. You hold down the fort up front here?"

"Why, sure," George said.

Sheriff Lonegran marched me down the corridor. He didn't have a gun and he didn't need one. All he had, and all he needed, was the law of the state of Virginia on his side.

CHAPTER NINE

We went down the corridor to a small room in back. It was empty except for a pair of surplus army filing cabinets, a pair of surplus army cots and a small sink in one corner. The single small window was barred. Crickets chirped outside.

"Sit," Lonegran ordered.

I sat on one of the cots. The canvas sagged under me. "Now spill it, Drum. All of it."

Lonegran stood over me, leaning forward at the waist. He had a faint smell of sweat and white salt marks crusted his khaki shirt at the armpits. His droopy lids made him look sleepy and morose. I was used to that by now. It meant trouble.

"Why?" I said. "The State Board'll ask me the same questions you ask—with a steno taking down my answers."

"The hell with that crap," he shouted. "I'm through taking that kind of crap from you. I took it all I'm going to. You killed a man, Drum. Maybe there isn't any law going to say you did, but as far as I'm concerned you killed a man in my territory and you belong to me tonight. Now talk."

There are Sheriff Lonegrans in all the countries of the world, just as there have been Sheriff Lonegrans in all the ages of history. Captain Masters had him pegged pretty well—a good peace officer, but he got riled too easily. A frontier needed his type, but civilization crowded him. When he got riled, his own personal code of ethics pushed the law from his mind. Hell, I thought with a faint wry grin, maybe he'd have made a crackerjack private eye.

The grin was a mistake. He wiped it off my face with a back-handed swipe that almost knocked me off the cot.

My vision jerked and blurred and I took a long time focusing on him. He didn't seem to have moved. The way I felt, with a power shovel I might move him an inch or two. But I had to grip the wood sticks of the cot hard through the canvas to keep from jumping him.

"Maybe I been too vague," he said. "Somebody paid you for that dossier on Dr. Lord. Who would that be?"

There wasn't any answer I could give him. If I told him the truth, that Mrs. Lord had been the only one to pay me, he would probably swing on me again, and if he did, he'd have a fight on his hands. Whether he won or lost, he could call the fight any way he wanted to. I sat with my lips tight and the whole left side of my face numb.

"I asked you, Drum."

No answer wasn't any better than the only answer I could give him. He got hold of the lapels of my jacket and jerked me to my feet. "Let me tell you where it's your tough luck to be standing," he said from a distance of half a foot. "In the morning they're gonna underplay their hand. There ain't nobody gonna want publicity on this thing. But that's the morning. Until the morning, you're my boy. If I can get a name out of you before they send a subpoena for you, then all the politicians in Washington won't be able to make them sit on this. I aim to get that name. Now, who was it paid you?"

I brought my hands up fast and broke his arms away from my jacket. He went back a step and swung on me, but he was off balance. I caught his arm and turned the wrist out from his body and then back. He found himself on the wrong end of a hammerlock. When I bent his wrist up between his shoulder blades he stomped down with his heel on my instep. He'd let himself in for a sucker play, but so had I. He jerked free, almost breaking his arm. I could barely stand on my right foot

He spun around and glared at me.

Then we both heard a car pulling up outside. The car door slammed, and a couple of seconds later there were footsteps in the corridor outside. Someone knocked at the door.

"Rog, it's Matt. Open up, will you?"

Lonegran swore under his breath, but opened the door. Captain Masters came in, looked us both over and grinned ruefully. "I guess I got back just in time," he said.

Lonegran was angry and didn't try to hide it. "Until they get around to serving papers, he comes under my jurisdiction, Matt."

"No he doesn't."

"Says who?"

Captain Masters took off his visored cap and ran a hand through wavy black hair. "The state attorney general, Rog. That's the way it goes."

"But Christ, be reasonable. Sure, I figure them to pull that kind of crap in the morning. Don't tell me you're gonna jump the gun for them?"

Masters shook his head. "It came over on short wave while we were driving back. They want Drum in Richmond, Rog. Not here. They're afraid of what might happen here."

"All they want to do is sit on it," Lonegran groaned.

"Don't I know it."

"What you gonna do?"

"Take him to Richmond with me. I've got to, Rog. Those are my orders. If I don't, you know what kind of stink it will raise."

"Then what'll they give him? A nice polite hearing?"

Masters nodded. "Hearing's the day after tomorrow."

"What the hell kind of hearing will it be, tell me that."

"I told Drum once we'd make him eat his license. That still goes."

"But a civil charge," Lonegran complained. "They're gonna sit on it, that's all they'll stick him with. You tell me, is it justice?"

"It's politics."

"Politics." Lonegran threw his hands up in a wide, helpless gesture. Then the three of us went out through the corridor to the large front room of the building. George was sitting at one of the desks with his feet up and a thick cigar stuck in his red face.

"No hard feelings, Rog?" Masters asked.

"Hell, it ain't your fault. But before you go I got something I want to say to Drum. All right?"

Masters had no objections.

"If they did it my way, Drum, they could of got you on a criminal charge. But up there in Richmond they got politics on the brain. So I tell you what," Lonegran said, looking more sleepy and more morose than I had ever seen him. "You go up there and get your license lifted and your goddamn wrist slapped. Then come back down here to Prince Charles County. Come back down here for any reason at all. I'll get you for parking on the wrong side of the street and I'll get you for spitting on the sidewalk and I'll get you for breathing out of the wrong side of your nose and then I'll take you in back where we were just getting warmed up and before I'm through I'll get you for resisting arrest and I'll have you put away for so long you'll grow a beard down to your toenails. That's all, Matt. You can take him now. He's your prisoner."

Masters turned toward the door. George swung his feet off the desk and stood up. I caught a movement out of the corner of my eye and stared to turn, but I wasn't quick enough.

Lonegran rabbit-punched me just under the left ear, and I fell forward against the door and then down.

"I guess he kind of tripped," Lonegran said.

"A guy ought to watch where he walks," George chimed in.

I got up with the taste of bile in my mouth. Blank-faced, Captain Masters looked me over and jerked a thumb toward the car waiting outside. I lurched out there, dragging lead shoes. Masters and I got into the back of the car.

"You come back," Lonegran called from the doorway like a storekeeper dunning a departing customer. "Don't forget you all come back."

If I wanted to do anything about what had happened to Duncan Hadley Lord, I knew, I'd have to take him up on it.

They went through the formalities of placing a criminal charge against me in Richmond. This meant booking, mugging and printing me in the middle of the night, then taking away my shoelaces and belt and what I had in my pockets and giving me a cell all to myself in the Richmond City Jail.

The cot in there was firmer than the one in Lonegran's rear office. Besides, sleep was what I had been put in there for. I stretched out on the cot and tried to think of what I was going to do in the morning. I couldn't think straight. My mind went around and around, the way it does when you're exhausted. I told myself what I did tomorrow depended on how the attorney general dealt the cards. They had left me my cigarettes, and I smoked a couple. A few cells down the block a drunk began to sing sadly and nasally in the tank. Then he stopped and either he or somebody else was noisily sick. I thought about my detective license and was reasonably sure they'd lift it in Virginia and lift it in Washington too. My brow burned where the stitches had been taken in it and I had two painful swellings on my neck from Lonegran's fists. I thought a little about Duncan Hadley Lord up there on his ledge before he had jumped. I shut my eyes and saw Bobby Hayst in the firelight and remembered how the firelight and the sound of the rain had gone away. Half asleep, I tried to call her name. She smiled at me.

Then I slept like a dead man....

In the morning they gave me corned beef hash, dark bread and coffee which tasted like it had been made with the grounds collected from every greasy spoon in Richmond. A little while after the trustee took away my breakfast tray a guard came for me.

"Your lawyer's here," he said.

I went with him without answering. My lawyer, who I had never seen before, was a little man in a rumpled flannel suit.

"The name is Bart Fox, Mr. Drum," he said. "I posted your bond."

"Who asked you to?"

"I can't hear a word you say."

"Okay. How much was it?"

"Five grand."

That was a good sign. Five thousand dollars meant that the criminal booking was regarded only as a technicality to be scratched out after the State Board held a hearing and decided what to do about my license.

"You put up Jerry Trowbridge's bail too?"

"Trowbridge?   I didn't put up any other bail."

"What about Dygert?"

"I don't know anybody named Dygert," Bart Fox said quickly.

"Where's Trowbridge?"

"I'm not supposed to have any truck with any names," he said, then lowered his voice. "But if you're looking for Trowbridge, I guess it won't hurt to tell you he's checked in over at the John Marshall. That's over on—"

"I know where it is, Mr. Fox."

"Your hearing's tomorrow morning at the Capitol. Caucus room C. You be there."

"I'll be there. They're not wasting any time, huh?"

"What I hear, they're holding the preliminaries today, both for the hearing and to see if they can turn what they've got over to a grand jury."

"Think they can?"

"How should I know? But they don't think so, if the size of the bond means anything."

"That's what I thought. Will I see you again?"

"Not unless they do turn it over to a grand jury, and you get indicted, and you need a lawyer, and pick me." Bart Fox grinned.

"Well, thanks."

"I'll give you a word of advice, though," he said, walking with me to the turnkey's desk, where I got my personal possessions and a signed receipt. "You better call up some friends and have some character witnesses down here tomorrow." We walked outside together. It was sunny and warmer than it had been all week.

I said, "Tell Dygert thanks for the bail. But tell him the way I figure it, he owed me that. I don't owe him a thing."

"I don't know anybody named Dygert," Bart Fox said, slowly and carefully this time.

"Well, in case you ever meet him, tell him."

We both grinned, and shook hands. Then Fox walked up the block, turned the corner and was gone. I took a cab over to the John Marshall Hotel.

The desk clerk at the John Marshall was a little leery of a guy with a stubble of beard on his face, no luggage and a suit which looked as if it had been slept in because it had been slept in. But the John Marshall is a big hotel, this wasn't the convention season and Richmond has never been much of a convention town, so in the end I got my room.

When I asked, they told me a Mr. Trowbridge had checked in alone last night, but there was no answer when they rang his room. Then I picked up a razor and a toothbrush and went with my room key to the bank of elevators while the whole lobby stopped what it was doing to watch the big guy with the stitches on his brow and the bruises on his face make like a paying guest.

Upstairs, I shaved, showered and stretched out on the bed in my underwear, communing with the ceiling. That didn't help me any more than it helped the ceiling, so I lit a cigarette, flipped the phone off its cradle, and asked for long distance.

Five minutes later I was talking to Jack Morley at the Protocol Section of the State Department in Washington.

"Chet!" he said. "My God, man, where've you been since you got back from India?"

"Up to my ears in work at first—"

"Well, I'm glad to hear the old private op's making out."

"—until recently. Now I'm up to my ears in trouble, Jack."

Jack Morley didn't ask me to name the trouble right off. The first thing he asked was, "Anything I can do to help?"

He'd graduated from the FBI Academy with me, then we'd each served a hitch with J. Edgar's boys and I'd decided to put up the shingle while Jack had gone to work for the State Department. He and his wife Betty were my favorite married couple in Washington. To prove it, I ate Betty's corned beef and cabbage every couple of weeks. I guess I was their favorite bachelor.

"I need a character witness tomorrow," I said. "If Mr. Dulles isn't too busy, could you tell him to hop a bus down here? Seriously, Jack, can you get the time off and come?"

"One of us named Morley will be there. Better tell papa about it, Chet. Plenty trouble?"

"Plenty," I said, and sketched it in for him. The first thing I heard was a groan, then he asked: "They going to pull your license?"

"It looks that way."

He didn't say anything.

"We're about the same size," I said. "If you could bring down a suit of clothes and a shirt and meet me at the John Marshall in the morning, I'd go in there without looking like I rode the rails all night to make it. Okay?"

He said okay and added, "I hope to hell you're wrong about how it'll turn out tomorrow. What about Trowbridge?"

"You knew his old man too, didn't you?"

Jack said that he had known him slightly.

"Money and a misdirected idealism," I said. "And the wrong connections."

"That Dygert," Jack groaned. "He plays rough, Chet. Watch out for him."

"Who's he working for? Who'd send that kind of letter to the U.S. Information Agency?"

"I could make a pretty good guess, but why don't we wait till morning and find out for sure? Uh-oh, Chet. They want me. The Finnish foreign minister's flying in today and old Jack's got to roll out the red carpet. One thing."

"What's that?"

"I know how you feel about old man Trowbridge. But don't let the kid railroad you for it, huh?"

I said I wouldn't, and we hung up.

Jerry didn't show up at the John Marshall all day. As near as I could figure, Dygert had put up my bail through Bart Fox so I'd be free to talk to Jerry about that breaking-and-entering alibi. But if Fox had told the truth, Jerry hadn't been arraigned at all. That didn't make much sense. But his not showing up began to make sense: they had changed their mind and didn't think they'd need me to set up Jerry's alibi.

I ate dinner at a little place on Maymont Avenue across the street from William Byrd Park, then took a long walk on Broad Street because I knew I'd feel caged back at the hotel. For almost the first time in my life I admitted to myself I was lonely. A private detective who runs a one-man agency as I had done most of the time has to be a lone wolf. He likes working alone or he wouldn't be in the business. But this was different. This was being cut off from everyone including yourself, because I could form no picture in my mind of anyone named Chet Drum forbidden by law to practice his trade. Yet starting tomorrow that was the Chet Drum I'd have to learn to live with.

That began to smack of self-pity, and I ran away from it. I went into the first grill I passed on Broad Street and tanked up on a few beers. When I hit the street again it was almost eleven o'clock. Neon made glowing patterns in the cool autumn night. Trolley cars rumbled by. I went around the corner, heading for Franklin Street and the John Marshall. A panhandler with a tic in his face stepped out of a dark doorway. I gave him a dollar knowing he would booze it before the night was over. He almost slobbered his thanks. That made the difference: I belonged to the human race again and self-pity moved off furtively and invisibly to find another victim.

"He come back?" I asked the desk clerk who had come on in the late afternoon.

"Not yet, sir."

"But he hasn't checked out?"

"No. Of course not."

"Ring me if he comes in any time tonight."

"Yes, sir."

I went up in the elevator. The desk clerk didn't ring me. Around dawn I fell asleep.

60   STEPHEN MARLOWE

CHAPTER TEN

The man from the Virginia attorney general's office was named Jefferson Lee Jowett. He was a big fellow with a mane of hair graying picturesquely at the temples and a soft, persuasive voice. He was as southern as hominy grits. He dominated caucus room C because that was his job. Except for the four men from the State Licensing Board, everyone else was there reluctantly.

Jefferson Lee Jowett's opening speech set the stage. He didn't get to Jerry and me at all. He wouldn't get to us until much later. He phased us all in on the history of the private detective in America, starting all the way back with Wells Fargo and the Pinkerton guards, letting us know how important private investigations were in a free society, pointing out that our obligations to society were as important as society's debt of gratitude to us, and making us all feel, by the time he finished, that any private detective who deviated one atom from the high standards set by Wells Fargo and the Pinkerton guards was a disgrace to the profession and a menace to free society, a mad dog who had to be muzzled and restrained.

After that, but only after that, they got down to business.

Early in the morning, I'd climbed into the dark-blue suit Jack Morley had brought down for me. It was a pretty good fit. Jack and I had breakfast in the John Marshall Coffee Shop, where Jack said:

"I did some G-twoing for you, Chet. Got a friend over at USIA." USIA was the United States Information Agency.

"What he say?"

Jack sipped from his second cup of black coffee. "Well, here it is. You won't like it. As long as Duncan Hadley Lord was alive and kicking, Judson Bonner had the agency over a barrel. But—"

"Judson Bonner!" I gasped.

"Oh, didn't I tell you? Bonner's our boy."

"He must be seventy if he's a day. I thought he retired years ago."

"He did, Chet. But he's got money and he's got some pretty strong convictions. Like, for example, any American dollar spent east of the Statue of Liberty and west of the Golden Gate Bridge is being thrown down a bottomless well with the stink of corruption in it."

"Guys like him play right into the Reds' hands. Doesn't he know there's a cold war going on? Doesn't he know if we don't get the American point of view across, the Reds will get across their version of it?"

"Don't I know it. Doesn't USIA know it. That's their function, and I don't have to tell you how important they are. But Judson Bonner doesn't know it. Anyhow, once Lord killed himself, the whole picture changed. The one thing USIA never wanted, for understandable reasons, was a bad press. With Lord alive, Bonner was going to see they got one. Either that, or he was going to be the piper to the tune they sung. But Lord died before his tie-in with the Agency was official. That didn't leave Bonner with much of a case against them."

"Well, at least that's a good deal," I said.

"Maybe. Maybe not. Bonner's a bulldog, and he's still digging. But to get back to your hearing. With guys like Bonner around, sensitive agencies like USIA fear adverse publicity morbidly. On the other hand, with a case that kind of blew up in his face, Bonner wouldn't exactly jump for joy if the kind of digging and snooping he makes a practice of got much play. You begin to see it?"

I made a face.

"Well, don't draw the wrong conclusions about the Agency. I know a lot of the boys up there, and they're a good bunch. But they don't know you from a hole in the wall, and the circumstantial evidence *does* make it look as if you were Bonner's paid assistant, and they'd like to just get the hell off the hook. Besides, in a way they think they're doing you a favor."

"A what?"

"A favor. Sure. I don't have to tell you the attorney general has an option of bringing charges against you two ways. Civil charges, in which case if found guilty you lose your license. Or criminal charges, in which case they truck you off to the hoosegow. The charges will be merely civil if it can be shown you violated the confidences of a client—say, for ideological reasons. But if it can be shown you took money to do it, the charges are criminal and you go to jail."

"They're rationalizing themselves up a tree," I said. Then I added: "Jack, you haven't exactly been letting any moss grow. Thanks."

"Anyway, from where I sit it looks like a deal. Bonner doesn't get mentioned and Bonner doesn't show up. The agency had an anonymous informant. You, or an unknown intermediary. The only one who gets hurt is you, and you don't get hurt as much as you would if they drag in everything and show you took money."

"What about Dygert?"

"Who? Oh, the private eye you mentioned yesterday. Far as I can see, he doesn't fit into the picture at all. Hell, how could he? If he gets dragged in, then Bonner gets dragged in."

"What am I supposed to do, sit quietly by and let them railroad me?"

"My God, Chet, what can you do? If I hadn't mentioned Bonner you'd never have tied him in."

"There's Dygert."

"Yeah, there's Dygert. But Dygert could claim, if you get nasty, that he paid you to do a job for him in all innocence. That he thought it his patriotic duty to expose Lord's lack of moral judgment. That he never knew you'd been hired by Mrs. Lord. That would leave friend Dygert in the clear—and you facing a criminal charge. Then what?"

I finished my coffee. I looked at Jack through the smoke of my cigarette. "I guess," I said after a while, "the State of Virginia collects my license."

"It's worse than that, Chet. My boy over at the Agency said the District Licensing Board got wind of it. They're sending a man down. My guess is if you lose your license here they'll lift it in D.C. too."

We paid our check and left the coffee shop. Jerry still hadn't showed up at the hotel, so I drove over to the Capitol with Jack in a taxi.

Caucus room C was in the basement under the Old Hall of the House of Delegates, where Aaron Burr was tried for treason a hundred and fifty years ago. I knew a little of how old Aaron had felt.

Then we went into caucus room C and took our seats and listened to Jefferson Lee Jowett's opening speech.

The rest of it was short and savagely precise. Jack had done remarkably well guessing some of it, but he hadn't guessed all of it. So we both sat with our jaws hanging and listened to the neatest frame ever put around the head of a man who spells his name S-u-c-k-e-r. Even old man Euclid would have approved.

An elderly lawyer named Stapp, who had a corduroy forehead and wore his glasses on a ribbon, spoke up for USIA. Yes, he said in answer to Jefferson Lee Jowett's question, USIA had received an anonymous tip on the moral shortcomings of Duncan Hadley Lord. Would he hazard a guess as to the sender of the tip? No, he did not feel qualified to do so. Expediently, no one thought to ask for the letter which the USIA director must have received. I kept my mouth shut: if I aired the dirty linens I'd find myself on the wrong end of a criminal indictment. But don't get it wrong. USIA was understandably acting in its own best interests. They weren't part of the frame.

Neither was Professor McQuade, who testified as to why he had felt compelled to hire me. All through his testimony he stared at me with cold hatred. When he was through, they called Mrs. Duncan Hadley Lord. She wore black and spoke in a voice choked with emotion, verifying McQuade's testimony. Then Jefferson Lee Jowett asked:

"Did Mr. Drum contact you in any way after your husband's death?"
Answer: "Yes. Yes, he did."
Q. To say that his report on your husband's activities was ready?
A. Well, yes.

Q. Anything else?
A. Yes, there was something else.
Q. Could you tell the board about it?
A. Mr. Drum asked if I wanted him to destroy the report.

The four board members went into a huddle. They broke it up when Jowett asked another question.

Q. Have you any idea, Mrs. Lord, why he asked you this?
A. He said that since my husband was dead he thought I might want to forget about the whole thing. Something like that.
Q. But you told him...
A. That I wanted to see the report, of course.
Q. What would you say was his reaction to that? Would you say he was glad?
A. No. He definitely was not glad.
Q. He would have preferred to destroy it?
A. Well, yes. I think so.

That hadn't nailed up the frame, either. Mrs. Lord was testifying to the truth as she saw it, and if opinions were asked for and accepted in evidence, you have to remember this was a hearing before a board from the attorney general's office, not a court of law.

It was Jefferson Lee Jowett's next witness who brought the frame into caucus room C with him. Jowett said: "The State Board now calls Mr. Gerald Trowbridge," and Jerry, who had been sitting across the large room from me and not meeting my eye, went up there. He looked young, earnest, troubled. He seemed to be fighting a great battle with himself. He was a reasonable facsimile of Jack Armstrong, the All-American Boy. Compared to him, with my bruised face and the swollen gash stitched over my eye, I was a charter member of Murder, Inc.

Q. Mr. Trowbridge, could you state precisely your relationship with Chester Drum?
A. I worked for him as a private detective.
Q. Licensed where?
A. In Washington, D.C., sir.
Q. But not here in the State of Virginia?
A. No, sir.
Q. Didn't that strike you as strange?
A. I don't think I get what you mean.
Q. Why didn't Drum apply for a Virginia license for you?

A. I was bonded to him in Virginia. He said it was the same thing.

Q. Because he wanted to have at least one member of his agency immune from just the sort of thing which is going on here today?

Before Jerry could answer, one of the board members suggested that that was purely supposition. Jowett shrugged and let it ride.

Q. You did the leg work for Drum on the Duncan Hadley Lord case?

A. That's right.

Q. Did Drum say who he was working for?

A. For Mrs. Lord. I saw her myself. But—well, I don't know if I should say this.

Q. Go ahead, please. That's what you're here for.

A. Well [reluctantly], the more information I brought in on Duncan Lord, the more agitated Chester got.

Q. Agitated?

A. Well, like he was mad at Lord. You know.

Q. For ideological reasons, perhaps?

A. You mean, that he thought a man in Duncan Hadley Lord's position shouldn't be carrying on the way he was?

Q. I'm asking the questions, young man. You're supposed to answer them. [Laughter] I asked, was he angry for ideological reasons?

A. Maybe. I can't be sure. Chet's a patriotic American. There's nothing wrong with that.

Q. No. Of course not. Unless he allowed his patriotism to blind him to the ethics of his profession. You were with Drum when he asked Mrs. Lord if she wanted the report on her husband's activities destroyed?

A. Yes, sir. I was.

Q. It was in a telephone conversation that he did this?

A. Yes. I—I listened in on the extension phone.

Q. Was Drum aware of this?

A. No.

I wanted to get up and shout that that was a lie, but nothing could have made a worse impression since Jerry looked so earnest and troubled. Jack Morley wisely gripped my arm until he felt the muscles relax.

Q. Can you remember how the conversation went?

A. No, I don't think so.

Q. But Drum did urge Mrs. Lord to permit him to destroy the report?

A. Yes, sir.

Q. Eloquently?

A. Sure, but...
Q. With more eloquence, perhaps, than the occasion demanded?
A. I never thought of that.
Q. What would you say Drum's reaction was when she refused?
A. He was angry.
Q. Very angry?
A. Yes, sir. [Sadly] I guess so.

Sheriff Lonegran, who didn't like Jerry but who liked me even less, finished the job. He testified that Jerry seemed terribly upset the night Duncan Hadley Lord jumped, so upset that they had to restrain him from going up there after the professor. He also testified that, in the trouble which followed, I set the pace and Jerry merely followed it obediently. His parting shot got a laugh, but some sober looks too. He said, "In Prince Charles County we got jails for guys like Drum. And we got plenty of room."

After that, I was asked to testify. I told the story pretty straight but left out Ernie Dygert and Judson Bonner. I knew I had to: the only kind of evidence I had against Dygert was purely circumstantial—the fight in Hamling's Bar and Grill. I testified that the first time I'd heard the taped recording of the report on Duncan Hadley Lord was after he had jumped. I looked around the room. Stone faces looked back at me.

I saw a fight once in the Washington Arena. It was an over-the-weight match between a clean-cut, unmarked welterweight and a stocky, almost gnarled middleweight who was older, whose face was masked with scar tissue and who plodded around the ring with the heavy tread of an old warhorse. The clean-cut young welter had a way of tearing up the book of rules, gouging, thumbing, hitting on the break, rabbit-punching. Somehow he got away with it. The hulking middleweight fought a clean fight, but the kid was a skilled technician: he made the bigger man look bad, look dirty. Three rounds which should have been taken away from the welter were taken away from the bigger man, and the welter won a split decision. The welter danced around the ring, light on his feet, happy, very sporting after the decision. He even went over and shook the bigger man's hand. They gave him a standing ovation. The middleweight plodded from the ring with a police guard keeping the angry crowd away from him. It was a little like Beauty and the Beast minus sexual overtones. It was clean-limbed, clean-living David slaying the giant Goliath.

I had ten long, hard years on Jerry. Ernie Dygert and a police doctor with small pink hands and Sheriff Lonegran had temporarily changed the patterns of my face. If I smiled, it would look like a gargoyle's mask. I didn't smile. I took my swollen face and sat down. My neck was still very painful where Lonegran had rabbit-punched me.

Jack Morley got up and spoke for about fifteen minutes. What he said impressed the hell out of me, not because of what he said or the way he said it but because he had taken the trouble to dig. He had all of it and I guess it sounded pretty good—my combat service during the war, my good record with the FBI, the few times in my P.I. career I'd helped the State Department overseas, particularly that business in India which I'd closed up a few months back. Then Jack finished with a few personal references, ending on a little joke which fell as flat as a blowout on the rear wheel of a two-ton car. He said: "Drum's the only private eye I've ever known who I'd let babysit with my kid."

It was my battered face, of course. The way I looked in caucus room C, I'd have scared any kid who walked into the room. All they had to do was look at me and look at Jerry. Jerry was the Lone Ranger with his mask off.

The board took fifteen minutes. Then the chairman, a slat-thin lawyer named MacReady, spoke. "This isn't a court of law," he said. "We do not admit evidence here on the basis on which it is admitted before the bar of justice. But we have a certain obligation to society, and this obligation is made doubly important due to the nature of the accused's profession. To put it another way, a reasonable doubt in a court of law is sufficient to merit acquittal. But a reasonable doubt before this board is, and must be, sufficient to merit conviction. The board unanimously believes that a reasonable doubt exists as to the defendant's innocence. The board must therefore rule that the license under which Chester Drum has been permitted to practice private investigation in the State of Virginia shall be declared null and void this day and until another such board, meeting under the direction of the attorney general of the State of Virginia, with the power vested in it by the attorney general, shall rule otherwise. The office of the attorney general, Mr. Jowett, is so instructed."

Jefferson Lee Jowett thanked the members of the board. Jerry left in a hurry as soon as the verdict was handed down. I was told a man from the Virginia attorney general's office would call at my office in the near future for the original of my Virginia license.

The representative of the District of Columbia board, who had sat through it all taking notes furiously, left without a word. I didn't like the look on his face.

Outside, Jack told me, "My God, what a raw deal you got. What are you going to do, appeal it?"

"Yeah," I said. "The only way I know that might work."

"How's that?"

We walked across Capitol Square together in the bright sunshine. Lawyers with bulging briefcases hurried by. A big car pulled to the curb on Capitol Street and a woman got out the back. Flashbulbs popped as press photographers took her picture. Then a covey of reporters clustered around her, hiding her from view.

"I'm going to see Judson Bonner," I said.

CHAPTER ELEVEN

I returned to Prince Charles County with a gun and a gadget, because that's where Judson Bonner lived. The gadget was a pocket recorder that had a tie-clip mike and worked on batteries. The recording unit, which fit with the batteries in a case not much bigger than a breast-pocket billfold, was a tight spool of wire that could run for two hours. I had received it through the mail about a year ago along with a covering letter which congratulated me for being one of a dozen private detectives in a dozen cities receiving a complimentary model. Until now it had stayed put in the deep drawer of the desk keeping the office bottle of Jack Daniel's company because that isn't the kind of detective work I do. I had to give it a trial run to check the batteries out, but they were okay.

This was after I'd gone back to Washington with Jack Morley by train.

"You can't see him," Jack had said. "You're out of your mind if you try."

"Who?"

"You know damn well who. Judson Bonner."

"You know some other way?"

"No."

"Me neither."

"In the first place there's the Prince Charles County sheriff. You said yourself he was out to get you. That's where Bonner's living these days, Prince Charles County."

I watched the telephone poles slip by. Jack lit a cigarette and said, "Also, what the hell good would it do you? You think maybe Bonner will go to bat for you and implicate himself?"

"I got to see him, Jack."

We said good-by at Union Station in Washington. I told Jack I'd bring the suit over one of these nights, and took a taxi home. I made myself a big drink and called Bobby Hayst on the phone. There wasn't any answer. I was almost glad. I didn't know what to say to her. I made another drink. Before you knew it, I had four or five and no appetite for dinner. I called Bobby again. No answer, which meant another drink. Somewhere along the line I drifted off to sleep stretched out on the sofa in the living room.

I got up in the morning as hungry as a horse, as brave as a lion and as smart as an elephant. At least that's what I told myself. The hungry as a horse part was easy. I put a pot of coffee up, grilled six strips of bacon and fried four eggs in their fat. While I was waiting for the toaster to pop, the telephone rang.

It was Jack. "I wish you wouldn't, Chet," he said.

"You know I've got to."

He sighed and told me where Judson Bonner lived. It was on Route 60 a few miles from Toano. I hung up, finished eating and drove over to the office.

Jerry had come and gone, probably last night. His desk was clean. He had even taken his girlie calendar off the wall.

I strapped on my shoulder rig, loaded every chamber of my Magnum .357 except the one under the hammer and thrust it into the holster. Then I tried out the pocket recorder. Figuring out how to get the wires to the tie-clip mike without showing was harder. I finally put the recorder in the inside breast pocket of my jacket and made a little hole in my shirt right under that. I drew the wires out through a button hole and attached them to the tie-clip. But that wasn't any good because a half inch of wire stuck out around the edge of my tie. I dug a hole in the tie with the desk letter-opener and ran the wires through that. I covered the hole with the tie-clip. It looked pretty good.

That's the elephant part. Or maybe it's a fox that's smart. Anyway, then the lion took over, locked up the office, went downstairs and outside, and drove down into Virginia.

A dreary autumn rain was falling when I reached the Judson Bonner estate. From Route 60 you couldn't see the house at all. A dense hemlock hedge about twelve feet high bordered the road for a quarter of a mile. It must have taken Judson Bonner twenty years to grow a hedge like that. It was as thick as a wall. I drove slowly by, then stopped. Metal gleamed inside the hedge. I got out and went over for a closer look. The hemlock had been planted around a cyclone fence. It was ten feet high and topped by two feet of barbed wire, three rusted strands of it, almost hidden by the hemlock. Judson Bonner was a man who liked his privacy.

There were two gates in the fence, both of heavy black wrought iron and about two hundred yards apart. One had massive white brick gateposts. A plaque on one of them said: *Judson Bonner.* The other didn't have any gateposts except the uprights of the hidden cyclone fence. Here the plaque was fastened to the wrought iron and said: *Judson Bonner, Service Entrance.*

I drove up to the service entrance and beeped my horn. In a little while a figure came running along a muddy path on the other side of the gate. He wore khakis and a lumber jacket and carried a big black umbrella. When he came close I rolled down the car window and stuck my head out. He was a young, good-looking guy, a pale blond. He didn't seem happy about being out in the rain.

"What is it?" he said.

"I have to see Mr. Bonner," I shouted back at him.

"Got out of there so's I can have a look at you. "

I opened the car door and got out. The rain soaked me in seconds. He seemed to get some satisfaction out of that.

"Who are you, pal?" He had a cocky way of talking and his accent was not native to the Commonwealth of Virginia.

"The name is Drum."

"Who says you got to see Mr. Bonner?"

I smiled at him. He had a wolf's grin with nothing behind it.

"I say so."

The wolf's grin prowled off. "Got an appointment?"

"I don't need an appointment."

He sneered. "Climb back in your pushcart and go home, pal. All you'll get if you stay here is a soaking."

He started to walk away. The rain drummed on his umbrella.

"Tell him it's the private dick who lost his license in Richmond yesterday," I shouted. "Tell him that."

He turned around and came back. A gust of wind lifted the umbrella and he got wet. He wiped the water off his face as if it was acid.

"Drum, you say?"

"Yesterday in Richmond. I didn't say boo. He knows I could have. Tell him that."

"All I hear is words, pal. I don't know what you're talking about."

"Tell him. If you don't he's liable to take away your umbrella."

He went away without a word. I climbed back into the car and lit a cigarette. He was back in fifteen minutes. He opened the gate.

"Pull her through and wait," he told me.

I drove through the break in the hemlock hedge and stopped. The blond lad pulled his umbrella shut and got into the car alongside of me.

"Drive slow, pal," he said.

It was a muddy dirt road that curved twice before running straight between twin rows of sycamores. On the first curve we passed a white clapboard gatehouse that I might have made the down payment on with every cent I had in the bank. After the road ran straight we drove for almost half a mile before we saw Judson Bonner's mansion through the low dripping arch made by the sycamore branches.

The house was red brick with a white-pillared portico out front not quite the length of a football field and a slate gambrel roof as big as a circus bigtop which dominated the red brick and white pillars and made the house look as if it was sinking into the ground.

"Stop here, pal."

I pulled to a stop on a driveway which circled around behind the house. It was flanked on the other side by a garage big enough for a dozen cars.

"Now, out you go."

The gateman pointed to a door in the side of the house. He ran over to the garage and went in. I figured he had done his day's work.

I opened the door and went in. There wasn't any bell or knocker. I found myself in a long dim hall with foxhunt murals on the walls, a carpet which almost hid my shoes, and no windows.

When I took three steps down the hall a man came toward me. He was young, like the gateman, and even better looking. He was good-looking enough to have been in pictures, but he didn't look like any pushover. He wore a lightweight turtleneck sweater which showed his muscles and a pair of avocado chinos a little too tight. He had wavy black hair and long eyelashes. He didn't look twenty-one. Judson Bonner, or whoever did the hiring, liked the hired help tough but decorative. It was worth thinking about, but at the time I didn't come up with any bright ideas.

"Frisk job, dads," he said, and ran his hands over me in the usual places. His left hand paused for a split second on the pocket recorder, but he must have finally decided it was a thick billfold. He yanked the Magnum out of its shoulder holster, thumbed the cylinder away from the barrel and tapped the bullets out on the palm of his hand. Then he handed the gun back to me. He put the .357 slugs in his pocket. He smiled.

I smiled too. "Maybe I got a pocketful of them myself," I said.

"Maybe you have. But you'd never get the chance to load up, dads. Come on."

I followed him. He didn't seem to mind turning his back on me at all.

CHAPTER TWELVE

He knocked on a door and waited. I stood behind him, leaking rain-water on the deep carpet. A voice, muffled through the heavy door, told us to come in. This time the kid in the turtleneck stepped to one side, so I turned the door handle, pushed the door open and walked. I wondered if getting out would be as easy.

It was the kind of room you'd pay four bits to see, without thinking you were bilked, in Sagamore Hill. The walls were paneled with dark, glossy wood—probably teak. From the teak, trophies glowered down at me. There must have been two dozen of them, the best being a huge Kodiak bearhead with gaping jaws and hanging tongue. The Victorian furniture was cumbersome and cluttered, with high stiff chairs and ornate inlaid tables. An enormous teak and leather desk at the far end of the room almost hid a fireplace big enough to roast a steer whole.

A man sat behind the desk and just in front of the hearth, brooding, his elbow on the desk and his chin on his hand, as we started out on our safari across the trophy room. That would be Judson Bonner.

The desk was eight feet across. That was as close as you could get to Judson Bonner.

He wore a cashmere smoking jacket with a satin shawl collar. He had a lot of white hair. He needed a haircut. He had a thin white two-piece mustache you could hide under a matchstick. He had a gaunt face and a narrow, high-bridged nose. His eyes, which were not deep-set, took ten years off his face. They were young eyes, curious eyes, but eyes which had not done much smiling. His mouth was small and bitter.

I reached for a cigarette, thumbing the starter on the pocket recorder as I did so. That would give us two hours of recorded conversation.

"Don't smoke," he said. "I have never smoked in my life. I see no reason for you to contaminate the air."

I put the cigarettes back in my pocket, marveling at Judson Bonner's voice. It was deep and well modulated. It had the clarity of a perfect belltone. Before retirement four or five years ago, Judson Bonner had spent three terms in the U.S. Senate. His voice, made for oratory, had probably got him there and kept him there.

He waved a hand before I could talk. "Please feel no need, Mr. Drum, to recapitulate yesterday's hearing for me. I have my informants. Now, what is it you wish to say?"

He didn't offer anyone a chair. They were that kind of chairs: they looked as if they had never been sat in, as if they had been made for a museum. I wouldn't have been surprised to see ropes tied across the arms.

"All right, then you know," I said. "I didn't mention Ernie Dygert yesterday. I didn't mention you. I could have."

"And if I said I never heard of anyone named Dygert?"

I leered at him. "Go ahead and say it. That would make three people in this room who know you're a liar."

Turtleneck, who stood a couple of paces behind me, sucked in his breath. But Judson Bonner's face changed expression exactly as much as the Kodiak bear's. "Suppose we say I knew him. Then what?"

"Suppose we say you hired him. Suppose we say he gets a thirty-grand-a-year retainer from you. Suppose we say he used part of this year's thirty grand to buy information I didn't know one damn thing about from my man Trowbridge. Suppose we say you put that information in a letter and sent it to USIA along with certain requests which they feel free to ignore now only because Duncan Lord is dead."

He stood up. I had not realized how tall he was. "Do you not know that men like Duncan Hadley Lord, who see fit to fritter away our resources and our money overseas, are a menace to the security of our nation?"

"Suppose we say," I went on, ignoring his rhetorical question, "that if I open my mouth to the right people you're all washed up as a one-man morals lobby or anything else in D.C."

"That's extortion!" he shouted. Spots of angry color flared on his cheekbones.

"What do you call the kind of deal you tried to make with USIA?"

"That's different. I was acting in the best interests of our nation."

The more I riled him, the closer what he said came to what I wanted to get down on the recorder. I asked: "When did you decide what the best interests of our country were? The last time you were out of this room? When you shot that bear, maybe? Around 1925?"

His eyes narrowed and his mouth formed a tight thin line. "Gilbert," he said, "throw this man out of here."

Turtleneck moved forward and grabbed my arm. I planted my feet and said: "Go ahead. And read all about it in the Washington *Post-Times* in the morning. Come on, Gilbert. Show me the door."

Bonner moved his hand. Gilbert let go of me. I lit a cigarette and this time Bonner didn't say anything about it.

"Precisely what is it you wish, Mr. Drum?" Bonner asked.

"First let's get our cards up out of our laps, huh? Dygert works for you, right?"

"He has done some work for me, yes."

"And you were out to get something on Duncan Lord?"

"A public figure's life should be an open book, Mr. Drum."

"They never are. Answer me."

"Well, yes. But you are putting the matter crudely."

"Pardon me for my lack of education. And Dygert got that information for you?"

"Yes, of course. You already know that."

"Got it how?"

"Apparently you know more about that than I do."

"You didn't come to me for any payoff. I came to you. Let's hear you say it so you know why you're paying me."

"Mr. Dygert has never revealed his sources to me."

We had reached an impasse, but I thought I could coast on what I had for a while. It was more than enough to appeal yesterday's hearing. It could use a clincher, though. It could use an outburst. I grinned and said, "That sounds as if you're working for Dygert, not the other way around."

Bonner's small mouth fluttered. Color leaped into his cheeks again. Unexpectedly, I had hit a bull's-eye. It was the first real bull's-eye I had hit in there. It was also the last.

A door behind Bonner's desk, between the fireplace and the first trophy, opened. Ernie Dygert stalked into the room. The door slammed shut behind him. Purple bruises marred his face. His left eye was swollen shut. A lump on his jaw made his face look lopsided.

"I can handle this, Ernie," Judson Bonner said.

Dygert ignored him. He had a gun in his big fist, a .45 automatic which could blow a hole through a six-inch beam of oak. I was no six-inch beam of oak. The gun was pointing at me.

"I wish you would let me handle this, Ernie," Judson Bonner insisted.

"Don't make me laugh," Dygert said. "You really believe Drum came here for a payoff? He never even got around to naming his price."

"That's easy," I told Dygert, staring at him steadily. "It's ten thousand bucks, cash on the barrelhead."

All he did was laugh. With anyone but Ernie Dygert I might have got away with it. But he was that kind of detective. He probably carried a pocket recorder around like I carried a notebook and a pencil. For him it was probably the greatest invention since Edison took down his shingle.

"You got some mighty interesting stuff there," he admitted. Then he stopped smiling. "I want it."

He came in front of me. The .45 was well oiled. I could smell the oil. He held out his free hand. "Give."

He let me play it dumb for a few seconds while he looked me over. He liked my tie-clip the minute he saw it. His hand reached out, he gave a yank, and six inches of wire dangled from my shirt. He smiled condescendingly.

I flicked the cigarette in his face. Sparks flew. I turned and made a run for the door.

It was Gilbert who brought me down with a flying tackle. We rolled over on the floor and got tangled in a polar bear rug. Gilbert had muscles, but he was no heavyweight. I clubbed him once with the edge of my hand where his jawbone meets his ear, and he was all through. I got up.

Dygert stood over me with his .45.

"Unbutton your jacket," he said. "Then put your hands on your head and keep them there."

Gilbert sat up, groaning. Judson Bonner was frozen half-rising out of his chair, like one of his trophies. I opened my jacket. The right side hung heavily.

"Heeled too, are you?" Dygert said.

"Gun's empty," Gilbert said thickly.

Dygert removed the recorder from the inside breast pocket of my jacket. "Nifty little gadgets, aren't they?" he asked no one in particular. He tossed the recorder to Gilbert. "Lift the spool," he said.

Gilbert did so with fumbling hands. He stood up.

"Now let me have it."

Gilbert obediently did that too.

"Give Mr. Drum back his recorder."

Gilbert walked in front of me and used the recorder against the side of my jaw. My knees went rubbery but I didn't fall down.

"You ought to put on some weight, Gilbert," Dygert said. Then he jerked his head at me. "Turn around, Drum."

I turned around and stared at the door it had been so easy to enter through. Conversationally, Dygert asked: "What do you think happens to you now?"

I shrugged.

"Go on. Take a guess."

I didn't hear Dygert's footsteps. I did hear a low vocal sound which came from Judson Bonner.

For a split second I smelled the oil on Dygert's .45. Then the ceiling came down to slam the floor like a punch press. I was caught between.

It was the last day of the planet earth. The sky was lurid. The sun was swollen and bloated. It hung very close. The earth was going to fall into it. The last man in the world, his head swollen and bloated from too much swollen and bloated sun, opened his eyes. At least, he thought he opened his eyes. He couldn't see anything. He heard an impossible sound. It was almost like rain banging away at a metal roof. It was almost like a car engine. It was almost like tires thumping and whispering over wet pavement. It was almost like wipers swishing and thumping on a windshield. It was almost like all four.

A voice said: "Cold as a son of a bitch, ain't it?"

Another voice answered: "I don't know. It's not so cold back here."

"Some rain," the first voice said.

"The trouble with you, George, you don't like being dragged out of your house on a night like this."

"Ah, it ain't that."

"But what the hell," the voice next to me in the back seat of the car said. "He's desperate. He can be violent. I don't have to tell you. I couldn't bring him in alone, could I?"

The last man in the world groaned. He couldn't help it.

"Coming out of it, Drum?"

I opened my eyes cautiously. The lurid red haze retreated. Sheriff Lonegran and I were seated in the back seat of a speeding car that had the wet highway all to itself. I mumbled something and wished I was the last man in the world again.

Sheriff Lonegran settled himself comfortably. Seated in the rear of the car with his dwarfed legs bent he looked bigger than he was. Every now and then he leaned forward to stare out the windshield of the car. The rain fell like molten gold in the headlight beams.

We drove through a small town, then the road went straight across flat farmland. Lonegran had a big automatic on his lap with the fingers of one hand draped loosely on the butt. If you didn't know who he was, you'd think he was asleep sitting there, sunk morosely in an unpleasant dream. In a little while he lit a cigarette.

"What time you got, Sheriff?" George asked.

"Almost eleven-thirty."

I wondered what had happened to the rest of the afternoon and the early evening. I moved my shoulders and tried to get comfortable. Pain moved in pulsing waves at the base of my skull. When Lonegran finished his cigarette he rolled the rear window on his side of the car down far enough to flick the butt out. Then he rolled it up again. The wet cold air made me feel a little better.

The windshield wipers were a pair of metronomes measuring the slow black passage of time and space. George whistled tunelessly and interminably through his teeth. Then I heard another sound, faint and far away through the rain. It was the lonely moan of a train whistle, and it came closer.

We drove another mile or so. A red light winked on and off ahead of the car. I felt myself shifting forward as George stepped on the brake.

"Train coming," George said disgustedly. "We ain't never gonna get home."

We stopped before the tracks. There wasn't any gate, but the red warning lights blinked on and off, on and off. No cars pulled up across the tracks. No headlights glowed behind us. The locomotive came hurtling by, roaring and hissing, with an aura of rainwater dancing about its great black bulk. A long line of freight cars rumbled by. George lit a cigarette and cursed them in the fluid way that only a Southerner can curse. Sheriff Lonegran was leaning forward slightly, the automatic gripped tightly in his fist.

"Just sit still, Drum," he said.

I didn't say a word. I hadn't moved.

The long freight slowed down, its couplings clanking and squeaking. After about ten minutes, you could see the red light on the caboose. Then the caboose drew up even with us.

Lonegran half got up in the back seat of the car and slammed the automatic down on George's head. As he did so he shouted: "Hey, look out, damn it!"

George slumped in the driver's seat, his head falling on the horn ring. In one motion Lonegran yanked at George's collar until the horn stopped blowing and turned to face me with the gun. He jerked the muzzle toward the door on my side of the car.

"Okay. Out."

Death waited out there in the darkness and the rain. I knew it, and Lonegran knew I knew it.

"I said out."

George groaned. If he regained consciousness in the next few moments, I might live. He slid to the right and fell out of view on the front seat of the car. His breathing was deep and low.

"I'm supposed to make a break for it?" I asked.

"Just get out."

"What will you tell George I hit him with?"

"Out, damn you."

Lonegran leaned across me and opened the door. He was very close but I didn't try anything. I figured it wouldn't have made too much difference to him if he shot me in the car. Cold wind blew a gust of rain in at us. The caboose light of the train was a tiny red pinpoint fading into the night.

I got out and took two dejected steps, head down, shoulders sagging. That was easy. Standing up had turned the waves of pain in my head into hammers.

After the first two steps I fell into a low crouch and ran. My shoes pounded on concrete, then crunched on gravel. I didn't hear Lonegran behind me at all. It was as if the night had swallowed him, gun and all.

When my shoes hit wet grass, Lonegran's gun roared.

Simultaneously, my feet flew out from under me and I went down headfirst on the grass. Maybe that was why Lonegran missed. He fired again, at shadows. Down on the ground he couldn't see me.

I stayed there, but I was too close to the road, too close to Lonegran and his gun. I began to crawl.

When I had gone about ten feet I heard Lonegran's shoes striking gravel. I didn't turn my head to look at him. I thought my face might shine in the rain. If I turned, and if it did, he'd blow a hole in it. I kept going on hands and knees.

Then I didn't hear his running steps. That meant he was on the grass, coming after me. I knew he couldn't see me. If he saw me I was a dead man. I did not know how long it would be before he saw me.

I crawled. Something whipped across my head and stung me just above the stitches the police doctor had taken in my brow. I stopped crawling and reached out with one hand. I felt a strand of barbed wire.

I heard a movement behind me. It was almost completely dark. I could see—dimly—about five feet, and that was all. To my left at the farthest range of vision I saw Lonegran's shoes. He had stopped at the barbed wire. He wasn't more than five or six feet from me. I didn't look up. All I saw was his shoes. I didn't move. I held my breath, then let it out very gently through my mouth and breathed in that way.

Lonegran did not know I had fallen. He was looking for me, but he was looking too high. For all he knew, his first shot or his second might have got me. But if they had, I wouldn't have come this far. His gun was a .45, and you do not crawl more than a few feet with a .45 slug in you, even if it means your life.

Lonegran's left shoe stepped down on the barbed wire. He stood that way a long time. He must have been trying to pierce the gloom of the rain and the night with his eyes. His weight made the wire creak where it was attached to an unseen fence post.

His foot shifted. I followed it with my eyes. It stepped up to the second wire and the wire sagged and then went taut under it. Then, crouching, Lonegran went through between the middle and upper strands of wire.

He muttered softly when his jacket caught on a barb. I heard cloth rip. Then he was through.

He began to walk on the other side of the barbed wire fence. He stopped right in front of me. If the fence wasn't there I might have chanced jumping him. Then he walked away from the fence. He had heard something. I don't know what it was. I didn't hear it. He started to run.

I got up and ran back to the car.

George met me coming out.

His eyes widened, and he shouted. He was groggy but he had a gun too. I hit him in the belly with everything in me that said I wanted to go on living. He jack-knifed and fell back against the fender of the white and black sheriff's car. His gun clattered on the pavement. I made a dive for it, but George bounced off the fender and fell on top of the gun.

I plunged into the car. The engine was still idling. George had never shut it off waiting for the train, and Lonegran had been in too much of a hurry to come after me to worry about the car.

Orange fire blossomed in the night as Lonegran's gun roared. The right rear window of the car turned into an opaque spiderweb with a small round hole in the middle of it.

I swung the car across the tracks and back in a lurching U-turn. As I came around, Lonegran was silhouetted in the headlights. I ducked my head below the level of the dashboard and tried to run him down. He fired wildly. He must have waited until the last moment and then flung himself off the road.

In less than ten seconds I was doing sixty. I kept my foot to the floor and watched the speedometer needle climb to seventy, then eighty, then eighty-five. I kept it there, driving into a wall of rain with only one headlight. Lonegran's final wild shot must have got the other one.

"That's fine," a voice said. "That's really swell. Now we've got a crooked sheriff who wanted to kill you."

It was my own voice, and it was too high. My arms began to tremble as reaction set in. I slowed to seventy-five. It still felt like flying. Rain beat furiously against the windshield, clattering like hail, making it all but impossible to see. I slowed to fifty and that was a little better.

I couldn't keep quiet. It didn't matter that no one was there, I had to talk. "Take it easy," the strange, too-high voice said. "You're all right now. They wanted to kill you. They wouldn't dare to take you alive. It's like the hearing all over again. Because you could raise a stink that would make every paper from here to D.C. and back again. So why don't you? Why the hell don't you?" Two of me sat there arguing in the car, both tired and hurt and lonely. "Because I can't. Because I can't prove a thing. And because there's still only one way to get my license back."

But why Lonegran? I couldn't answer that one. At the moment I hardly cared. All I wanted to do was get away.

I slowed the black and white official car down driving through Toano. Near the north end of town a cop coming out of a restaurant waved. I waved back and kept driving. Pretty soon I reached the big hedge of Judson Bonner's estate. A car followed its headlights out of the driveway just as I passed. It started south toward Toano, but I heard the complaint of abused brake-linings and gave a look through the rearview mirror. The car skidded to a stop on the wet pavement, fishtailing close to the right shoulder of the road.

Whoever was driving began to see-saw it back and forth and then swung it around in a U-turn. By then I was a quarter of a mile away with my foot to the floor. I kept it there and saw the headlights way back.

The miles slipped by. The car behind me couldn't gain, but I couldn't lose it either. Just this side of Richmond I swung around a wide curve that I knew would hide me from view for maybe half a minute. I braked and drove off the road and down a steep muddy path to a culvert. I rolled the window down and waited. In a few seconds I heard whoever was following me go speeding by. This seemed as good a place as any to ditch the sheriff's car, so I left it there on the bank of a boiling, rain-swelled stream and climbed back to the road.

A mile of walking along the shoulder of the road through the rain brought me to a gas station. No cars passed me. There weren't any cars at the pumps. I walked across the asphalt and opened a glass door. Warmth and light flooded over me.

When I opened the door there had been a kid at a desk with his feet up and his eyes in one of those exposé magazines. He dropped the magazine and stood up.

"Whisky," I croaked.

He took another look at me and produced a bottle without a word. I took off the cap and drank until the bottle made gurgling sounds and I started to cough.

"What the hell happened to you, mister?"

"I got lost. You have a number for a taxi garage?"

He had a number, and called it. Then he asked: "You sure you-all don't want an ambulance?"

I grinned and shook my head. Whatever the grin did to my face made his face turn white.

Ten minutes later the taxi came. I took it into Richmond and over to the bus depot on Broad Street. Before the bus for Washington pulled in, making the long Tidewater run from Norfolk through Newport News, I had time to clean up in the washroom. The barbed wire had opened another gash on my forehead and the rain hadn't washed all the blood off my face. I did what I could in the washroom and went upstairs to wait for the bus.

I was hungry, but too tired to do anything about it. I dragged myself into the big white and blue bus when it was announced on the P.A. system. By then it was almost three o'clock. I found a seat in the rear of the bus. No one bothered me. I slept all the way through the four-hour run into Washington. The driver had to shake me awake. He must have smelled the whisky. "Come on, buddy. Come on. End of the line."

I stepped out into a gray cold dawn, found a taxi, and went home.

CHAPTER THIRTEEN

The apartment wasn't much, but it was home. It seemed as if I'd been gone a year. The place had a clean, unused look. Everything was tidy. The furniture in the living room gleamed as if it had just been waxed. You cleaned up this morning, I told myself. So what? Make that yesterday morning.

But I hadn't cleaned up. Despite that, the living room and kitchen would have got the Good Housekeeping seal of approval.

I went into the bedroom like papa, mama and baby bear.

Someone was sleeping in my bed too.

"Is it morning?" she asked, rubbing her eyes sleepily. "You're home. Oh, you're home!"

She sat up. The blonde hair was tousled. The blue eyes were instantly, beautifully alert. The lovely body was clad in a nightgown not quite as substantial as an industrious spider's web.

She got out of bed and drifted over to me with her arms wide. She came over and squeezed me. I squeezed back. The way I felt, it was like two bears trying to hug each other to death.

She drew back and said, "I tried to call you. All day yesterday, I tried. I couldn't get you. I decided to camp on your doorstep. I hope you're not mad, Chet."

Then she saw my face. She touched it with her fingers. "What did they do to you?" she gasped. "What did they do to you?"

She had a warm, healthy smell, made of equal parts of sleep and perfume. She made clucking sympathetic sounds and her eyes went watery. Then they got a determined look in them and she said, "I don't know what you've been doing the last few days, but now you're going to listen to Bobby." She pouted. I hadn't said anything. "You understand?"

"Yes, ma'am," I said, and she led me into the living room. She was gone only a moment, but consciousness was dim and I began to think I had dreamed her up. I blinked. There she was again, Bobby Hayst, leaning down over me. A glass was thrust into my hand. Four ounces of whisky, neat. I drank it.

"Now get up and march into the bedroom. Get undressed."

I went into the bedroom. I was going to get undressed. It had seemed like a fine idea. But when I sat down on the edge of the bed it seemed like an even better idea to kind of stretch out for a moment. I stretched out. From the bathroom I heard the sound of water rushing into the tub. I drifted.

Bobby was taking off my shoes and socks when I came out of it. "Come on, up. Sit up."

I sat up. She removed my jacket and shirt. "Where's your robe?"

I told her.

She brought it to me and I slipped into it. "Now take off your pants and march into the bathroom. Hot bath waiting for you."

She was wearing a robe too, a no-nonsense blue thing that buttoned up to her neck. Still, she looked lovely enough to kiss. I kissed her.

"None of that now, mister. Let's get you fixed up first." She leaned down to kiss the lobe of my ear. "I'll see you later."

I wandered into the bathroom and made my way through a cloud of dense steam to the tub. When Bobby shut the door behind me, I took off the robe and dropped into the tub. At first it was too hot, but pretty soon it felt great. For the second time, I let myself drift.

... door opening and closing.

"What are you trying to do, drown yourself?"

I sat up and coughed water out of my throat. "Hey!" I said.

Bobby started to laugh. "You look so funny, sitting there and blushing."

"Who's blushing? You made the water hot enough to boil a lobster in."

"Well, soak for a while. When you're parboiled, come out. It'll do you a world of good."

"Git," I said, lifting a dripping arm out of the water and threatening her with it.

She went out and closed the door. I soaked and scrubbed and soaked again. I felt more sleepy than ever, but less fatigued.

"Breakfast's ready!" Bobby called.

After toweling myself I slipped into the robe and left the bathroom. By comparison the rest of the apartment was cold. I went into the kitchen.

"First you drink this," Bobby said.

It was a steaming cup of coffee, laced with brandy. I took a sip. Maybe it was a steaming cup of brandy, laced with coffee. I drank it down and felt warm and drowsy.

"Three soft-boiled eggs and toast," said Bobby.

That's what I ate. Then there was more coffee, without brandy this time, and a cigarette. All the while Bobby watched me like a proud mother.

"How'd you get in here anyway?" I asked.

"Later. We'll talk later. Finished? Then just crawl into bed."

"Alone?"

This time Bobby blushed. It was worth seeing. "Alone, Chester Drum," she said. "For now."

She kissed me good night and tucked me in and kissed me good night again. It was the last thing I remembered for some time....

Her hair tickling my chin awoke me.

I was lying on my side with my arms around her. She felt warm and softly supple. She fit into my arms beautifully, with her head tucked under my chin and the rest of her lined up just where you'd want. She scratched my foot with her toes.

"Sleepyhead," she said.

I leaned my head back far enough to tilt hers up, and kissed her on the mouth.

"How long you been in here?" I mumbled against her lips.

"Too long, with you sleeping. How do you feel?"

"Good enough to make a habit of this. What time is it?"

"Eleven o'clock—at night. You slept all day. To make a habit of what?"

I showed her.

We had a one A.M. supper of steaks, French fries and salad. During the day Bobby had done some shopping.

"Good?"

"Delicious."

Bobby grinned. "I'm doing what the psychologists call reinforcing the habit."

"It doesn't need any."

We sat over our coffee-with-brandy and cigarettes. "I read about the hearing in the papers," Bobby told me. "Just a small article on the next to the last page of the first section."

"The only reason it got in was Dr. Lord. He was big news."

"They railroaded you," Bobby said angrily.

I shrugged. "It was convenient for everybody."

"But that isn't all they did to you. You could barely stand on your feet when you came in here. What happened?"

I told her over a second cup of coffee and another cigarette.

"You mean they actually tried to—kill you?" she said. Suddenly she looked up. "Are you safe here? They know where you live. They know where to come and get you."

"Sure I'm safe. Killing me when they could make it look like I sapped a deputy sheriff is one thing. Murdering me in cold blood, that's something else."

"But if they arrested you once, they could do it again."

"How? They arrested an unconscious man and were going to kill him before he ever reached jail. That was all they wanted. There won't be any charges now. As far as they're concerned, I never even visited Bonner. Since I got away."

"What are you going to do now?"

"I haven't thought about it."

"More coffee?"

I drew a line across my gullet. "It's up to here."

"Chet," Bobby said, her face grave and troubled. "Did Dr. Lord really get that letter from the Agency, the USIA, like you said? Or did you make it up?"

"Make it up? Don't be silly."

"And the Agency got a subtle threat from Judson Bonner?"

"Sure. I told you. But from where I stand it looks like Dygert's calling the signals, not Bonner."

"Anyhow. And that's why Dr. Lord—jumped?"

I nodded. Suddenly I knew what Bobby was driving at. She stood up and went to the sink with a handful of dishes. She didn't say anything. I came up behind her and touched her shoulder, but she stiffened.

"Listen, kid," I said. "I know what was bothering you. Well, it's over now. We know why Dr. Lord took his own life. It had nothing to do with you or how he felt about you."

She swung around. Her hair looked very light against the dark blue robe. Her eyes gleamed with tears.

"But I helped them," she said. "Don't you see, I helped them."

"It could have been anyone."

"No! I did it. It was me."

"All they wanted, all they needed, was—"

"I know that. You don't understand what I'm trying to say. I led Dr. Lord on. It was part of my—technique." She made it sound like an ugly word.

"You're imagining things. You told me you liked him."

"Of course I liked him. I thought he was the most interesting man I'd ever met. I told you that."

"Then what's eating you?"

"Because I led him on, because I didn't discourage him about feeling the way he did, he... kept seeing me."

"I told you, Bobby. If it wasn't you it would have been somebody else."

She smiled at me. It was a bitter smile. "Do you really believe that?"

"No."

"Then I helped them kill him."

"You've got it all tied up logically," I said, "with a cockeyed kind of logic. The only thing it isn't, is true."

"I'm quitting," she told me all at once in a rush of words. "I've got some money. I'm all through. I don't have to do it. I'm finished with being a fancy telephone whore."

She started to cry.

She ran into the bedroom, flung herself on my bed and cried into my pillow. Sitting down near her, I took her hand. She turned over and I bent down and kissed her gently. Snuffling like a little girl, she knuckled her eyes. I gave her a handkerchief and she blew into it in an unladylike fashion.

"So quit," I said. "Is that something to cry about?"

She grinned up at me, and I wiped the tears off her cheeks. "I—I guess it sort of calls for champagne."

"That's better. Here, blow your nose again."

"Oh, Chet. Being with you makes me feel so wonderfully—clean."

Under the circumstances, that was about the nicest thing a girl had ever said to me, but I didn't want her getting solemn again so I said: "There goes my reputation."

She took it half seriously. "I don't mean it like that at all, silly. You know what you do to me."

"Step one," I said. "The lady quits. Step two. Where does she go from here?"

Bobby sat up and looked away from me. "I wasn't going to tell you," she said. "I mean, I don't have any long-range plans, but—"

"I'm listening."

"No. Forget it. You've got your own worries. You're a private detective without a license to practice."

"They haven't taken it away in D.C. yet."

"But you said they will. Didn't you?"

"Don't worry about me. What about you?"

Instead of answering, she got up, went into the kitchen and attacked the stacked dishes furiously. I dried them for her. "You should have seen your building super," she said. "I told him I was your secretary. He nearly swallowed his teeth. They are false, aren't they?"

"Yeah. But stop changing the subject."

She started to scrub the sink. "Sure," she told me, "I have some plans. But I'll be darned if I'll talk about them now."

"Why not?"

She grinned. "I know you. You'll try to talk me out of them in a weak moment." The grin faded. "Well, there aren't going to be any weak moments."

We took the conversation into the living room, but I couldn't get anything out of her. Sometime around the middle of the night we sent some brandies down to put the steaks to bed, had a final cigarette, and turned in. There wasn't any funny stuff about who should sleep where. The only comfortable sleeping place in the apartment was the double bed in the bedroom, so we both used it. She had seemed so preoccupied that I decided not to touch her, but after about ten minutes lying there in the dark she came into my arms with a funny kind of little growl.

Afterwards, she cried softly.

"What's the matter?"

"I'm so happy when I'm with you. Nothing's the matter. I'm just so happy."

I kissed the back of her neck and slept holding her in my arms. She must have turned over in her sleep, because I awoke later facing her. Her breath was like a baby's and in the darkness I thought I saw a little smile on her lips. I went to sleep again....

In the morning she was gone.

I found her note in the kitchen, read it and called myself some ugly names. The note said:

Chet darling,

I have a luncheon engagement this afternoon with Jerry Trowbridge. This is hard for me to explain. I tried to tell you but couldn't. I don't want to crawl off with my tail between my legs. Remember once I told you I was free, white and twenty-one? That still goes, but it means something else now. When I first contacted Trowbridge I told him I'd propositioned you about doing some work for your agency—the kind a girl like me has been known to do. I said you hadn't told me anything definitive one way or the other, but now that you were forced to close up shop I was turning to him. He seemed pretty eager to buy what I had to sell. I'm not altogether sure where it will lead, but I've got to find out. You see, after what happened to Duncan Lord, I feel this is the only way I can retire (that's a funny word to use, isn't it?) and still look into a mirror without throwing things. I don't have any specific plans really. The only thing I know is I've got to try and make them pay for what they did to Dr. Lord, because no matter what you say, I was to blame too. Call it a self-imposed penance, if that makes sense.

There's one other thing I wanted to say. I think I'm falling in love with you. We'll find out about that later. Won't we, Chet?

Bobby

P.S. I'll get in touch with you again after I establish some kind of a relationship with Trowbridge and, I hope, Ernie Dygert.

I read the note again over a cup of strong coffee. I looked at the part where she said she thought she was falling in love with me. The words didn't change. I tried to get a clear picture of my own feelings toward Bobby, and couldn't. We'd never been together when the only thing that mattered was the two of us, and how we felt; never been together long enough to see if it would wear thin after the incredibly strong physical attraction we felt for each other simmered down some; never been together where there wasn't a bed, and our need and a desire to make the rest of the world go away.

"We'll find out about that later," Bobby had written. She hadn't added, but could have: "Right now I'm too busy sticking my head in the lion's mouth."

I called her apartment. There wasn't any answer, of course. I dressed and went to the office.

CHAPTER FOURTEEN

"First really cold day, ain't it, Mr. Drum?" the elevator starter in the Farrell Building said conversationally. "I'll bet we get some snow this year by Thanksgiving. Well, that's the way it is, I always say. Late summer, early winter. You get a late summer like we had, they kind of forget all about the autumn. Too bad," he added dolefully. "Autumn's my favorite season. How's about you, Mr. Drum?"

I mumbled an answer.

"By the way, guy was asking about you. He went back up to wait. Going out of town for Thanksgiving, are you?"

I said I didn't think so, then the elevator doors closed and we went up. I got off on the sixth floor and walked down the hall to my office. The outer door, which leads into the little waiting room, was not locked. I never lock it, so the potential cash customers have a place to park themselves if they want to wait for a private eye one of whose virtues is not steady hours.

He was seated in the waiting room and got up as soon as I came in. He had a hard face and thin, almost fleshless lips. He had the knowing, cynical eyes of a cop.

"Mr. Drum? I'm McGrath, District Licensing Bureau."

"Come on in," I said, and opened the door to the inner office. In a moment we were seated facing each other across my desk. The room had a stuffy, dusty, unused smell. I opened the window and brisk, cold air blew in.

"Now, then, Mr. Drum. This won't take a moment. As I believed you know, one of our men attended your Richmond hearing."

I opened my mail, waiting for him to go on. He had that this-is-a-painful-duty tone of voice, so I had a pretty good idea of what was coming. The only mail of any interest was a letter asking me to join the Baker Street Irregulars.

"Do you intend to appeal it?"

"Yeah, sure. I guess so. I've been too busy to do much thinking about it."

"Busy doing what?"

"Personal stuff," I said.

"Good. I'm glad you aren't involved in any investigations, Mr. Drum, because I'm afraid that until such time as you appeal the decision of the Richmond hearing the Bureau considers it necessary to suspend your license in the District of Columbia. If the appeal is refused, we could then give you a full-scale hearing here in Washington. If it is approved, why then, naturally, we would return your license to you."

"You guys take a lot of chances," I said.

"I beg your pardon? Oh, I see. You must have your little joke. But I needn't tell you that the relationship between the law and the members of your profession is a delicate thing and that, in order to merit the privileges granted you under the law…" He made quite a speech about it, lit a cigarette, gave me an extremely faint apologetic smile and asked for my license. I gave it to him. That left a pale-green rectangle on the dark-green wall where it had been hanging.

"Of course, I don't have to tell you not to use your photostats illegally?"

"Don't worry," I said. "I was planning to turn a neat profit selling them."

He was a man without a sense of humor, or maybe it wasn't so funny. Anyway, he gave me a severe look, shook his head and left with my license, frame, glass and all, tucked under his arm.

Before I had time to feel sorry for myself, I had another visitor.

I heard her high heels click-clacking in the hall, heard the outside door open, and saw a woman's silhouette behind the pebbled glass of the connecting door. For a moment I thought it was Bobby. But the silhouette wore a large picture hat which had a brim as wide as her shoulders, and Bobby wouldn't wear a hat like that.

The connecting door opened, and she came in.

She was the kind of redhead that makes them make up all those stories about redheads. She wore her hair long and it made the skin of her face look almost the color of milk. She had green eyes. A green-eyed redhead, she was, with a figure that would stop the shadow on a sundial. She wore a severely simple gray dress, three-inch spike heels that would make her about five-ten, and too much lipstick but no other make-up. When she smiled she showed a little too much in the way of teeth, but considering all her other assets you could forgive her that.

She smiled and said: "You must be mad."

"I haven't gone to my psychiatrist yet today," I said.

"No, I don't mean that kind of mad." She smiled again. "I mean angry."

"Why, does it show, Miss…"

"Mrs. Bonner. It doesn't show. I know all about you."

"Sit down, Mrs. Bonner," I said. "It *is* Mrs. Judson Bonner?"

"The only one in this whole business," she said, acknowledging the full name with a nod, "who has a right to be madder than you." She sat down, crossed her fine long legs and displayed her knee. "I'd like a cigarette."

I gave her one. While I lit it she held my hand a little longer than necessary. "And a drink too, if you're like all the private detectives I've read about."

Out came the office bottle and two paper cups. "Pros't," I said.

"I haven't heard that in years. Pros't to you." She tilted her head, and the drink was gone. There were faint wrinkles on the skin under her jaw and I realized for the first time that she was a good deal older than she looked. Thirty-four or -five, I thought, with a teenager's taut, high-breasted, long-limbed figure.

Putting the paper cup down, she said, "I followed you the other night, you know. If it was you in the sheriff's car."

"Guilty as charged."

"They were going to do away with you. Gilbert told me. He wasn't crazy about you, but he liked the idea of killing you even less. I'm glad you managed to get away."

"What's your beef, Mrs. Bonner?"

"Beef? Oh, I see. Because of what I said. In a word, Mr. Drum, my beef is Ernie Dygert. Give me another drink."

I poured it for her, half the paper cup this time. She sipped it steadily, like most people sip iced tea. "My, that's good. Might I have one more?"

This time I filled the paper cup, without comment. I was still working on my first drink. If she had much more I thought she might float out over the transom into the hall.

"Ernie Dygert," she said, after drinking half of the full cup, her voice not thick but her words spaced further than they had been when she first came in, "is a no good son of a bitch."

"Granted," I said.

The smile showed her gums this trip. It seemed a shame that someone hadn't told her about that.

"My husband was a very great man," she told me, "an independent conservative in an age when most conservatives get their ideas from either *Time* magazine or the Chicago *Tribune*. He was doing an important job, and doing it well. I helped him. We were a pretty good team, I thought. A few years back I was just his secretary, you know." She held out her glass. "I needed that. One more, please? Just a small one; I'll say when."

I poured. A small one turned out to be half the cup. "Say it again. I like the way you say it."

"Pros't."

"Pros't, Mr. Drum. We were a fine team, as I said. The work we were doing became so important that I convinced my husband to retire from the Senate and devote full time to it. You might call him a one-man lobby for the preservation of the American way of life."

That didn't get anything out of me. The way some people saw Judson Bonner, he was a one-man lobby for the preservation of the American way of life as Judson Bonner had decided the American way of life ought to be.

"Then Ernie Dygert came along." A look of drunken hatred, exaggerated almost to the point of burlesque, contorted her face. "Listen to me," she said.

"You can say what you want about my husband, but he has standards. He's a good man. A great man." Mrs. Bonner looked around slowly in drunken suspicion, then leaned forward across the desk and waggled a fingernail the color of her hair in front of my face. "Judson's got a theory. There's a skeleton in every man's closet, he says. So, if the government makes a mistake, puts someone in a position where he's liable to hurt this country, Judson feels it's time the skeleton, or the dirty wash, or whatever you want to call it, was aired. Like Duncan Hadley Lord. In a hypothetical case—say, Duncan Lord—Judson goes to the man first. If he agrees to do the right thing, if he will alter his policies in line with the best interests of the country, what we've found will go no further. But if he refuses—and Duncan Lord refused, Mr. Drum—then Judson has no recourse but to air the dirty wash. You see? He's fair."

She repeated: "A great man. But Judson was never a great one for details. That's where I came in. You believe it, a great li'l old head for details?" She tapped the side of her head to prove it. "Then Dygert." She said an ugly word and hoped Dygert could apply it to himself. "I didn't turn up anything in my investigation of Duncan Lord. Maybe I would have, but Judson became impatient, because if we didn't hurry, Lord and what Lord believed would become entrenched in USIA. Around that time, Dygert came to my husband."

She paused, smoothed her red hair with one hand and went on. "Oh, Christ, Judson wanted to get something on Duncan Lord. Because Lord was dedicated to the shameful misuse abroad of government funds, something Judson's been fighting all his life. Anyhow," she admitted grudgingly, "Dygert's a good detective. It was Dygert who got the goods on Lord, not me. My methods are old-fashioned and soft, that's what Dygert said. He actually laughed."

She stuck out her chest. "Me, old-fashioned." There was nothing old-fashioned about her chest. "The son of a bitch sold my husband a bill of goods. He was taking over. He was going to handle our investigations, not me. He got a fat retainer to do it. He—"

"Even after the Lord affair backfired?"

"More so then. Because"—here she stopped, set her lips firmly, and went on—"Judson became frightened. If we weren't going to be involved in the Lord thing, after it went wrong, only Ernie Dygert could keep us out. That's what he said, and Judson believed him." She glared at me in drunken fury. "Before you knew it, Dygert was practically running the show. That did it. It—it was like retiring me to the farm. Do I look like I'm ready to retire to any old farm?"

"Exactly what do you want me to do, Mrs. Bonner?"

"You have your reasons for hating Ernie Dygert, just as I have mine. You're in his business. You know how he operates. I want you to get him for me. I want you to ruin him. I don't care what you do. I won't care how it's done. I just want you to get Dygert."

I took a wild stab. "What about your boys—Gilbert and the blond fellow? Can't they do the job?"

First her face reddened. Then she smirked, and the smirk turned into that smile which did the wrong things to her face. "You see?" she said triumphantly. "You're astute. I knew it! I knew you would be."

"Thanks, but that doesn't answer my question."

"Them? They're a couple of kids."

"But they work for you? You hired them? You pay their bills?"

Her smile wasn't pretty now, and it had nothing to do with how she showed her teeth. "Oh, I see what you're getting at. Money. It's money you want to talk about now." She leaned forward, and the plain gray dress obediently fell away from her skin to show the deep shadow between her full breasts. "Well, I don't have much money of my own. Not that Curt and Gilbert ever needed much of that to satisfy them."

The wild stab had been a good one. If Mrs. Bonner thought she had the merchandise I wanted, I'd have an ally—and maybe some information. "Curt and Gilbert work for you, then?"

"Yes. What difference does it make?"

"And get paid for their efforts in the nearest bed, of which there must be plenty in that big house of yours?"

She got up, still smiling, and came around the desk and stood in front of me. Then she slapped my face so hard the swivel chair made a quarter turn.

"That's for being too smart too fast," she said. Then she dropped in my lap and her lips started grazing on my face. When they reached my lips she gave me what she must have thought was a bride's kiss. I thought it was a whore's kiss.

"And that," she said, "is for proving you're smart enough to be the man I need." She sat up straight, still on my lap, and pulled my head against her breast. She was trembling with excitement, but that was no credit to my virility because she had something else on her mind. "Ruin him for me, Chester!" she cried. "You can do it! I know you can, I just know it." She stood up and leaned on the desk. "Forgive me," she said, "I'm a little drunk. But that way you can get down to fundamentals so quickly. Can't you?"

I said that you could. Then I said, "How do I go about ruining your friend Ernie Dygert?"

She licked her lips. Then, while she applied more lipstick to them, I wiped it off my face with a handkerchief.

"You'll do it?"

I leered at her. She lived in a simple world with an old man for a husband and two strong young punks barely out of their teens as lackies-of-all-trade.

I said, "If you get fundamental enough, often enough."

That was what she wanted to hear. She stood in front of me with her hands planted on her hips and said in hardly more than a whisper: "I'll bet you know how to do things Curt and Gilbert haven't even dreamed of." She waited. I smiled. It must have been the right kind of smile. She said, "We'll have to do it together," then laughed nervously but brazenly. "To Ernie Dygert, I mean. Because he's going to get himself out on a limb again, and when he does I'll be there."

"And when he does, you'll let me know."

"I'll let you know. You'll drop everything and come running?"

"I'll come running."

The words sounded familiar. For a moment I couldn't place them. Then I remembered.

Call me, Chet.

I'll call you.

I'll come running.

And Bobby Hayst blowing me a kiss outside her apartment building.

"...because, naturally, I wouldn't have to pay you," Mrs. Bonner was saying. "You want to get Dygert as much as I do. You, because of what he did to you. Me, because I want things to be how they were before Dygert horned in. Right?"

"Right as rain," I said.

Mrs. Bonner went to the door.

"Don't forget."

"How could I?"

Satisfied, she took her nymphomania and got out of there. I hadn't even learned her first name, but she had left the scent of her perfume in the office. I couldn't open the window wide enough to get rid of it.

CHAPTER FIFTEEN

Thanksgiving weekend came and went. There was no snow in Washington, though it grew cold enough to snow. In the papers they told about early snows blanketing New England and Northern New York and wrote copy about a real old-fashioned winter and copy about the satellite race and more purges in Red China and fruitless talk in the U.N. and how the consumer price index had gone up another fraction of a percent.

I lived off what was left of my bank account and drank too much and never managed to be tired enough for a good night's sleep. After a week, I closed the office and listed the telephone number with an answering service which I checked every afternoon out of habit. Now that I was out of business, cases really piled in. I referred them to friends in the trade and got words of thanks and sympathy and a few free lunches.

It was one of those times in your life when you'd chew a dinosaur's leg if you had a dinosaur's leg to chew, just to break out of the lethargy that was smothering you. I called Bobby every day, but there was no answer. I went over there the day after Thanksgiving, but the building manager told me she had checked out leaving no forwarding address. I glared at my dwindling bank account and called Hank Marshall, who runs a two-man agency on New York Avenue and asked him to trace Bobby for me. Because I'd given Hank a couple of cases in the last few days he insisted on doing it for free.

Hank Marshall called me on a Sunday afternoon. "Chrissake," he complained, "what did you get me into?"

It sounded like trouble. I thought of Bobby. "What's the matter?" I said.

"Chrissake, boy. I go up there. The Hayst dame, her place. I show the buzzer and give the building manager a fin. He just looks at me. It winds up being a sawbuck."

"What happened?"

"The apartment ain't been rented yet. He leaves the passkey on his desk and turns around to mumble at the wall. You know the old pitch."

"Why didn't you just ask to see the place, to rent it?"

"Couples or single broads. That's all. Don't you think I tried? Anyhow, I take the key and go up there. Chrissake, they'd been through the place with a bulldozer. Bedding torn. Rugs ripped up. Frames stripped off the pictures."

"Had she left anything behind?"

"Chrissake, if she did they got it. Whoever the hell they were."

"No, I mean clothes, things like that."

"You already told me she checked out. It was bag and baggage, boy. Well,

then this manager gets a kind of guilty feeling, you know how they sometimes get. And me standing there with my goddamn hand in the cookie jar
someone else took all the cookies out of. He almost passes out on me. He
starts in hollering bloody murder. I finally shove it through his thick skull that
I wouldn't of had the time to do a job like that. Chrissake, I was only in there
five minutes. Five minutes. Six guys working with bolos couldn't of done all
that damage in five *hours!* What the hell were they looking for?"

I said I didn't know.

"You want I should make like a skip-tracer, Chet?"

"If you've got the time, Hank. It's important."

"Time I got. But she left a trail as cold as a frigid bride's first night. Chrissake."

Hank complained some more, but knowing him, that meant he was mad
at himself for not being able to find Bobby. I thanked him in advance for anything he could do, and hung up.

I took a long, stiff drink. That didn't help. I was scared, because Bobby was
up to her lovely blonde hair in trouble. She'd propositioned Jerry Trowbridge
for a job, and he'd agreed. Too willingly, of course. Which meant that either
Jerry or Dygert had seen right through her. What they'd been hoping to find
in her apartment I didn't know. Something which would explain what she
really wanted, maybe. Or something from me. There probably hadn't been
anything to find, but that didn't matter. They were on to her.

They were on to her.

I called Jerry Trowbridge's apartment, intending to play the heavy. Lay off
Bobby Hayst, or else. Deliver her safe and sound, buddy, or you're dead. I was
that scared, and I would have meant it. But there wasn't any answer.

Dygert's office would be closed on Sunday, so I looked up a home address
for him in the directory. There wasn't any. Information told me it was an
unlisted number. No, sir. Not under any circumstances. We cannot give it
out. That is why it is unlisted, sir. I'm sorry.

I tried Jerry again that night. When there was no answer, I drove over to his
apartment just off Rhode Island Avenue in a big old house which had been
split up for eight or ten tenants.

"He's gone," the landlord said.

"What do you mean, gone?"

"Don't jump down my throat, mister. Been gone three days. Out of town."

"Where out of town?"

"Search me, mister. Just out of town, he said."

I held out a five-dollar bill, which disappeared the usual way. "Look," I said,
"give it some thought. He must have done something which would tell you
where."

The landlord was a stout man with a face made for scowling. He scowled. "Can't think of anything right off."

"Well," I said desperately, "if he was going fishing, he might take a fishing pole."

"He didn't take no fishing pole."

"I just meant that to give you an idea. Was there anything in the way he packed which might have indicated where he was going?"

"I didn't watch him pack, mister. Saw him come down."

"Yes?"

"Got picked up in a cab by a real big guy. Not the driver. The guy waiting in back. He got out to help them load up Mr. Trowbridge's stuff. That's how I happened to see him. I don't snoop."

"Of course not. A real big guy? Bigger than me?"

He considered it. "Yup. Even bigger."

"Dark hair, beetling brow and a broken nose?"

"Well, heck, mister. I guess you know him."

"What kind of cab was it?"

"Heck, I don't remember. You sound like a detective."

"Veterans' Cab? Capitol Transit? Durant's?"

"I just don't remember, mister."

"He traveling light or heavy?"

He scowled again. "Light, I guess. A couple of pieces, but he couldn't stuff all his gear into them. There were these ski boots."

"Ski boots?" I said. I almost grabbed him.

"Yeah, like I said. Had the laces tied and the boots over his shoulder. Can't miss ski boots, can you?"

That was all I got out of him. Jerry and Dygert had gone north. For skiing. And Bobby?

Monday morning I called Dygert's office. He was out of town, indefinitely, whereabouts unknown. I tried my luck with Ike Wilson, the gossip columnist for the *Star-Courier*.

"Bobby Hayst?" he said. "Oh, my, the hard life you detectives lead." Apparently he hadn't seen the small article in the papers. I didn't have the heart to disillusion him. "A funny thing," he said. "She just walked out. I happen to know, because a friend of mine just flew in the other day from Caracas with a bundle of money and—the wife should only hear me—a hankering for a blonde girl. I thought of Bobby right away, but her number's been disconnected." Ike stopped talking. I could picture him blushing. "Hey, don't get the wrong idea, I do this only for my friends, I assure you. Anyway, two or three of her girlfriends didn't know where she was, either. They said she'd been out of circulation for a couple of weeks." Ike paused again. "Come to think of it, ever since you asked me for her number."

He tried to pump me to find out if that was a coincidence. The idea seemed to both startle and amuse him. "Pumping a dry well, huh?" he said finally. "I can take a hint. Well, so long."

The posters in the window of the Capital Travel Bureau on E Street showed gay young things in scarlet or aqua ski togs swooshing down white hills. The skiing season was on its way, all right. I went inside and got taken in tow by a tall mannish woman with severely plastered-back black hair with a wide white part as straight as a ski jump, or maybe I was just projecting.

"Skiing?" she said, in answer to my question. "Oh yes, we know a number of good places this time of year."

"I'm interested in a place where there's bound to be snow, even now, in November." Jerry, I thought, had taken his ski boots. They're bulky and get in the way, and if skiing or not skiing depended on the weather, he could have rented boots as needed. I began to feel like a detective again.

"Well, I could recommend some mighty fine places in New England or upper New York State." The mannish woman frowned. "But to tell you the truth, don't believe all you hear about all the fine skiing snow in those districts this early in the year. They have wonderful press agents. If you really want a guarantee of good skiing snow, in November, I'd say the Laurentians every time."

That sounded reasonable enough, because the Laurentians were due north of Montreal, Canada. "There many places up there?" I asked.

"Goodness, I could give you a list of seventy or eighty. What sort of place did you have in mind?"

"I don't exactly know. Luxury, probably. Sure, a luxury place. I like to ski, but I like to rub elbows with people who count, if you know what I mean."

"Yes, naturally. I know what you mean."

"Like, if there was a place you just knew had some VIPs right now, because you booked them... congressmen, maybe, or big operators around Washington? The wife would go for that."

I waited. The mannish face frowned. "Umm, no, I can't recall right off any people like that I booked."

"Well, I guess that really doesn't matter." I let it go for a second, then asked: "Say, what's the best way to get up there, anyway?"

"You'd be flying? Anything else just takes days."

I said I would be flying.

"Well, there are three airlines flying from Washington to Montreal. From there smaller chartered flights take you to Mont Tremblant or the other skiing areas." She brought out some brochures and quoted airline rates. She gave me an envelope so full of brochures it was almost as thick as a telephone directory. I said I'd let her know and got out of there.

I struck paydirt on my second telephone call.

"That's it," I said, after I'd been put through to the right person. "I'm Mr. Dygert's assistant. You see, we left these goggles out of his bag, and while I know you can get ski goggles anywhere, these are special goggles, made in Austria. Mr. Dygert is prone to snow-blindness." I waited. Then I said in a rush, "Frankly, it was my fault. I mean, Mr. Dygert told me to see that the goggles were packed, but I just forgot." I tried to sound worried. Hell, it was easy. I *was* worried. "I'm liable to lose my job," I said.

"Exactly what do you wish us to do, sir?"

"I want to know where to send the goggles."

"But surely you know where your employer went."

"That's the funny part of it. You don't know Mr. Dygert," I groaned. "When he finally does get away, he really wants to get away. He didn't leave any address. All I know is he went skiing in the Laurentians."

"Well, just a moment, sir." I waited, and sweated. Then: "I'm sorry, sir. Trans-Canada booked a party of six, including your Mr. Dygert, as far as Montreal. We did not book them further. You see, although we do run a service into the mountains, it's only a short run over good roads and a party of six might well have decided to hire a private car in Montreal. That method of travel, especially for a party of that size, is very popular in the Laurentians."

The string had run out. I thanked Trans-Canada's man and hung up. I had a destination now, which was something. The Laurentians. And a party of six. I mulled it over. Dygert and Jerry, of course. And Bobby makes three. Judson Bonner and his wife would bring the total to five. If they were going to Canada to put the screws on someone as they had put them on Duncan Lord, the sixth man wouldn't be their victim. He'd already be there, waiting. If there was to be a victim. Because Bobby Hayst could be enough. But why Canada? And how the devil could I find out where, among all the skiing resorts in the Laurentians, they had gone?

I had one more call to make, long distance to Toano, Virginia....

"Bonner residence." It wasn't Curt and it wasn't Gilbert. It was a voice I had never heard before.

"Hello, this is Mr. Hauser," I said, "the baggage master of Trans-Canada Airlines at Washington International Airport. Something extremely embarrassing has happened. You see, on our weekly check of unclaimed incoming luggage we found a piece of outgoing luggage. Investigation determined that it was checked aboard on your Mr. Bonner's recent flight to Montreal and we'd like to send it right on to him but have been unable to find a forwarding address."

"How sure are you it belongs to Mr. Bonner?"

"We're positive."

There was a pause. Then: "I'm not. Mr. Bonner's luggage isn't marked." I didn't know why he was suspicious. Probably, because he was paid to be suspicious. He added, "Better describe the piece to me."

"I don't have it here in my office," I said in a slightly annoyed tone. "All I have is the report."

"Well, go take a look at it and call me back. Or better yet, I'll give you fifteen minutes and call you back at Trans-Canada. Mr. Hauser, huh?"

And the phone went click in my ear.

I stared at the wall across my living room. A Gauguin reproduction showing two nude Polynesian girls wading in a stream hangs there, but the wall I had reached looking for Bobby was a blank one.

With death on the other side.

CHAPTER SIXTEEN

The telegram came just before midnight.

MEET ME MONT TREMBLANT POST OFFICE, MONT TREM-
BLANT P.Q. CANADA, THREE TOMORROW AFTERNOON.
                                        DOROTHY BONNER

I smiled at the little sheet of stiff yellow paper and read it again. She had
never told me her first name, but I didn't need her first name to know that
Mrs. Judson Bonner was sending for her ally.

A phone call to Trans-Canada got me a reservation on the ten A.M. Viscount. After that I cleaned, oiled and loaded my Magnum .357 and felt some-
what melodramatic doing it. Then I thought of Bobby and the feeling went
away while I paced around the apartment, made a drink and left it standing.
I read the telegram a third time. A day's work, much of it on the phone but
still the kind of work a detective does, had narrowed the trail and left me
with a couple of hundred square miles of Quebec Province. Mrs. Bonner's
telegram had made the day's work superfluous—or had it? I felt ready and
reasonably sure of myself again, for the first time since they'd lifted my
license. That was important. Telegram or no, I'd have flown up to Canada in
a funk otherwise. Just hang on, Bobby, I thought. Hang on.

Cocky bastard, I told myself. I went to sleep....

The Viscount put down at Montreal International Airport shortly after one
the next day. It was a cold day with a lead gray overcast and the smell of snow
in the air. With three ski buffs I was directed across the field to a small twin-
engined plane. As soon as a baggage cart brought our luggage and it was
loaded aboard, the engines started with explosive spurts. Moments later we
were winging across the field and toward the snow country to the north.

Ten minutes this side of Mont Tremblant, the view far below of white-
mantled hills and clumps of spruce and hemlock was obscured by a swirling
snowstorm. "Gonna be perfect skiing tomorrow," someone said happily.

"If it stops snowing."

"Hell, man. I only have four days. It better stop."

We landed bumpily at Mont Tremblant's small airport. The runway was
very close to the town itself, on the only flat ground I could see. Great soft
feathers of snow were falling in the cold, almost windless air. I turned up the
collar of my trenchcoat, pulled my hat brim down and carried my suitcase

over to the post office, passing through half of Mont Tremblant to get there. The town was Swiss chalet style, the buildings made of logs with high peaked roofs and ornate half-timbering and colorful exterior wall murals. Despite the snowstorm, the skiers were out in force, thrusting ahead on the powdery snow in the streets or carrying their skis on their shoulders or riding in horse-drawn sleighs with jingling bells and skis racked behind. I reached the post office at ten after two, went inside, stamped off my shoes and waited.

An hour later, I was still looking at the wanted posters. It grew dim outside and the snow still came down. The post office wasn't busy. A couple of tourists in heavy ski boots clomped in for their mail. At about four-thirty a man wearing a plaid mackinaw brought in the sack of mail that had come up on the plane from Montreal with me. At five the clerks began to put on their outer clothing and I heard a clanking as one of them opened the fire door and spread the embers in the pot-bellied stove that heated the small post office.

"We close now, *monsieur*," one of them said apologetically as he headed for the door. "There was something... ?"

I looked at my watch. Five o'clock. But the clock on the wall had already told me that.

And no Mrs. Bonner.

The door rattled and opened before the clerk reached it. A stout, bespectacled French-Canadian wearing a floppy knitted toque hat, a double-breasted overcoat with a fur collar and a bright *ceinture flechee* sash around his ample middle came into the post office and looked around myopically. He squinted at me.

"Monsieur Drum?" he asked.

I nodded.

"*S'il vous plait?*"

He led the way outside. A small horse-drawn sleigh was waiting. The stout French-Canadian waited in the snow while I climbed aboard. He followed me, almost tipping the sleigh. He smiled, blew his white breath in my face, and flicked the reins. Its harness bells jingling, the horse began to trot through the snow, the sleigh runners hissing.

We went to the end of town and up a little hill. You couldn't see the roadbed because it was covered with new snow, but the towers and cables of a ski lift followed the road up the hill to a large Swiss-chalet-style building. There was a small parking lot with a dozen cars almost hidden under their burden of snow. More sleighs, unharnessed, were waiting in the driveway. The gay music of an accordion playing "Alouette" drifted out into the snow and the night.

"The Grand Hotel Hemlock," my driver said with a flourish, and climbed down with my suitcase. *"Monsieur stays long?"*

"Mrs. Bonner sent you?" I asked.

"Ah, *oui, oui,* Mrs. Bonner." He made a long face. "The tragedy, *monsieur.* The tragedy of it."

I followed him inside. We went through a lounge where skiers in slipper socks and furry mukluks were seated sipping hot drinks and listening to a man with the reddest face and biggest smile I had ever seen playing "Alouette" on the accordion.

At the desk I was given a registration slip to sign. The clerk smiled at me. "Of course a room with bath on such short notice we could not give you," he said.

"What about Mrs. Bonner?" I said.

"Yes, yes. They have the grand suite."

"She in now?"

"But of course." The clerk gave me a sad smile. "And with all this—how you say?—gaiety in the lounge." He turned and snapped his fingers. He was a precise little man in a suit so dark gray it looked black. Maybe it was black. "Boy!" he called in French. "Show Monsieur Drum to his room."

"No. I want to see Mrs. Bonner now," I almost yelled.

The clerk gave me a searching look. Then he shrugged. "Show *monsieur* to the grand suite, then take his bags."

The bellboy turned out to be a middle-aged man wearing a satin-backed vest and a green apron. I went with him to an open-cage elevator and up in it to the second floor. We walked down the hall and he stopped and knocked at a door, then stepped diffidently back.

A homely young woman I had never seen before opened the door. She gazed at us blankly. I began to think the plane had set me down in the wrong world. *"Oui?"*

"This is Monsieur Drum," the man in the green apron said.

The woman looked at me distastefully. "You are late," she said severely in English. "Well, it does not matter. He lingers. He—just—lingers. You are a relative?"

"I want to see Mrs. Bonner. She sent for me."

"Naturally. Come in, please."

She stepped back so that I could enter a large French provincial living room. Three closed doors led off it. On one wall big logs burned on a bed of ash in an enormous fireplace. The door closed behind me. The woman left the living room through one of the other doors, opening and shutting it softly. I lit a cigarette. There was a tray of whisky and glasses on an end table, and I made myself a Scotch and water and waited. Presently the door through which the homely young woman had disappeared opened and shut again. Mrs. Bonner came out.

She wore a flannel shirt and slacks which made her hips look too big and too low. Her hair was not combed. Her eyes were red and swollen from crying.

"He just sat down and said he wanted water," she said after a while. "Just a little water. Then he clutched his chest. The doctor is with him now." She spoke in little confused fits and starts, as if she had lost all touch with time sequence. "He is in an oxygen tent. They brought it up from Montreal this afternoon. The doctor won't leave him."

All I had for her was a blank stare.

"Judson," she said. "It is Judson. This morning they had an argument. Judson. And Ernie Dygert. When he cracks his whip even Gilbert jumps now. Even Curt." She paused. "They don't come out and say it, but I can see it in their faces. The doctor. The nurse. Judson. He's going to die. Judson is going to die."

She made a stiff drink for herself. I took it away from her and gave her a cigarette instead. "Get hold of yourself," I said.

"Judson had a coronary," she said.

The nurse came out. "Madame Bonner." She pronounced it Bone-ay.

Without another look at me Mrs. Bonner followed her through the doorway. The door closed. I finished my drink and walked in front of the fire to stare at the flames. Judson Bonner was dying. It didn't mean anything to me one way or the other. But it did mean delay. At least I knew that Dygert was here or had been here this morning. I saw a phone on a table in one corner of the room. I picked it up.

"S'il vous plaît?"

"Is a Miss Hayst registered here?"

"Yes, sir."

I let out a long breath. "Connect me with her room."

"She is out, monsieur. She left this afternoon."

"With her baggage?"

"No. No, of course not."

"The minute she comes back, tell her I'm here. This is Mr. Drum. Send her to me. No, keep her down there and call me. I'll be here or in my own room. You got it?"

"Of course, sir."

I hung up. Mrs. Bonner came into the room, followed by a tall man carrying a satchel. He looked dignified and grave. "There is nothing, madame," he said in French. "Nothing we can do that we have not done. In such cases, you wait with God. I will be in the hotel tonight. If there is a change... if I am needed..."

"His face," Mrs. Bonner told me. "As if he must fight for every breath he takes. As if he is in great pain."

"There is no pain whatsoever," the doctor assured her in English.

"Oh, get out!" Mrs. Bonner screamed at him suddenly. "Get out, get out! You talk of pain. He is dying. Dying! What does a little pain matter—if he could live?"

"Madame, under the circumstances, I would like you to take a sedative."

"Get out!" Mrs. Bonner cried. "I don't want a sedative. I don't want... oh, I'm sorry. I'm sorry. I didn't mean to shout at you. I just don't want..." She began to cry.

"*Monsieur?*" the doctor said to me, heading for the hall door.

Mrs. Bonner looked up. "No. I want him to stay. You'll stay, won't you, Chester?"

I said I would stay. The doctor went out. "If only he had listened to me," Mrs. Bonner said softly. "Then this wouldn't have happened." She picked up the drink I had taken away from her a few minutes ago. She drank it and sat down on the carpet in front of the fireplace. "I ought to be in there with him," she said. I didn't say anything. "Give me a cigarette."

I gave her one, and lit it. She smoked for a while, then threw the butt in the fire and turned to look at me.

"The argument began last night," she said slowly. "I can't go in there now. I want to tell you about it. Even Judson, by then, had begun to treat me like a useless little girl." She stood up. When she spoke again her voice had come down in pitch and she was no longer crying. She seemed to be talking about something that had happened a long time ago, perhaps to someone else or in another life. "The man's name is Goheen. He's an assistant secretary in the Canadian Foreign Office and the new Canadian liaison man to the U.S. on atomic energy. He's here on vacation before reporting to his new post. At least Judson and Dygert agree on that: Why should there be any liaison on atomic energy? Why should we give our secrets to foreign powers, even Canada? But Judson's usual investigations hit a blank wall. Goheen had led an exemplary life. We had hoped that if he had been discredited after he came to Washington, then..."

"Tell me about Dygert," I urged. "But don't expect me to jump on your ideological bandwagon."

"This much we found out about Goheen. He's an ambitious career man. If we could get something on him, threaten him with what we had—"

"There would be a payoff," I finished for her.

"Well, all right. All right, it was Dygert's idea. Goheen, you see, comes from a rich family. Dygert tried to convince my husband they could put Goheen in the same sensitive situation they tried to put Duncan Lord. But I don't have to tell you there's a basic difference. Because Lord would have been in a policy-making position, while Goheen is only a liaison officer. But since Dygert had managed to discredit me and Judson had learned... well, not to think for himself, he went along with Dygert.

"A few days ago, Dygert sent Curt up here. Not to this hotel. To the Hotel St. Laurent, where Goheen is staying—with instructions to become friendly with Goheen. Curt's a skier—and charming. He was successful. Do you begin to see?"

"Bobby Hayst," I said, without thinking. "Setting him up for her."

"How did you know about her?" Mrs. Bonner asked.

"Okay. I know. She's the main reason I'm here."

"But you said—"

"Never mind what I said. Now I'm telling you that still puts us on the same side."

She laughed. It was not a happy sound. "Even you," she said. "Even you don't take me seriously. You only pretended to want to help me."

"To get Dygert or to help Bobby Hayst, what difference does it make?"

She sighed, then looked at her empty glass and went over to the liquor tray to fill it. I got in the way. "That's enough," I said. "I want you to talk."

"You have no right—"

"None at all," I said, and smiled at her.

"All of you," she said with self-pity. "Every last one of you, while he lies dying in there."

"Just talk."

The door to Judson Bonner's room opened and the homely nurse came out. "He's resting comfortably for the first time," she said. "I think, with God's help, he is going to be well." The nurse smiled at us, a hopeful, optimistic smile which lit up her homely face, then returned to the sickroom.

"Then if he's going to be all right, all I have to do is wait," Mrs. Bonner said without logic.

I grasped her shoulders and shook her. "They never trusted Bobby Hayst, did they?"

"I don't have to say anything now. Leave me alone. Get out of here."

I let her go. I thought that was her vanity talking. I went to the door.

"Wait."

I turned around. "All of it," I said. "The works."

"You lied to me. You tried to trick me."

"I love you too, Mrs. Bonner. Sure, I lied to you. What difference does it make?"

She turned and spoke to the fire. "I knew it would happen like this. I knew it. It wasn't good enough for Ernie Dygert to be an investigator. If he couldn't find what he was looking for, he'd manufacture it. That's what he was going to do—here. That's what the argument was about. Last night. This morning. Judson wouldn't be a party to anything like that. I don't have to tell you with Duncan Lord it was different. He made his own bed. What he did he did of his own free will. But this would be—"

"Dygert's had plenty of experience as a divorce detective. Go ahead."

"You're right, they never trusted your little whore. They tried to find something that could tie her to you. They even went through her place. From what I overheard they took it apart. They couldn't find a thing, but that didn't change what Dygert thought. He didn't trust her. Still, as long as she played along, he could use her. If she stopped playing along, if she tried to make trouble... Anyway, Judson wouldn't hear of it. They argued and Judson—was stricken." She turned around. Her eyes were bright with fear and hate. She was almost crying. "The girl was supposed to go over there tonight. It would be easy for Curt to drug Goheen. They became friends. Skied together. Drank together. Then, in his room, they would undress him and take pictures of him in bed with the girl."

"He married?"

"Curt found out. His wife is pregnant, or she would have joined him here. Curt mentioned it this morning. It seemed to amuse him." She added in self-defense: "I never knew he was like that. Anyway, you know what happened to Judson."

"What about tonight?"

"In the confusion after Judson was stricken, the girl got away. I don't know what she was planning to do, originally. I think she would have gone along with Dygert for her own purposes—whatever her own purposes were. But when Curt mentioned the pregnant Mrs. Goheen, that was a mistake. She changed. You could actually see it. She went over there early this afternoon. To the St. Laurent."

"To the St. Laurent? Why?"

"Suppose you tell me. Did you send her up here to trap us? Because if you did, what better way than that? She tells Goheen, then both of them play along—and go straight to the police before Dygert has a chance to leave Canada with his film."

I nodded slowly. Bobby could have decided to do just that.

"Well, Dygert went after her," Mrs. Bonner said spitefully. "Right before it started snowing. It's two miles to the St. Laurent. If you ask me, she never got there. I looked out the window. All the horse sleds were in use. She went on skis, but she isn't much of a skier. Dygert's an expert, and so is Curt. She never even got there, I tell you. They stopped her. They had to stop her. She knew all our plans. They had to stop her for good."

She was yelling after me when I reached the door. "Wait, please! We're still in this together. Don't you see, Judson was torn between going on the way he was and breaking with Dygert. He said he was going to tell the police in Virginia what Dygert had done. If it wasn't criminal, at least it would get Dygert out of our hair. Then Judson had his coronary. Then—"

"Who was he going to tell, Sheriff Lonegran?"

"Wait! You've got to wait."

But I slammed the door behind me and ran for the stairs. She opened the door and called me a name. I took the stairs down three at a time.

When I got outside it was really snowing. A stiff cold wind had sprung up and the sleigh driver I found told me, "From the northwest. From La Verendrye it comes. It will snow all night and bring the Arctic cold." He puffed a big pipe complacently. He was warmly bundled in a mackinaw and a heavy wool scarf. Winter was his friend.

"Take me to the Hotel St. Laurent," I said.

"Two miles, *monsieur!* My little horse is tired. I am tired."

"Twenty dollars," I said, "if you make it in half an hour."

He grinned and tapped out his pipe. "For ten dollars a mile I would take you to La Verendrye itself. *Allons!*"

I climbed aboard. "Haya! Hey!" he shouted to the horse. The harness bells jingled.

CHAPTER SEVENTEEN

It took us forty minutes, the sleigh slipping and lurching up hills and down and around steep turns, to reach the St. Laurent. We drove through a blizzard of swirling snow and shrieking wind. The driver gave me a thick plaid blanket, but still I was almost numb with cold when we pulled to a stop. The horse shook itself. Despite the snow and the cold, it was lathering. I gave the driver twenty dollars and ran inside.

The Hotel St. Laurent was larger than the Hemlock, its lobby more crowded, noisier. Three groups clustered around three different accordionists. The resulting music was a discordant confusion of sound; and because the evening was older, more drinking had been done. Everyone looked amazingly healthy and slightly high. I had to push my way through to the desk.

"Mr. Goheen," I said. "It's urgent."

The clerk looked at me professionally, at the snow melting on my trenchcoat, at my gloveless hands. "You are not a guest?" he said. He had white hair and a pink face with dewlaps. He wore small rimless glasses and they perched too low on the bridge of his nose.

"I said it was urgent."

"Two-seventeen, *s'il vous plait*," he called behind him to a PBX operator. I waited. The operator shook her head. "Mr. Goheen is not in his room," the elderly clerk told me.

"Maybe he's in the lobby."

"Then you do not know him, *monsieur?*"

"No. He here?"

The clerk looked around, adjusting the glasses higher on the bridge of his nose. "Ah, ah," he said, "the clothing they wear." He clucked his tongue.

The lobby was a confusing sea of bright reds, blues and yellows, of plaids and overplaids, of dancing, singing, drinking vacationers. A lithe girl jumped up on a table in her slipper socks and toasted a deerhead on the wall with a steaming mug. An accordionist played an arpeggio as she came down in a man's arms. He kissed her, and the crowd swirled around them.

"*Alouette!*" someone shouted.

The accordionist played and they sang a chorus of "Alouette," clapping their hands and stamping their feet.

"Every year younger," the clerk said, shaking his head. "Or I am growing older." He smiled, then the smile faded. "There is Mr. Goheen," he said, pointing across the lobby a little reluctantly.

I looked where he was pointing. A tall man only a few years older than most of the others was sitting with a mug in his hand. Three very young, very happy girls were holding court around him. He wore a red and black plaid shirt and looked happy. I went over there.

"Mr. Goheen?" I said.

"Who're you?" one of the girls asked me with a big grin. She had long yellow hair and flushed red cheeks and looked a little drunk. "Whoever you are, get undressed. I mean, get out of those silly clothes and into something sensible. At least come on and sing. Stop looking so serious. Do you play the accordion?"

"I'm afraid she's had a bit too much to drink," Goheen told me. "Yes, I'm Goheen. Why?"

The blonde took my hand and pulled me toward her chair. "At least sit down. Why—you're freezing cold." She patted my hand. Someone thrust a mug in my hand. It was hot and it was a good idea. I drank.

"Did a girl come looking for you this afternoon? A blonde? Pretty?"

"The place is crawling with blondes," one of the other girls said. She was, of course, a brunette.

"What's the matter with blondes?" the blonde girl asked indignantly, raising her voice.

"I'm afraid I can't hear you," Goheen said with a smile. "But no one came looking for me this afternoon. No blondes or anything." The brunette smiled at him. He smiled back, but in an amused fatherly fashion. I decided Dygert knew his business: the only way they would have got Bobby into bed with him was if they drugged him.

"You have a friend," I shouted over the noise. "You met him up here. Named Curt?"

Goheen frowned. He wasn't angry, but he was puzzled. "Say, what is this?" he asked me. "Just what do you want, mister?"

"What would he need any old blonde for?" the brunette demanded. "He's married. Happily married," she added sulkily.

"Curt's a blond lad," I told Goheen. "Twenty-one or -two. Maybe that isn't the name he used."

"I know the man. He isn't here. What's this all about?"

Before I could answer, someone nearby dropped a mug on a cocktail table with a loud crash. I looked up. The girl who had dropped the mug seemed very embarrassed. She brushed at her slacks awkwardly. "Now look what you did!" she accused someone standing near her. About ten feet behind her, in another small group, I saw Gilbert.

"Well?" Goheen asked.

I didn't answer him. I put my mug down and walked over to Gilbert. He had his arm around a girl's shoulder and she was saying: "Then, on account of the fence down there, you have to christie. I mean, *have* to. The snow sprays and you miss the barbed wire by inches. Just *inches*. There ought to be a law."

"What's christie?" Gilbert asked.

"My goodness, don't you know *anything* about skiing?"

Gilbert patted her arm. "In the morning, why don't you teach me?"

I put my hand on Gilbert's shoulder. My other hand was in the pocket of my trenchcoat, gripping the Magnum .357. I thrust it, through the coat, hard against the small of Gilbert's back.

"Hello, Gilbert," I said.

He turned his head slowly. He was wedged between me and the girl. He did not turn his body. His eyes widened and then narrowed.

"My, doesn't *he* look solemn," the girl said. She eased her shoulder away from Gilbert's arm and started to move off.

"No, stick around," Gilbert said.

But a fellow in a turtleneck sweater offered her a drink. They seemed to know each other. The fellow told a joke about a girl skier caught out in the snow and a logger from La Verendrye. Everyone laughed, even Gilbert. I moved my hand down from his shoulder to his biceps. While they were laughing I said softly, "It's a gun. Don't bet it isn't."

The crowd around us followed turtleneck as he went toward the fire beginning another joke. Their laughter drifted back.

"Where's Curt? And Bobby Hayst. All of them."

"Screw you, Drum," Gilbert said.

"Let's go up to Curt's room," I said.

"Screw you," he said again.

"Have it your way." I jabbed with the Magnum. "But you ought to see the statistics on people who get hurt in crowds."

"The arm," he said. "You're hurting the arm."

"Curt's room."

"All I have to do is holler."

"Then holler. Which would leave you holding the bag if anything's happening to Bobby Hayst. Go on and holler."

"What the hell," he grumbled, "I'll take you upstairs."

We pushed through the crowded lobby to the stairs. I never let go of his arm. But across the lobby I saw Goheen watching us as we went upstairs.

"Who says I got a key?" Gilbert whined as we paused outside the door of room 215. He sounded like a juvenile delinquent collared by a tough police sergeant. Hell, he was young enough still to be one if he had gone around in the right circles.

"If you don't open that door I'm going to slug you and search you," I told him.

He fumbled in his pocket, then thrust at the lock with impotent anger. A moment later we stepped into the darkness of Curt's room.

"The light," I said.

There was a click, and a ceiling fixture went on, showing a small room with two twin beds, a wing chair and a dresser. When Gilbert turned around to face me, I hit him. He sailed back toward the nearer bed, his arms flying out, and bounced on it. I hit him again coming up. This time he huddled on the bed, covering his face with his arms. I grabbed the front of his flannel shirt and dragged him to his feet. He swung out blindly and ineffectually with his right fist. I caught it and pivoted him around, forcing his hand up between his shoulder blades.

"Go ahead and horse around," I said.

He hunched over to minimize the strain in his arm. He began to curse me in a soft, steady voice. His selection of words was colorful and graphic, but it was cut off when I moved his arm upward an inch.

"Where's Bobby Hayst?"

"How in hell should I know?"

"When'd you get here?"

"...Afternoon."

"Who with?"

"Dygert. Lay off, will you please? And that guy Trowbridge."

"Chasing Bobby Hayst?"

"Yeah. Yeah."

"Did she reach the hotel before you?"

He tried to wrench free. I pushed the arm up. He sobbed.

"Did she reach the hotel before you?"

"No. We caught her."

"Where?"

"About a quarter mile down the road."

"Then what happened?"

For a moment his bluster came back. "I'm gonna kill you for this, dads."

"Kill me tomorrow," I said, forcing the arm again. "Now better concentrate on talking. After you caught her, what happened?"

"I don't ski so good. They sent me ahead to get Curt. I got him. He took my skis and... told me to make myself at home."

"He went back to the others?"

"Yeah."

"Had they talked about what they would do with Bobby Hayst?"

"I don't know."

"Had they talked about it yesterday? This morning?"

"You're gonna break my arm!"

"Then answer me."

"They talked."

"Spill it."

He sobbed and didn't say anything.

"What you going to get out of this—besides a broken arm?"

"Old man Bonner pays us in peanuts." He spat the words. "His nympho wife... in tail. Dygert showed us real bread."

"What were they planning to do with Bobby Hayst?"

We stood between the door and the closer of the two beds. Gilbert craned his neck to look around desperately. I heard a noise behind me. The door opened and shut.

Goheen came into the room angrily. "What are you doing to that boy?" he said.

I let go of Gilbert, who collapsed on the bed and put on an innocent, boyish look the way other people put on a hat. "He must be nuts," he said.

Taking out the Magnum, I stepped to the foot of the bed so I could cover Goheen and Gilbert. Goheen stood about six feet away from me. He looked at the gun and then up at my face. He took a step toward me.

"You're making a damn-fool mistake," I said.

"Give me the gun and we'll talk about it."

"I told you you're making a mistake."

"The gun, mister."

"A girl was coming here to see you," I said quickly. "She had been hired to pose in bed with you for pictures. She balked. This man and his friends, who had done the hiring, came after her. To stop her. To kill her. This one couldn't ski very well. Your friend Curt could. They changed places."

Goheen said nothing, but his face told me what he thought. He thought I was crazy, but that gave him new respect for the gun in my hand. He stood still, three feet in front of me. He could have reached out and touched the gun. His eyes wavered from my face to it.

"I told you he was nuts," Gilbert said.

That must have made me take my eyes off Goheen for a split second. He lunged for the gun. Just as he grabbed it, I hooked my left hand at his jaw as hard as I could. His eyes went out of focus. He let go of the gun. He wobbled but didn't fall. When I moved back a step he came after me. Then his knees buckled and hit the floor.

Gilbert jumped off the bed and ran for the door.

I got there a step after he did. He yanked the handle and the door started to swing in. I kicked it shut so hard the wall rattled. He spun around and landed a hard right over my heart. He was no good to me dead. Maybe he was beginning to realize that. His left hand clawed at my right wrist. Pulling it free, I laid the gun barrel along his jaw. He went over sideways with the force of the blow and then down on his face.

That was when Goheen jumped me.

He wasn't much of a fighter, but he was a big man and he had guts. I was worried about the gun. It might go off by accident and hurt someone. Goheen had a mugger's grip on me. Staggering under his weight, I reached the bed and dropped the gun there. Then I fell to one knee and sent Goheen cartwheeling over my head. He landed on his back with a thud they must have heard halfway to Montreal.

I put the gun back in my pocket and dragged Goheen to the bed. I wrapped him in the bedspread as tight as a mummy. His eyelids were fluttering, but he was still unconscious. In the closet I found two of Curt's belts and a pair of suspenders. I fastened the belts around Goheen's legs and the suspenders around his torso and arms. After that I got a glass of water from the bathroom and took it over to Gilbert. He was sitting on the floor now, looking dazed and hurt. The left side of his jaw was blue. When I threw the water in his face he spluttered and gasped.

Just then someone knocked at the door.

"I say, is anything wrong in there?" It was an English voice, clipped but concerned. "Heard a dreadful noise."

"I'm sorry," I said. "Just an accident."

"You're quite positive?"

I said I was sure. His footsteps went away.

"What were they going to do with Bobby Hayst?" I asked Gilbert.

He glared up at me, water dripping from his head. But he didn't have any fight left. He said, "The Park. Mont Tremblant Park. It's a wilderness. For cross-country skiing. They were going to take her in there. She can't ski any better than me. They said they were going to leave her in there. You figure out what would happen to her in a storm."

"They took her there tonight?"

"This afternoon. Figure it out, Drum. The girl's as good as dead already."

CHAPTER EIGHTEEN

It was Goheen who called the Mounties. They had a small post at the entrance to Mont Tremblant Park. Goheen did the calling because his name was known and, at his word, any preliminary investigation could be dispensed with. Goheen had regained consciousness while Gilbert was talking. He had asked to be untied in a very small voice. I had had Gilbert do it. After getting loose, Goheen had hit him so hard with his open hand that Gilbert fell down. He got up whimpering and Goheen hit him again.

"How can you ever forgive me?" Goheen had asked me.

"I don't want an apology. I want help."

That was when Goheen called the Mounties. They came inside of fifteen minutes. I had expected scarlet tunics, breeches with a stripe down their seams, top boots and World War I style campaign hats. That must have been the picture Hollywood had given me. They came in hooded O.D. parkas and ski boots. Two of them took Gilbert into custody at once. He began to yell that he wanted a lawyer, but he was told that none of his rights were being infringed unless they placed a specific charge against him and then refused him legal counsel. For twenty-four hours they could hold him on an open charge, and that was what they were going to do.

The Mountie who stayed behind was a tall wiry sergeant named Moriarity. He wanted to hear my story and I gave it to him, all of it, in ten minutes. The words tumbled out almost of their own volition. The only thing I could think of was Bobby out there in the blizzard, alone, freezing, trying to thrust forward on skis she barely knew how to use. The picture in my mind became so vivid that I couldn't keep talking. I stopped to light a cigarette. I felt all choked up inside.

"Our men are out there now," Moriarity told us. "But don't expect miracles. It isn't midnight yet. We won't really be able to do anything until dawn. Does this man Dygert know the park?"

I shook my head.

"That's bad. If he knew the park, we might know the best places to look, the places a man with knowledge of the park might leave her, the deep gullies where the snow piles in soft high drifts." He frowned. "Or the ridges where she'd be exposed to the wind. Or..." He paced around the small room, an active outdoor man who suddenly felt constrained and helpless. "There are almost four hundred square miles of wilderness out there, Mr. Goheen. Of course, on skis in one afternoon they couldn't get very far into it. And they haven't returned yet that we know of. That's a good sign, I think."

He went to the window and lifted the curtain. He stood there a long time watching the snow come down, listening to the wind. "If they're successful," he said, "if they leave her to freeze and get out themselves, the snow will cover their tracks. If that happens, we'd only have your word against theirs."

"It would be murder," Goheen said.

"It would be murder, Mr. Goheen, and they'd stand a good chance of getting away with it." Moriarity turned away from the window. "Well, I'm going to call in, and then I'll get some rest. There's no sense talking about it if talking won't do any good. I suspect they'll be sending me out there at dawn."

"I want to go with you," I said.

He shook his head at once. "I appreciate the gesture, but this is our job, Mr. Drum. We spend five months of the year on skis. You could only hamper us."

"It isn't a gesture. I want to go."

Goheen rubbed the back of his neck and showed us a wry grin. "Mr. Drum is a stubborn man, Sergeant, who doesn't like to take no for an answer."

Moriarity shook his head again. "This time he takes it, Mr. Goheen." He used the room phone to call Mountie headquarters at the entrance to the park. A patrol had already gone out into the storm. They had a walkie-talkie with them but had not yet reported in.

"Get some sleep," Moriarity urged me. "That's what I'm going to do. You'll see things my way in the morning. Well, I guess it's good night for me. The station will contact you, should anything develop. I hope to God they have good news for you before very long."

After the sergeant left, Goheen took me down to the bar for a drink. I don't remember what I had. I went back upstairs with Goheen at a quarter to one and said good night to him outside his door. There was absolutely nothing I could do now, at night. One man alone wouldn't have a chance in the blizzard at night, even if he could handle himself on skis a good deal better than I could. And blundering out there in heroic helplessness wouldn't help Bobby—if she was not beyond help already.

I got short snatches of sleep interspersed with long periods of wakefulness, trying to will myself to sleep because I would need all the rest I could get when morning came. But it didn't work. I saw Bobby huddled in a blanket in Duncan Lord's old farmhouse and Bobby looking beautiful but fussing over me like a mother hen the night I had returned exhausted to my apartment. Then I saw her out in the snow and the wind, her skis moving slowly, agonizingly, her face a mask of pain.

Then I would drift off and three times during the night I thought she called my name and I would sit bolt upright and have to will myself to sleep all over again, listening to the wind which was Bobby's voice calling.

At four o'clock I got out of bed, opened the closet and found a sweater and heavy windbreaker among Curt's things. They were a tight fit but would probably keep out the cold.

When I had put them on, Goheen knocked at the door and came in. He wore ski clothing and an unzipped lumber jacket. "Thought I heard you prowling around," he said. "You're going out there, aren't you?"

"I've got to."

He took a brochure out of his pocket and said, "This comes compliments of the hotel. It's a map of the park with the cross-country ski trails marked out." He put on the night-table lamp and spread the map out. "The X's are shelters along the trail."

That was the first optimistic news I'd had about Bobby. "Then if they left her out there, and if she could have made her way to one of the shelters..."

"Don't get your hopes up. There are hundreds of miles of skiing trails in there, and the shelters are few and far apart. You any good on skis?"

"I managed to get in some skiing in New England the last couple of winters. I'll make out."

"I was practically weaned on hickory," Goheen told me. "I'm going with you."

"That's crazy. This isn't your fight."

Goheen showed me a hard, cocky grin. "Don't waste your time trying to stop me. Are you ready?"

I looked at him, then silently held my hand out. He clasped it. "What time do you have?"

"Four-twenty."

"Then it will be light in an hour and a half. Come on."

Goheen zipped up his jacket. We went downstairs.

At first I thought it was still snowing, but that was the wind whipping flurries off the high-piled drifts. The air was cold and very dry, so that you didn't realize how cold it really was until you had gone a little ways. Then your nostrils became thick with the frozen moisture in them.

We made our way through knee-deep snow to the hotel ski shed. The door was fastened with a rusted padlock which I broke with my gun butt. The hinges needed oil. Once inside, Goheen lit a small pocket flashlight. With its help he found his own skis on a wall rack. While he was busy with the bindings I took the flashlight and went over to the racks of rental skis. They were painted orange and had white numbers stenciled on their trailing edges. About half of them had ski boots already in the bindings. I found a pair which I thought would fit me, took off my shoes, removed the ski boots from the bindings, laced them on my feet and stuffed my trouser bottoms in. Then I took the skis down from the wall, set them out parallel on a plank bench and reclamped the bindings. Goheen brought me a pair of ski poles.

"Let's get going," I said.

"Wait a minute." He took the flashlight and searched around behind the counter which ran the length of one wall in the shed. His skis made clomping noises on the wood floor. He came back with about a dozen bars of chocolate, stuffing some of them in the pocket of his lumber jacket, peeling the wrapper off one and giving me the rest. I ate some chocolate and put the remainder in my pocket.

"If you're going," I said, "you must think she has a chance."

He shrugged. "I don't think Moriarity thought so."

"That's the impression I got."

"Better have some more chocolate now."

"Then why are you going?"

Again he shrugged. "It was something Moriarity said. The Mounties know this park. Dygert—that's his name, isn't it?—doesn't. Maybe a couple of amateurs blundering in there as Dygert must have blundered in will be able to think of something the Mounties might miss. Hell, aside from that, the entire post doesn't have more than twenty-five men. Mont Tremblant is a lot of park for them to cover."

"What about the trailside shelters?" I said.

"Well, what about them?"

"If she was out all night, without protection, she's dead. The Mounties know that. We know it. But we probably draw different conclusions. The Mounties will look in the places Dygert might have left her to die. They'll be looking for a body. They'll be looking for murderers. Especially if there aren't many of them to look. I'll be looking where she might be—if she's alive."

"But they wouldn't have—oh, I see. You mean she might have managed to reach one of the shelters?"

"Maybe. You got the map?"

"Yes."

"Come on."

I was awkward on the skis at first. The trail to the park entrance went down a slight grade. I stumbled along, using the poles for greater speed, in Goheen's tracks. He must have known the area very well, because it was still too dark to see much. We were heading north, into the wind. It was icy cold, and the wind blew flurries off the drifts at us.

When we reached the first steep drop, Goheen shoved down with his poles and went up and over in a spray of snow. Now I had to get out of his tracks or risk breaking a leg. I came to a stop on the crest of the hill and stamped both feet to kick snow off the bottoms of my skis. Then I dug my poles in, pushed, and went swooping down after Goheen. The snow hissed under my skis and dark masses of spruce and hemlock slipped by on both sides. Before I reached bottom, where Goheen was a faint dark blur in a world of snow, I realized I had tried to go too fast too soon. I brought my weight up on the balls of my feet and the inner edges of my skis, turning the points together in a braking snowplow. Just before I reached Goheen the points crossed and I went over headfirst, rolling to a stop on my back with the skis sticking straight up into the air.

I got to my feet and brushed the snow off me. "We're not in any race," Goheen said. "Take it easy. Snowplow all the way down if you have to. Can you christie?"

"Yeah. But I wouldn't win any medals."

When he grinned, I realized it was beginning to grow light. "No, I guess you wouldn't. Well, let's get moving. The park's just ahead, over that hill."

Going uphill on skis is backbreaking work, especially if you're in a hurry. The technique is the reverse of snowplowing: it's called herringboning because of the pattern your skis make in the snow. You draw the trailing ends of your skis together and dig in with the inner, metal edges, the points thrusting up and outward at almost a forty-five-degree angle from the direction you're moving. I once saw a trick-skier do it carrying a stepladder slung on one shoulder and a full pail of water in his free hand. But I'm no trick-skier and I'm no expert. When I reached the top I was panting like an old horse making his way to the glue factory on top of the hill, but despite that I'd gained some confidence. I began to feel more at home on the long, gliding extensions of my feet. I grew more adept with the ski poles for balancing, for increasing speed on slight declines, for digging in, right pole and left ski, left pole and right ski, uphill. And on the final long slope leading down to the park, I plummeted fast in Goheen's wake, the snow hissing, the runners thrumming, crouching, leaning forward, keeping the center of gravity low and maintaining my speed until the very last, when I came to a sudden snow-spewing stop with a pretty fair christie.

Goheen nodded his approval. "Better take a breather," he said, peeling another candy bar. I munched on my chocolate in a cold silent world, all ghostly gray-white in the predawn light. Then the eastern sky became pink over the smooth white snow-covered hills, and the hills in the west burned with pink fire.

We got under way again at a quarter to six and in a few moments passed a sign which said, in French, Le Parc de Mont Tremblant. The Mountie post was a big log building about a quarter of a mile to our left and then, all at once, the first long pass of the cross-country park lay before us. It was dazzling white under a bright, brittle, almost crystalline blue sky. It undulated between the higher Laurentian peaks in low white ranges of hills. There was a lot of evergreen growth in there, and in the shadows of the trees the snow looked blue.

We went down, swooping swiftly, dropping fast with that express-elevator feeling you get in your stomach. Then we thrust forward for several hundred yards over flat tundra. Then we climbed a hill, herringboning quickly because the snow was soft, there was no crust, and the edges bit deep. Goheen held up his hand, so I didn't stamp my skis and push off for the next long drop.

"First shelter's about a mile and a half"—he pointed, panting for breath—"that way. The only trouble is, there are two major trails cutting across the park."

Over his shoulder, I looked at the map. One of the trails went northwest, in a more or less straight line, toward a town on the edge of the park called La Macaza. The other zigzagged over rougher country due north to a body of water called Lac du Diable. Lake of the Devil. I pointed at that trail with my finger.

"Lake of the Devil," Goheen said, nodding. "That's the way I see it. That's the real wilderness run."

"Take a look over there," I said.

Far below us and to our right, a patrol of six men was skiing. They moved swiftly in a formation, the tiny figures spaced about fifty yards apart in two straight lines of three men each. That would make them Mounties.

"They aren't following the trail," Goheen said. "See, down there, the markers?" The markers were nailed on high posts and cut roughly in the shape of arrowheads. From this distance I guessed they were spaced at quarter-mile intervals.

"I was thinking," Goheen told me. "Maybe we ought to let the RCMP know how we've figured it."

"I didn't know we really figured it any way at all."

"Well, how I figured it, then. If Dygert doesn't know the park, wouldn't he have to stick close to the trails?"

"Maybe. But the further afield he went, the more certain he'd be that when he left her he'd leave her to die."

Goheen scowled. "That's what the Mounties must be thinking. They can only cover so much ground. If this patrol's any indication, they're ignoring the trails entirely. What do you think?"

I didn't answer for a minute. Then I said, "I'm with you. But I'm not all the way with you. We have an idea. The Mounties have an idea. We could be wrong, they could be wrong. If we stick to the trail, and follow it up to the Lake of the Devil, and if they go their own way across country, that increases the odds in favor of finding her, doesn't it?"

"I hadn't thought of it that way. Then we don't tell the Mounties?"

"Right. Unless you have any better ideas."

When he shook his head, I put my leather shell gloves back on.

"Also," Goheen pointed out, "if we stopped to tell them, and if they knew what we were doing, they might kick us the hell out of the park."

"There's that, too," I said, kicking the snow off my skis. I stood poised for a moment on the brink of the hill until Goheen came up parallel with me. Then we dug in with our poles and dropped toward the Lac du Diable trail.

CHAPTER NINETEEN

We reached the first shelter a little before eight. I hadn't known what to expect, so the shelter surprised me. It was a small log cabin with a porch on which the snow had drifted high. It had a brick chimney painted bright red. If you were lost in the snow, you could see that chimney a long way. That gave me a surge of hope for Bobby, until I realized if they had abandoned her during the night, all the bright red brick chimneys from here to British Columbia wouldn't have mattered.

I started to unclamp my bindings, but Goheen touched my arm. "See how the snow's drifted over on the porch? You'd have to shovel your way in."

"Unless she got here last night," I said.

Goheen didn't answer. What he thought was clear: she never could have found her way here last night. I removed my skis and shouted: "Hello! Anybody there?"

My voice echoed off the white hills. There was no answer. I floundered waist-deep through snow on the porch to get to the door. Inside, there were four bunks and three canvas cots in a single large room dominated by a pot-bellied stove. On one wall, piled almost to the ceiling, was cordwood. I touched the stove. It was cold.

Goheen smoked a cigarette while I fastened my ski bindings. In the early morning the wind had slackened off, but now it sprang up again, blowing so hard that the flurries of snow lifted from the drifts all around us, drifts piled sometimes twice a man's height against outcroppings of rock in the lee of the wind.

It was cold as we started out once more. As long as you keep skiing, you stay warm, but when you stop the sweat on your body has a chance to evaporate and the chilling wind knifes through you. That made me think of Bobby, left out here somewhere to die, without food and after a while without the energy or the ability to keep moving. Gliding along behind Goheen I felt a sudden chill that had nothing to do with the biting wind.

We covered the four miles to the next trailside shelter in not much more than an hour. As long as we went with the wind it wasn't so bad, but the trail twisted and turned through the hills making the wind seem to change direction every few minutes. Sometimes it was like skiing against a wall of ice. That was when you went into the teeth of the wind. Sometimes, with the wind blowing from the side, we had all we could do to keep to the trail. Twice we lost it altogether and had to circle back until we found the last marker and begin all over again. The wind tore at our clothing, numbed our faces, made our ears sting with pain. It took the breath from our lungs and the strength from our legs. At times it even drove all thoughts of what we were doing out here from my mind. There was only the snow and the wind and the next hill to be climbed and the fast soaring drop down the next slope.

At the top of a small rise, Goheen thumped my shoulder and pointed. Nestled in the blue shadow of a copse of spruce was the shelter. Because the trees protected it from the wind we could see the thin blue-black wisp of smoke rising from the chimney.

I pointed off to the left, down the flank of the little hill. Straight, it wasn't much of a drop, but the flank was a long gradual slope of several hundred yards. "Down that way," I said. "If it's them, we could get in among the trees before they saw us. We could get right up to the cabin without being seen."

Goheen nodded. We lifted our skis and turned them. The snow was virgin white, unmarred by ski tracks. Whoever was in that cabin had been in there since last night.

Crouching low, with the shoulder of the hill between us and the cabin, we went down. In five minutes we were in among the dark blue spruce shadows. The cabin was a solid dark bulk fifty yards ahead of us, through the trees. You could smell the smoke of the wood fire.

"I'm going first," I told Goheen.

He shook his head and came on right behind me. Because the cabin porch was in the lee of the wind, only a few inches of snow covered the boards. I held up my hand and stopped. The snow had been trampled on the porch. And from here we were able to see what we could not see from the top of the hill: ski tracks led through the snow parallel to the cabin and a couple of feet away from it, turning and disappearing behind the cabin. I said two words. I said: "This morning."

Goheen moved his head up and down.

We crouched and duck-waddled on our skis laboriously to the porch, keeping below the level of the two windows. I had my right glove off and the Magnum in my hand. The wind made a faint keening in the higher spruce branches. Aside from that it was a dead world, without sound, almost without color. The bright red chimney looked like an apparition.

When I reached the two steps leading up to the porch I removed my skis. I heard Goheen struggling with his bindings. One of them had iced over. Finally he nodded. We both stood up. One long stride took me to the porch. Another, to the door. I turned the handle and kicked. The door swung in.

A woman screamed.

It was her blonde hair that did it. At first I thought she was Bobby. She stood in the doorway and then her head came up. Her eyes were wide with surprise and fear.

"Who are you?" she gasped.

A man's voice called: "Carol! Carol, what is it?"

Goheen and I entered the cabin. The woman's eyes got bigger when she saw my gun.

After hours on the snow, it was almost suffocatingly warm in the cabin. The potbellied stove glowed a bright, cheerful red. A man was sitting up on the edge of one of the bunks. His left foot was bare and even from the other end of the cabin you could see how swollen it was.

"Do you usually burst into shelters like that?" the woman asked. Quick anger replaced the fear in her voice. She was young and quite pretty. She wore ski pants and a ski sweater with a big Indian head on a blue background.

I put the gun away. The woman had been close to hysteria. She turned on the man almost savagely. "All this wouldn't have happened if we'd gone to Stowe. You never hurt your leg in Stowe. But no, you had to try the Laurentians."

"Carol, for crying out loud."

The woman started to cry. "I'm sorry. I'm sorry. They scared me out of my wits. First last night, then this. Oh, Howie..."

Howie got up, hobbled over to her and patted her shoulder. She looked up immediately. "Sit down. Sit right down, will you? For all we know the leg's broken."

"No it isn't. Just a bad sprain." The man winced with pain and sat on the edge of the bunk again.

"What happened last night?" I asked.

"What a night!" Carol said, laughing suddenly, uncontrollably, with the tears glistening on her cheeks. I looked at Goheen. He looked at me and shrugged.

"About a mile from here," Howie said. "Yesterday, just before dark. I had a bad fall. We were making for the cabin anyway. Going to spend the night here."

"Romantic," Carol said, getting rid of the word as if it was a bad taste in her mouth. "In Stowe, you're never too far to get back to the hotel. In Stowe—"

"Shut up about Stowe, for crying out loud," the man said wearily. "That's all I've been hearing all night."

"What about last night?" I urged.

"We got about halfway here," Howie said, his eyes bright with memory. "I was beat. Carol couldn't possibly have supported my weight the rest of the way. I couldn't have gone another five steps if my life depended on it." He smiled. "Heck, it probably did."

"Then we saw these people," Carol said.

"It was pretty dark by then. They were far off on a hill, four of them, skiing down at an angle so they'd have crossed our path maybe two, three hundred yards ahead—if I was able to move."

"I waved," Carol said. "I shouted. I screamed at them. It was dusk, like Howie said. The wind had died down. They heard me. I know they did. They would have heard me twice as far away. I have a voice that can carry."

"It sure as heck can," Howie chimed in, the suggestion of a grin tugging at the corners of his lips.

"But they just continued on the way they were going. It was maddening. After a few seconds I left Howie here and skied after them."

"Yelling like a banshee all the way," Howie said.

"Well," Carol said, "finally one of them turned around and they came down. They didn't look very happy about it. Especially the girl. If I ever saw anyone scared to death in my whole life, it was that girl."

"You should have seen your own face when these fellows busted in on us," Howie told her.

"I know what I'm talking about, Howie Unger. That poor girl was scared of something. Really scared. Anyhow, they helped us down to the cabin. The men talked a little, among themselves. The girl hardly said a word. It was like they were watching her. She was scared to talk, I tell you."

"But I thought you told me last night it was the girl who finally answered you up there," Howie said.

"It was. So what? I have eyes. I have ears. Something was going on."

"A blonde?" I asked. "Hair about your color? And three men, two of them pretty young, the third a very big guy, say in his late thirties?"

"I knew it!" Carol cried triumphantly. "I knew they'd done something wrong. You men're the police, aren't you?"

"They left here how long ago?"

"That's the crazy thing," Carol said. "One of the younger men wanted to leave as soon as we got here. The other young one didn't say a word. The big fellow told the first one to shut up. Then... well, there are provisions stacked in these cabins. Beans, coffee, tins of beef, things like that. We tried to make Howie comfortable, then the girl and I made supper. I tried to get her to talk, but everything she said was a monosyllable. Also, one of the men—usually the big guy—kept hanging around us. Finally, we all turned in. I was worried about Howie. And scared, I guess. I tried not to show it, but I didn't sleep much."

Carol stopped talking long enough to light a cigarette. I didn't ask her any more questions. She was a girl who liked to talk and it would be quicker this way, I decided. "Here comes the crazy part," she said. "At night the stove gives enough light so you can see. They should have been bushed, just like we were. They were skiing most of the afternoon, they said." She dropped her cigarette on the floor and stepped on it. The floor was littered with cigarette butts, more than she and her husband possibly could have smoked. "But still, all night long one or the other of them was up. Every time I dozed and woke up I could see him there, sitting near the stove. Sometimes it was one of them, sometimes another. Never the girl, though. The girl was sleeping. I heard her moan in her sleep. Once I even went over to her. The man near the stove came over. It was the very young one, the fellow who wanted to leave last night. He just looked at me. I—I've never been looked at like that before. I went back to bed.

"I thought perhaps I'd get a chance to talk to the girl in the morning. But they were up before dawn, putting more wood in the stove, getting breakfast. The young fellow who didn't do much talking waxed all their skis. I didn't get a chance to go near the girl. They went just as they came and just as they'd been all night—as if they were sorry they ever laid eyes on us. I didn't ask them to take us out, which I would have done, Howie being injured and all. They didn't offer it. The big fellow promised to tell the Mounties where we were."

Carol took a breath. I don't know what else she had in mind to say. She looked like she was quite willing to talk all day.

I said, "They left at dawn?"

"Around five-thirty. Going to La Macaza, they said."

"This isn't the trail to La Macaza," Goheen pointed out.

I was already zipping my windbreaker. "What time is it?" I asked Goheen. My own watch still said six-thirty. I'd forgotten to wind it.

"Almost nine forty-five."

Four hours and fifteen minutes, I thought, not liking it. In that time, moving steadily, they could have covered a lot of distance.

"Don't worry," Goheen told the couple in the cabin. "We'll let the Mounties know where you are. Just sit tight."

"Listen," I said. "If the Mounties come for you, tell them to follow those ski tracks outside. Tell them it's urgent. Tell them a girl's life depends on it."

"You're going after them now?"

I nodded.

"You see!" Carol cried. "I knew it. I knew it! What did they do, mister, rob a bank or something?"

"Sure," Howie said with a grin. "They're hightailing it on skis clear up to Hudson Bay, where a kayak will take them to their hideout in Greenland."

"Oh, shut up, you," Carol said indignantly.

I crossed the porch in two steps, looking down at my skis in the snow at the bottom of the stairs. I turned around to say something to Goheen. Then something made me look up. I started to say, "Bobby's had two good breaks—"

And saw a figure skiing toward us, not fifty yards away, coming with a rush down the slope of the hill.

Simultaneously a gunshot cracked across the snow and a bullet thumped into the logs a foot from my head.

CHAPTER TWENTY

I dove back into the cabin and slammed the door. "Get down!" I bawled.

They didn't need any instructions. They had heard the gun. Howie and Carol squatted on the floor in front of the bunks. Carol didn't look surprised, just scared. Howie's face would have looked the same if he had just seen the sky fall. "Hudson Bay," Carol said.

Goheen was crouching near the potbellied stove. I rushed to the window, drawing my Magnum and breaking the glass with it. The lone skier out there had executed a ninety-degree stem turn and was cutting diagonally across the flank of the hill toward the cover of the trees. Crouching low, he dug hard with his ski poles. He hadn't done the shooting unless he had a third arm.

"Stop or I'll shoot!" I yelled.

He kept going.

When he was about forty yards from the trees and eighty or ninety from the cabin, I steadied my elbow on the window sill and fired. The kick of the Magnum slammed my hand against the jagged edge of broken glass and blood began to flow. The skier kept going. Hitting a moving target at ninety yards with a pistol takes luck, not skill. His luck was better than mine. He kept going. His ski cap had come off, probably when he made the stem turn. I could see his blond crew-cut hair silhouetted against the dark trees. I steadied my arm a second time, sighting on his legs. Just as I squeezed the trigger, Goheen came up behind me and pushed my arm, forcing my elbow through the window and off the sill and sending the bullet into the snow ten feet from the porch.

Seconds later, the fleeing figure disappeared.

"You—you couldn't just kill him in cold blood," Goheen said. "That was Curt."

I didn't reply. Goheen looked at my face. "Jesus, I'm sorry," he said. "I should have let you alone. I guess I'm not cut out for this."

"Get away from the window," I told him. "Get down."

He did so. I hunkered down near the window. Carol was crying softly while Howie awkwardly tried to comfort her. They had us, I thought. But we had them. If we opened the door and tried to get to our skis, we'd be sitting ducks. But if they shot us, they'd have the kind of murder on their hands they'd been trying to avoid with Bobby. Still, was there anything else they could do?

"What the hell," I said suddenly. I'd made a fine target framed in the window. They hadn't done anything about it.

"Give me your hat," I told Goheen. He threw it along the floor and I raised it slowly above the window ledge on the barrel of my Magnum. I held it that way for a minute or two. There wasn't any gunfire. I removed the hat, stood up and fired blindly at the woods, then dropped to the floor again.

"What you do that for?" Goheen asked.

"To keep Curt in the woods."

He scowled. "What difference does it make?"

"Plenty of difference," I told him. "Are you willing to take a chance?"

"What kind of chance?"

"Well, I think I can figure out—more or less—what happened."

Goheen showed me a frown. "If you can, you're a better man than I am. I'm all confused. Why the devil'd they come back here? I don't get it."

"Try to put yourself in their place. The last thing they wanted to happen yesterday was some other skier to cross their path while they had Bobby with them. But that's just what happened. They couldn't just run when it was pretty obvious they heard Carol calling for help, not if they were going to leave Bobby out there to die. So they had to come down and spend the night here, like any other cross-country skiers would. They had to help Carol and Howie."

"That much I figured out. So what?"

"All right, first thing this morning they took off. They were still going ahead with their plan, but they had to change it because they'd been seen with Bobby."

"Change it how?"

"Sooner or later the Mounties were going to find Carol and Howie. That much they could be sure of. Sooner or later the Mounties were also going to find Bobby—frozen to death—that much they could be sure of too. And what if Carol and Howie were still around?"

"Sure. Sure, now I get it. Carol and Howie might put two and two together, their suspicious behavior during the night, the fact that they didn't let Bobby do any talking."

"Now you're getting there. They'd have to convince Carol and Howie there wasn't any dirty work."

"How could they do that?"

"They did it. Or they were going to. They just turned the whole thing around. Instead of mysteriously disappearing after leaving Bobby out there, they decided to come back here. Probably they had some story cooked up explaining how Bobby got lost, separated from them. Probably, they were going to act concerned, scared. Maybe they were even going to ask Carol to help them."

"Hold on," Goheen said. "Now you're going off the deep end. Because it isn't snowing. Because all Carol would have to do is follow the ski tracks to where they left Bobby. Then what? If they found her too soon, she'd still be alive. Heck, get right down to it, they've only been gone less than five hours. It's daylight. There isn't any blizzard. Why couldn't Bobby come back here under her own power?"

I shook my head. "I can't answer either of those questions, but if you're willing to take a chance, maybe I can answer them before the day is up."

"Go ahead. I'm listening."

"Okay. Grant they came back?"

"That's easy. We know they're out there."

"They came up over the hill. They didn't have any reason to hide in the woods, not knowing we were here. Then one of them—Curt—came down the hill to ask for help. They couldn't very well be accused of killing Bobby if they asked for help finding her. Got it?"

"Sure. I'm still listening."

"The others are waiting up on the ridge. Watching. Then I open the cabin door. They can see me. They know who I am. On impulse, one of them takes a shot at me. That wouldn't be Dygert. He's too cool. It's the one you don't know anything about." I paused. "It's Jerry Trowbridge. Dygert stops him from shooting. Then what?"

"Curt goes off into the woods," Goheen said bitterly, "and I stop you from taking a potshot at him."

"I show them the hat, and of course it would look like someone's head out there. Still, they don't fire. Because they're not going to, if they can help it. Not that they know what they can do next, except maybe just wait us out. Anyhow, I can take it up to there."

"Then what?"

"Then I don't know. But Curt figures he's covered, figures he's a dead duck if he tries to come out of the woods and make his way back to the others. That's why I took a blind shot at the woods. To give him something to worry about. As for the others, they're better off where they are, on top of the hill where they can watch us and see what we'll do. They could work their way down the flank of the hill to the woods and keep out of sight, like we did, but what's in it for them?"

"I got you, and it makes sense. Two of them are on the hill and Curt's in the woods. So what?"

"So I'm willing to bet there wouldn't be any shooting if I walked out the door, put on my skis and went into the woods looking for Curt."

Goheen didn't say anything for a moment. Then he said, "Why not bet we could both walk out of here, mount skis and take off after those ski tracks? What do you want Curt for?"

"For his gun. He's probably armed."

"You have a gun."

"You don't. And there's no telling what they do after I leave. They might follow me. They might wait, but I doubt that. They couldn't just wait. They might come down here. They might split up."

"Let's say you get his gun. Then what happens?"

"I bring it back to you. Then I take off after Bobby. If I don't draw any fire by then, I won't draw any—until I find her."

"But two of us—"

"Use your head," I interrupted. "We don't have any guarantee they won't finally decide to come down here. Because then we wouldn't be sweating over what they were going to do next, they'd be sweating over our next move. We couldn't leave Carol and Howie alone to face them. So somebody has to stay here."

"Fellow named Goheen," he said, a little sadly.

"Right. Fellow named Goheen. There's only one way into the cabin. The front. If they came down you could pick them off. They wouldn't have a chance."

Goheen stood up. I must have convinced him: he wasn't afraid of the window now. He said, "Would you?"

I didn't get it. I looked at him blankly.

"Would you have a chance?"

"I told you. I'd bet my bottom dollar there wouldn't be any fireworks if I went out there."

"It isn't your bottom dollar you'd be betting," he told me. "It's your life."

I went to the door. "If you have a better idea, spill it."

"I don't have any ideas at all. But hell, Curt'll see you coming. If you get that far. You wouldn't see him."

"That's not how I figure it. Why should he wait in the woods? He'd try to make his way around the slope of the hill and back up. He wouldn't be looking for me. The last thing he'd expect is someone to come in there after him. All right?"

"No, damn it. It's not all right. There's a dozen ways they could kill you. From the hill. From the woods. As soon as you poked your head out. After you'd gone a ways. After you got clear of the cabin. As you reached the woods. I can't let you—"

"You can't stop me. There's one more thing. I have to leave you without a gun for a few minutes. But they saw me and they won't know I'm alone. They won't know who else is in the cabin. They won't know you're not armed. They ought to stay put, for a while at least. Just don't get cocky. Keep under cover and wait."

He nodded glumly, then raised his head and grinned. "Jesus, the way you have it all figured. Clausewitz has nothing on you."

I smiled back at him. It took some doing. I opened the door and shut it behind me. It had all sounded splendid, in theory. But in fact it was dazzling sun and snow and the big white hump of the hill and the dark woods and a cold keening wind in the trees and death waiting everywhere you looked.

I went down to my skis and fastened the bindings awkwardly with one hand. In my other hand I held the Magnum. I was exposed. I was vulnerable. I had done some pretty good guessing, but I could have been wrong ten ways from Sunday. One way would have been more than enough. Any moment I expected to hear the crash of a gunshot. It wouldn't surprise me. It wouldn't surprise me because I wouldn't have time to be surprised. It would be the last thing I'd ever hear.

One of the bindings had frozen over. I had to bang it with the butt of the gun. Sweat ran down my back. The wind wailed and the sun glared. Something snapped in the woods. A branch, I told myself. Breaking under the weight of snow and frost. But was it?

I shoved my boots into the open bindings, flipping them forward and down until they clicked into place. I stood up. So far, it made sense for them to wait. They wanted to see what I was going to do. So far. I squinted against the bright sun-glare and saw the place in the snow where Curt had made his stem turn, a gash in the unmarred whiteness of the hill. I glanced, just once, at the top of the hill. They were there, waiting, watching. It was absolutely certain that they saw me, and just as certain that they had a gun. I didn't see anything.

I thrust forward over the snow and poled toward the woods.

CHAPTER TWENTY-ONE

If I entered the woods right behind the cabin it would be safer. That would give me cover, but Curt had cover too. And if I didn't follow the parallel ruts of his ski tracks through the snow I might blunder in the woods for hours without spotting him. I decided to follow the tracks .

Pretty soon I was climbing a slight rise on the flank of the hill, to reach Curt's tracks about fifty yards beyond the gash in the snow where he'd made his stem turn. From that point the tracks ran slightly downhill all the way to the woods and I figured to make the best time skiing down after it. But I had reached the point of no return. I was now halfway to the woods. I looked back once over my shoulder and saw the dark square mass of the cabin silhouetted against white snow and blue sky. It seemed ineffably snug and peaceful with a tendril of smoke curling lazily from the red chimney. It stood for a warm stove and a hot drink and the sanctuary of four walls. I looked ahead to the spruce woods, the branches feathery with snow, the boles of the trees dark and straight, the shadows between them so dark blue they were almost black. I had my skis and my gun. I was vulnerable from the hill and vulnerable from the woods. I kept going.

Then I reached the first few scattered trees. Here only a few inches of powdery snow blanketed the ground, for the thick spruce overgrowth had kept most of last night's heavy fall twenty feet off the floor of the woods. I snowplowed to a stop, squatted and unfastened my bindings. I could make better time in the woods on foot. I trotted through the snow and the silence, in and out among the trees, following Curt's tracks .

Before long I heard something. I couldn't identify the sound at first, then I realized it was someone's labored breathing. It seemed to hang in space ahead of me, not growing fainter, not coming closer.

I began to stalk him. My heavy ski boots made crunching noises on the snow. I couldn't help that.

Ahead of me, quite suddenly, the zigzagging tracks through the snow ended. He stood there in dim shadow with his back turned and his head slumped forward. His breath made a steam-engine sound through his slack mouth. I could even see the white plumes of it in the still, cold air. He stood with one arm against a tree trunk as if he were keeping it from falling. Every now and then he would jerk his head up and look in one direction or another. He was lost and he was scared.

He wore a turtleneck sweater, black, with a high red collar. His shoulder moved in unison with his panting. The back of his neck, above the collar, gleamed with sweat.

I was almost between the tails of his skis with the gun in my hand when he whirled around. One of the skis caught my shin and we both tumbled to the snow. He swung wildly with a ski pole, numbing one side of my face from temple to jaw. I brought the Magnum down flat on top of his head. He collapsed as if all the bones had been drawn from his body, leaving him as limp as an empty gunnysack.

Swiftly I went through his pockets. He had a .32 automatic with a nickel-plated handgrip. I ejected the clip. It was full. I slammed it up into the butt and put the .32 in my pocket. Then I left him there and followed our tracks back to my skis. There were three people in the cabin back there and Bobby ahead on the snow somewhere who said I couldn't stop to worry if Curt might freeze to death before anyone found him.

I carried my skis through the woods to the copse which sheltered the cabin. There I put the skis down and sprinted around to the door. A gunshot cracked hard and flat in the silence. The bullet thumped against the logs ten feet from me and whined off. They wanted to scare me, I thought. If they had meant to hit me, it would have been much closer. I tried to tell myself that because I had to go out there again.

The door opened. I went in. The door shut behind me and I gave Goheen the .32 automatic.

"Curt?" he said.

"In the woods."

"Did you kill him?"

"He's unconscious."

"They shot at you. You were lucky once. You can't go out there again."

"They wanted to scare me."

Carol brought me a hot cup of coffee and Goheen gave me a cigarette and lit it for me.

"I could use something stronger," I admitted. "About ninety proof stronger."

Howie grinned and hobbled over with a hip flask. When I had drunk half the hot coffee off, he poured what was in the hip flask into my tin cup. I gulped it down and felt the warmth flood through me. It was rum.

I hadn't sat down. All I had to do was walk four steps over to the door. It looked like half a mile. I shook Goheen's hand. Howie wanted to shake too. That was easy. Carol came over and touched my arm. She was a small girl. She stood on tiptoe and brushed her lips against my cheek.

"Hey, you'll make a guy jealous," Howie said. But he was grinning again.

Carol's eyes held mine for an instant. "That's for being how you are," she said.

I took the map from Goheen, opened the door and shut it quickly behind me. I ran at a crouch along the porch and vaulted the porch rail. No one took a shot at me—this time.

I put on my skis and moved slowly out over the snow toward the hill. At the top of it and skirting the woods on their right was the Lac du Diable trail. Somewhere up there, waiting, watching me, were Dygert and Jerry Trowbridge.

That was the hard part of it. Herringboning up the hill, I was a step closer to them every time I moved.

Two men, desperate, high on a hill. One of them scared enough to shoot. He had proven that. He had taken one shot at me already, and maybe two. Was he up there now, waiting, hunched over with a stiff cold finger on the trigger of his gun and fear sending the tiny electric impulse from his brain along his arm to the hand that held the gun and the finger that would squeeze the trigger?

I let go like a locomotive getting rid of excess pressure at the top of the hill. It had been a long, hard climb. Curt must have felt like that in the woods, right before I hit him. I shaded my eyes and squinted. There were dips and gullies in which they could be hiding. There was a higher shoulder of hill to my left. They could have been down behind that, out of sight from the cabin and out of sight from where I stood. I was looking for the glint of sun on gunmetal, but didn't see it. The shoulder of the hill was the most likely spot, I thought. If I spoke in a conversational voice, they would hear me. If I looked straight at them they could see the color of my eyes. And if I turned my back on them, which I had to do to pick up the markers of the cross-country ski trail, they could stand up, take dead aim, and empty their guns at me. My life hung on a thin thread which said they didn't want to commit that kind of murder—yet.

I turned my back and skied down the back slope of the hill to the Lac du Diable trail.

The sun was weak and watery and an hour past its zenith when I reached the lake. A few hazy white clouds hung against the blue of the sky. The wind was very strong, whipping the branches of the spruces and birch which bordered the frozen lakeshore. I had followed the tracks of their skis all the way. I hadn't stopped once. It was the toughest journey I had ever taken, anywhere, anytime. My arms were like lead. My knees trembled so much I hadn't been able to ski in a straight line for the last half hour. Not once had I seen or heard Dygert or Jerry Trowbridge pursuing me, but I knew they were there, behind the low hills, taking cover in the copses of trees along the trail.

Every step I took could have been my last. I knew it, and they knew it. Yet they hadn't done anything about it. Why?

I found out why when I reached the lakeshore.

The ski tracks ended there. They had gone out with Bobby over the frozen surface of the lake. It was the color of mercury with bluish glints here and there. Only an occasional patch of snow marred the solid surface of ice, for the fierce wind had blown the snow off the exposed lake as soon as it had fallen, piling it high in drifts against the trees on the shore.

I could see clearly where Dygert, Jerry and Curt had come off the lake a dozen yards to my left, but the lake was at least half a mile wide and so long I couldn't see the other end of it. They could have taken Bobby in any direction. And left her.

This far I had come. I could go no further. Left? Right? Straight ahead across the frozen lake? No wonder they hadn't tried to stop me. They would have been crazy to.

The wind moaned in the trees. It was a sad, bitter sound, a minor key wailing for the dead, the dying and the defeated.

I sat down against the bole of a big birch which slanted out over the lake. I put the Magnum on my lap and got out a cigarette. My hands were shaking so badly I used up half a pack of matches to light it.

I threw the cigarette away and stood up. "Come on!" I shouted. "Come on down here!"

It was a foolish, melodramatic gesture. It said I had lost and knew I had lost. The sound of the wind changed. It was laughter rattling the gaunt birch branches. I took off my skis and prowled along the lakeshore, my boots silent as death on the ice. There was just enough snow to keep it from being slippery.

After a few minutes I turned around and went back. It would take days for one man to search along the shore. That was the worst part of it, knowing that. Because if they had followed me back here, it meant they knew Bobby might still be alive.

Lake of the Devil, I thought. The thought drifted, and for a few moments my mind was an absolute blank, barely aware of the cold, the wind, and hopelessness.

Then I heard something.

I don't know when I first heard it. It wasn't there and then it was, a sound which the wind could not quite hide. I must have heard it for some time before I realized it didn't belong to the wind in the trees.

A noise. A faint scraping.

I stared out over the lake. Gray mercury. Blue glints of deep ice. Tattered white cobwebs of snow. And the watery yellow reflection of the sun.

A dragging sound. Then scraping, silence and scraping again.

Her ski jacket was white, like the snow. Her hair was yellow, like the watery reflection of the winter sun. I saw her.

I saw her.

White and yellow movement a quarter of a mile down the lake. Dragging itself with agonizing slowness across the ice. And something trailing behind the white ski pants. A matchstick, scraping. A single ski still fastened to one of her boots.

I ran out across the ice, and fell. Skidded a few yards on my belly and got up and ran again. She wasn't very far out, but she wasn't making for the shoreline either. She was dragging herself roughly parallel to it, using her arms to pull her weight, using one leg, bending it and straightening it, the ski dragging, making a few inches, maybe half a foot, with each intense effort.

When I reached her, she looked up at me. Her eyes were wide, but she didn't see me. Her face was covered with snow. Her hair was frozen. There was a red streak in it that was frozen blood.

"It's going to be all right, Bobby," I said. "It's going to be all right now."

Her wide eyes just went on staring at me. Then, silently, she started to cry.

I couldn't get the single ski off because it was frozen solid to her boot. I picked her up the way she was and got her in a fireman's carry. Staggered across the ice with her like that.

Forty yards. Fifty. The birch branches rattled, beckoning.

A shot rang out. The bullet hit ice three feet to my left and ricocheted away. I ran with her then toward the trees, slipping, sliding. Another shot. The bullet tugged at my sleeve. I saw him. One of them, and he wasn't on skis. He came running among the trees on the lakeshore, firing as he ran. If he stopped, if he got down on one knee and steadied his elbow on the other—

He kept running.

I reached a drift of snow which the wind had piled high against the trees on the shore. I stooped and dropped Bobby there, took the Magnum out with stiff, half-frozen fingers, and waited.

I could hear him coming. Dygert?

Then I saw him, head and torso above the drift, his eyes scanning the lakeshore anxiously, desperately, a big automatic in his hand.

It was Jerry Trowbridge.

I think I had known somehow, ever since the fight with Dygert in the bar and grill in Washington, that it would come to this. He didn't look like a college kid now, with his pale good looks and his short-cropped dark hair. His face was haggard with a two-day growth of beard on it. His eyes were wild. I thought of his father, and of the way he smiled when he was pleased with something he had done. I thought of Duncan Lord, and of Bobby, and of how he had helped them drag her out here to die. Maybe I weighed it all, but if I did, I did so unconsciously. He had a gun. I had a gun. One of us was going to die.

I stood up and brought the Magnum in front of me, my arm extended, the way they teach you at FBI school. He saw the motion. His eyes narrowed and he whipped the automatic around.

I squeezed the trigger once. The Magnum roared and bucked back against my hand.

Jerry fired twice. Two quick shots, at the sky, as he fell.

Seconds later, I saw Dygert. He was a dark bulk crashing through the frozen, winter-dead scrub that poked up stiffly through the snowdrifts. He wasn't on skis. He came fast. He was still too far off for a good shot. I waited. Then he stopped and went out of sight behind the drifts. When he appeared again, he was gliding on hickory, poling hard, away from the lake. I stood up, climbed the high drift, sinking to my knees in the soft snow, and watched him go. After a while, he was a minute speck sliding across the white vastness of the snow. Then he was gone.

I went to Jerry. He had fallen on his back near a big white birch. One of his legs was twitching. It stopped when I reached him. The bullet had entered his head below the chin, driving up because I had been below him on the lake. His head rested on a red stain in the snow. The stain grew, and darkened. He was dead.

I took the .45 from his slack fingers. It was a U.S. Government Issue Colt. I put it in my pocket and went back to Bobby.

Goheen's map showed a shelter about three-quarters of a mile down the lakeshore. I carried Bobby up and over the snowdrift. There didn't seem to be any life in her, but I could feel the faint ruffle of her breath against my neck.

I set her down gently in the snow and fastened my skis. Carrying her, it took me an hour to cover the three-quarters of a mile to the cabin. I lurched like a drunk, slipped and slid like an ice-skating comic at a winter carnival.

For a long time the cabin didn't appear any closer. Then, all at once, it loomed just ahead of us. I put Bobby down on the porch steps and unfastened my skis. I opened the door and carried her inside. The ski frozen to her boot caught crosswise in the doorframe. I pulled it clear. I went inside carrying Bobby cradled like a bride.

The groom had almost been death. But I didn't think of that till later.

CHAPTER TWENTY-TWO

The potbellied stove glowed cherry-red. Bobby lay near it on a cot I had dragged across the cabin with every blanket I could find piled on top of her. She was trembling, and still very cold. Once she opened her eyes, and whimpered, and shut them again. I made coffee from a tin on a shelf in the cabin. I tried to spoon-feed it to her, but she gagged and choked and the hot liquid ran down her chin.

I sat down to wait on a wall bunk. Neither the blankets nor the stove could stop Bobby's trembling. Pretty soon I got up, lifted the covers and climbed into bed with her. Even through her ski jacket I could feel how cold she was. I took her into my arms, trying to give her some of my body warmth. We lay that way a long time. She didn't move. I could feel her breath faintly on my cheek. Then she stirred and one of her cold hands came up and touched my face. She sighed.

Exhaustion washed over me in warm, drowsy waves, like an ocean of lead. I couldn't sleep, because Dygert might decide to come back. It wasn't likely, but he might. The way he had fled wasn't likely either, but he had done it. I thought about Jerry. I should have felt the guilty gnawing bite of remorse, but it didn't come. I was too tired, or too much had come between me and Jerry. Beyond Bobby's head I could see her ski boots on the floor. I'd had to cut one of them away with a knife because her ankle and instep were swollen almost twice their normal size. Dygert, I thought. Dygert. Don't sleep. You can't sleep. The tide of exhaustion rose and engulfed me. I tried to fight it off. Get up, I thought. But I couldn't get up. Bobby needed my warmth. Coffee, I thought. Get up and have some coffee. I could still smell it. I didn't get up. I didn't have it. I slept.

The cherry glow of the stove, and darkness through the windows. I was sweating.

"Chet," Bobby said.

Her cheek lay against mine. It was feverish.

I touched her with my hand. Her skin was dry and burning with fever.

I got out from under the blankets, threw more wood into the stove and rewarmed the coffee. Bobby turned her head to watch me. She watched every move I made. My arms and legs were stiff and sore. I found a can of juice and an opener. I gave the juice to Bobby and drank the coffee myself. Then I sat down on the edge of the cot and peeled the blankets off her. She removed the ski jacket and sat up holding her knees.

"You've got a fever," I said.

"I know it. I can feel it. But I'm all right. I just feel so weak. My leg doesn't hurt now. It's numb." Her eyes widened as she relived her ordeal. "They took me out there," she said. "On the lake. He held me down. Jerry. Then Dygert... jumped... my leg." She licked her dry lips. Sweat stood out in little beads on her forehead. "I had to... it was freezing... drag myself along."

"Take it easy," I said. "Don't talk about it." I kissed her hot brow. Her fingers fluttered against my cheeks.

"If I could just keep moving. That was what I thought. If I could keep moving... stay alive. You would come. I didn't know where you were. You were still in Washington. But I knew. If I could stay alive. If I could keep from freezing, you would come. You would come, Chet."

I held her. Her tears were hot against my cheek. Then she started to cough. She held her chest and went on coughing. Her face got red. It was an ugly hacking cough, deep in her chest. When she finished she lay back weakly, her eyes shut, her breathing shallow and rapid. The redness drained from her face quickly after that. She looked gray. She gasped and tried to sit up, tried to smile at me. It looked like a death mask.

She spent a hard few minutes gasping for breath. She opened her eyes. They looked frightened. She was limp and pale, and panting for breath as if she had run a long way.

"It's so hot," she said. "It's so hot in here. I can't breathe..."

I opened the windows and let the cold night air in. She coughed a little, but her breathing was better. After a while she fell asleep. I covered her with two of the blankets and paced back and forth across the cabin, five steps to the wall and back, trying to think. I'm no doctor, but I know the symptoms of pneumonia. And Dygert—Dygert might come back. But I had no reason to believe he *would* come back. And Bobby needed medical help. Antibiotics. Oxygen, maybe.

I knew I had to wait for morning. In the morning, if it didn't snow during the night, I could pick up Dygert's ski tracks. If he doubled back, I would know it. If the wind didn't obliterate his trail.

Twice during the night Bobby woke up coughing. Once I gave her some juice to drink. She complained of pains in her chest. Her fever had risen. I found some canned corned beef and wolfed it down. I slept a little, fitfully.

It was a bleak gray dawn that threatened snow. Bobby's face was ashen. She was already awake, her breathing harsh.

"Pneumonia," she asked me, "isn't it?"

"It looks like pneumonia," I admitted.

"Did Judson Bonner die?" she asked me abruptly. "He had a heart attack."

"I know. Last I saw, he was hanging on."

"I heard them talking, Dygert and Jerry Trowbridge."

"Just lie still and rest. Don't talk."

"No. I want to," she said as I tossed more logs into the stove. "Dygert was scared. Not of Mrs. Bonner. If the old man died, he said, he thought he could handle Mrs. Bonner. If he got there in time. He was scared that Judson Bonner might live, though. Scared that if he did he would make a clean breast of everything. I didn't..." She broke off, started to cough.

"Listen," I said. "Lie still and shut up or, so help me, I'll spank you."

She smiled up at me weakly. "Chet," she said. "Chet, you're the gentlest tough guy I've ever known. But don't you see, if Bonner lives, and does talk, he'll exonerate you? Don't you realize that?"

"I said be quiet. You're a sick girl."

"...said a funny, frightening thing. It would be easy, he said. Just as easy to kill Bonner, in his bed, in his oxygen tent, as it was to kill me."

"Yeah. After a heart attack, he could probably scare Judson Bonner to death."

I waited a half hour. I went out on the porch. It was bitter cold and almost windless. The sky was the color of the frozen lake. It wasn't snowing yet, but you could smell the snow.

Had Dygert gone on skis back to Mont Tremblant then? It figured, after what Bobby had told me. Following his trail, I'd know for sure. If the snow didn't cover it. If the snow didn't make it impossible for me to get Bobby the kind of help she needed.

I heard her coughing, and went back inside. I took her hot hand in mine. Her fingers clutched my fingers. "Look," I said, "I'll lay it on the line for you. What you've got is probably pneumonia. I could stay here with you and do what I can. But there isn't much I could do. Or I could go for help. If I go for help, that means leaving you alone—I don't know how long."

"Go after Dygert," she said.

"I'll go after help, if you tell me to. Dygert can wait till later."

For a while she didn't say anything. I made some fresh coffee. I could hear her breathing hard, through her mouth. I gave her some hot coffee. She took a sip and said, "I want you to go. I think you ought to." Her voice was weak and she had trouble focusing her eyes on me. "But only under one condition. I'm a sick gal, Chester Drum. You'll have to humor me."

I had to lean over to hear her. She tried to smile up at me. "Name it," I said.

"That if you get help... you don't come back with them. They'll be able to take care of me. I want you to go after Dygert. Well? Promise?"

We stared at each other, solemnly. She tried the smile again but couldn't quite make it. For a while she said nothing. She concentrated all her efforts on the job of breathing. "It's a promise?" she asked finally.

I nodded. "It's a promise."

We drank our coffee together. Then I made her as comfortable as I could. Her eyes were too bright and her cheeks had that dead gray look they get with pneumonia.

"Can you get out of bed?"

"...if I have to."

"You'll have to keep the fire going."

"That's easy."

I gave her Jerry's .45 and said, "Dygert isn't coming back. But anyway." She took the gun. I turned the cot around so that she could see the door.

I kissed her cheek. She held me for a moment, then let go. I looked back once. She lay very still, as if afraid any movement might start her coughing again.

I stepped outside, put on my skis, and went looking for Dygert's trail. An hour after I found it, the snow started to fall.

CHAPTER TWENTY-THREE

I lost his trail on a ridge west of the shelter where Goheen was waiting. It had been snowing for two hours now, not hard, but it showed no signs of stopping. About a quarter of a mile back, I had found an old, run-down cabin. It was too old and too dilapidated to be part of the park's shelter system. It had probably been standing long before Mont Tremblant Park had a name. Dygert's tracks had stopped there. The cabin had no stove, but there was a fireplace with ashes in it. The ashes were still hot, and when I'd opened the door, the wind had fanned them into brief flames. Dygert had spent the night there, and had gone on. It gave me some little satisfaction to know he'd been as tired as I was.

Dygert's tracks—made this morning, the ruts deeper—had gone on from the cabin. But on the ridge, in the snow, they vanished.

He had headed overland on the shortest route back to Mont Tremblant, gambling he could make better time than on the trail, gambling he wouldn't get lost. I took the same gamble. There was a frozen stream below the ridge on my left. I saw a stream on the map. I kept going.

Up over high snow-covered hills. Down long slopes, gliding. Across flat tundras, with the wind blowing again. Skiing was reflex now. I belonged to the snow and the cold. There was nothing else. Nothing behind me and nothing else ahead of me.

Then I climbed a hill, like any other hill. Like a thousand others. I stood panting on the top. I stamped my skis and pushed down and back with the poles. And saw the long low Mountie station leaping up at me.

A patrol starting up the hill met me. I talked. They talked. I showed them the map, pointing. They told me to slow down. One of them smiled. They led me back to the station and inside. One of them said a helicopter had finally arrived from Montreal, to help in the search. It was grounded, though, until the snow stopped. It was a two-seater, and if the snow stopped it could pick up Bobby and bring her out, to the small hospital in Mont Tremblant, in minutes.

"'Copters," a corporal said. "We used to have dog teams. Not anymore. You never saw a dog team the snow stopped."

The door opened. It was still snowing. Sergeant Moriarity came in. He looked beat, but his face lit up when he saw me.

"You went in," he said.

"I went in."

"I figured you would."

I drank three cups of black coffee and spread the map out on a desk for Moriarity. I showed him the cabin where Goheen, Howie and Carol were. Marked the cabin where Bobby was waiting. Told him that Curt might be dying or already dead in the woods. Told him Jerry Trowbridge was dead.

"You killed him?"

"We shot at each other, I didn't miss."

He rubbed his chin. He hadn't shaved. His beard was stiff and wiry and made a scraping sound when he rubbed it. "Don't leave Mont Tremblant," he said.

He looked at a man seated before a shortwave radio set. "We still have any units in the field?"

"Two patrols, Sergeant. I've called them in."

"Near Lac du Diable shelter?"

"O'Connor called in about two miles from there."

"Get him back, if you can. Send them to the shelter."

The radio operator called. "Patrol Four. Patrol Four. Do you hear me? Over."

The radio squawked and a voice said faintly: "This is O'Connor with Four. We're coming back. Over."

"Don't. There's a sick girl at Lac du Diable...." The operator gave instructions.

"Better phone the Grand Hotel Hemlock," I told Moriarity. "One of them is loose. He might try to go back there."

"To do what?"

"To kill Judson Bonner, if he isn't dead already."

Moriarity grabbed for the phone. I opened the door.

"Where the hell you think you're going?"

"Over there."

"For Christ's sake, we can take care of it now.... Hello, Hemlock? Just a minute." He cupped the phone. "Haven't you had enough?"

I didn't answer him. I went outside and put on my skis. I heard Moriarity talking on the phone. Then the door slammed behind me. I started moving. Moriarity shouted something after me. I kept going.

The lobby of the Hemlock was almost deserted when I got there. A small group sat quietly, subdued, in one corner. A girl was saying, "Then why don't we go over to the St. Laurent? This place is like a morgue." A boy and a girl were talking about the first winter carnival down south in Ste. Agathe. I passed the desk, where the elderly desk clerk was complaining to the doctor who had been in the Bonner suite the night before last.

"...my business. Ruining it! You must move him."

"We can't move him yet, Bouvet. It would be dangerous."

"But a dozen guests have checked out already. More, in the morning...."

The doctor shrugged. The clerk, Bouvet, shook his head sadly, his wattles quivering. "How long?" he asked, when the doctor just stood there.

"I don't know how long."

"Mont Tremblant is no place for a heart attack," Bouvet said stubbornly.

I went upstairs.

The Mountie sitting on a chair outside the Bonner suite was wearing the red-coat uniform that Hollywood had immortalized. He had a revolver on a lanyard in a shining leather holster.

"You can't go in there," he told me politely.

"Been quiet?"

"They don't even know I'm here. I wasn't supposed to scare anybody. Who're you?"

"Drum," I told him. "I'm the guy who suggested they put a guard here."

He looked at me. He was very young, but he had smudges under his eyes and lines on his face as if he'd gone without sleep for too long. His eyes narrowed then widened. He stood up. "Say that again."

"I'm Drum. I—"

"I just let a man who said he was Chester Drum go in there."

I got to the door a step before he did. I turned the handle. The door was locked. He shouldered me aside and used a key on it. We went in together, the Mountie fumbling with his polished leather holster.

He never had a chance to use his gun.

Mrs. Bonner was just getting out of her chair. She looked angry. She stood up in the Mountie's line of fire. Ernie Dygert stood behind her, a few feet from the door to Judson Bonner's room. "...to reason," he was saying. Then he saw us. His reflexes were very good. In two steps he had reached Mrs. Bonner. He circled her waist with his left arm. An automatic appeared in his right hand. He looked out on his feet. I must have looked like that too. He had been going on nervous energy. But he had enough left to know we wouldn't let him walk from that room.

"I'm getting out of here," he said.

The door behind him opened silently. I saw it and the Mountie saw it, but Dygert didn't.

Judson Bonner crouched in the doorway behind him.

He looked ghastly. His wrinkled pajamas were draped on a frame of bone. His eyes were sunken into his pale face, like dark holes punched in a ball of raw dough. His left hand twitched, clawlike, on his pajama jacket, then clutched out at the doorjamb for support. In his right hand he held a small automatic. He lurched out of the doorway on bare feet and started to fall forward from the waist. That was when Dygert heard him. As Dygert started to turn, Bonner's left leg slid forward, supporting him.

He shoved the automatic against Dygert's side and pulled the trigger. He pulled it five times, his frail body jerking with each shot he fired.

Dygert's arm slid down Mrs. Bonner's dress. She opened her mouth to scream. She didn't make a sound. Dygert fell back away from her. He teetered for a moment on his knees. He dropped the automatic and went down after it on his face.

Bonner made a noise which might have been a cry of terror or a cry of joy. Then he collapsed, falling across Dygert's body.

Mrs. Bonner never moved, never made a sound, not even when the Mountie went over to examine them. "This one is dead," he said, indicating Dygert. "The old man's breathing."

Then Mrs. Bonner really cried.

I ran for the phone.

They had draped a blanket over Dygert and returned Judson Bonner to his bed and his oxygen tent. The doctor came out. "I don't understand how he ever had the strength to get up," he said. "His heart is bad, but he has a slight chance."

"He wouldn't want any kind of chance at all," I said.

His wife was at his bedside until the end came. Judson Bonner died just before dawn.

A little later it stopped snowing. The helicopter went out for Bobby and flew her in to the Mont Tremblant hospital. Judson Bonner's oxygen tent was the only one in town, so they brought it to the hospital and put Bobby in it. All morning the helicopter was busy, ferrying back and forth to the other cabin, bringing out Carol first, then Howie, then Curt, who had walked into the cabin to surrender a couple of hours after I had set out after Bobby, and finally Goheen. I heard about that later from Goheen and Sergeant Moriarity.

They let me stay with Bobby until she passed the crisis. In the early afternoon her breathing was better, easier. Then, later, she smiled up at me through the plastic of the oxygen tent.

When Gilbert and Curt were brought into the hospital two days after that and confronted with Bobby, they confessed their part in the attempted murder. The inquest on Jerry Trowbridge was brief and ruled that I had shot him in self-defense.

In a week, Bobby and I said goodbye to Goheen and flew back to the States. He promised to look us up when he got to Washington.

There was another hearing in the building where Aaron Burr had been tried for treason. Jefferson Lee Jowett presided. This time he didn't bother with oratory. It wasn't necessary.

Mrs. Lord and Laurie, wearing black, attended the hearing with Professor McQuade. I was surprised to see them in mourning clothes. So much had happened, it seemed as if months had passed since Duncan Lord's death. They didn't try to talk to me before the hearing or after it. They had come to see the men responsible for Duncan Lord's suicide punished, but Dygert, Jerry Trowbridge and Judson Bonner were all dead. The bleak, bitter hostility they had left they aimed at me. I don't think they were ever quite convinced I wasn't responsible for what had happened.

The only surprise at the hearing came in Mrs. Bonner's statement. She also wore black and already in her mind she had built a legend of her husband. He had only wished to serve his country, she said. Everything he did, he had done for his country. I was too weary to argue with her. For all I knew, she was right. Maybe Judson Bonner really had believed that. It didn't matter—now. No one at the hearing tried to take away from her the little she had left.

The surprise came a few minutes after her expected eulogy of her husband. She went on talking compulsively, as if the sheer volume of her words would give her the absolution she sought. She had had an affair with Sheriff Lonegran, she said. They had been very careful about it, very smooth, all but once. It had nothing to do with how she felt about her husband. She was how she was. Then one time, they had been very clumsy. Dygert had walked in on them. He never said a word—not right away. Lonegran had wanted to tear him apart, but Mrs. Bonner calmed him down. Then later, when I visited Bonner with my pocket recorder, Dygert told Lonegran I wasn't to reach the Prince Charles County jail alive. Or else.

They gave me back my license. Mrs. Bonner went to live alone in her big house. Maybe she's still there.

A week after the hearing. Captain Masters of the Virginia State Police came into my office. He made a gun of his thumb and forefinger and shot at me with it. Then he grinned ruefully.

"We sure gave you a hard time, Drum," he said.

I said something about being used to it, in my line of work.

"I heard about Canada. It must have been rough."

I waved at a chair, and he sat down. It had been Jerry's chair. I brought out the office bottle. We had a drink, toasting each other silently with our glasses.

"I got to thinking you'd like to know what happened to Lonegran."

"What could have happened to him? Mrs. Bonner's evidence was only hearsay. It wouldn't stand up in court. You know that, I know it, and so does Lonegran."

"He didn't act like he knew it," Masters said.

I filled his glass and said nothing.

"The day after the hearing, he didn't show up at his office."

"So?"

"So this came in on the teletype yesterday." He handed a yellow sheet of paper across the desk. It was a teletype from the office of the Policía Federal of Mexico in Guadalajara, Jalisco Province. A man identified as Roger P. Lonegran, sheriff of Prince Charles County, Virginia, had crashed his car into the abutment of a bridge spanning a river on the highway from Guadalajara to Ajijic. They had to get his body out of the wreck with blowtorches.

We talked for a little while, then Masters shook my hand and left. I never saw him again.

I told Bobby about it that night at her new apartment. She's been talking lately of leaving Washington. It has too many of the wrong kind of memories for her. She may decide to leave in a week, or a month, or not at all. Except for that, we don't talk about the future. It might spoil what we have. What we have, now, for as long as it wants to last without us pushing it, is each other.

We drank to that.

THE END

Turn Left for
MURDER

by STEPHEN MARLOWE

PROLOGUE

On the night of Tuesday, January 13, 1942, at a little after eleven o'clock, Norm Fisher dusted his hands with talcum powder, then ran them down the long, tapering length of the number twenty cue stick. He chalked the tip carefully until it was completely blue. He then bent over to squint along an imaginary line he had drawn from the white cue ball to the fifteen ball to the far left corner pocket.

"Cripes, Norm," one of the boys said, "I could sink it behind my back."

Ignoring him, Norm Fisher stroked the cue stick smoothly along the bridge he formed with the fingers of his left hand. He waited for the moment when his right eye and his stroking right hand would be in perfect coordination along the imaginary line he had drawn. It was almost as if he were shooting a gun, Norm thought. You don't pull the trigger, you squeeze it. You don't jerk the cue stick back and lunge forward with it; instead you follow through gently on the stroking motion when everything is just right.

At the moment Norm decided to follow through and make his shot, someone placed a hand on his shoulder. The tip of his cue stick was deflected a fraction of an inch, and he struck the cue ball with too much English. The cue ball described a brief curving path a foot or so to the left, then came to rest on the green felt of the pool table.

"Scratch!" one of the boys cried jubilantly.

Norm straightened up slowly with a pained, scathing look twisting the features of his face. He had learned that look from some of the older guys who hung around on the street and up here in Sunny Jim's. Giving that look was more mature than cursing and less dangerous than fighting. It really let them know you were pissed off.

The look froze on Norm's face as if he were in a moving picture and someone had stopped the camera to study one of the frames. Then Norm tried to smile.

The man who had laid his hand heavily on Norm's shoulder and made him scratch the shot was Big Danny Cooper. You definitely did not scowl at Big Danny or snarl or anything.

"Hiya, Pretty," Big Danny said. "I was looking for you."

"Hiya, Dan," Norm said casually, resting his cue stick down on the tabletop. He tried to make it sound like the most natural thing in the world, saying hiya to Big Danny like that. He could see awe in the eyes of the other boys.

Big Danny wore a double-breasted blue overcoat and a gray woolen scarf. His shoes were hand-stitched. They were classy just like all his suits and silk shirts. It was said Big Danny had twenty-five silk shirts, each a different color. He was twenty-six years old, eight years older than Norm. He wore his hair long with a pompadour up front, high over his right eye. Most of the boys in Sunny Jim's wore their hair that way, too.

"Me and Buggsy was wondering if you'd want to do a little driving for us tonight," Big Danny said. "How about it, Pretty?"

Six weeks ago, Norm had borrowed fifty dollars from Buggsy Green, the Street's shylock. Yesterday he had gone down to the candy store which Buggsy's mother owned and had told Buggsy he couldn't pay. At the six-for-five shylock rate, he now owed Buggsy a hundred and ten dollars. All along, he had never intended to pay Buggsy a cent. It was a dangerous thing to do, but it had worked. Now he was in.

If you failed to pay six dollars a week for every five you borrowed from the shylock, you usually got a schlammin, a beating. But sometimes, particularly if you had been hanging around the shylock and his friends for a long time, they figured you could repay them with some kind of favor instead.

Then you were on your way. If you kept your nose clean you wouldn't remain a punk kid for long. Hadn't Big Danny called him Pretty, the name Buggsy had dubbed him with because of his curly hair? Wait till the girls down at the luncheonette heard that, coming from Big Danny Cooper, too.

"Sure, Dan," Norm said.

Someone sank the fifteen ball and called, "Hey, rack 'em up, Skatbootch!" As Skatbootch began plucking the colored balls from the trap at the foot of the pool table, Norm got his mackinaw from the wall hook and followed Big Danny Cooper toward the stairs. He knew that everyone in Sunny Jim's was looking at him.

"The bum in the car asks you anything," Big Danny told Norm, "we're taking him to find Buggsy. You got me?"

"Yeah," Norm said. "We going to Buggsy's house?" He was disappointed. The house where Buggsy Green lived was just up the block. He hardly knew why they needed to drive.

"No," said Big Danny. "You know that garage under the El across from Kelly's?"

Norm nodded. The Brownsville Garage had an office on one side and one of those big, corrugated metal roll-up doors at the other.

"You drive us there," Big Danny said as they reached the sidewalk. A sudden flurry of snow had swirled down on the Street, but it wasn't sticking yet. "Then go across to Kelly's and have some cream soda or something."

"I drink beer," Norm said.

"Then beer. Here's a buck, Pretty." He gave Norm a crumpled dollar bill. "When I wave my hand outside the garage, you come back. And don't drag your tail, kid."

Big Danny pointed to a car at the curb, a late model black sedan, a Buick. Norm opened the door for Big Danny, then went around to the driver's side and slipped in behind the wheel. There was a man sitting in the back of the car, but Norm couldn't make out his face in the darkness.

Norm kicked the car over, shifted the gears and accelerated smoothly away from the curb. He was very conscious of Big Danny sitting next to him, and he was a little nervous.

"Are you sure we won't be waking up Mr. Green?" the man in the back of the car asked.

"Naw," said Big Danny. "I'm telling you, he's working." As far as Norm knew, Buggsy Green never worked a day in his life, except on Sundays when he sometimes helped his mother in the candy store. He certainly never worked in the garage under the El.

"He can give me the money? I need it pretty bad."

"Don't worry about nothing," Big Danny said. From the corner of his eye, Norm could see that Big Danny had put on a pair of gray gloves.

By the time they reached the El, the snow was coming down hard. Norm pulled the car up outside the corrugated metal door of the garage. There was no light coming from the office. Through the snow, he could barely make out the neon sign of Kelly's Bar across the street. He watched as Big Danny and the man walked over to the corrugated door, Big Danny fumbling in his pocket, probably for a key. Then Norm turned and walked across the deserted street.

Norm showed his draft card to the barman, then sat down at a stool close to the door. The plate glass window of the bar was fogged over and he could not see through it. He wouldn't be able to see when Big Danny waved to him.

Norm gulped his beer quickly, paid for it, and walked outside. The snow was beginning to stick.

From where he stood, he could barely tell that the corrugated door of the garage had been opened and swung up by Big Danny. Unable to see Big Danny or the other man, Norm headed back across the street. A train rumbled by overhead, and shattered the late evening silence. For a while Norm stood outside the garage, but then the cold began to get to him. There was nothing under the mackinaw but his shirt. His teeth were beginning to chatter, and he figured there wouldn't be any harm if he went into the garage.

Inside, there was the smell of gasoline fumes. A light from somewhere up ahead barely revealed the gray cement-block walls. Three or four cars had been left in the garage overnight, one of them with a badly damaged front end. Some accident, Norm thought, wondering if anyone had been hurt. He kept walking toward the light.

It was an overhead lamp, hanging on a chain which dangled from the high ceiling just over the hydraulic grease-rack. The shadow of the rack was like a giant letter H on the floor.

Big Danny was standing on the bar of the shadow H. He was mugging the man whom Norm had driven to the garage. His left arm circled the man's neck from behind and held him. The man's legs were drumming up and down very hard as if he were running some place as fast as he could go. But his traveling days were over. Big Danny was plunging an ice pick into the man's chest, his right arm swinging back and forth, his fist clenched around the handle of the pick.

Norm leaned against the cement block wall. The beer rose up in his throat and made him gag. *Run away,* he told himself. *Don't get sick. You can't get sick now. You ought to run away. Any place. Just keep on running. Don't stop.*

But Norm just stood there against the wall and watched. *Run, you punk kid.* He watched while the man stopped running in place. *Get the hell out of here!* He watched while Big Danny let the man fall over the grating on the floor.

What's the matter you can't move? He watched while Buggsy bent over the man on the floor with a tire iron and slammed it down across his forehead, making a sound like a baseball bat hitting a fastball squarely.

Run, run, run, run, run....

He watched while Big Danny dragged the man off the grating and Buggsy turned on a water tap on the wall and got a broom from somewhere and swept the blood down the drain.

If you run, they'll find you and kill you. That's why you're not running. He watched while Big Danny and Buggsy carried the dead man out to the car, opened the back door and squeezed him inside.

Big Danny's calling you now. "I'm coming," Norm said. What a strange voice he had!

Snow had mantled the Canarsie dunes with white when Norm braked the car to a stop. He sat still and looked straight ahead. He kept the motor running. He watched the windshield wipers chasing the big powdery snowflakes from the windshield. He avoided the rearview mirror when Big Danny got out and opened the back door.

"Go around the trunk and get the can of gasoline," Big Danny told Buggsy. Buggsy took the keys from the ignition switch of the car. The car shuddered, then the motor was silent.

Buggsy came back with the five-gallon can while Big Danny dragged the dead man ten yards off among the dunes. Norm could barely make out Buggsy sloshing the contents of the can over the dead man. Then Buggsy was running back toward the car with the empty can banging against his leg. Big Danny dropped a match on the gasoline-soaked clothing of the dead man and started running too.

"Get moving," Big Danny told Norm as he got in the front seat beside him.

Buggsy climbed in back and slammed the door. "I spilt gas all over my pants," he complained.

The funeral pyre was burning bright and orange there among the Canarsie dunes when Norm swung the sedan around in a wide U-turn, skidding briefly as he drove back down the road toward Brownsville.

"That bum walked right into our hands," Big Danny told Buggsy. "Funny, huh?"

"What do you get gas out of pants with?"

"We been looking for him three days to hit him," Big Danny went on. "So he comes looking to make a touch from you. Louis will be very happy we did the contract so quick."

"Do you use Carbona or something?"

"Shut up about the pants. It evaporates, I tell you."

"They cost me fifteen dollars."

Big Danny grunted something, then lit a cigarette. He offered one to Norm, but Norm shook his head. If he took anything in his mouth now, he would puke. "You were all right, kid," Big Danny said.

"Thanks," Norm said automatically.

"You notice him, Buggsy? The way he acted?"

"You ain't no punk, kid," Buggsy admitted.

"He was cool," Big Danny said. "Forget about the six for five, Pretty. You're even with Buggsy. Ain't he, Bug?"

"Don't call me that, willya? Yeah, I guess so."

They drove north through Brooklyn, reaching Brownsville before one o'clock. The snow was coming down more slowly now. Norm hoped it would snow long enough to cover their tire tracks. When they drove under the El he could see the neon sign above Kelly's Bar. He did not look across the street at the garage.

"Drive yourself home, Pretty," Big Danny said. "We'll worry about the car." Then he turned around and faced Buggsy over the rear of the front seat. "Did you see the way the bum was jumping up and down? I ain't never seen that before."

"He sure was surprised," Buggsy said.

"I mean, the way he jumped."

"Do you have to talk about it?" Norm said. Immediately, he was sorry. He should not have said anything.

"Everything's going to be O.K., kid," Big Danny told Norm. "Just drive yourself home. You'll get used to it."

Norm stood on the curb, watching the taillights of the car fading through the snow. He wanted to think about absolutely nothing. He wanted to curl up in bed and sleep. Already, the memory of Big Danny holding the dead man was vague. Buggsy leaning down and hitting the fallen body with the tire iron was like part of a dream. Had Norm really driven the corpse out to Canarsie and watched them burn it?

Everything was vague and formless in his mind. Only the sight of Buggsy sweeping the water, running pink with blood, down the drain in the garage floor was so clear Norm thought if he squeezed his eyes shut he could reach out and take the broom from Buggsy.

In the window of the bakery outside the four-floor walkup apartment house where Norm lived with his mother was a poster. It had a big picture of Uncle Sam on it, looking very serious and pointing a finger and saying WHAT ARE *YOU* DOING FOR DEFENSE? For some reason Norm got suddenly sick when he looked at the poster. He leaned over and threw up in the snow, then walked up the three flights of stairs to the apartment and let himself in.

He lay on his bed in his underwear. The bed was an old iron poster, the white paint peeling from it, the spring flat, the mattress sagging. The dresser was maple but old. Years ago, Norm had carved his initials in it with a penknife. NF in big letters, two inches high. His father, who had died of cancer two years later, had walloped him for it.

Mrs. Fisher was scrambling eggs for him when Norm walked into the kitchen.

"What's the matter, Norman?" she said. "All night in your sleep you were moaning."

"It's all right, Mom."

"You came in late, Norman."

"It wasn't so late."

"I heard you. What do you do out on the Street so late?"

"Nothing much." Norm sat down and shoveled forkfuls of scrambled eggs into his mouth without appetite.

"You forgot your orange juice, Norman. You were up in the poolroom?"

"Leave me alone, Mom."

"Your father never went to poolrooms."

"It's all right, Mom."

"There's nothing better you can do?"

"Please leave me alone."

"Shooting pool when you could be studying for the City College test?"

"I don't want to go to college."

"You don't want. You don't even want to go to work, Norman. You don't want."

"I'm going to be drafted soon, Mom."

"I should work to support you while you go to poolrooms? You're eighteen, Norman. A man."

"I don't want to talk about it, that's all." Could he tell her everyone along the Street looked up to Big Danny and Buggsy and the others because they wore silk shirts and custom-made suits and drove flashy cars and had all the girls practically falling all over them but never worked at all? Maybe he ought to tell her about Buggsy and the broom and how Buggsy had swept the garage floor so sparkling clean.

"You sit around all day until the poolroom opens at one o'clock. You live there, Norman. Why don't you take your toothbrush and sleep there? You should think more of your father. An example."

"Shut up!" Norm shouted, pushing his chair back from the table and standing. "He's dead. My father's dead. You just ought to shut up about him."

"Norman... Norman... I should wash your mouth with soap. If you was smaller."

"I'm sorry," Norm said. "I didn't mean it." He was almost a foot taller than his mother and still growing. He towered over her. He leaned down awkwardly and tried to hug her. He could feel her stiffen and pull away from him. She was sobbing.

"Mom," he said. "Listen, Mom. None of the guys are working. They're all waiting to be drafted. That's all, Mom."

"I only make forty dollars a week. We need the money."

He looked at his mother, who was still sobbing, but all at once he saw Buggsy and the broom, and the way Big Danny had held the dead man around the neck. He remembered the drive to Canarsie with the wipers brushing away the snow, and how the funeral pyre had blazed brightly against the night. Everything was not vague as it had been last night. Now, everything was clear in his mind, clearer than his mother in the print housedress and the chipped enamel-topped table and the old four-burner gas stove in front of him.

"I won't wait, Mom," he said. "I'm going down to join up right now."

He took the subway to Grand Central Palace in New York. He read a paper on the train and looked around furtively when he read the article about the torch-murder. The man, burned beyond recognition, was still unidentified.

At Grand Central Palace, Norm was examined and sworn into the Army. He requested immediate active duty. His serial number began with the numerals 1-2 because he had volunteered.

CHAPTER ONE

The distance from the gatehouse to the main building of the Tudor Hotel and Country Club was less than a quarter of a mile, but Big Danny Cooper jammed his nylon-mesh shoe down on the accelerator pedal and felt the surge of power as the big Caddy engine responded eagerly. He waved cheerfully to a few hotel guests as they stopped to stare at the brand-new turquoise convertible as it sped down the private road. Then he patted the power-brake pedal and brought the gleaming two-and-a-half-ton machine to a screeching stop in front of the hotel.

"Mr. Moore is expecting me," Big Danny told the desk clerk, leaning across the marble counter and smiling at him. Marble, yet. "Cooper is the name."

"Of course, Mr. Cooper. It's Room 401 for Mr. Moore, 403 for you. I hope you'll be happy, sir."

The bellhop followed Big Danny into Room 403 and deposited the three tan leather bags on the carpet. He flicked the air-conditioner switch and Big Danny heard the soft hum as cool air was forced into the room. He gave the bellhop two dollars, waited until the boy left, then opened the smallest valise and took out his comb and brush. He spent five minutes in front of the mirror getting his hair exactly right. It was beginning to recede at the forehead and was thinner in the back than it used to be. Big Danny brushed a few flecks of dandruff off the shoulders of his pale-green jacket and smiled at himself in the mirror. *For a gent pushing forty you can still make the dames howl, yes sir.*

Whistling, Big Danny spent another hour unpacking his bags and placing everything just right in the drawers and closet of the room. Then he strolled to the French doors, opened them and walked out on the terrace. There was a fine view of the swimming pool, the eighteenth hole of the golf course, and the Catskill Mountains, fading from green to purple in the distance.

"Hey, Danny. We're over here."

A three-foot-high stone ledge separated this terrace from the next one. Big Danny looked in that direction and saw Buggsy Green, Louis Fassolino, Li'l Paisan Ucci and Eugene Moore all sitting around a table. They were sipping tall drinks and smoking. It was Buggsy's gravel-throated voice that had called to him. For a guy still on the good side of forty, Buggsy sure didn't look so good.

Big Danny crossed the ledge and joined his associates on the other side. "You're an hour and fifteen minutes late," Louis Fassolino said. He wagged his round head from side to side as if he were Danny's father or something. "Have a gin and tonic?"

"You know I don't drink." Big Danny kept on standing because he was a head taller than anyone else there, even Fassolino. The name Mr. Fats certainly fit him. Mr. Fats made up in girth what he lacked in height. Big Danny could really look down on them when he was standing.

"You miss the good things in life," Mr. Fats said, pouring more gin for himself and opening a fresh bottle of quinine water. "They say the food here is splendid, by the way."

"It's kosher," Li'l Paisan Ucci reminded him. "Give me the good pasta or chicken cacciatore and some Chianti. Ahh." And Li'l Paisan smacked his thin lips.

Eugene Moore cleared his throat and said, "Gentlemen, I would like to get back to business. We have the whole weekend ahead of us here at the Tudor."

"Some hotel," Big Danny said.

"Now, about Mr. Stanley Harris, the special prosecutor."

"Hit him," Buggsy growled. "I say he's gotta be hit." Buggsy flinched. A fat striped bumblebee was buzzing around the terrace. "Look at that goddam bee."

"He's afraid of the bee," Big Danny chortled. Buggsy was scared of so many things, Big Danny thought, it was surprising how he managed to survive so long.

"I'm allergic to bee stings," Buggsy said. "I almost died once." He took an ineffectual swipe at the bee with his big hand, then relaxed when it left the terrace for more peaceful territory.

"Buggsy wants the prosecutor executed," Eugene Moore said. "Before we vote, I would like to remind you of several things. In the first place, the prosecutor hasn't actually done anything yet."

"He will," said Buggsy. "He's gonna. You see what he said in the papers."

"Here," Li'l Paisan said. "Here is a drink. Cool yourself off. You don't see me getting excited, do you?"

Big Danny smiled. When Li'l Paisan got excited, he really blew a full head of steam.

"It's all right for you to talk," Buggsy growled. "You ain't in Brooklyn. You don't care what happens in Brooklyn."

"But you're wrong, Buggsy," Eugene Moore told him. "We all care what happens in Brooklyn. We will not lose sight of the rest of the country, though. Since Mr. Ucci's business interests lie in New Jersey, his reticence is understandable."

"That's just it," Buggsy protested. "He's over in Jersey. What does he care what Harris does in Brooklyn?"

"It affects us all," Eugene Moore said. "That's why I called this meeting. It's significant that three of you are from New York, isn't it? Mr. Ucci, from New

Jersey, represents other local interests. Since my own enterprises are on a national level, you can trust me to be objective. Gentlemen," Eugene Moore went on in a soft voice, taking off his glasses and wiping them with a white handkerchief, "this is our problem. If Harris is allowed to live, our extensive New York interests may well be in jeopardy. If Harris is executed, on the other hand, the entire national organization may have to absorb and care for gentlemen on the lam from New York, not to mention the bad publicity Harris' death will give us from coast to coast."

"He means it will raise a stink, boys," Mr. Fats said. There was a cool breeze on the terrace, but his silk sports shirt stuck to his body with sweat. You could see the thick, wet clumps of chest hair right through it. "Let me tell you how I feel, Buggsy. I am as much Brooklyn as you are."

"Hell," Buggsy said, glowering. "You're the boss."

"No, Buggsy. I ain't the boss. No one is the boss, not even Mr. Moore. We all got our jobs, though, what we're best suited for. I say this, Buggsy. To hit Mr. Harris now, when he gets so much press he's more in the newspapers every day than the President, is stupid. To hit Harris at all unless we got to, also is stupid. To hit the little people, that's different. To hit the witnesses the prosecutor needs to make strong cases, that's good. Nobody knows them yet. You do not see their faces on the television yet. Hit them that way, the little guys, so Harris ain't able to do a thing but puff and blow, that's excellent."

"We don't have to take that kind of crap from Harris, that's all!" Buggsy shouted savagely, standing up. "You lookit the papers, don't you? I'm a... a..."

"Leech," Eugene Moore supplied.

"Yeah. A leech on half of Brooklyn, he says. The son of a bitch, who does he think he is?"

"So long as he can't prove anything," Li'l Paisan said, "what do you care, Buggsy? They call me worse than that in New Jersey, but they can't lay a finger on me. I like it. I tell you, I like it."

"We can hit that bum," Buggsy said. "Me and Big Danny could do it ourselves. You think I wanta wait till it's too late? Already the bum sends my ma to jail. She's been holding the shylock kitty fifteen years in her candy store, but the bastard makes a drive on shylocks, and where's my old lady now? In jail she is. Now he's making noise about me. Maybe he don't like our whole family. You think I want to go nuts? I'm going nuts, I tell you!"

"I like Mr. Fats' suggestion," Eugene Moore said, holding his glasses up to the sunlight and examining the polished lenses. "Wait and see what happens, Buggsy. Without witnesses, the prosecutor won't have any case."

"I got to hit that bum for my mother," Buggsy said.

"What do you think, Danny?" Eugene Moore asked.

Big Danny shrugged. "If we don't hit the prosecutor, we got to hit somebody else. It ain't I don't like to think, just that I let Mr. F do some of the thinking for me. That's right, ain't it, Mr. F?" The prosecutor would be an interesting contract, though. Big Danny would have to study Harris' habits carefully. He would have to learn the pattern of his life, the way he spent his working days and what he did on weekends. He'd also have to know of any little quirks he had. It was the quirks which often set them up for the hit, the little things. There would be one right minute of all the minutes in the day, all the days in a month, to hit a man like the prosecutor. Big Danny would strike in that minute after careful study.

"Then you don't care?" Eugene Moore asked him.

"Naw."

"You're a good boy, Danny," Mr. Fats said. *Almost forty,* Danny thought. *What a boy.* "We're missing all that fine sunshine," Mr. Fats went on talking. "Why don't we vote?"

"Better let the prosecutor alone," Li'l Paisan said. "I vote we don't kill him."

Eugene Moore nodded. "And I agree. The prosecutor means trouble, Buggsy. But your way means more trouble."

"It's all right for you," Buggsy growled. "The bum's driving me nuts. We got to hit him."

"Not for me," said Mr. Fats. "I'll take my chances with a living prosecutor. There's more ice in the bucket, boys." So saying, he dropped two cubes into his glass and made another gin and tonic.

There would be other interesting contracts, Big Danny thought. Almost with regret, he realized he had come so far in the organization he didn't work on many contracts himself these days. They were relegated to punk kids instead. He was too important to make the hits himself. He was an executive. He sighed and said, "I vote with Mr. F."

"You're a good boy," Mr. Fats said, smiling an oily smile of approval.

"I'm the guy taking all the crap," Buggsy said, walking to the edge of the terrace and staring down at the swimming pool. "You guys don't give a damn. Your old ma ain't behind bars on account of the special prosecutor. You don't know what it's like. I'm Brooklyn. I'm the guy he's after. You wait, Fassolino. You'll wish you voted to hit him."

"Oh, now, Buggsy," Eugene Moore suggested. "Why not make it unanimous?"

But Buggsy shook his head.

"Four to one against," Eugene Moore said. "Motion defeated. Gentlemen, why don't we get a good suntan?"

"Not me," Buggsy told them. "I got to go back home. Me and the wife are moving out to Long Island."

"You ain't through with Brooklyn?" Big Danny demanded.

"Hell, no. The noise and the stink makes me sick, that's all. I'll drive in on a parkway every day. They don't read the New York papers out there maybe; my wife won't have to take Harris' crap, too."

"You really care?" Mr. Fats wanted to know.

"She nags the crap out of me, that's all," Buggsy said. He shook hands all around and crossed over the parapet on the other side of the terrace, where he entered his own room.

"No hard feelings?" Li'l Paisan called after him.

Buggsy stuck his head out on his own terrace. "The bum's got to go," he said, and disappeared into his room.

"It would be a calamity at this time," Eugene Moore told his associates. "If we kill the prosecutor, there would be more lammisters than places to hide them."

"Buggsy is a stubborn man," Li'l Paisan said. "You heard him."

"He's a good boy," Mr. Fats protested. "A worrier, but good."

"He'll need watching," Eugene Moore said. "We can't take any chances. We wouldn't want Buggsy to throw a monkey wrench into the national machinery, would we?"

"No," Mr. Fats admitted. "He's going to be busy moving out to Long Island, anyhow."

"Watch him," Eugene Moore said. "Keep an eye on him, Danny. He trusts you."

Big Danny grinned. "Buggsy? He don't trust anyone."

"Watch him," Eugene Moore said. "I would hate to call a contract on Buggsy, but if he puts his own interests before the national interests... You watch him, Danny."

Going a round of golf with Mr. Fats later, Big Danny couldn't concentrate on his game. He was hooking too much on the drives. His stance was good, though. He knew it and held it longer than necessary. He watched Mr. Fats waddling across the fairway ahead of him. He could feel the excitement building up inside him, his whole body tense and expectant, like a clenched fist.

The idea was so new and unexpected, it left him dizzy with anticipation. It might never come off, he thought. Probably, it wouldn't.

Buggsy Green and Big Danny Cooper: two guys who had come up the long hard way together; organizational executives who headed the troop of killers whose members were fanned out, on demand, to fulfill nationwide contracts. They got the contracts from Mr. Fats, who probably got them from Eugene Moore and other national bosses. There wouldn't be a gang killing in Brooklyn without Mr. F's approval. But there wouldn't be one, either, unless Buggsy and Big Danny gave the nod.

Now Buggsy might try to cross the organization. Just might. If Buggsy

went too far, Big Danny might be given a very different kind of contract—
Buggsy, his pal, his partner, who bossed the troop with him. *Hit Buggsy.*

You could kill the Chief of Staff of the United States Army easier, Big
Danny thought. You could parachute into the Kremlin and assassinate that
guy—what was his name, Malenkov?—a lot easier. Buggsy, who had shared
a few dozen contracts with Big Danny over the years, knew the score. How
would you go about killing Buggsy? Big Danny wondered. It would be the
climax of his career. It would take originality and consummate skill.

It would be an orgy.

CHAPTER TWO

Norm Fisher swung the overhead garage door down and walked around to the front of the house. It was two o'clock in the morning. He didn't mind working the night shift, though, not if it meant an extra twenty dollars a week. They could use the money, what with two-year-old Debby growing so fast, and another baby almost ready to be born.

Norm padded quietly up the five stairs to the bedroom floor of the split-level house. Arlene had left the night lamp burning in the hall, but he heard her voice. "Norm? It's all right, honey. I'm up."

He walked into the bedroom, leaned over and kissed his wife on the cheek. She drew his face down with her hands and kissed his lips. "Don't you like to kiss pregnant women?" she said. He could barely make out the grin on her face. Arlene was a small girl, brunette and pretty. Sometimes when he was working at the factory he would think of how he would soon be going home to her and Debby. The thought would make him feel good all over. They had been married almost five years, but it was still the same.

"Just one certain pregnant woman," Norm said.

Norm got into bed. He didn't have the dream so much anymore, but sometimes it came unexpectedly. He would wake up yelling and then he would be faced with the job of telling Arlene everything was all right. It bothered him because of Arlene more than anything else. Twelve years was a long time. He didn't know much about psychology, but he figured the scar was someplace inside him. A trauma, it was called. But he had learned to live with it. Only when Arlene said, after he had dreamed of Buggsy and Big Danny and that night back on the Street in Brooklyn, "Norm, sometimes I hardly think I know you"—then it was hard to live with.

The vast supermarket, covering almost an acre of ground about a mile south of Hicksville on Long Island, shared the shopping area with a few dozen smaller stores on Oyster Bay Road. There were great gleaming plate glass windows outside and a parking lot which could hold almost two thousand cars. Inside, row after long row of displays seemed to stretch endlessly.

Norm was pushing Debby in the food cart while Arlene studied her shopping list, making some last-minute changes with a pencil. "The meat counter is down there," Arlene said, and led her family along the aisle.

Norm smiled. *Me*, he thought. *Domestic. Really domestic.* It was a long way from Brooklyn. A long way from a lot of things. His mother would have liked to see him like this, pushing his daughter down the aisle of a supermarket in a food cart. But his mother had died of a heart attack while he was in service. His mother would have loved Arlene.

Up ahead, Arlene was busy at the meat counter. Norm let Debby lean out of the food cart to play with the stacks of canned foods along the way.

"Excuse me," a woman said in a whining voice.

Norm steered the food cart out of her way.

"What kind of crap," the man with her grumbled loud enough for Norm to hear, "I got to go shopping with you!"

"Once a week," the whining woman told him.

Then the man saw Norm. He scowled and said, "Don't I know you from somewheres, mister?"

"You look familiar," Norm said. He wished the man would go away, but the woman's food cart blocked the narrow aisle for all of them. There was something about he man he recognized, something frightening.

"Hey, wait a mo!" the man said. He had a square face and kinky hair. His eyes were very small and close set. His nose looked like it had been broken. But it was the mouth you saw most of all. Thick, petulant lips, down-drooping at the corners—cruel lips, self-indulgent.

"Wait a mo!" he said again. "I'll be damned, it's Pretty Fisher."

Norm's knuckles whitened on the cart handle. All these years in all those dreams, Buggsy had been almost faceless. He had not realized it until today. Big Danny's face he remembered vividly. But with Buggsy, it had been the rasping voice that bridged the years.

This man was Buggsy Green.

"No, I don't know you," Norm said.

His hands were trembling. His voice sounded different again, strange. Like that night in the big garage.

"You're Pretty Fisher. I don't forget a face. It's me, your old pal, Buggsy."

"Norm!" Arlene called. "I'm down here. Bring the cart, will you?"

"Coming," Norm said.

"You live around here?" Buggsy asked him.

"I'm telling you, you've got the wrong man. I don't know you."

What the hell, Norm told himself as they drove back home. It was almost twelve years ago. You're not the same guy. You were just a punk kid then. You didn't know why they wanted you to drive. You wanted no part of it. There was nothing you could do.

You could have gone to the police.

You could still go to the police.

Why did you wait almost twelve years, Mr. Fisher? We'll buy the first part of it. You didn't know where you were driving that man, or why. But you saw them kill him. After he was dead, you knew.

I am just a material witness with a wife and one and nine-tenths children, sir.
You drove the murder car. You waited twelve years.
I was in the Army three years, sir. I was discharged a captain. It's funny, sir. There
was a platoon leader in my company who used to say if everyone surrendered to the
police for the crimes he committed, there wouldn't be a soul left on the streets.

Norm toted the packages into the house for Arlene and placed them on the kitchen table. Debby scurried about their legs while they unpacked and put away the groceries. Suddenly, Arlene sat down. She looked very pale.

"The baby?" Norm said.

"Yes. Turning around. I'll bet he's a big guy, Norm."

"Maybe it's time to go. Maybe you're a week early."

"No. It's stopped."

"You sure?"

"Of course, I'm sure."

"Listen. Would you mind if I left about three hours early for work? There's something I have to do."

"It's about that man in the supermarket, isn't it?"

"Will you please forget all about the man in the supermarket? Well, can you manage without me or can't you?"

"You don't have to get angry."

"I'm not angry."

"Then stop shouting. Go whenever you want."

Norm called the New York Public Library. Yes, they had newspapers twelve years old. No, he didn't need a card. The *Tribune* and *Times* were in microfilm at Forty-second Street, but he could go down to the Newspaper Division at West Twenty-fifth and see any newspaper he wanted. He was welcome.

He drove along the parkway to Kew Gardens and took the independent subway to Manhattan, getting off at Twenty-third Street. Inside the Newspaper Division, an elderly man was dusting the shelves of bound newspapers with a feather duster.

Norm found part of what he was looking for in the January 19, 1942, *Daily News*. He read:

TORCH VICTIM IDENTIFIED

Police came one step closer to solving New York's latest gangdom slaying today when the body of Leo Rose, an unemployed fur-dyer who had been reported missing on Wednesday, was identified through dental records.

After an autopsy performed by Assistant Medical Examiner Morris Grover, it was determined that Rose had died of multiple puncture wounds about the chest, made with an ice pick or other sharp instrument. Rose's skull had also been fractured.

The body was found five days ago in the Canarsie dunes area of Brooklyn, burned beyond recognition. Police believe the murder shows all the earmarks of a gang-style slaying.

Now, at least, he knew the man's name. It seemed a futile bit of knowledge, twelve years later, but it made him feel better. Although he spent another hour and a half with the bound newspaper volumes, Norm could find no further mention of the killing.

He thanked the old man, who was now dusting the three long tables with his feather duster. He took the subway back to Kew Gardens, paid the parking lot attendant and drove home. It was already too late to go to work, but he hadn't taken a day's sick leave in months and thought he had one coming.

A Buick Roadmaster sedan with tinted, wrap-around windshield was parked in the driveway of his house. It sure was a nice car, he thought. He didn't know anyone who drove a car like that.

He opened the front door.

Buggsy Green was just getting ready to leave.

"Oh, there you are, Norm," Arlene said.

"You got a nice little place out here," Buggsy said. Debby had brought out her new doll, the one she got for her birthday, to show him. Buggsy sat down again.

"She winks," Debby said proudly.

"I looked you up in the phone book," Buggsy said. "Ain't it like old times, Pretty?"

Arlene laughed. "Pretty, is it? That's cute."

"Well, forget about it," Norm said.

"Would you like something to drink, Mr. Green?" Arlene asked. "I'll make lemonade. Come on, Deb." Mother and daughter walked into the kitchen.

"Why the hell don't you leave me alone?" Norm said. "There's nothing you want here."

"Lemonade," Buggsy said, as if the idea were entirely original with Arlene. "What do you do for a living, Pretty?"

"I'm an inspector at the Fairless Camera factory."

"The pay good?"

"All right."

Buggsy grinned. "Hundred a week?"

"Around."

Buggsy dug down into his pocket and came up with a thick green roll in a money clip. A portrait of Grover Cleveland was etched on the first bill. It was a thousand-dollar bill. "This is money," Buggsy said. "Real money. It would take punks in camera jobs like yours a year to make what I got in my hand."

"We manage," Norm said. "Look, Buggsy. I don't know what you want, but I don't want you coming around here."

"Your castle, huh? Your fourteen-thousand-buck castle with a thirty-year mortgage. You guys make me sick, Pretty."

"So, I make you sick. So, get out of here."

"Here's the lemonade," Arlene said. She came out from the kitchen with a tray on which was a pitcher, three large glasses and a small one.

"We're practically neighbors, Mrs. Fisher," Buggsy told Arlene as she passed around the lemonade. Debby drank hers immediately and asked for more. Norm filled her glass. "Say, that's a nice kid there. Polite and all. You're gonna have your hands full with two, Mrs. Fisher. You'll need money, I'll bet."

"Norm's got a nice job."

"Yeah, I heard. Inspecting cameras."

"Oh. Are you in the same line, Mr. Green?"

"Take Debby out back," Norm said.

"Naw. I work for a big national outfit. Kind of like an executive, you'd say. Wouldn't you, Pretty?"

"Pretty," Arlene said. "I can't get over it."

Just then the telephone rang. Arlene went to answer it.

"Will you get out of here?" Norm said.

"Still drive like you used to, Pretty? I could use a guy like you."

"No thanks."

Buggsy reached into his pocket again and peeled a couple of bills off the inside of his roll. "Here's two C's," he said. "You think about it, Pretty."

"I don't want your money."

Buggsy tossed the bills on his lap. "No strings. Like that old six for five, remember? All free and clear. We never paid you nothing for that job."

"Just—get—the—hell—out—of—here."

"I'm going," Buggsy said. "But wise up, kid. I want you should work for me, you'll work for me. Well, I'll give your regards to Big Danny."

"You can shove it," Norm said, losing his temper. He was about to wad up the two hundred-dollar bills and throw them in Buggsy's face, but Arlene was coming back from the kitchen. He stuffed the money in his pocket.

"It was Nancy," Arlene said. "She and Abe want us to play bridge Sunday night, if we can get a baby sitter. That is, if I'm not in the hospital yet."

"You want I should sit for you?" Buggsy said, winking at Norm.

"You're not serious?" Arlene wanted to know.

"Sure. I ain't got kids of my own, see? I like kids. I always liked kids, didn't I, Pretty?"

"Mr. Green was just going," Norm said.

"If you're really serious about baby sitting," Arlene said.

"Good-by," Norm said, holding the door for Buggsy. "Don't come back," he whispered fiercely. "I'll call the cops."

"The cops? What the hell for? I'm just a business executive. Well, Pretty, see ya. I live in Syosset, so we're practically neighbors." Buggsy climbed into his Buick. The motor growled. The Buick backed down the driveway and streaked away along Greenview Lane.

"That's quite a car," Arlene told Norm.

"Just a Buick."

"What does your friend do for a living? Just a Buick, the man says. A four-thousand-dollar Buick."

"I don't know what he does for a living. I haven't seen him in twelve years."

"Outside the supermarket, you said you didn't know him."

"All right. All right. He's a rotten, no-good, stinking crook. He's been a crook all his life. Now will you leave me alone?"

"Norm. Tell me what's the matter."

"I was only fooling. He's not a crook. I just don't like him, that's all. You don't have to like everyone you know, do you?"

"Norm, you sound so funny."

He did, all right. His voice was strange again.

CHAPTER THREE

A low, one-story structure of cinder block, the Fairless Camera and Instrument Corporation sprawled over half a dozen acres of a one-time Long Island potato farm. The Fairless factory specialized in commercial cameras on government contracts. Norm supposed there was good reason for the security measures, but the uniformed guard at the guardhouse always irked him. He showed his badge and followed the stream of other workers into the rambling building.

"Hey, Fisher. Foreman says he'll want you to start on the lens housings again tonight."

"O.K.," Norm said. He stopped at the first department where a dozen turret lathes were boring, facing and turning the magazines of the lens housings.

"Hi, Norm."

Mechanically, Norm took the checking setup off the bench near the screeching turret lathe. He set up the height gauge with size blocks and began evaluating the man's first piece. "Swell," he nodded, and followed his shadow, cast by the overhead fluorescents, down the aisle.

"First baby tonight," a man at the automatic screw machine said an hour later. "Here you go."

Norm turned the housing lug in his hands, examining it. Automatically he poked a thread gauge into the hole. It was almost a week since Buggsy had visited them. Had Buggsy's talk of baby sitting somehow been a veiled threat? *What the hell, calm down.* Buggsy had never been subtle. Norm jammed the no-go member of the gauge against the opening of the threaded hole. There was a hum of machinery around him, a smell of oil. His hands were trembling slightly.

The P.A. system blared. A loud but sleepy voice said, "Norman Fisher to Inspection Office. Norman Fisher to Inspection Office."

He walked past the rows of busy machines to the wallboard partition of the Inspection Office. Mac O'Reilly, the foreman, was waiting there for him. O'Reilly was a big, powerful man with a red face that got redder very easily. He didn't say a word. He handed Norm a memo from the Assembly Department. Norm read:

> H-109-12 lens housing,
> Hole spec. .0943 plus .0005 diameter
> .0000
> Hole o/s .0095

O'Reilly picked up the offending lens housing, which had been turned back by the Assembly Department. "Gimme that plug gauge," he told Norm.

Norm went to the wall and got the plug gauge, handing it to him. O'Reilly, his face very red, thrust the no-go member into the hole. It slipped in easily, sloppily.

"I'm sorry," Norm said.

"You're sorry. You were sorry last night and the night before, too. What do you do, just look at 'em, Fisher? You gotta do more than look."

"I'll be more careful."

"Got something on your mind, boy? I don't want to be hard on you."

"All right. All right."

"New baby any night, now, huh? Anytime now."

"Yes," said Norm.

"Oh, I almost forgot," O'Reilly said. "There's a call for you from the guardhouse down by the parking field. You can pick it up here." O'Reilly shuffled from the partitioned office.

Norm picked up the phone. "This is Fisher," he said. "The guardhouse has a call for me.... Hello?"

"Hi, Pretty. It's your friend, Buggsy."

"What are you doing here?"

"I remembered where you work. I want to talk to you alone. Without the old lady. You have a lunch hour or something?"

"Nine o'clock," Norm said. "But I don't want to see you."

"Yeah? You come out here at nine or I'm going in there. Which is it?"

"I'll be out at nine," Norm said, and hung up.

Outside, O'Reilly said, "I wanted to tell you. It's getting slow since Korea stopped."

"I know."

"They been laying people off on a basis of seniority."

"I heard."

"On a basis of efficiency, too. They're up the creek, the boys upstairs. This ain't the only camera corporation, you know. They got to turn out good work. You better watch your step, Fisher. I'm the guy they holler at. I'll holler louder at you."

"Sure," said Norm. "Sure."

"Lemme know when the kid gets born."

"I'll pass out cigars," Norm said.

He went to the punch-press department and inspected the first pieces off the presses until the eight-fifty-five warning buzzer sounded. He went to the men's room and washed his hands. That's all he'd need, Buggsy coming in here now. Instead of following the workers down to the cafeteria, he went outside.

It was almost fully dark now, with faint traces of the summer sun in the western sky. He followed a few overtime day workers past the guardhouse, forgetting to sign out. Buggsy came out of the shadows behind the guard-house and took his arm and steered him toward the parking field.

"I only have half an hour," Norm said. "What do you want?"

"Just relax, Pretty." Buggsy led him to the Buick Roadmaster. "A four-hole job," Buggsy said. "A beauty. No Caddy for me. You get a Caddy, the tax boys start sniffing after you."

A few minutes later, Buggsy stopped the car near a roadhouse along the Jericho Turnpike. They went inside, where Buggsy ordered a double Old Overholt. Norm ordered two hamburgers, all the way, and a bottle of Schlitz.

"I'll lay it on the line," Buggsy told Norm. "I got a job for you."

"I'm not interested."

"Listen, will you? There's five thousand bucks in it for you. Five grand, free and clear."

Five thousand dollars. As much as Norm made in a year. He sighed, sipping his beer. It was ice cold. "I'm still not interested," he said.

"There's no sweat, kid. A cinch."

"No."

"You don't even know what. Ask me what."

"I just don't care."

"Here." Buggsy scribbled a telephone number on the back of a table card advertising Schlitz beer. He gave it to Norm. "This is the number you can call me at after you change your mind."

"Give me your address," Norm said. "I'll mail you the two hundred dollars."

"Keep it, kid. I don't want your money."

"It's not my money."

"The boys didn't want to call a contract on this guy. I think they ought to, that's all. So I'll call my own contract."

"I'm not listening."

"Funny guy. You know why I got to tell you?"

"I don't know why."

"That nutty law. Like a wife can't be made to testify against her husband. An accomplice's testimony ain't no good, unless it gets corroborated. That's what you'll be, an accomplice. What a nutty law, huh?"

"I'll be late," Norm said.

"The bum's name is Stanley Harris. He got to be hit."

"Just drive me back." Norm stood up.

"Sit down, will you? And don't go getting any ideas. You ain't forgot that old Brownsville Garage thing?"

"You can't scare me. You can't talk about it, just like I can't."

"There's your family, Pretty." Buggsy smiled at him.

Norm lunged across the table, grabbing the lapels of Buggsy's jacket. Buggsy slapped his hands away, rapped his knuckles across Norm's mouth.

"Sit down, Pretty. Don't try that crap. I ain't playing games. I stopped playing games a long time ago."

Norm patted his lips with a handkerchief. He was bleeding. When Buggsy ordered a second drink, Norm asked for a double Old Overholt, too.

Someone had dropped a nickel into the juke box. It was a smooth orchestral arrangement of "I'll Be Seeing You." Paul Weston, Norm thought. Arlene liked to dance to that record. The waitress brought their Old Overholts, humming along with the record.

"You gentlemen ought to buy the whole bottle," she said, grinning.

Buggsy grinned back at her. She let her hand touch his as she put the shot glass on the table. "You're O.K., baby," Buggsy said. She smiled again.

"Now get lost," Buggsy told her. Looking hurt, she retreated. "It's corroboration," Buggsy said to Norm, "what you got to worry about."

Norm gulped the Old Overholt in one swallow. The whiskey burned his bruised lips.

"I could get a punk to drive me," Buggsy said. "It wouldn't cost so much, either. But I know you'll do a good job. You'll have to. Y'know what that bum calls me? A leech. Can you imagine that? Me. A leech. He's going to get hit by a leech."

The two double Old Overholts had gone to Buggsy's eyes. The way he went right on talking, though, he could drink two more without feeling it. "Me, with my nervous stomach," Buggsy said. "I can't take it. The boys ought to know I can't."

Norm finally had to promise Buggsy he would call him. Buggsy left a ten-dollar bill on the table while the waitress was still totaling up their check. When they had covered half the distance back to the Fairless Camera and Instrument Corporation, the Buick got a flat tire.

Buggsy pulled up on the shoulder of the road. "Well, goddam," he swore. "A brand-new car. I should have got puncture-proof tires."

"That's too bad," Norm said. "Maybe I'd better walk from here. I'm late already."

"Don't leave an old pal stranded out here, Pretty. Give me a hand."

Norm was surprised by his own response. It was automatic, like one of Pavlov's dogs, after twelve years. Buggsy was one of the neighborhood big shots. Norm was a punk kid. Norm went around obediently to the rear of the car, waited while Buggsy opened the trunk, then took out the spare tire and the jack. Twenty minutes later, they were rolling again. Norm would be almost an hour late.

"I'll be waiting for your call," Buggsy said as he left Norm at the Fairless parking lot. "I hope it's a boy, kid."

Norm walked by the rows of cars and through the gate.

"Hey there. Hold on, bo." It was the guard.

"I'm sorry." Norm showed his badge. "It's all right. I'm night shift."

"Fisher, huh? You didn't sign out, Fisher. Your foreman called down here wondering. He's plenty mad. Next time you better sign out, Fisher."

"Sure," Norm said.

Inside, O'Reilly was waiting for him. "Where you been, Fisher?"

"It was that call. An old friend."

"You didn't sign out. You didn't say you might be late."

"We had a flat."

O'Reilly's face was flushed. "Assembly found another one. A mistake. I got yelled at, Fisher."

"I'm sorry."

"You're a lousy, stinking excuse for an inspector."

O'Reilly was shouting. Norm could see the punch-press operators looking at them. "We got too many inspectors as it is."

"What do you want me to do? I already made the mistake. I can't take it back."

O'Reilly turned his face away. "God, did you tie into one. That's a flat tire, huh?"

"Damn you, stop needling me."

"That's my job, needling."

"Then find another pincushion."

"I don't have to take no back talk."

"You're keeping me from my work," Norm said.

"Who says you're still working here?"

"So fire me!" Norm shouted.

O'Reilly grinned. He was enjoying himself. "What are you, threatening me?"

"You goddam bastard." It was Buggsy. Buggsy had frayed his temper. He didn't know what he was saying. "Hell, Mac. I'm sorry."

"You're crap. I oughta take you outside."

"I'm trembling." This is how he should have reacted to Buggsy. What did he want from O'Reilly? O'Reilly was only doing his job.

"You're through, Fisher. You're finished here. Come around tomorrow for your check. Two weeks so the union won't squawk."

"That suits me," Norm said. He didn't look at O'Reilly. He started walking toward the exit. A few of the machine operators came over and thumped his back, said nice things to him. They could square it up with Mac. They could talk to him before he sent the report to Personnel. They could have Norm back on the job tomorrow.

"Don't do me any favors," Norm said and went out to his car.

"You're forgetting to sign out again, Fisher," the guard called after him.

"You can take that sign-out book and shove it," Norm said.

You're some big shot, Norm told himself. Why don't you walk up to Mr. Fairless himself and punch him in the nose? Aren't you going to get five thousand hard-earned bucks from Buggsy Green? You don't need this crummy job.

He drove home and took out a bottle of bourbon. He drank it straight from the bottle and it went down burning but hit his stomach like water. He couldn't touch Buggsy's offer, or Buggsy's money. Another baby was coming. He'd go out tomorrow and look for a job. Fairless wasn't the only light industry on the Island.

God, Arlene. I'm sorry, Arlene. How am I going to tell you I was fired?

Suddenly the bourbon went to his head. He reached out for the bottle, knocking it over. He got down on hands and knees with a dishrag, sopping bourbon from the kitchen linoleum. His bruised lips were burning. He reached into a pocket for his handkerchief. He touched something stiff and rectangular.

It was the Schlitz card on which Buggsy had written his telephone number.

CHAPTER FOUR

Louis Fassolino, called Mr. Fats by the members of his organization, blinked his eyes at the sunlight streaming in through the windows of the bedroom, snuffled phlegm up his nose and swallowed it. His sinus was a real pain.

Sighing, he jabbed a large elbow against the ribs of his sleeping companion. "You up?" he demanded.

"I'm up."

"Then roll out of bed and fix us some breakfast."

He rolled over and planted big, blubbery lips on her mouth. The over-sized bed creaked. "How does it feel sleeping with the fattest man in Brooklyn?"

"You're cute, Louis."

"Cute she says. The boys should only hear it." He pinched her well-padded posterior. She yelped and sprang from the bed, a small girl, lushly curved, with a vapid face. She was wearing a black lace nightgown. Nightie, he always called them.

"Breakfast," he said again, aware that he had started to salivate copiously. He felt suddenly embarrassed. He had forgotten her name. He was always forgetting girls' names. "I want juice, any kind of juice you find in the box. I want kippers and baked potato. Put up the potato now, Dimples."

In the bathroom, he showered and shaved. He applied a perfumed after-shave lotion to his face. It gave him a pleasant stinging sensation. He shot deodorant from the squeeze bottle under his arms, then shuffled into the bedroom on a pair of mules. He selected striped silk undershorts, a loose-woven basque shirt in powder blue, darker blue slacks, powder-blue socks, navy-blue suede loafers, size thirteen-and-a-half triple-E. As he walked into the kitchen, he could already smell the broiling kippers. His mouth was watering.

"There's somebody to see you," Maxine said.

"This early in the morning?" He drank the tomato juice, scorched his finger splitting open the baked potato, knifed a generous chunk of butter on each half. He watched it melt, running down the potato skin in little golden rivulets, while he removed the backbone from each of his two kippers with a knife and fork.

"It's eleven-thirty," Maxine said.

"Who wants to see me?"

Maxine straightened up and smoothed the silk robe over her nightgown, her nightie. "It's Big Danny Cooper." The way she said it, he knew she thought Big Danny was handsome. Her voice said she was impressed by Big Danny's reputation. Her eyes glittered with thoughts and dreams of Big Danny.

"Maybe I'll give you a formal introduction sometime," Mr. Fats said. "Now, scram out of here."

"I was going to scramble myself some eggs."

"Are my eggs ready?"

"On the stove."

"Fine. Here's a little money." He gave her a hundred-dollar bill. "Take a taxi to Flatbush Avenue and eat in the cafeteria. I'll call you."

"You sure are cute," Maxine said, and went into the bedroom to dress.

"Danny!" Mr. Fats shouted. "Come on in here, Danny."

Big Danny sauntered into the kitchen and sat down across the table from Mr. Fats. "You're looking great, Mr. Fats," he said.

"I lost three pounds." Mr. Fats scooped up a generous heap of baked potato, dripping butter, and forked it into his mouth. "Get me the buttermilk out of the refrigerator," he told Big Danny. Mr. Fats took the cardboard cap off the buttermilk and drank it straight from the bottle.

"Some of Buggsy's punks are casing Stanley Harris," Big Danny said.

"You don't tell me."

"That's right."

"They told you?"

"They told some of my punks."

"After all the years I spent training Buggsy," Mr. Fats sighed. "It's too bad Buggsy was 4F during the war, Danny. He should have learned the hard way how to take orders. Get me the bacon and eggs over the pilot light, will you?"

Big Danny went to the stove and got the dish, then lit a cigarette. Mr. Fats said, "Not while I'm eating, for crying out loud."

Big Danny crushed out the cigarette and said, "Am I going to hit Buggsy?"

Finishing the quart of buttermilk, Mr. Fats belched and patted his fat lips with a napkin. "I'm surprised at you, Danny. You're as bad as Buggsy, you are."

"What kind of business is that? I do like I'm told."

"No one told you to hit Buggsy. No one said hitting Buggsy would be necessary."

"I can think about it, can't I? I got to make plans if I'm going to hit Buggsy before he can do anything stupid about Stanley Harris."

"You make plans when you're told."

"I got to be prepared. It ain't like hitting a bum."

"You don't even know I'll give you the contract, if the Combination gives me a contract."

"I'm the only guy who could pull it off."

"Tell me, does Buggsy come to Brooklyn much since he moved?"

"Every day. He still works here."

"Are you going to see Buggsy today?"

"Sure."

"I want to see him. You tell him for me to come over to Brighton Beach—the usual place—will you, Danny?"

"Sure."

"Be a nice boy, Danny. I'll do nice things by you."

Big Danny nodded.

"You want Maxine's phone number? A good word from me?"

"And how," said Big Danny. "Some kid."

Mr. Fats gave it to him.

Armed with Maxine's phone number, Big Danny sallied forth to find Buggsy.

Shutting his eyes so the sunlight looked pink through his closed lids, Mr. Fats stretched out on the blanket near the handball courts at Brighton Beach Baths. He could hear the slapping of the little black balls against the wall and against leather-gloved hands, the pounding of sneakered feet on the concrete of the handball courts.

"It's me—Buggsy," a rasping voice said. He could have said it was Rumpelstiltzkin. Mr. Fats would have known. That voice. Mr. Fats opened his eyes, propped his head up on one elbow. Buggsy was standing in front of him with a cardboard box, containing two paper cups of cream soda and four hot dogs with sauerkraut.

"Peace offering?" Mr. Fats said. "Buggsy, did anyone ever tell you in a bathing suit you look like an ape? Exactly like an ape or a Neanderthal caveman?"

Buggsy put the box down and stood blinking into the hot sun.

"You're going to get hit in the head," Mr. Fats said between mouthfuls, between swallows of cream soda, "if you don't watch your step."

"I ain't done nothing."

"It's what you're thinking of doing. The Combination does not want Stanley Harris touched."

"I ain't even thinking of Stanley Harris. Honest I ain't."

"Sit down, Buggsy," Mr. Fats said. He grabbed Buggsy's ankle with one huge hand and tugged at it. Buggsy came tumbling down on the blanket, his feet spraying sand on Mr. Fats' hot dogs.

"Don't lie to me," Mr. Fats said. "I hear you've been having the punks case Stanley Harris, so you can just cut out that lying crap. What's the matter, you got no sense in your noodle? Or maybe you think you got too much sense. If the Combination calls a contract, I'll let you know. Are you a one-man army, Buggsy?"

"Which one of my punks told you? He'll get hit in the head, not me." Buggsy punched his right fist against his left palm.

Mr. Fats had met Buggsy's punks once, in Brownsville. Girls' names he could never remember, they were all the same, all beautiful. But punks' names he always remembered. You made a punk feel he was going places if you remembered his name. "It was the one called Crazy Sammy," Mr. Fats said, selecting a name at random.

"That crazy bastard."

It was a test, Mr. Fats thought. A fine test for Buggsy, only Buggsy didn't know it.

"I'll take care of that crazy bum bastard," Buggsy said.

Mr. Fats finished his hot dog and glared at Buggsy. "You drive Crazy Sammy around to my place on Ocean Parkway tonight."

"I still think I ought to do it myself."

"You don't do anything yourself. You listen to me." If Buggsy didn't bring Crazy Sammy around tonight, Mr. Fats would know he had to think seriously about getting a contract called on Buggsy. If Buggsy did bring the punk around, Mr. Fats would play along with him. Crazy Sammy just had the dumb luck to be caught in the middle. "Bring Crazy Sammy around," Mr. Fats said again.

Later, Mr. Fats drove over to Sheepshead Bay in his Lincoln Capri. At Lundy's he had a shore dinner—a basket of steamed clams, clam chowder, half a broiled lobster, half a broiled chicken, salad, shoestring potatoes, pie a la mode and iced tea.

Mr. Fats was treated like a king. King Louis Fassolino, he thought, remembering all the newspaper stories. King Killer. Three times they had picked him up for murder, three times they had tried him. Once, in the old days, he had even languished in the death house up at Sing Sing for fourteen months. The smart lawyers got him a new trial, though, and by then the witnesses were conveniently dead, buried where they wouldn't be found in the Combination's cemetery over in Jersey. Li'l Paisan Ucci sure had helped in that one. Li'l Paisan and him were like this—brothers.

Mr. Fats drove home smoking a cigar. He put the Lincoln Capri in the garage and went inside. He put an LP opera on the phonograph and sipped a glass of tangy muscatel.

The doorbell rang.

Mr. Fats looked at his wristwatch. Seven fifty-five. Jacqueline was expected at nine-thirty. Jacqueline? Well, some name like that. Some man's name with two French syllables at the end of it, making it feminine. They would have plenty of time with Crazy Sammy, though.

Mr. Fats opened the door. "I brung Crazy Sammy like you said," Buggsy greeted him.

Crazy Sammy stood there, shuffling his feet self-consciously. Every now and then a muscle in his left cheek would twitch violently. It was one of the reasons they called him Crazy.

"Holy mackerel," he said, awe in his voice. "It's Louis Fassolino. You got an important job for me, Buggsy?" Twitch. "Something I can handle?" Twitch. "You won't be sorry you picked me."

"Come in," said Mr. Fats. "Down the cellar, please."

They followed him across a hall and into the kitchen, then down a flight of steps to the cellar. The walls were paneled with pine. In one corner there was a bar with a tinted mirror behind it. A rack of pool cues leaned against the wall. The center of the room was taken up by a pool table.

"I would like to thank you for the information you gave me," Mr. Fats told Crazy.

Crazy shrugged. "What information?"

"Maybe you figured you were doing the right thing," Mr. Fats went on. "But, Crazy, you must learn this: in the Combination, your loyalty should be to your immediate superior, Buggsy."

"I didn't give you no information," Crazy said.

Buggsy slapped his face. "You no-good stinking rat."

Crazy's face turned white, the pimples on his cheeks standing out red and ugly.

"Buggsy," said Mr. Fats. Buggsy leaned against the pool table and lit a cigarette. Mr. Fats waddled to the cue rack and selected a heavy stick. Holding it in the middle, he walked over to Crazy and slammed the thick end across his cheek. Crazy fell down.

"Get up," Mr. Fats said. Buggsy had passed the test, but it seemed a good opportunity to teach Buggsy a lesson at Crazy's expense.

"I want to get out of here," Crazy Sammy pleaded. "You got the wrong guy." He stood up, gently probing his numb cheek with his fingertips. The blue mark was three inches long, from cheekbone to jaw. He walked toward the stairs which led to the kitchen.

Mr. Fats swung the heavy end of the cue stick at the back of Crazy Sammy's head. He hit just below and behind the ear. Crazy fell and then rolled over and sat up, his cheek twitching furiously. Mr. Fats struck him in the mouth with the cue stick.

"It ain't me," Crazy Sammy cried. "It ain't me you want."

Mr. Fats smashed his mouth with the cue stick again. It made a noise like kicking a football. Crazy Sammy spit out three teeth and a lot of blood.

The cue stick caught him across the bridge of his nose. He fell over on his back and held his hands up in front of his face. Mr. Fats turned the cue stick around and jabbed the tip at his eye. Crazy Sammy screamed.

He could yell till he ruptured a blood vessel, Mr. Fats thought. Behind the pine paneling was Celotex. There were all-year-round storm windows because the house was airconditioned.

"He passed out," Buggsy said.

Crazy Sammy lay on the floor with his mouth open, blood leaking down on his shirt from the space where three teeth had been. There was a smear of blue cue chalk on his eyelid.

"What are we gonna do with this Crazy?" Buggsy asked.

"You, Buggsy, not me. Take him back to Brownsville. But first I want to tell you something, Buggsy."

"Yeah?"

It would serve two purposes, Mr. Fats thought. First, Buggsy would relearn fear and respect. Second, Buggsy wouldn't be able to trust his punks. If he didn't have any punks he could trust, he wouldn't be able to try a private contract on the prosecutor, Stanley Harris.

"Yes," said Mr. Fats. "It wasn't Crazy Sammy who told me."

Buggsy put out his cigarette. "What?"

"It wasn't Crazy. Somebody else."

"Who?"

"You know, I forget his name. I'm always forgetting names."

"Then why did you knock hell out of Crazy here?"

"Now you know what happens when a punk goes nuts. Maybe he doesn't get hit in the head, but he gets hurt. To you, Crazy Sammy's a punk. To me..."

"I get you," Buggsy said.

"You better start looking around for some new punks," Mr. Fats suggested. "You don't know who to trust, do you?"

"I can't trust no one. No one. Those guys. I brung them up from the gutter," Buggsy cried in self-pity. "It ain't bad enough I got all this trouble with my insides."

"What trouble?" Mr. Fats wanted to know.

"I'm a sick man," Buggsy said. "Real sick. Now I got to worry about the punks. You're the only guy I can trust even a little, Mr. F."

"Thank you, Buggsy."

"No, I got me one other guy I can trust," Buggsy went on. "Why? On account of he's scared, that's why. The only time you can trust 'em is when they're scared so much they're afraid to breathe."

"Who is that?"

"Aw, a guy. I knew him around Pearl Harbor, that's all."

"What's his name, Buggsy?"

"It ain't that I don't want to tell you, only... I don't have to tell you everything, do I?"

"Look at Crazy," Mr. Fats said. Crazy Sammy showed definite signs of coming to. He was beginning to moan. His swollen cheek was twitching again. "If you don't trust me, I won't trust you. I'll start thinking, maybe Buggsy is keeping too much of the shylock take in Brownsville or something like that. Look at Crazy Sammy."

"Pretty, that's his name. Pretty Fisher from Hicksville."

"Hicksville, Long Island?"

"Yeah."

"They don't call him Pretty in Hicksville?"

"Norm Fisher, they call him. If I said spit, he'd drown himself in it."

"That's interesting," Mr. Fats admitted. If Buggsy still had any ideas, he must remember that name. Norm Fisher of Hicksville. "Buggsy, you better take Crazy back now. He's coming around."

Buggsy got his hands under Crazy Sammy's arms and lifted him to his feet. The blood was still trickling sluggishly from his mouth, down his shirt. Mr. Fats was sure Crazy would need some stitches. He opened the cellar door and watched Buggsy walk out, supporting Crazy Sammy.

Norm Fisher of Hicksville. Mr. Fats would remember that name, in case Buggsy defected. He got a rag and soaped it up at the basement sink, then began to clean the blood from the asphalt tiles of the finished basement. He was hungry, but it was already nine o'clock. He would barely have time for something to eat before Carlotta arrived. Carlotta? Something like that. A boy's name with a few letters after it in French or something, making it sound feminine. What a name.

CHAPTER FIVE

"One of the aircraft plants is probably my best bet," Norm Fisher told his wife. "There are plenty of them on the Island."

"You ought to go around to their employment offices," Arlene said.

"I know. I will."

It was worse telling no one. He could have gone to the police anytime during these twelve years. He could go to the police now. Or he could contact a lawyer and find out how the law might be expected to interpret his role in the Leo Rose slaying.

Or he could tell Arlene. *Arlene, I thought you would like to know your husband was an accomplice to murder.* Sure, he could tell her—in a pig's eye.

"What's got into you, Norm? You just sit there and, well, mope."

"Just leave me alone, will you?"

"I'd feel better if you went looking for a job," Arlene said. "Don't worry about me."

His mind refused to function about anything else. Every time he closed his eyes, he saw Buggsy. They said things like that were dangerous. Obsessions. You had to take the bull by the horns.

He decided to take Arlene's advice—get out, look for a job... anything.

It was late when he got back. He had no job. There were possibilities—nothing definite. He had also stopped for some beers. And time had moved too fast. The house was dark. He went up the walk and wondered if Arlene could be asleep already. It was only ten forty-five. She usually remained up for the eleven o'clock news on the radio.

Arlene wasn't in the bedroom.

The overnight bag she had packed for the hospital wasn't in the closet. Debby's little bed had been slept in, but she wasn't there now. He found a note on the kitchen table.

Norm: I'm taking Arlene to the hospital for you. She's fine, don't worry. Debby will sleep over with us tonight. See you in the morning. I'll bet it's a boy.

The note was signed *Abe.*

Norm fumbled through the phone book for the number of the hospital on Horace Harding Boulevard in Queens. The night operator switched him to Maternity. Yes, Mrs. Fisher had been admitted. At ten-forty. No, there was nothing to report yet. Was he the husband? He might as well stay home and get some sleep. He could call the hospital every hour or so.

He peered through the window. There was a light on in the kitchen of Abe's place. He started walking to the door, then realized he couldn't go in there smelling of beer. Anyway, Nancy had two children of her own. She could take care of Debby.

He walked into the bathroom and ducked his head under the cold water tap. He toweled himself dry, then went into the kitchen and found some cold chicken in the refrigerator. In the cabinet over the sink was a bottle of Seagram's Seven. He took it down and poured himself a large drink in a water glass.

He had to meet the payments on the washing machine, the clothes dryer, the television set, and the car.

Their banked money would cover it, and the mortgage, for a few months. But he didn't have a job and he wasn't going to get one so easily, not after what happened.

Buggsy. He sloshed another drink from the bottle. The four-hole Buick... the way Buggsy could spend money.

Buggsy had him by the well-knowns, anyhow. No, he would not call Buggsy.

But then he stood up and went to the phone and dialed Buggsy's number. He had thought of it so much, he didn't have to look at the card.

The line was busy.

He had another drink, lit a cigarette, called the hospital. Nothing yet, Mr. Fisher. She's not in the delivery room. The labor room. Sometimes it happens like that. The contractions come fast for a while, but the woman isn't ready. Nature takes its time, Mr. Fisher.

Buggsy's line was still busy.

What the hell, it wasn't only Buggsy. Sure, Buggsy belonged in jail—the untouchable assistant to the King Killer of the murder machine. The newspapers said so. But a lot of palms had to be greased for the murder machine to go on functioning all these years. The quiet ones were worse. The pillars of the community—they made Buggsy possible. If he didn't help Buggsy, someone else would. Buggsy had him, but good.

He dialed the number again. *Buzz-click, buzz-click.*

He hurled the phone across the room. He walked after it on unsteady feet. The automatic busy signal was still buzzing and clicking. Carefully, he placed the receiver back on its cradle and replaced the phone on its stand.

It was just that he didn't want to drag Arlene into this mess. But if he didn't do what Buggsy wanted, they might be in more trouble.

He put on a jacket and went outside. The sky was clear and full of stars. This far from the city, you could see the pale irregular band of the Milky Way spanning the sky.

He pulled the car out of the garage and headed north toward the parkway. Driving fast, he would reach the hospital in about forty minutes.

For the time being, he forgot about Buggsy.

CHAPTER SIX

Norm found a parking space two blocks from the hospital on Queens Boulevard. Nearby, colored bulbs, like the strung-out decorations for an unseen Christmas tree, called his attention to a used car lot.

The night receptionist at the hospital was reading a confession magazine. She probably believed all the stories were true and received a vicarious thrill from them. "Fisher," Norm said. "Maternity."

Her involved directions led him to the maternity section of the hospital. "Fisher," he told the nurse on duty.

"Yes, Mr. Fisher. You called me once or twice." She had a pleasant voice but was sweating in the oppressive heat. Norm had hoped for Arlene's sake the hospital would be airconditioned. "Your wife is in the delivery room now, Mr. Fisher. Please have a seat in there." She indicated a waiting room.

"Is everything all right?" Norm asked.

"We'll call you."

"Can't you tell my wife I'm here? You see, I couldn't drive her and—"

"Your wife is under ether now, Mr. Fisher."

The waiting room was square and large, lit irregularly by three torch lamps. A pair of pay phone booths stood unused in one corner. Two men were pacing back and forth. A third was sitting on a sofa and smoking a cigar. Norm went to the window and looked out on an alley in which an ambulance was parked.

Just then a white-smocked doctor entered the waiting room. "Mr. Allerup?" he demanded. The cigar-smoking man came over. "Your wife has presented you with a lovely baby daughter."

"Oh God, four," Allerup said. But then he was beaming and pounding the doctor's back as he followed the white-smocked figure out into the hall. It was something nice to worry about, Norm thought. The sex of your child. *If it's a boy, I can call it Buggsy.*

At twelve-fifty, Dr. Weems came into the waiting room. Sweat stains darkened the armpits of his smock. He was still wearing the little white cap. He looked like a well-fed Claude Rains. "Mr. Fisher?" he said. "Oh, there you are."

Norm had met him once at his office here in Queens. "How is she, Doctor?" he said.

"Fine. Just fine. You have a son, Mr. Fisher. A fine boy."

"That's... wonderful. Can I see Arlene now?"

"She's still sleeping. Ether. Why don't you come back in the morning? Meanwhile, go out and have a good time. Celebrate."

"I'll do that," Norm said automatically. He watched Dr. Weems disappearing down the corridor, removing the white cap from his head and shaking his long gray hair. Probably he wore the cap to the waiting room for its dramatic effect.

A boy, Norm thought.

He hated Buggsy more in that moment than he ever had before. Sure, it was one of the big moments in a man's life: the first job, the first girl you had, getting out of the Army, getting married, the first child, and now—having a boy.

But he was without a job. And there was Buggsy.

"A boy," he said.

Outside, Norm walked the two blocks to his car and kept going. He didn't feel like driving home now. Celebrate, Dr. Weems had said. He walked to the intersection of Queens Boulevard and Broadway. A bar—Hymie's Place— was still doing business. Norm followed the neon arrow in through the door.

"Rye," Norm said.

He gulped the rye and had another. A third. He left a ten-dollar bill on the bar. Every now and then the barman would make change for him. When the ten had dwindled to four dollars and change, Norm got up, went to the phone booth in the back, and called Buggsy. It was now one forty-five.

There were six purring rings on the phone before a whining woman's voice said, "Hello? Is anything the matter?" At this hour, Norm couldn't blame her.

Buggsy's wife. It suddenly occurred to him he didn't know Buggsy's first name. He couldn't help smiling. He said, "I'd like to speak to Buggsy." He smiled again. He was good and drunk.

"Harold is in Brooklyn," the whining voice told him. "You know, Sunny Jim's. Harold's always up there, playing pool."

Norm dialed 411 and got Sunny Jim's phone number from Information, then called it.

"Yeah?" a voice at the other end of the line demanded.

"Buggsy," Norm said.

"Who's calling?"

"Tell him it's Norm... Pretty."

"Sure thing, Pretty." The voice made vocal eyebrows at him.

A moment later: "This is Buggsy."

"Pretty talking."

"Well, well, well," Buggsy said.

"You told me I should call you. I'm in Queens."

"I don't know Queens from a hole in the wall. You'll have to come over here, Pretty."

"To Brooklyn?"

"Sure. Sunny Jim's."

Norm felt a sudden masochistic desire to see the old neighborhood. He was wallowing already. He might as well drown himself. "I'll be there in half an hour," he said, and cut the connection.

The Coca-Cola people had given Sunny Jim's a shining new sign. The stairs were more rickety than Norm had remembered them. But the sounds of the poolroom were the same: the explosive break of fifteen racked balls in rotation, the loud click of cue ball striking numbered ball, the thump and roll of a ball landing in a pocket and rolling through the tunnel to the trap at the end of the table, the hushed talking.

In twelve years, Buggsy had graduated to three-rail billiards. He was squinting under the green-shaded lights hanging above the billiard table, lining up a shot with the two white balls and the red one. Two young punks stood behind him. They were smoking cigarettes and silently admiring him.

"Hello, Buggsy," Norm said.

Buggsy smiled at him. He gave his cue stick to one of the punks and said, "You finish out the hour, Foggy. It's on me."

"Gee," Foggy said.

"Pretty Fisher," Buggsy said. His body had stopped growing too early in life. The neck was almost nonexistent. The arms belonged to a man a head taller than he was. When he walked, they rocked in front of him from side to side. The small eyes were pugnacious and calculating.

"We'll take a ride in my car, Pretty." Buggsy nodded to Sunny Jim, who had aged, and Skatbootch, who seemed ageless, as he followed Norm downstairs.

They got into the Buick and soon roared away from the curb. Buggsy lit a cigarette and said, "Today is Tuesday. On Friday afternoon we're gonna hit the bum. I got it all cased."

"I didn't say I would help."

"What are you here for, a handout?"

"You said five thousand dollars."

"Five G's. Yeah."

"We just had a boy. I need the money."

"I'll give you five hundred on account. You know, Pretty, I wouldn't want you to cross me."

Holding the wheel with one hand, Buggsy grinned and tossed a fat roll of bills at Norm. "Take it," Buggsy said.

Norm counted off ten fifty-dollar bills. Each bill made it harder for him to turn back. When he pocketed the five hundred, it would be impossible. Buggsy didn't even watch to see if he took the right amount. Norm put the ten fifty-dollar bills in his pocket and gave the roll, still thick, back to Buggsy.

"Just one thing," Norm said. "Don't come to my house and bother me. I want to leave my wife out of this."

"Business is business," Buggsy said. "Your old lady don't have to know."

"Let's keep it that way."

"Anyhow, she'll still be in the hospital, won't she? Which hospital, Pretty?"

"Never mind."

"In Queens, huh? Well, I could find it."

"Shut up," Norm said.

"I should care? Friday afternoon I'll pick you up at your place. Then you drive."

"Why can't I meet you here?"

"Because I ain't got a drop for the car. It's a hot car, stupid. There's plenty of room I can park it out in Syosset."

Norm said nothing. Buggsy had parked under the El, a block from the garage. Overhead, a train rumbled by, heading for New Lots Avenue. It was strange Buggsy had no drop, no rented garage, for the hot car. Norm knew how those things worked. You used a jump box to start the car and heist it. You got another license plate from a more remote neighborhood, removing it from a car which you had cased and knew would probably not be used until the weekend. You put the stolen plate from the second car on the first car. You then put the car in the drop and left it there until you were ready to use it.

Buggsy did not have a drop in Brooklyn. It might mean a lot of things. It might mean Buggsy was going to steal the car at the last minute. But that was doubtful because it placed an unnecessary uncertainty on the whole operation.

It probably meant Buggsy was afraid to leave the car in Brooklyn, even in a legally rented drop. It probably meant Buggsy couldn't trust his punks. It probably meant organized gangdom was opposed to Buggsy's plan.

Norm said, "How's Big Danny these days?"

"What the hell do you care?" Buggsy snapped.

"I just wondered, that's all."

"Stop bothering me, willya? I got my own problems. I'm a sick man, Pretty. At my age."

"Will Big Danny be with us on this job?"

"Stop it! Stop that crap. You let me handle the details and do like you're told. I could drop dead tomorrow, Big Danny wouldn't bat an eyelash. My pal. Well, screw him."

"Sure," Norm said.

"You don't know how it is," Buggsy wailed in self-pity. "Me, a sick man. The bum of a prosecutor keeps running off at the mouth how he's gonna serve up my head to the D.A. on a platter. I got to hit him. My heart can't take it. You think I'm a healthy man or something?

"I can't trust no one," Buggsy went on. "That's what I got to worry about.

That and the prosecutor and my ticker. If you cross me, I'll kill you. Don't forget, Pretty."

Buggsy drove Norm back to his car and Norm got out of the Buick. "If there's a change of plans," Buggsy called to him, "I'll let you know."

"Fine," Norm said.

Fine. Great. Norm reached into his pocket and felt the ten fifty-dollar bills there. Did it really matter how many murder cars you drove? And if Buggsy wanted to hit the prosecutor, Buggsy would hit him no matter what Norm did. The prosecutor was as good as dead—unless Norm went to the police and told them what Buggsy was planning.

An early morning fog had rolled up from Massapequa Bay, shrouding the first level of all the split-level houses in Hicksville with white. The bedroom levels looked like small bungalows, their foundations driven into smoke. Norm parked in the driveway and went into his house. He called the hospital. Mrs. Fisher was doing fine. She was sleeping. She'd be getting her first nourishment soon. The baby had been foot-printed but would drink only water for twenty-four hours. That was best. That was the hospital policy.

Norm took his shoes off and flung himself across the bed without undressing. In the morning he would see that everything was all right with Debby. Thoughts strayed through his brain: *Nice of Nancy and Abe. Now we have a boy....* Gary Fisher they would call him. Little Gary... Norm wondered if he would look like his mother. Gary... Celebrate, Dr. Weems had said. *The poor kid.... The poor helpless little kid.... Why did he have to have me for a father?*

CHAPTER SEVEN

The trouble with beach parties, Eugene Moore thought, was that people were too demanding. It was expected of him, he knew. He was a socialite, wasn't he? The newspapers called him a socialite.

Three of Eugene Moore's ten acres were white and sandy beach. From here where the gentle waters of the Sound lapped softly on the white sand, you could see the promontory on which the Moore mansion stood. The house, of gleaming white stone and glass brick and window walls of tinted glass, was perched at the very edge of the promontory. A world-famous architect had built it at a cost of a quarter of a million dollars just after World War II had ended. Steps carved in the stone of the promontory led down to the beach, the beach house, and the jetties which formed an artificial yacht basin.

"I love to swim in your sound," the Pretty Young Thing purred. She had detached herself from a group of panting admirers and stood next to Eugene Moore, hands on round flaring hips, long dark hair gleaming wet, shoulders back, breasts thrust forward with nipples pushing out against the fabric of the scanty swimsuit.

"I'm glad you like it," Eugene Moore said, patting her bare bronze shoulder. It was wasted on Eugene Moore, but that was one of the things you didn't talk about.

Now the Pretty Young Thing scooped two martinis off a tray carried by a passing waiter.

Eugene Moore sipped his drink. The Pretty Young Thing sipped hers. When Eugene Moore did not make conversation, she finally dropped her empty glass on the sand and skipped back to her former group of admirers.

Eugene Moore didn't like men, either. You would assume, he thought now as the men in bikinis and the women in bikinis romped together across the sand and into the water and back out again, dripping wet, that if a man didn't like women, something might be wrong with him and he would like men. The wrong hormones. But Eugene Moore was indifferent to both sexes. He wondered if that made his success possible.

Eugene Moore turned around, the blue waters of the Sound behind him, the white sails looking like confetti. The sand was dotted with beach umbrellas and handsome men and pretty women. He faced the promontory. It was an apparition. It had to be an apparition.

Coming down the rock-hewn steps were Big Danny Cooper and a younger man Eugene Moore did not know.

Eugene Moore smiled affably when Big Danny reached the bottom of the stairs. But his voice was not affable. "I told you never to come here unless it was important."

"So, it's important," Big Danny said.

He was wearing a charcoal-gray shirt with DC monogrammed over the pocket, and pink flannel trousers. Big Danny Cooper, the fashion plate of the murder machine. The other man was younger, a punk kid. Eugene Moore couldn't see much of his face because the nose and the cheeks were covered with thick bandages, and the punk wore dark glasses. He was dressed cheaply in a well-pressed forty-dollar suit.

"What is it?" Eugene Moore asked in a polite voice. That same polite voice had ordered the execution of more than fifty men in the past twenty years, men whose defections had made their continued living dangerous to the well-being of Eugene Moore's acquisitive empire.

"I want you should meet Crazy Sammy," Big Danny said. The bandage-masked punk offered his hand, which Eugene Moore did not shake.

"Crazy Sammy is one of Buggsy's boys," Big Danny said as they walked down the beach.

"Oh?" Eugene Moore was mildly interested. Buggsy was a problem. Up in the Catskills, they had voted not to hit Stanley Harris, the prosecutor. The vote had been a foregone conclusion: Eugene Moore had not approved of the execution at that time. Buggsy, though, had disagreed. Well, even the best of men were expendable.

"*Was* one of Buggsy's boys," Crazy Sammy said in a surly voice. The bandage on his cheek shook, as if the flesh under it was twitching.

"What he means," Big Danny said, "is that for no reason at all, Buggsy gave him a schlammin."

"Please lower your voice," Eugene Moore cautioned him. "You were working on the Harris thing for Buggsy?" Eugene Moore asked Crazy Sammy.

Crazy Sammy shook his bandaged head. "Not me. No, sir. Buggsy only made believe I was."

A Pretty Young Thing with blonde hair came running across the sand toward them. She bounced so fetchingly that Big Danny let out a long, low whistle as she approached.

"Tell me, Sammy," said Eugene Moore, "what is Buggsy doing about Stanley Harris?"

"I don't know." Crazy Sammy's bandage twitched. "I mean, he's doing something. I don't know what."

"Then why did you bring Crazy Sammy here?" Eugene Moore asked Big Danny.

"Because of the schlammin he got. Don't worry, boss. I know what Buggsy is up to."

"I'm not your boss. Louis Fassolino is your boss. Why didn't you tell all this to Mr. Fats like you were supposed to?"

"Now you're getting there," Big Danny grinned, thumping Eugene Moore on the back.

He's utterly transparent, Eugene Moore thought. *He's working up to something. Killing gives him more joy than anything, although he tries to hide it. He's working up to a contract. He thinks this meeting is going to end in my giving him a contract.*

"I couldn't tell it to Mr. Fats because Mr. Fats helped give Crazy Sammy the schlammin," Big Danny said.

Eugene Moore took off his glasses, holding them at arm's length and rotating them slowly. The lenses, which corrected his sight for astigmatism, distorted the beach and the seascape like a moving trick mirror. He polished the lenses with a handkerchief and returned the glasses to his eyes.

"What do you know about Buggsy's plans?" he asked Big Danny.

"Plenty. One of his punks says he's gonna hit the prosecutor this Friday."

"Friday," said Eugene Moore. If true, it was imperative they stop Buggsy. "One-of his punks let you know this?"

"Yeah."

"But not Crazy Sammy here?"

"Nope."

"Then why did you bring Sammy to see me?"

"For the same reason I couldn't take him to Mr. Fats. The night before last, Buggsy brings Crazy Sammy out to see Mr. Fassolino on Ocean Parkway."

That's definitely not adhering to proper channels, Eugene Moore thought. In any big organization you had to go through channels. Crazy Sammy should never have met Louis Fassolino. "What did Mr. Fats want to see him about?" Eugene Moore demanded.

"It was a nutty thing," Crazy Sammy said. "I walk in. I'm impressed. I say, 'Gee, if it ain't Louis Fassolino.' I seen his picture in the papers. I figure this is damn important. I'm going places. I ain't no punk now. 'Thank you for the information,' he says to me."

"Who said to you?"

"Mr. Fassolino. 'What information?' I ask him. 'You know what information,' he says. I don't know from a hole in the wall. 'But Buggsy is your boss,' he says. 'You got to be loyal to your boss.' The son of a bitch slams me over the head with a cue stick." Crazy Sammy fingered the bandages on his face. Crazy Sammy twitched.

"What information was he talking about?" Eugene Moore asked.

"The prosecutor business," Big Danny said. "Fassolino claimed Crazy Sammy was telling him what Buggsy was planning to do about Stanley Harris."

"How do you know he didn't?"

"I know, that's how. Earlier that day, I told Mr. Fats. I was watching Buggsy like you told me up at the Tudor, remember? I figured you didn't want me to bother you, so I told Fassolino. I ought to hit them both," Big Danny said.

Eugene Moore lit a cigarette. The five-piece band the caterer had supplied was coming down the stone steps. The musicians wore silk shirts, tight black trousers, and maroon sashes about their waists. Latin American motif, Eugene Moore thought. Nice, but expensive. Their instruments were already waiting for them on the float a hundred feet out in the Sound. A motor launch would take them there from the yacht basin.

"If there is any hitting to be done," Eugene Moore said, "I'll let you know."

"If you don't, you're making a mistake. I know what Buggsy's doing. He can't crap without me knowing it. On Friday he'll try to hit Harris, see? Mr. Fats was trying to show him he couldn't trust none of his punks."

"What's wrong with that?" Eugene Moore asked.

"Plenty. He knows what the Bug is up to, but he's keeping it secret. We're all liable to get hurt while he's trying to calm Buggsy down."

"Why don't you let me decide that?"

The bandsmen had climbed into the motor launch. The Pretty Young Things waved to them as the launch roared away from the yacht basin.

"They kicked hell out of Crazy Sammy," Big Danny said. "An example, Mr. Fats thought. He could show Buggsy his men weren't loyal. Buggsy couldn't tackle a job like the prosecutor himself. Also, Mr. Fats could show Buggsy what happened to a guy when he didn't do what he was supposed to. Only it didn't work."

"Why not?"

"Because Buggsy's got someone else. A guy we used to know in the neighborhood. His name is Norman Fisher and he lives out in Hicksville now. He's going to drive for the Bug."

The band on the float broke into the strains of "El Mambo." The sound carried well across the water of the Sound. Couples began dancing barefoot on the hard-packed sand at the water's edge to the provocative rhythm of the mambo beat. Briefly, at times like this, Eugene Moore regretted his sexlessness. He wondered if he could take hormones or something. No. You couldn't keep a thing like that secret.

"Is this Fisher person reliable?" Eugene Moore asked.

"Buggsy's got him by the short hairs over something he done a long time ago."

"That's too bad," said Eugene Moore.

"But so have I," Big Danny said. "There ain't a thing Buggsy can make him do I can't make him do."

"Really," said Eugene Moore. "That's interesting."

"You want I should hit the Bug or shouldn't I?"

"I'm not sure yet," Eugene Moore said. He smiled. It was a mild grin, a bookkeeper's grin or a clothing salesman's. Eugene Moore had mild blue eyes, too, and a modest way of standing. He shifted from one leg to the other as if he weren't sure of himself. Occasionally he took off his rimless glasses and polished them abstractedly.

"You wait for Big Danny upstairs," Eugene Moore told Crazy Sammy. Crazy Sammy slouched off toward the stairs and climbed them.

"The last thing we want," Eugene Moore told Big Danny, "is a gang war. That was the main reason for forming the Combination, Danny. We have a national organization. Law and order within the ranks of organized crime. We do not start shooting up the sidewalks of New York or Chicago or any-place."

"That nutty Bug will lead us all to the electric chair. You got to make exceptions."

"I didn't say my answer was no. I merely want to suggest there are methods and methods. Danny, this will be the most important contract you ever carried out. I don't want Mr. Fats to know. I don't want any of your punks to know, which is why I sent Crazy Sammy away. This Fishman fellow—"

"Fisher," Big Danny said, his thin lips parted in a grin. "Norman Fisher of Hicksville."

"Yes, Fisher. What is it you and Buggsy got on this Fisher fellow?"

"Aw, some old thing. Some contract," Big Danny said. "It don't matter. He's scared so much he needs rubber bands around his pants cuffs."

"Good, Danny. That's very good. You said Fisher is going to drive for Buggsy on Friday. That's exactly what I want him to do."

"I don't get you." Big Danny seemed confused and disappointed. He'd be a terrible poker player, Eugene Moore thought.

"It's simple, clean, efficient. Fisher will drive for Buggsy. But Buggsy won't get a chance to hit Stanley Harris. I want you to arrange it so Fisher sets Buggsy up for you. I want you to hit Buggsy."

Big Danny grinned. "Hey," he said, "that's all right. That's damned good."

"The important thing is, I want it to be clean. No repercussions, no dangling loose ends. I'll take care of explaining things to Fassolino. But after, not before. Don't let me down, Danny."

"Not this boy," Big Danny said cheerfully. "Not me. As far as I'm concerned, this is it. This is the big thing."

"You don't like Buggsy?"

"It ain't that. What a contract, to hit Buggsy..."

"Yes," said Eugene Moore. There was something satisfying about being able to read a man so completely.

A few minutes later, Big Danny climbed the steps and joined Crazy Sammy at the top of the promontory. Then he disappeared with him.

"This is some beautiful party, Geney boy," a nameless Pretty Young Thing said to Eugene Moore.

CHAPTER EIGHT

"Fisher," Norm told the stout nurse at the hospital nursery door. "I'm the father."

He waited at the long, shade-covered window. Three women ahead of him were jabbering excitedly as the shade was suddenly rolled up. A white-masked nurse held aloft a red-faced infant for their scrutiny. The child looked like either Uncle George or Aunt Harriet. See? See the nose? Not like the parents' at all. The baby was withdrawn. The three women oo'd and ah'd. The shade descended.

The outside nurse opened the door a crack and said, "Fisher, number fourteen." The door closed. The outside nurse smiled at Norm, who nodded. The shade was rolled up. The masked inside nurse chucked the infant's chin. The infant's muscular reaction looked almost like a smile.

Norm smiled back. He didn't wait for the shade to descend. He turned and walked away from the window quickly, a lump forming in his throat. He lit a cigarette and drew the smoke deep into his lungs. The floor nurse said there was no smoking in the corridors, please. Norm went to Arlene's room and stood outside the doorway for a long time. He could hear the women talking inside—the new mothers. He heard the pages of a magazine being turned.

Norm suddenly wanted to get out of the hospital. He wasn't the Norm Fisher that Arlene had known before the baby was born. He looked at his watch. Arlene had given it to him for their second anniversary. Two-ten. Weekdays, the afternoon visiting hour brought few people to the hospital.

"Please, Mr. Fisher," the floor nurse said. "There's no smoking in the corridor."

Arlene called. "Is that you out there, Norm?"

"Yes," he said. Mechanically, he moved into the room. There were four beds, all occupied. There were flowers on three of the nightstands. The fourth nightstand, near the window, Arlene's, was empty. He hadn't even thought to bring Arlene flowers.

He reached the bed and leaned over, kissing her lightly on the lips. The mattress was cranked up. She had been sitting and reading a slick-paper magazine. She was pale and her lips looked very red with no makeup on. She looked younger than any of the other women in the room.

"Some kid," Norm said.

"You can say what you want," Arlene told him, laughing. "I don't care what you say. I think he's funny looking. Did you see the ears?"

Her smile was contagious. Norm grinned back. "How are you feeling, kid?"

"Bored to tears," Arlene whispered so the other women wouldn't hear. "I only want to get out of here."

"When will they let you go?"

"On Sunday, Dr. Weems says."

Sunday. Forty-eight hours after he helped Buggsy kill a man. He found it hard to think of anything else. He stood next to Arlene for a few more minutes, answering her questions about the house, about Debby. He didn't tell her he hadn't dropped in to see Debby at Abe and Nancy's place.

"Did you find a job?" She was smiling. She believed in him no matter what.

"Sure," said Norm. "Not too much but a swell opportunity."

A lie. He couldn't tell Arlene there was nothing. Not now. He wanted to leave, but Arlene would start wondering about things unless he stayed with her the full hour. Thirty minutes to go, he thought, looking at his watch again. That was a hell of a note: in a hurry to leave his wife who had just given birth. Buggsy's fault.

Queens Boulevard was crowded with afternoon traffic when he left the hospital. Everything from semitrailers to motor scooters. A big Buick glided smoothly between the mall and the sidewalk, the horn tooting. The Buick came to a stop at the curb. Buggsy was sitting at the wheel.

Norm turned and walked down the street.

"Hey, Pretty!"

He walked back to the car, leaned in through the rolled-down window. "You're supposed to pick me up Friday, Buggsy. What the hell do you want now?"

"Don't get sassy. Just come in and sit down. You think I'm an amateur or something? You think I want something to go wrong? We're gonna have a dress rehearsal. Right now."

Norm opened the door and got inside the Buick. Buggsy pulled away from the curb. "For someone who doesn't know his way around Queens," Norm said, "you sure were able to find the hospital." The more he thought about it, the less he liked it.

"There ain't too many hospitals in Queens," Buggsy said. "It took an hour on the phone, but I kept on asking for Mrs. Norman Fisher till I got the right place. They said afternoon visiting hours was two to three, so I figured you wouldn't be in Hicksville. Smart, huh?"

"Just leave my wife out of this."

"Who said anything about your old lady? I only wanted to find you so we could go through the motions, that's all."

Norm told Buggsy to turn right on the Interboro Parkway service road. Here the parkway was in an underpass. They drove along between it and long rows of apartment buildings.

"Here's the setup," Buggsy explained. "Every weeknight, the bum gets out of the subway on Avenue J, in Brooklyn. The BMT. It ain't really a subway there. It kind of runs above the ground but it ain't elevated, either. You know what I mean?"

Norm said he knew. He told Buggsy to make a left turn and a half right. They came out on the parkway.

"Every night at a quarter to six, like he was a clock, Harris gets off the subway. He walks up Avenue J seven blocks to East Twenty-third Street. At the rush hour there's an exit open on the north side of Avenue J. That's where the bum comes out of. He usually reaches the fourth block, the corner of Ocean Avenue, at six minutes to six, give or take a minute. That's a busy street, Ocean Avenue, with a bus line. You've got me so far?"

"Yes," Norm said.

"Swell. If we was to double park on Ocean Avenue, just south of Avenue J and facing J, nobody would suspect something was wrong. The bum will be coming down the far side of the street on our left. We wait till he crosses the street, then make a right turn and cruise along slow. It don't matter if the light is green or not. We got time. He still has three more blocks to go. You got it? Now, this is important. We got to hit him before he turns left on East Twenty-third because it's a one-way street running the wrong way."

"Yes," Norm said.

They had now reached the curving length of the parkway which cut through the cemeteries. Queens County's six million corpses. Buggsy was whistling through his teeth a song which had been popular years ago. Norm lit a cigarette and told Buggsy to turn left on Pennsylvania Avenue where the parkway ended.

"That's pretty good," Buggsy said, grinning. "You know the way better than I do. That's real fine."

They made a right turn on Linden Boulevard, went past hospitals and light industry and billboards and an old residential section which had become rundown. They turned left on Kings Highway, where the neighborhood was better. When they reached the intersection of Avenue J, Buggsy turned the corner and parked. "It's a couple of miles to Ocean Avenue," he said. "But you better drive the rest of the way. Get familiar with it, huh, Pretty?"

Norm got out of the car. Buggsy slid over. Norm started the Buick up again, the Dynaflow roaring. Buggsy told Norm to make a left turn on East Twenty-first Street, a right on Avenue K, then up one block and a right on Ocean Avenue. When they reached the next corner, Norm double-parked next to an ice-cream truck.

"This is the place," Buggsy said.

Across the street to their left was an apartment house. Across from it on the northwest corner of Avenue J and Ocean Avenue was a vacant, weed-grown lot with a cyclone fence running around it. It was there, on that corner near the lot, they would first see the victim. He would cross Ocean Avenue and keep walking, thinking about what he was going to eat for supper, or about his wife, or the work he had done in the office. They would make a right turn and cruise up Avenue J, keeping him in sight. "I'll be sitting in the back," Buggsy said. "I'll have to sit in back because the left side of the car will be facing the bum. Get a move on. Turn the corner."

The light changed to green. A boy and girl were buying ice-cream pops from the truck. Norm drove around the corner. Buggsy said, "Wait a minute. Stop. Let's do it right."

Buggsy went around to the back seat of the car and got in, rolling down the left rear window. Norm drove, passing the corner of Twenty-first Street at ten miles an hour. When they approached Twenty-second Street, Buggsy faced the window and said, "Bam, bam, bam!" as if he were a small boy playing cops and robbers.

"He's dead," Buggsy said in a hoarse voice. "Now the bum is dead. We hit him. You know what you do now?"

"I guess I drive up Avenue J to Kings Highway—"

"The hell you do. We'll go home the long way, so I can get rid of the gun. You'll keep driving up Avenue J to Bedford Avenue.... Now make a right turn."

They drove in silence, heading south on Bedford Avenue. They turned left on Avenue U and right on Flatbush Avenue. Soon the stores gave way to a boat basin on their left and city garbage dumps on their right.

"In the old days we used to get rid of packages out here in Flatlands," Buggsy said. Norm said nothing. "But now they got a police station," Buggsy pointed out.

Coal yards loomed up on their left at the end of the boat basin. Beyond the coal yards was a golf driving range. Norm could see the tiny figures standing on the driving lines with their matchstick clubs. On their right was a low red brick building with shining red police motorcycles lined up in front of it. Some of them were with sidecars.

"The parkway police," Buggsy said.

They crossed a bridge over the Belt Parkway and took the turn which swung around and down in a wide cloverleaf to the parkway. "That's it," Buggsy said. "On Friday when we cross Mill Basin Bridge, I get rid of the gun. You got any questions?"

"No," said Norm. They were driving along Belt Parkway, eastbound, but all he could see was the corner of Avenue J and Ocean Avenue in Brooklyn. There, on Friday, they would wait for Stanley Harris. There they would shoot him dead.

After leaving Buggsy, Norm dropped in at Abe and Nancy's place in Hicksville. It was a split-level house just like his own: eight rooms and no basement. Fourteen thousand dollars with seven hundred down on a GI mortgage and thirty years to pay. He'd be an old man when he finished paying.

Nancy opened the door. She was a pleasant-looking woman, but a little too plump. Debby came running across the living room toward him. When she reached him she hugged his knees and said, "Daddy! Daddy! Daddy!"

"Are you a good girl?" he said.

"Congratulations," Nancy said, shaking his hand. "Abe and I were very happy. We called the hospital and spoke to Arlene. She's thrilled, Norm. Really thrilled. Say, listen. If there's anything I can do, some shopping or something, just let me know."

"That's all right," Norm said. "Thank you."

"Why don't you come over and have lunch here tomorrow?" Nancy said. "Some home cooking will do you good."

"Maybe I'll do that. And thanks again, for everything."

"Oh, I almost forgot. Someone was around looking for you. I think he's waiting for you in your backyard. A nice-looking man, dressed to kill. Debby acted like she never saw him before."

"I'll go over and see," Norm said. "You be a good girl, Debby." Debby wanted to go with him. She began to pout as he walked away from the door, but Nancy held her hand. Soon she was smiling and waving good-by.

Norm walked around to his own backyard. It had been almost twelve years, but he recognized the man at once. Sitting on the beach chair, smoking and making himself at home, was Big Danny Cooper.

CHAPTER NINE

"Pull up a chair, Fisher," Big Danny said. "Sit down." He was the same Big Danny. He had changed even less than Buggsy, although his hair was thinner than Norm remembered. He was wearing a dark, light-weight summer suit flecked with white.

"What do you want?'" Norm said.

"Whatever the Bug is paying you, forget it. You're not going to earn a penny of that money."

"I don't know what you're talking about."

"Look, Fisher. I know every move you made the last few days. So don't make me laugh, will you?"

"I still don't know what—"

"You met the Bug in the supermarket. He didn't proposition you then. He came over here to your house after, but you practically threw him out. A couple days later he went out to where you was working, the Fairless Camera and Instrument Corporation. You both drove in his car to a roadhouse on the Jericho Turnpike, where he offered you five thousand dollars to drive the murder car so he could kill Stanley Harris, the special prosecutor for the Kings County D.A.'s office.

"You went looking for another job. You had some beers. Meanwhile, your wife went to the Horace Harding Hospital and had a baby. Congratulations. This afternoon you visited her, and Buggsy met you outside. You drove to Avenue J and Ocean Avenue in Brooklyn, where Buggsy went through the hit with you. You came back here the long way, I guess. I came straight out here on the Northern State Parkway."

"All right," Norm told Big Danny. "You know what I've been doing. What do you want?"

"That Buggsy, he's all right. I like him. We been buddies all these years. But I'm telling you, Fisher, he's all of a sudden become a mad dog. Like he has rabies, you know. One bite from him and you're through. Don't let him bite you, Fisher."

Norm stood up. "Please leave me alone. You know why I have to do exactly what Buggsy wants."

"Sit down, Fisher. The Bug, you know why we call him that. He's got a bug in his ear. He's a worrier. He can't sleep; the prosecutor gives him night-mares. The Combination doesn't want Harris hit, but Buggsy still wants to kill him. So, we got to hit Buggsy."

Norm thought that was the best thing he ever heard. They were going to kill Buggsy. It was better than getting out of the Army, better than getting married, better than anything. Big Danny had come here to tell him he wouldn't have to go through with the job, as scheduled.

"We had different kinds of education, you and me," Big Danny said. "You don't just decide to kill a bum and kill him. There's only one way you can do it with a good percentage of getting away without being made on the job." Big Danny rubbed his hands together as he spoke. His voice had become more expressive, his eyes were two wicks of bright-burning flame.

"We got it figured the best place to hit Buggsy would be just before he hits the prosecutor. It's dangerous. If we slip up, he gets a crack at Harris. But he'll be so busy seeing everything goes right, he won't have time to think of anything else."

Big Danny leaned forward. "You'll be driving the car. You'll make that murder car a hearse—for Buggsy. The minute you see the prosecutor coming down the street, don't wait till he crosses. Just turn up Avenue J and start moving, slow. The Bug will start hollering at you. He'll think, this damn kid is gumming up the works. He won't be thinking of nothing else. I'll be in a car on Avenue J. As you go by, slow, I hit the Bug. He's in the back seat, so you got nothing to worry about. Then you stop the car, jump out, hop in my bus and we get away. You want I should run through it again?"

"Jesus," Norm said. "No."

"What's the matter, Fisher?"

"Buggsy will kill me."

"Buggsy's going to get killed, Fisher. He's bucking the national organization. He can't win. You're shaping up on one side or the other. You want to be on the winning side, don't you? There's your family to think of."

"I don't know what to think. I can't think. I don't know. I don't know."

"You're thinking the Bug will kill you as easy as eating breakfast. Listen, Fisher. With us it's business. As easy as turning over in our sleep. We don't want to hurt you. We don't want to hurt your family or nothing. It's business. If you cooperate, we'll hit Buggsy on Friday. If you don't cooperate, we're still going to hit him. Maybe not Friday, but soon. Only then, we'll have to hit you too. And listen, boy. If Buggsy gets a shot at the prosecutor on Friday, I'll be right around the corner. I'll hit both of you, so help me. You got it clear?"

Norm nodded. He couldn't think. Buggsy held one end of the net. There was always the hope that he could get out, somehow. Somehow. Now Big Danny held the other end of the net, and the net was closing.

"Well, Fisher," Big Danny said. "I'll call you Friday, early in the afternoon, to remind you. If you're thinking of telling the Bug I was here, don't. If you're thinking of doing anything but what I told you, don't. Remember, the Bug's only one guy. I'm working for an organization that don't take no for an answer. You got it?"

"I understand," Norm said. He would still be helping a killer, but could forget all about the five thousand dollars.

Big Danny stood up and shook hands with him. Big Danny walked to his car, which was parked down the block. It was a convertible Cadillac with wrap-around windshield.

Norm went over and talked about nothing important with Ray Lafferty, his next-door neighbor. The words spilled off his tongue without effort, as if the tongue were grooved and a phonograph needle were spinning around the grooves. He borrowed Ray Lafferty's power mower and took it around to his front lawn. The mower handle vibrated pleasantly against his hands as he marched up and down the lawn. He'd have to fill up the little gas tank for Ray Lafferty. It was only fair.

"You know how it is, Norm. You sit around here and have nothing to do. I wish it was time to leave already. I feel strong enough to leave right now," Arlene said.

It was Thursday afternoon, the visiting hour. Arlene looked fine. He had forgotten how slender she was.

"You just have a good rest until Sunday," Norm said. He figured she was safest in the hospital, anyway.

"Normie? You look worried."

"I—it's nothing."

"Look at me. This gal is your wife, remember? She knows you. She says, right now, you're scared stiff about something."

"You're imagining things."

"I am not. Is it about your new job?"

"No."

"Keep looking at me. I want you to look right in my eyes when I say this. I got a call from your friend Mr. Green this morning."

"He called you here?"

"Yes. But that's what I mean, Norm. When I said it, you looked even more frightened. Whatever is bothering you, it has to do with Mr. Green, doesn't it?"

"What did he want?"

"He said a peculiar thing. He said you were working for him. If that's true, how come you didn't tell me?"

"What else did he say?" He was Buggsy, sure enough. He was the Bug. No one else would speak to Arlene under the circumstances, but Buggsy might. Buggsy had. Buggsy was a worrier. He worried so much about things, he couldn't sleep. Buggsy wanted Norm to worry. Buggsy figured if he told Arlene a little, not too much but a little, it would make Norm worry. It would make Norm worry the way Buggsy worried, so much he couldn't think of anything else.

"Nothing much," Arlene said. "He congratulated me about Gary. Normie, I don't know why, but I don't like that man."

"You don't have to pay any attention to him," Norm said.

"Is what he said true? Are you working for him? What kind of work is Mr. Green in, Norm?"

"Just forget it," Norm said.

"You're in some kind of trouble."

"Nothing I can't get out of."

"That's not the truth."

"Just forget it," Norm said again.

"I love you, Normie. Do you understand that? I'd do anything you asked me. Anything at all."

"Then I'm asking you to forget it."

"Is Debby all right?"

"Debby is fine. I mowed the lawn."

"It sure needed it."

Their conversation went on meaninglessly. It was like passing the time of day with Ray Lafferty or anyone else on the block.

He was beginning to hate the astringent, antiseptic smell of the hospital. He left with half an hour of visiting time still remaining.

CHAPTER TEN

"Some more shots, Mr. Ucci, if you don't mind."

"I don't mind it at all," Li'l Paisan Ucci said. He reached up and draped his arm across the tall showgirl's golden shoulder. He had to stand on tiptoe to do it.

Flash bulbs popped. Li'l Paisan was exactly five feet tall. He had to look up to see the tall showgirl's face, but he obliged the photographers. His eyes were on a level with the girl's collarbone. She wore spangles and tassles and not too much else.

"What kind of show are you putting on here at the new theater, Mr. Ucci?" the reporter asked.

"A classy show. The kind Jersey ain't had in a long time."

"How do you manage to have time for all your enterprises?" a girl reporter demanded.

"He's very smart," the showgirl said.

"Myrna, you shut up." Li'l Paisan pinched her rump, then smiled affectionately at her for the reporters. "She's a nice girl," he said. "They're all nice girls. You can tell your readers when he was younger, Rocco Ucci used to go all the time to the burlesque in Newark and Union City. He thought it was tired—tired jokes, sagging dames. You know what I mean. He thought some day he could open a burlesque which was different. New jokes. Nice young girls, you know. You can tell your readers it is a present from Rocco Ucci to them."

The reporters began to shuffle out.

"Come back anytime," Li'l Paisan said.

He had Jersey sewed up, Li'l Paisan thought. He took his cut from the shylock rackets in the cities, from the dock unions on the Hudson, even from the truckers who hauled the cabbages and asparagus up from the South Jersey farmlands. He practically owned that town down near the big military reservation, Fort Dix. About the only thing he didn't control in the state was the Turnpike. He'd have to look into that someday.

"You shouldn't open your trap near the reporters, Myrna," he said. "You know what they say about little girls."

Myrna rolled her eyes and other things. "I'm no little girl."

"That's cheap," Li'l Paisan said. "What's the matter with you, I thought you had class? Please don't be a slob."

"Why, you little bastard," Myrna said. "You think I can't get other jobs? You think I have to work for you?"

"Shut up," Li'l Paisan said. The veins on his neck were taut blue cords. "If I say you're a slob, that's what it makes you—a no-good slob."

"I just don't like to be called names, that's all."

"Come here," Li'l Paisan said. "Bend down."

She crouched. He kissed the smooth clear skin of her cheek, then tilted her chin with his left hand and slapped the other side of her face. "I can give you a kiss or kick your big white teeth in. It's all the same to me. Which do you want, Miss Slob?"

Her face was red. The white imprint of his small hand, all five fingers, was on her cheek. She took a deep breath and she tried to talk, but no sound came out.

"You think you can get a job someplace else maybe in Jersey? Where?"

"In Union City," Myrna mumbled, rubbing her cheek.

Li'l Paisan pointed to the phone. "Call them for me, please," he said.

Myrna walked over to the phone and dialed a number. Wordless, she handed the receiver to Li'l Paisan. "Get me Carrell," he barked. "This is Ucci. You know a big dame, a real big tomato named Myrna Wilson? Good stuff, huh? She wants to work for you. I don't want you should hire her, you get me? Good boy. Here, I'll let you talk to her." He gave the phone to Myrna.

"Hello?" she said, and listened. She hung up.

"Guys like you," she said. "Guys like you."

"What about me?" Li'l Paisan was smiling.

"There ought to be a law against guys like you."

"Now maybe you know on which side all the bread in Jersey is buttered."

"Yes, Mr. Ucci."

"Call me Paisan. Informal. I like all my girls should call me Paisan."

"Yes, Paisan."

"Come here now."

She walked to him expecting to be slapped again. He patted her chest. "You got nice equipment, kid. I don't want to be hard on you. I want you should learn how to use it."

"Yes."

"I will have a job for you sometime and maybe it won't have nothing to do with burlesque, but you'll do it. Yes?"

"Anything you say."

"You will meet all kinds of people and stop being a slob. Be glad I took you out of Brooklyn. Modeling clothes in downtown Brooklyn, there ain't no future in it."

Just then the telephone rang.

"Hello?" said Li'l Paisan. "Well, Big Danny Cooper. How's the boy?... A little theater business. It's nothing. A hobby.... Sure, I got the time. I always have the time for Eugene Moore. You boys come right over, I'll be waiting." Li'l Paisan hung up.

"You, Myrna," he said. "Get yourself lost. Take a shower. Here. Here's twenty dollars. A gift from Paisan. Go buy yourself a hat. Come back later, looking classy."

Myrna folded slender fingers over the twenty-dollar bill. "It's only I have feelings," she said. "I want to be classy for you, Paisan. I'll try."

"You're going to be all right, with Paisan's help. Paisan is going to help you."

Eugene Moore sat down, placing the end of a cork-tipped cigarette between his teeth, worrying it with his lips, not lighting it. Big Danny took one of Paisan's cigars and rolled the empty aluminum cylinder on the desk.

"There's something special you need done in Jersey?" Li'l Paisan asked.

"Not in Jersey," Eugene Moore said. "Over in Brooklyn."

Li'l Paisan said nothing. He wondered why they needed a Jersey man to do a Brooklyn job.

"You remember that meeting we had at the Tudor, upstate?" Eugene Moore asked.

Li'l Paisan puffed thoughtfully on his cigar, nodding, watching the gray-blue smoke drift slowly in the still air of the room.

"It's that worry-wart, Buggsy. That crummy bastard," Big Danny said.

"Buggsy Green is going ahead on his own to hit the prosecutor," Eugene Moore explained. "We'll have to stop him."

Li'l Paisan blinked through the smoke. "You want some of my Jersey boys to hit the Bug for you?"

Big Danny looked hurt. He pointed the glowing end of his cigar at Li'l Paisan and said, "Hell, no. I'm gonna hit the Bug all by myself."

"We have to set the stage for Danny perfectly," said Eugene Moore. "The details are of no concern to you, but Danny has reason to believe a little postponement will line Buggsy up perfectly for him."

"Postponement?"

"On Friday afternoon at a few minutes before six, Buggsy will try to hit the prosecutor. Buggsy's driver, a man named Fisher, is still the big question mark. After a delay, we think Fisher will set Buggsy up for us. That's where you come in."

"Anything at all," Li'l Paisan said.

"We want a few boys whose faces aren't known in Brooklyn. They'll be at the corner of Ocean Avenue and Avenue J, at five-thirty Friday afternoon. At five-forty, they stage a fight, an automobile accident, anything you want. They've got to make enough noise to bring a whole precinct of cops down on them."

Li'l Paisan took out a pad and pencil, and jotted down the time and place.

"Your boys will get off with a suspended sentence or thirty days in the workhouse at the most," Eugene Moore promised.

"Don't worry. My boys do like Paisan says."

"That's half of it," Eugene Moore said, "We're also looking for a girl who can put on a white uniform and act like a nurse."

"A girl with class?" Li'l Paisan asked. "I gotta girl who will do anything to show me she has class."

"On Sunday morning I will come here and pick her up," Big Danny said. "See she's wearing a nurse's uniform. On the way I'll tell her the pitch."

"You can trust this girl?" Eugene Moore asked. "It's important."

"I'm telling you, she's trying to impress me."

Big Danny winked. "She don't go to church on Sunday morning?"

"What's the job?" Li'l Paisan demanded, shaking his head.

"Snatching," Big Danny said.

"Kidnapping!"

Eugene Moore finally lit his cork-tip cigarette. He inhaled the smoke deep into his lungs and let it trickle from his nostrils. "Don't worry," he said. "No one will be hurt. The 'nurse' will deliver a woman and her infant son from a hospital in Queens to a place Big Danny will designate. As soon as the woman's husband does what we want, the woman and the boy go free."

Eugene Moore stood up. Glowing with pride, Li'l Paisan showed his guests around the theater. "You come and see the show anytime you want, Mr. Moore. Real class, it will have."

"Maybe I'll do that," Eugene Moore said. He followed Li'l Paisan across the dark stage and down the runway and five steps which led to the sloping center aisle banked on either side by shabby theater seats.

After the cool moist air of the theater, the sunshine hit them like from an oven. Squinting in its bright glare, Li'l Paisan watched Eugene Moore and Big Danny enter the Cadillac convertible. Li'l Paisan stood out on the street until the car was lost in the downtown Newark traffic. Then he returned to the theater.

This was all right, he thought. Not once had Eugene Moore or Big Danny mentioned Louis Fassolino. It probably meant Mr. Fats was in some kind of trouble with the eastern representatives of the Combination. Li'l Paisan would play it cool. Jersey was nice, but he didn't have to stay in Jersey all his life. If he played it right, he might have Jersey and Brooklyn, too. If Mr. Fats was no longer reliable, the Combination would need someone to take over Brooklyn. Buggsy they could forget about. Big Danny was a good hatchet man, but nothing else. Of the local big shots, geography favored Li'l Paisan Ucci.

"How do you like the hat?" Myrna said. She was waiting for him in the theater office, sitting on the desk with her legs crossed. She had a set of legs you could get excited just thinking about. The hat looked like a pie plate with feathers.

"It's very nice," Li'l Paisan said. He sure knew how to treat the dames. First you call them a slob, then you compliment them. They're grateful for the compliment. If they get too sure of themselves, you call them a slob again and start all over.

"How would you like to earn five hundred bucks?" Li'l Paisan demanded after he had called some of his boys and told them what they had to do on Friday.

Myrna stood up and hugged his face against her. She sure was a tall girl. Nice. "Paisan, I love you," she said.

"I ain't kidding, Myrna." Eugene Moore would throw a fit if he realized Li'l Paisan hardly knew the girl. She'd do anything he said, though. It was one of those things you just knew.

"Tell me, Myrna. When you was a little girl, did you ever think of being a nurse? You know, like Florence Nightinghood?"

"Nightingale," Myrna said. "You're cute."

"Nightingale, that's right. Already you ain't no slob. Myrna, for five hundred dollars on Sunday you're going to be a nurse. Go out and buy yourself one of those classy white uniforms."

"For five hundred dollars," Myrna said, "I'd be Joan of Arc."

CHAPTER ELEVEN

Norm looked at his watch. It was a quarter to four. Fifteen minutes. Buggsy wouldn't be late.

It hadn't been too bad until last night. It had all been unreal, like a dream, until last night.

Last night he had seen the prosecutor's picture in the newspaper. Stanley Harris, the caption said, rackets-busting young Special Prosecutor sent by the governor to clean up Brooklyn. The article went on to say how Harris was cooperating with a special Kings County grand jury which, unlike most grand juries, had realized the extent of its own power. This grand jury was not going to stop, the article said, until all the rackets had been kicked out of Brooklyn. Stanley Harris would devote his life to the destruction of those rackets, the article said.

Right now, Norm thought, Harris was probably cleaning up some work in his office. Another hour and fifteen minutes or so, he'd board the crowded rush-hour subway, with barely room for him to read his newspaper. The special prosecutor made headlines, but in the subway he was just another straphanger. Maybe he was thinking about what Mrs. Harris would prepare for dinner, or about watching television with the two boys later. Maybe he'd take the family down to Sheepshead Bay if the night was hot. Then, at Avenue J, he'd tuck the newspaper under his arm and swing along the street with his briefcase.

Closing his eyes, Norm could see exactly how Stanley Harris would look coming down the street alongside the empty lot. He would be a dark figure against the cyclone fence. They would see him there, waiting to cross the street....

A car door slammed outside. Norm held his breath. The next house? Or maybe they parked on the wrong block and were going around back to see Ray Lafferty or someone... anyone.

The door chimes rang.

Norm walked across the small gallery and went downstairs to the living level of his house. It wasn't happening. No? If he didn't think it was happening, why had he left a pair of worn work gloves on the table near the door? He took them in his left hand and opened the door with his right. The doorknob felt clammy.

"Hiya," Buggsy said. "You don't look so good." His close-set eyes blinked shut as he laughed. "You got gloves, I see. A regular pro." Buggsy was wearing skin-tight gray gloves. "Buck up, Pretty. It'll be all done in a couple of hours and you'll have five G's in your pocket."

"Whatever you say." Norm took a handkerchief from the back pocket of his gabardine slacks. He dabbed at the sweat on his forehead as they went outside together.

"I'll get in back right now," Buggsy said. "You might as well get used to driving this bus on the ride in."

"Sure," Norm said. The hot car was a 1952 Oldsmobile Rocket 88, four door, black. There was plenty of power under the hood of that car. It was new enough so the power was still there, but not so new it would be conspicuous.

Norm put on the work gloves and opened the car door. He slid behind the wheel and pressed the starter button while Buggsy settled himself in back.

"Take a look," Buggsy said.

He was holding up a large, gleaming blue pistol.

"Put that thing away," Norm said. "Someone will see you."

"Naa," Buggsy told him. "Some roscoe, huh? It's a Magnum .357. The Feds use these roscoes. Buggsy and the Feds. You like it?"

"I don't know anything about guns."

Norm looked at his watch. The hair on the back of his wrist was clumped together with sweat. It was ten after four.

"You know where I got the roscoe?"

"I don't care where."

"Overseas shipment, Pretty. They won't miss it till God knows when. Some crummy South American revolution, I figure."

Norm pushed the Hydramatic shift lever to Drive and stepped on the accelerator. The big Olds sped away from the curb.

"It looks like we're a little early," Buggsy said.

Norm had pulled up on Ocean Avenue, near the corner of J. Everything was exactly right. They were even double-parked next to the ice-cream truck. It was ten after five.

"Better not stay here," Buggsy said. "Drive down to the park and back. You don't want to attract attention, do you?"

Norm waited for the light to turn green, then drove down Ocean Avenue. Most of the houses lining the street were big and old.

A small boy, chasing a pink rubber ball, darted out in front of the Olds. Norm jammed on the brakes.

"Are you nuts?" Buggsy said. "Be careful, willya? That's all we'd need."

"Maybe you better drive," Norm said. Suddenly, he was shaking. His right leg was trembling so much he could hardly keep his foot on the accelerator pedal. His hands had sweated through the work gloves. He wondered if the police could trace a man through his sweat.

"You're doing fine," Buggsy said. "Relax."

Just before the entrance to the park, Norm swung the big Olds around the block. When he turned back on Ocean Avenue, he heard a *snick-snick-snicking*, from the back seat. In the rearview mirror, he could see Buggsy calmly loading bullets into the .357 Magnum.

"Lookit these pills," Buggsy said. "They ain't as big as forty-fives, but they got power."

Snick-snick-snick. Buggsy placed one bullet in the breech after loading the magazine. He put the Magnum off safety and laid it on his lap.

"Get over to Bedford Avenue," Buggsy said. "There's a dead end on Twenty-first Street. Then come down Avenue K and down Ocean."

Norm turned left and headed five blocks over to Bedford Avenue. This was some classy neighborhood. It must take plenty of money to live here, he thought.

They hit Ocean Avenue again. He turned right one block. This was it. No backing out. Nothing he could do.

"What kind of crap is that?" Buggsy suddenly said.

Up ahead, a crowd of people was milling about. Traffic was piled up for half a block.

"Get out and see," Buggsy said. He would remain in the Olds with his .357 Magnum.

Norm left the car in the unmoving lane. Horns were blowing, harried drivers shouting. The street was so full of people, Norm thought all the apartment houses must have disgorged their tenants at once.

There had been an accident at the corner of Ocean Avenue and Avenue J. A cream-colored Chevrolet convertible had hit a Studebaker Starlight coupe, 1950 model, broadside. The front fender and the door of the Studebaker were crushed.

Four men were staging a free-for-all in the middle of the street, standing close in a circle and pounding away at one another. The damaged cars were empty.

Police whistles shrilled. Norm saw two patrol cars driving up, sirens wailing. Three cops came on foot, sprinting toward the fighters, yelling, trying to keep the crowd back, trying to unsnarl traffic.

The four men kept right on fighting. Both cars had New Jersey license plates.

Everything's going to be all right, Norm thought. *Everything's going to be fine. Stanley Harris will be along any minute now. Buggy's back there someplace. He's got to stay with the .357 Magnum and the hot car. He can't make a shooting gallery out of a crowded corner crawling with cops.*

And the other thing, the thing Norm had hardly thought about, was going to be all right too. If Big Danny was waiting somewhere nearby to kill Buggsy, the wait was for nothing. You could as easily shoot a man and get away with it in front of a police station.

Two big policemen, their uniforms plastered to their backs with sweat, swung their nightsticks and charged into the four fighting men. All about him, Norm could see the slack faces, the jaws agape, the eyes mirroring violence. This happened so rarely. You might go all through life without seeing it. This was something to tell the wife about.

Someone tapped Norm's shoulder. He wheeled around.

"The stupid bastards," Buggsy said. "That sure ruins everything."

"Yes," Norm said. "It sure ruins everything."

"Lucky for us, the bum goes through his routine every weekday like he had an alarm clock inside his head. We'll hit him Monday, that's all."

The police had forced the four men apart. One of them was bleeding from a cut on his face. One of the policemen was asking questions and writing in a notebook. The ice-cream truck was doing a land-office business.

"Take a look over there,'" Buggsy said. "That hurts."

Norm looked where Buggsy indicated, diagonally across the street. He recognized Stanley Harris from his pictures. The prosecutor came swinging down Avenue J with his briefcase dangling from one hand and a newspaper tucked under his other arm. He stopped for a moment to see what was going on, then crossed Ocean Avenue and kept going.

"The bum," Buggsy said. "The lucky bum."

Norm nodded. "He sure is." Norm's mouth was so dry it was hard for him to swallow. He wanted to get Buggsy back in the car. Maybe Big Danny was crazy enough to start shooting with all those people around and all those cops. Then, suddenly, he didn't care. He almost looked hopefully for Big Danny's face. Let them shoot it out right here, right now. Norm's worries would be over. Let Big Danny squash the Bug once and for all, then let the police get Big Danny. Norm was just part of the crowd. No one would associate him with Buggsy. He could take the train home to Hicksville and resume his life.

A patrol wagon drove down the wrong side of the street on Avenue J. The four men were herded aboard. Now they appeared docile, almost as if they didn't care.

"Son of a bitch," Buggsy said. "I know that guy." One of the men had leaned out of the wagon to say something to a policeman.

"That's Hymie from Jersey City," Buggsy said. "One of Li'l Paisan's boys. I used to shoot craps with him over on the docks."

Police got behind the wheels of the damaged cars and drove them toward the curb. Moments later, traffic began to move smoothly in both directions along Ocean Avenue. Ignoring the traffic light, a policeman waved the cars forward until the bottleneck was broken. Several policemen went around, getting names and addresses of witnesses.

"Listen," Buggsy said. "It stinks, Pretty. I'm telling you, it stinks. Both cars are from Jersey. Hymie, a Jersey City hood I know, is in one of them. You know what I think?"

"No," Norm said.

"It's the Combination, that's what. They put up a goddam smokescreen so the bum could get away. But they know I'm gonna try again. It figures. I been a good man for almost twenty years, so now they're gonna try and hit me. That's gratitude."

"We'd better get out of here," Norm said. Some policemen were still on the corner. Big Danny wouldn't be coming now.

"Well, I got news for them. They don't know where I live on Long Island. On Monday, we try hitting the bum again. They can't fake an accident here every day, can they? After I hit the bum they'll forget about it. They don't kill a guy unless it pays off. This ain't like the old days."

The big eyes blinked. Norm could almost see the gears meshing inside Buggsy's skull. "That's the thanks I get," Buggsy grumbled. "They want to hit me. I'm a sick man, but that don't bother them. I do everything I'm told for twenty years. The first time we don't see eye to eye, they want to hit me."

Buggsy had double-parked the car near the curb and now climbed in behind the wheel. Norm sat alongside him.

When they reached the corner, everything seemed very normal. Norm almost expected another car to cut them off, with Big Danny inside it, a twin to Buggsy's .357 Magnum ready. But they turned up Avenue J and headed for Kings Highway without anything happening. Maybe Buggsy was right. Maybe Big Danny and the people he worked for wanted to delay Buggsy's attempt at assassination. But why?

Then he knew the answer. It wasn't just Buggsy they didn't trust. They didn't trust Norm to set Buggsy up for them.

CHAPTER TWELVE

Norm left Hicksville at one o'clock Sunday afternoon to take Arlene and Gary home from the hospital. Nancy had insisted on having dinner ready for them at their own house, so Norm had given her the key. She'd be waiting there with Debby when he got back with Arlene and the baby.

Up ahead, lightning flashed against the black bottoms of the billowing thunderheads. The dull, muted thunder was a long time coming. Norm was driving toward the storm. He had a blue plastic raincoat in the car for Arlene, and an umbrella. He had made out a check to the hospital. His funds were running low but the check was in his pocket because the hospital insisted on prompt payment. He hadn't touched the seven hundred dollars Buggsy had given him.

Suddenly, the storm hit. Great drops of rain, still spaced far apart, splattered on the windshield, drummed like giant fingers on the roof of the car. Norm rolled up the glass as the rain came down harder and was blown in through the window by the wind. The wipers helped, but the thunderhead was squatting almost on the parkway. It was very dark.

The parkway was heavy with homebound beach traffic, moving slowly in the storm. Norm got off at Parsons Boulevard. He figured he could cut across to Horace Harding and make better time.

What happened on Ocean Avenue the day before yesterday was only a reprieve, Norm thought. Nothing had changed. He'd be back there tomorrow. Stanley Harris was granted three more days of life, that's all. Norm couldn't go to the police then. He couldn't go to the police now—now especially, when he'd have Arlene and the two kids at home. He wouldn't do them very much good in jail—or worse.

I can call Harris, Norm thought. *Tonight.*

An anonymous call from a pay phone: someone will try to kill you tomorrow afternoon at the corner of Avenue J and Ocean Avenue. A crank, Harris might think. No. The prosecutor couldn't afford to take the chance. He knew he wasn't exactly winning friends and influencing people in Brooklyn gangdom. He'd change his schedule. Or he'd have help waiting on the corner. Or both. Along with Buggsy, Norm would be captured or killed.

The traffic was much lighter on Horace Harding Boulevard. On Norm's right, the abandoned veterans' development lay spread out across the muddied flatlands, the windows boarded up, faded billboards from last year's elections on some of the walls, asking people to vote for the candidate who had already lost. Before long the city would think of taking down the shacks and erecting a ten-story housing project where the same families could come back to live at about the same rent.

Bright headlights glared suddenly in the rearview mirror. The damned fool was practically right in his back seat. Norm swerved to the right, but the other car had already begun accelerating to pass him on the left.

It was a long black job, a Chrysler Imperial limousine. Seven thousand dollars' worth of car—and a meatball behind the wheel who didn't know how to drive.

The Chrysler almost passed, then cut in toward him. He applied the brakes and felt the rear end of his car fishtail slightly. He almost went into a skid on the wet pavement. The Chrysler was still forcing him toward the shoulder of the road. When he reached the corner of a street cutting into the deserted development, the Chrysler angled in more sharply.

Cursing, Norm swung his wheel all the way to the right. He pulled into the badly paved street. Weathered and sagging shacks were on either side. He stopped a hundred yards off Horace Harding Boulevard and looked back. The Chrysler had followed him into the development. The Chrysler slowed to a stop behind him.

Norm got out of his own car and slammed the door. *Let them try and say it was my fault,* he thought. *I ought to kick their teeth in.* He smiled grimly. That wasn't like him at all. It was the same as his fight with the foreman, O'Reilly. It was Buggsy he wanted to kick, Buggsy he wanted to hurt.

The rain pounded down on him. It felt cold, but it felt good. It smelled clean. Norm shook his fist and approached the other car. The front door opened. The driver climbed out. He was a small man. He looked dark in the rain. The car was a limousine, but the man wasn't dressed like a chauffeur.

"What the hell's the matter with you?" Norm said, still shaking his fist. "The road isn't wide enough or something?"

The front door on the other side of the car opened, also the rear door on the driver's side. Two big men got out. The driver said nothing. No one seemed to mind the rain pounding down.

"You are Mr. Fisher?" the driver said. It was half question, half statement.

Norm opened his mouth to say something. He was going to say, "How the hell did you know?" The man who had come from the other side of the front seat of the Chrysler walked up to him and hit him in the face. Norm fell down. The asphalt pavement was broken and muddy.

When Norm started to get up, the man kicked him. He fell over on his back. He could hear the steady hissing of speeding tires on the wet pavement of Horace Harding Boulevard, a hundred yards away. He yelled and rolled over and got up.

"You don't have to hurt him too bad," the little man said.

Norm told the little man to do something which was impossible, then hurled himself at the man who had hit him. Norm felt it clear down to his elbows when his fists struck the man's face. The man cursed and lurched back away from him. Norm waded toward him, fists clenched and ready.

There was a movement behind him. Norm started to turn, but the edge of the second big man's hand slammed down across the back of his neck. It was as if all his nerves flowed through that spot, carrying orders from his brain. There was hardly any pain, but he couldn't move. He couldn't even fall down.

The man spun him around by the elbow. The man wore no hat. Rain was dripping off his nose. His fist buried itself in Norm's stomach. Norm doubled over slowly. The other big man came and struck him behind the ear. Norm sat down in the mud. He wanted to be sick but he didn't have the strength.

When the small man, who had driven the car, came over and bent down beside him, Norm remained sitting. Once he waved his arms as if he were going to hit the small man. He couldn't get them to move fast. It was like trying to push through water. The small man brushed the arms aside and started going through Norm's pockets.

He wouldn't get much. There was twenty-odd dollars in cash and the check made out to the order of the Horace Harding Hospital. Let them try to cash that.

The small man took the check out and put the wallet back in Norm's pocket.

Norm heard the back door of the Chrysler slam. He was lying on his stomach now, his face cradled on his folded arms. He was still not able to rise.

The woman wore galoshes. Above them, she had nice legs. She wore a transparent acetate raincoat a lot like Arlene's. She was carrying an umbrella. She was a tall girl. Blonde. Beneath the raincoat Norm could see a crisp white nurse's uniform.

"We almost lost him on the parkway where he turned off," the small man said. "This damn rain."

The girl said, "You've got it?"

"Yeah, Myrna. Here's the check." He gave the check to the girl. She put it in the pocket of her raincoat. She was at least a head taller than Arlene. She was built well, but looked strong.

"You're sure you can handle it?" the small man said.

"She just had a baby, didn't she? Don't worry about me."

"You're getting classy already," the small man said. Norm's arms and legs were beginning to tingle. He thought he could move them without any trouble now, but he waited. "See," the small man said, "the dame might get scared if anyone's with you. The same if the car's different. You take Fisher's car and drive over to the hospital."

Norm looked at the face of the second big man for the first time. The one who had hit him behind the ear. It was Big Danny Cooper.

"We'd better get out of here," Big Danny said.

The small man nodded. The woman wasn't in Norm's range of vision any longer. He heard the door of his own car close, heard the starter grind and the motor cough.

Norm called on his remaining strength. He jumped up and flung a handful of mud in Big Danny's face. He took two staggering steps toward his car, which was still idling. Suddenly the small man stuck out his leg and tripped him. Norm fell on his face in the weeds alongside the badly paved road. Something exploded against his ribs.

"Don't be so damned cute," Big Danny said.

"Let's go," the small man said. "Max, you stay here and watch this guy for half an hour. Then you can let him go."

Norm rolled over. He was soaking wet. It was still gloomy. The rain still came down.

The first big man, Max, nodded. "I'll get a soaking out here," he said.

Big Danny grinned. "You know, Max, that's tough."

Norm saw Big Danny and the small man get into the Chrysler, and he watched as his own car drove away. He heard the Chrysler engine purr. Then the Chrysler was rolling smoothly down the street and then it was gone.

Norm sat up. He struggled to his hands and knees. His head was throbbing with pain, and a flame seemed to burn against the left side of his body. He wanted to throw up.

"Just take it easy, boy," Max said. "Stand up and walk away a few feet." Max held a .45, pointing it at Norm.

"It sure is some rain," Max said. He jerked the gun and told Norm to walk sideways five paces ahead of him until they reached one of the shacks. The windows were boarded. A tattered sign, blowing in the wind, said the circus had been in town last spring. The door wasn't boarded up. Max found a rock and swung it at the rusty padlock. On his third swing, the lock broke.

"Open it," Max said.

Norm took off the rusty lock and pushed the door in. It was gray and dim inside. There was a musty smell.

"I'm drenched already," Max said. "Get in."

Something black scurried across the floor. Norm walked inside, out of the rain. The roof wasn't so good. A puddle of water was on the rotted board floor, with more water splattering down into it from above. Norm sat and leaned against the wall. He let his head slump forward. He wanted to do something. That woman was going to take Arlene and the baby from the hospital—*she was going to kidnap them.*

Max stood above him with the gun. Still holding his head between his knees, Norm looked up. All he could see was Max's trousers. They had lost their crease in the rain.

Norm rolled forward, moaning, as if he were about to be sick.

"Take it easy," Max said. "You'll be all right."

Norm kept on rolling forward, as if he couldn't keep his balance even while sitting. When his head struck Max's legs, he pushed his hands suddenly against the floor and lunged forward with his shoulders. Max started to yell. But when Norm got to his knees, Max tumbled down on top of him. Max hit him with the gun, down low on his back near his kidneys. Despite the pain, Norm managed to twist clear of him and stand up.

Max was crouching, pointing the gun at him, starting to say something. Norm kicked the gun out of his hand. Max scrambled after it like a big beetle might. Norm jumped on him, his momentum making Max's head strike the wall. Again Max yelled. Again Norm kicked the gun away. He hit Max in the face when Max got up. Max's nose looked crooked. Blood spurted from it. Then Max covered his face with his hands. Norm hit him in the stomach.

Falling down, Max clawed at Norm's legs. Norm kicked at his face, but Max still tried to crawl across the floor after the gun.

Norm picked the gun up, and threw it out the open door. What was left of an old chair—three legs and the seat and part of the wicker back—stood under the boarded window. Norm picked it up and slammed it across Max's head. That was all. The man fell flat on his back and lay without moving.

Outside, Norm took a deep breath. He felt winded and spent, but not like he was going to be sick. It was about a mile and a half to the hospital. He started running through the rain.

"I'm Mr. Fisher," Norm said. "My wife—"

"One moment, please." The woman was small, with frizzly hair, buck teeth and glasses. She looked as though she belonged in a library, not a hospital. She was busy checking a register and hadn't glanced up. When she did, she said, "Are you all right?"

Norm was panting for breath. He had jogged through the rain the entire distance down Horace Harding Boulevard to the hospital. From his waist up he was one stinging, burning ache. His legs were numb, but trembling.

"I'm here for my wife. Maternity. My wife and son." It was difficult to get the words out.

He watched the finger trace its way down the list of names in the register. The finger stopped. The woman said, "I thought I remembered the name. I wanted to make sure."

"She's ready?" Norm said.

"She's gone. A few minutes ago, with your nurse. Do you want one of the doctors from the dispensary to look at you, Mr. Fisher?"

"She's gone?" Norm cried. "What do you mean, she's gone?" He was yelling. An intern walked over and raised his eyebrows at the receptionist. The woman shrugged.

"What's the trouble, mister?" the intern asked.

Norm was still trying to get his breath.

"Your wife is with your nurse, Mr. Fisher," the woman said. "They were getting acquainted as they left. I distinctly remember. The nurse paid the bill."

"Yes," Norm said. He couldn't tell her. He couldn't tell anyone. Buggsy had been suspicious of that accident in Brooklyn. Buggsy had thought the accident was staged to make hitting Stanley Harris impossible. A delay. A delay so Big Danny could make sure Norm would do what was wanted. They had him. They had him by kidnapping Arlene and the baby.

The intern's fingers closed on Norm's elbow. "Do you want us to have a look at you?" he said.

Norm shook his arm loose. "There's nothing wrong with me," he muttered. His face felt warm and wet. At first he thought it was the rain, but he had been inside too long. He took out a handkerchief and dabbed at his face with it. The handkerchief made a sticky contact. It came away red.

Norm backed away from the counter. He tripped over an overnight bag and sprawled on the floor. There was a complete silence at the counter.

The intern stood over Norm and said, "You need some help, fellow?"

"No," Norm said. He got to his knees. The reception room spun. He didn't know in which direction he would find the doorway leading to the outside. He steadied himself and took a deep breath. The door was over there. He walked slowly, careful, as if the simulated marble floor were a minefield.

Outside in the waiting room, people were looking at him. He sure was a bad advertisement for the hospital.

Arlene, he thought. *Gary.* He'd seen Gary only once. *My son.*

The intern had followed him into the waiting room. He got hold of his elbow again. "We really ought to have a look at you, fellow."

"Just get your hands off me."

He went out into the street. The storm had passed to the east. The sky was still dark, but not so heavy. The rain was lighter. He could see an occasional flash of lightning far to the east, but he didn't hear the thunder. Norm walked along Queens Boulevard and he wondered if the rain would wash some of the blood from his face. He walked to Broadway and into the same bar from which he had called Buggsy that first time. He went to the men's room at the back.

The mirror was dirty and cracked, but he could see the reason for the reaction he had gotten in the hospital. Both his eyes were blackened. His mouth was a swollen, bloody smear. His nose had been bleeding. A large bruise, from which blood was seeping, discolored his left cheek.

He leaned over the low sink. The blood rushing to his head made him dizzy, made his head throb. The sink was dirty. He could hardly see the white tile under the layers of caked dirt. He ran cold water and splashed his face. It stung as if iodine were being applied.

A small fat man waddled into the men's room, looked at Norm without comment, and went over to the urinal. Norm took some sheets of paper towel from the dispenser, wadded them, then soaked them under the cold water tap. Then he sponged his face with them. When he finished, he still looked as if he'd been in a fight. But he looked better.

He went outside and sat down at the bar. "Gi' me 'ouble rye," he said. His lips were swelling more. He couldn't pronounce some of the sounds. "So'a chase'."

The barman sloshed the rye into a glass for him. It scalded his lips and seared his insides, but he waited for it to relax him. He felt nothing. Absolutely nothing. Outside the bar, there was nothing, too. No reality. No world, no Arlene, no Buggsy, no Big Danny, no hospital, no Stanley Harris. The world was right here, inside his head. The world was spinning emptily.

There wasn't anything he could really do. He could just go home and wait for Big Danny to contact him. Sooner or later, Big Danny would. He would say, "We've got them, Pretty. Your wife and kid. You better do like we say." Pretty. He didn't look so Pretty now.

CHAPTER THIRTEEN

Arlene said good-by to the other women in the four-bed ward. The hospital nurse dressed Gary for the outside, then gave him to the nurse Norm had hired. That was a surprise, Arlene thought. A pleasant surprise, if not a very practical one. They couldn't really afford a nurse, but Norm wanted to make things easy for her. She could tease him about the nurse, though. It was the best-looking baby nurse she had ever seen. She looked more like a chorus girl in a nurse's uniform.

"What did you say your name was?" Arlene said.

The nurse held Gary stiffly. "It's Myrna."

"I guess my husband hired you for two weeks. Would it be all right if you only stayed a week? Even a week would be a big help."

"I don't care," Myrna said. "Are you ready?"

"I'm still surprised my husband didn't come here with you."

Arlene smiled. The nurse acted as if she didn't like hospitals. As if, for some reason, she were in a hurry to leave. Arlene waved to the other women again. "Lucky stiff," one of them called after her. "A nurse yet."

Downstairs, Myrna took a check from her handbag. Arlene saw Norm's signature on it. A woman behind the counter gave Myrna a "paid" bill in exchange for the check. Arlene smiled. Normie had certainly figured things smoothly.

"Well, let's go," Myrna said. "The car's a block and a half down. Gee, it's still raining."

What a nurse, Arlene thought. *She wants me to go out in the rain with the baby and walk a block and a half.*

"Give me Gary," Arlene said. "You get the car and blow the horn outside. All right?"

Myrna frowned. "I don't know," she said. "I really don't know."

"Here." Arlene took Gary from the nurse and held him. "Better get the car. My husband will start worrying if we're not home soon."

"I don't know," Myrna said again. "Maybe if I stayed here with the kid and you went and got the car..."

What a strange nurse, Arlene thought. "You get the car," she said.

Myrna finally nodded. "Well, all right," she said. She went out through the revolving door with Arlene's overnight bag. She looked back once at Arlene standing in the waiting room with Gary; then she disappeared in the rain.

It was almost as if she expected Arlene to run away or something. Well, it would be good for some laughs. She'd have plenty to tease Norm about. She hoped Myrna would work out, though. If they were going to pay her, they at least ought to get their money's worth.

A few minutes later, Myrna came running up the outside hospital stairs with an umbrella. When she saw Arlene standing inside the revolving door, she seemed relieved. She let Arlene carry the baby outside but held the umbrella over them.

They got into the car, Myrna behind the wheel and Arlene, holding Gary, alongside her. The baby was still asleep.

"Can you tell me the best way to get to Syosset?" Myrna said as she drove up Queens Boulevard.

"Syosset? We live in Hicksville. You just drove here."

"I mean Hicksville, that's right. They're real close, though. I have a friend in Syosset, so I said Syosset."

"Just go back on the parkway," Arlene said. "Take it out to exit thirty-six, then I'll tell you."

"Let me know where to turn for the parkway."

"You just came from there. Don't you remember?"

"I never could remember driving directions." Myrna smiled, then peered intently through the pie-wedge shape made on the wet windshield by the wipers.

Myrna didn't even seem to know the way back home, Arlene thought. Myrna hardly acted like a nurse. And it suddenly occurred to Arlene that Norm rarely let a stranger drive his car, ever since the day Moe Fordin smacked up a fender on the Jericho Turnpike. The only one he let drive was Arlene.

"My husband might like it better if I did the driving home," Arlene said.

"No. Don't be silly. You just had a baby. You're supposed to rest."

"He doesn't like other people driving his car."

"He gave me the car and let me drive, didn't he?" Myrna snapped.

"Don't raise your voice, Myrna. You'll wake Gary. And don't raise your voice to me at all."

"I'm sorry," Myrna said.

They turned alongside the empty lot near Queensboro Hall, then went down the long incline toward the parkway service road. The parkway itself was flanked at this point by a high stone wall, but they could hear the cars hissing by on the wet pavement.

"Some intersection," Myrna said. "That's why I couldn't find my way."

"There's been a lot of construction going on," Arlene said. "Tell me, Myrna, have you had much experience as a baby nurse? I mean, you look so young."

"Oh, lots," said Myrna. "Just lots."

"Do you use lotion or baby oil? It really doesn't matter to me."

"I don't care," Myrna said. "Whatever you want is fine."

"They gave me a formula for Gary at the hospital. I suppose you'll want to make the formula as soon as we get home."

"Sure. The formula."

"When Debby—that's our daughter—when Debby was an infant, we used terminal sterilization for the formula. But if you want we could..."

"I don't care. They probably sterilized the kid at the hospital. Why don't you stop worrying?"

"What did you say?"

"I didn't mean it like you thought, Mrs. Fisher. I mean you should take it easy, that's all."

"No. What else did you say? About sterilizing."

"Oh. They take care of everything at the hospital. Really, it will be all right."

Arlene bit her lip. She looked at Myrna, who was intent on driving. Myrna had a pretty profile, but her face was hard. Arlene held closer the quiet warmth of the baby.

They were on the parkway now, the wet foliage a dark green on both sides. Occasional cars speeding westbound in the opposite lane splashed up walls of water across the low cement barrier.

"Where did my husband get you?" Arlene asked. "At an agency?"

"Yes, that's right." The white pavement gave way to gray asphalt as they crossed the city line into Nassau County. The storm was further east, driven by the wind out toward Montauk. But the rain was still falling.

"Which agency was that?" Arlene demanded.

"You know, the one in Hicksville."

Arlene didn't know if there was an agency which handled practical nurses in Hicksville or not. She doubted it, but her doubt was in no way conclusive. What was she worrying about? So Norm hadn't found the world's finest baby nurse. So what? It would only be for a week. *It's almost as if I'm trying to convince myself there's something sinister about this girl,* Arlene thought. Having a baby could make a person think crazy things.

"Seriously," Arlene said, "I hope terminal sterilization is all right with you."

"It's fine. You're the mother."

"I have some Evenflow nipples which Debby still uses. They should be good for the baby."

"Odd or even, I don't care."

Arlene bit her lip again. "I'm trying to be friends," she said. "I wish you'd stop making fun of me, if that's what you're doing. What's the name of the agency in Hicksville?" Arlene could call them for Myrna's references when she got home.

"Just the Hicksville Agency," Myrna said.

They drove along through the rain in silence. Once Gary stirred and made a few tentative cries, but Arlene patted his back to comfort him, and he fell asleep again.

"There it is, up ahead," Arlene said, finally. "That's exit thirty-six. You get off the parkway and turn right. Then it's about a mile down South Oyster Bay Road before you have to turn again."

"Now I know where I am," Myrna said. She drove Norm's car off the parkway on exit 36 and came to a full stop where the exit hit South Oyster Bay Road at right angles. She put the car in first and turned left, went up on the bridge and over the parkway.

"That's wrong," Arlene said. "You were supposed to turn right."

Myrna didn't answer her.

"I said you're going the wrong way. We live in the other direction, Myrna."

"Don't make it hard on yourself," Myrna said.

"What do you mean by that? Just turn around."

"Be quiet, Mrs. Fisher," Myrna said. "Nobody's going to get hurt."

They passed a low, sprawling ranch-type house on their right, and a development of split levels behind it. Then there was a stretch of farmland on either side of the road, the ground muddy from the heavy rain. The windows were fogging over. Mechanically, Arlene wiped them with her hand the way she always did for Norm when they were driving in the rain.

"Of course nobody's going to get hurt," Arlene said. "What kind of talk is that? Just turn around. You're heading toward Syosset."

"I know where we're going," Myrna said. She didn't look at Arlene. She kept looking straight ahead.

There were more split-level houses and a great drainage basin on their right, a few meager shrubs clinging to the cyclone fence which surrounded it. Further up the road, perhaps a quarter of a mile, Arlene could see a traffic light suspended on wires.

"Are you going to turn around?" Arlene cried. Gary stirred in her arms and began to cry. He opened his eyes and stared sightlessly up at her and screamed.

"Now look what you've done," Myrna said. "Be quiet, I told you."

"Stop the car. Stop the car or I'm going to yell."

Myrna said nothing. Up ahead, the wire-suspended traffic light changed to amber, then red. Myrna muttered something under her breath and braked the car to a stop. Sunday or not, there was a big semitrailer idled in the rain in front of them. Arlene leaned against the door and turned the knob, but Myrna reached across her body quickly and slammed the door shut. Gary was screaming louder.

When Arlene lunged against the door again, Myrna swung her handbag at her. The handbag struck the side of Arlene's face, but she kept trying to open the door. Myrna grabbed Gary away from her, leaned across the back of the front seat and deposited the infant on the rear seat of the car. Gary was still screaming.

"What are you doing?" Arlene shouted. "What do you think you're doing?"

She was going to cry. She didn't want to cry.

"Just shut up," Myrna said. The light turned green. The semitrailer began to accelerate. They followed fifty feet behind it, heading not for Hicksville but Syosset.

Arlene turned around and leaned over the seat to get Gary.

Oyster Bay Road led them north through Syosset, beyond the flat potato country into the rolling hills of the North Shore. Big rain-heavy trees and estate fences lined the road, screening large old houses of fieldstone, clap-board or brick. An occasional gravel road meandered off to east and west.

Perhaps the woman was insane. There was no sense in provoking her. She might be frustrated, childless... you read about people like that, who took someone else's baby and... But how could she have paid the hospital bill with Norm's check?

Myrna turned right and climbed one of the eastbound roads. Arlene sighed and shut her eyes tightly. This couldn't be happening. She was imagining things. If she opened her eyes suddenly and looked, Norm would be sitting beside her, driving the car. Gary stopped crying. It was suddenly the most important thing in the world to keep him from crying again. Arlene could feel hot tears on her own cheeks.

"Here we are," Myrna said. "Boy, that's a relief." The car lurched to a stop. Oaks and maples loomed huge and rain-glistening green. Fifty yards away through the trees, Arlene could see the front of a rambling fieldstone house. A muddy trail led toward it through the trees, but the car could never travel over the deep wet ruts.

"Well, let's go," Myrna said. She opened the door and walked outside around the front of the car. She opened the door on Arlene's side, reached in and got the umbrella. She motioned for Arlene to come out. Arlene's feet sank almost ankle-deep into the mud. Myrna kept at Arlene's side and held the open umbrella so that the baby would be shielded from the rain.

Warm yellow light shone through the windows of the fieldstone house. Although the season was summer, a dank chill was in the air. Arlene clutched Gary against her body to give him warmth. She almost stumbled in her haste to reach the house. Most of the light came from a great bay window with side panels of stained glass floral patterns.

Myrna jabbed her finger against the bell button. Arlene could hear the chimes ringing inside, then heavy footsteps approaching the door. The door opened.

He stood there in a quilted smoking jacket. He was stocky, thick-chested, small-eyed. He seemed relieved to see them.

"I didn't know if you was kidding or not, Myrna," he said.

Myrna grinned at him. "That Paisan Ucci is going to be awful mad when he finds out."

Arlene said, "Why—it's Mr. Green!"

Buggsy Green led them into the house. A small, harried-looking woman met them at the other end of the entrance hallway. She wore a dark blue hostess gown which started at bony shoulders and draped down on all sides, perfectly straight. She was barely five feet tall and had lifeless eyes until she saw Gary. Then her eyes sparkled.

"Look at the little fellow," she sighed. "Just look at him. I can tell it's a boy, that strong forehead. We've never had any children, Harold and I. But I've always hoped and dreamed. Here, let me take him. You're drenched. You'll have to change into dry clothes." She removed Gary from Arlene's arms and cradled him in her own bony arms. Quite efficiently, she rocked him gently and smiled down at him while she hummed a lullaby.

"Why don't she shut up?" Buggsy said.

Arlene felt weak. She sat down heavily on an overstuffed chair on one side of the bay window in the large living room. Myrna brought her a glass of water. She sipped some of it, then pushed the remainder away.

She said, "I don't know if you people are crazy or what. Gary is a newborn infant. He needs a special formula, a warm place to sleep, diapers..."

"I've got them all," the small, harried-looking woman beamed. "Everything, just as if it's my own baby. I'm sure you're going to like it here, both of you, for as long as you want to stay."

Myrna arched her eyebrows at Buggsy, who shrugged. "Rosie," he said, "you better go inside and fix up the kid's place."

Rosie left the living room through a hallway to the left of the fireplace.

"Don't mind Rosie," Buggsy told Myrna. "She thinks Mrs. Fisher is an old friend of the family whose husband is in the Army and who's gonna stay here for a while. That nutty wife of mine. Always asking me to tell her about my business. 'How is business going, Harold?'" He mimed her whining voice almost perfectly.

"I'm a little scared," Myrna said.

"I'm giving you a thousand bucks, ain't I?"

"Paisan isn't going to like this."

"So, you know what Paisan can do about it."

Myrna grinned. "When they were telling me what I had to do, that tall good-looking guy, Danny, mentions your name. Like they were going to foul things up for you or something. I says to myself, 'Buggsy will want to hear about this. Buggsy used to be very nice to me when I was modeling clothes over in Brooklyn.' Anyhow, I don't like that Paisan. The slob."

"Does the nurse want to come in here and look around?" Rosie called from another room.

"Naw," Buggsy hollered back. "She's all knocked out."

"Normie didn't tell you to bring us here, did he?" Arlene asked. It hardly seemed possible, but it was a straw she could grasp.

"I'm making the formula now," Rosie called in a happy, sing-song voice. "The baby is asleep already."

"Some nutty wife," Buggsy said. "She wanted four kids, all boys."

Myrna rolled her eyes at Buggsy. "You could probably give her forty kids."

Buggsy beamed. He rasped, "You remember, huh?"

"I want to make a telephone call," Arlene said. "I want to call Norm so he doesn't worry." She stood up. The room wavered as though she saw it through rippling water. Buggsy drifted over to her and pushed her back into the chair.

"I'm so excited," Rosie called in from the kitchen.

"You got nothing to worry about, Mrs. Fisher," Buggsy said. "You would-n't want to go out in a rain like this anyway. Tomorrow night Myrna will drive you home to Hicksville, won't you, Myrna?"

"Whatever you say. What I want to know, what happens to me after that? I can't go back to Jersey."

"So, don't. Jersey's a bargain?"

"It isn't that. Paisan will want to give me a schlammin, or worse."

Buggsy snorted. "Are you kidding? After the way you screwed up this deal for Paisan, he'll be lucky if the boys don't give *him* a schlammin—or worse. I can just see their faces, when you don't turn up with the kid."

"You still didn't say what about me."

"I'll get you a job dancing on Long Island somewhere, don't worry. If things work out, I'll be the top of the heap. They'll get to thinking, if I can thumb my nose at the whole Combination and make it stick, maybe I'm a guy they ought to follow."

"The formula is up," Rosie called to them. "I prepared dinner before the guests came. I only have to warm it."

Five minutes later, they were sitting down at the dinner table. Arlene filled her mouth, chewed, swallowed. She knew she needed the energy. She ate mechanically, filling her stomach out of desperation. Rosie popped up half a dozen times to tiptoe into another room to see if Gary was all right. Once, Arlene followed her, half expecting Buggsy or Myrna to call her back. But they let her go.

Gary was sleeping soundly. A spare room of the large house had been fixed up as a nursery. A portable crib had been strapped to the bed and there was a bathinette in one corner of the room. There was even a large diaper canister.

"See how peaceful he is?" Rosie beamed. "I hope you don't mind com-mercial diaper service. That's what I got, Cupid Service. The best. I would have had the diapers monogrammed, only I didn't know the little fellow's name, just that you're Harold's cousin from Reading whose husband is in the Army."

There was something pathetic about the harried little woman. She acted as though this was one of the big moments in her life.

"Listen," Arlene said desperately, "I don't have time to explain. They'll hear us talking. They're keeping me here against my will. I'm not your husband's cousin. I live in Hicksville. I—I think your husband and that woman masquerading as a nurse are keeping me here so they can make my husband do something he doesn't want to do. You've got to let me use your telephone! Please."

A look of compassion came into Rosie's eyes. For a moment, Arlene thought the woman would help her. But Rosie said, "There now, you just take it easy. Harold told me how upset you were after the baby came, what with your husband being overseas and everything. We'll take care of you and the baby, dear."

"Please," Arlene said. "I can prove it to you if you let me make a phone call."

Rosie smoothed the covers down over Gary. "There, now. After supper, why don't you write a nice long letter to your husband? It will make you feel better."

"Please, just let me use the phone. Please."

"Harold said we weren't to let you get excited. I'll make you some hot Ovaltine after supper so you can go to sleep."

"You've got to let me—"

"And don't you worry about the boy. I'm a light sleeper. If the nurse doesn't hear him when he cries, I will."

Rosie held a finger to her lips and closed the door quietly.

Arlene saw a telephone on a little grass-topped wrought-iron table in the hall. She picked up the receiver and began to dial. Her fingers were trembling so much she couldn't get the number right. She tried again. She couldn't hear voices in the dining room. When she finished dialing there was a moment of silence before she heard the buzzing ring in the receiver.

An arm descended over her shoulder. A stubby fist depressed the phone cradle. She whirled and faced Buggsy, who was shaking his head sadly.

"The poor thing," Rosie said. "Maybe we ought to have Dr. Travers see her in the morning."

"Yes!" Arlene cried. "A doctor. I need a doctor. Call a doctor."

But Buggsy was still shaking his head. "She just got examined, Rosie. Just take care of the kid. The nurse is here to look after my cousin."

They all went back into the dining room. Rose made more coffee.

Later, Gary awoke and began crying for some milk. Rosie gave him a bottle. Arlene watched Rosie change Gary's diaper and decided that at least Gary would be well cared for. After the baby was back in the portable crib, Rosie said:

"No buts about it, young lady. You're going to bed." Arlene's overnight bag had been put on the bed in another spare room. Rosie left her there with strict instructions to retire at once. "I can't get enough of that baby," she said. Humming another lullaby, she closed the door of Arlene's room behind her.

Arlene sat on the edge of the bed and kicked off her shoes. There was a hooked rug on the parquet flooring, a night table with a lamp and a fiberglass shade, a bureau and the bed, which had no footboard. A doorway led off to a small bathroom.

Arlene was tired. She could barely make out the voices coming from the living room. She stretched out on the bed in her clothing, her feet propped on the overnight bag. Her head was throbbing dully with pain, in back of the eyeballs. She massaged her temples with her fingertips. If only she could get Rosie to believe her.

This was Norm's past, sweeping up out of the years to engulf them. Norm probably understood it. He probably knew what was going on. Arlene didn't. She gathered Myrna was supposed to take them someplace else but had delivered them to Buggsy and his wife instead.

Arlene sat up and got off the bed. She padded in her stockinged feet to the window and looked out. It was still raining, and the sky was getting dark now. Wet green ivy climbed thickly on the fieldstone wall outside the window. She might be able to get out this way. The house was only one story. But she couldn't leave Gary behind, even if Rosie seemed genuinely willing and able to take care of him. Perhaps, later at night, she'd be able to use the telephone. It was right outside in the hallway.

Stretching out on the bed again, she looked at her watch. Seven-twenty. She hoped they would retire early. She didn't think she would fall asleep, but...

The lamp was still lit, casting a circle of light on the ceiling through the top of the fiberglass shade. The air was cold now, as if a lot of time had passed and some of the rain-dampened night had seeped into the house. She looked at her watch. It was almost one-thirty. Arlene stood up. She was trembling with the damp cold. Gary, she thought. She hoped Gary was covered properly. She went to the door softly. The phone was just outside. She turned the knob.

The door was locked from the outside.

CHAPTER FOURTEEN

"Some stinking night out," Buggsy said. He always felt grouchy on a night like this. His heart would start acting up. A lot the doctors knew. They said his ticker was sound. They said your heart doesn't act up with bad weather, anyhow. It has nothing to do with bad weather! The bastards. They didn't feel it, the wrenching pain as if his ticker was about to burst. What the hell did they know?

"It will probably be nice out in the morning," Rosie said, cheerfully. She sat in her slip at the other end of the long master bedroom, putting her mouse-colored hair up in curlers. She looked bad enough all the time, Buggsy thought glumly. Like this, she looked like something out of a nightmare. *I'm lazy,* he told himself. *If I had any sense I'd have left her long ago. I need something like her like I need a hole in the head. Boy, what a figure. Like four pipe cleaners with skin-colored cloth holding them together.* She was the only woman who had ever looked indecent to him naked. He must have been nuts when he married her.

"That's the cutest baby I ever saw," Rosie said. She was rubbing cold cream into the skin of her face with her fingertips.

"Go to bed," Buggsy said.

He hoped she wouldn't ask to come into his bed. She often did when she saw babies. She thought it would help, as if it were contagious or something. That was a good one, contagious. *Look at her. Of course she can't have babies. It's amazing she's got enough energy to walk around. She wants me to go and have some kind of test. If that ain't a laugh. Maybe my ticker ain't what it used to be, but any time I can't knock up a dame without batting an eyelash, it's time to throw in the old towel.*

He felt grouchy but restless. It was Myrna, that big blonde tart. Sure, she was stacked. She knew it. She went around throwing it in your face. That Fisher dame was stacked, too. Only Rosie was a bag of bones. Some Rosie.

"I'm not sleepy, Harold," Rosie said.

"Take a hot shower," Buggsy suggested.

"A hot shower."

"Yeah, a hot shower."

"What's the matter, Harold? You used to say I was the prettiest girl on Pitkin Avenue."

Oh, damn, Buggsy thought. *Here we go again. Sure, I guess I said it. I must have been drunk when I said it. Sure her old man had some money, pretty good money in the clothing store. How the hell could I know he was going to lose all of it in the depression? I've been supporting her folks since the war. Next thing you know, they'll want to live out here in Syosset with us.*

Sure, I'm restless. A thing like Myrna prowling around the house somewhere, why shouldn't I be restless? Maybe she's getting ready for bed right now, just like this bag of bones here. But she don't look like a hag of bones. Boy, I remember. What a chest on that one. And them legs...

"I'm not the least little bit sleepy at all," Rosie said. She eased the slip straps off her shoulders and climbed out of her slip carefully so that she wouldn't mess the cold cream on her face.

Rosie stood next to her bed for a moment. Buggsy sucked in his breath distastefully. He sighed. What a lousy figure. She could make a fortune being the "before" part of a vitamin ad.

Rosie misinterpreted the sigh. She came over to Buggsy's bed awkwardly and shyly, then got on the bed and sat next to him. She wrapped her skinny arms around him. He could feel the bones right through his silk pajamas. What was she trying to do, start something? Did she think he could look at her with that Myrna in the same house?

"Get your elbow off of my chest," Buggsy said. "My goddam ticker."

"I thought."

"You thought. Stop thinking already. Go to sleep. I'm all knocked out. I ain't young like I used to be."

Buggsy lit a cigarette and watched Rosie, looking disappointed, get into her own bed. He ought to watch his smoking. Those things he read about cancer. Every place you looked, they said cigarettes caused cancer. He had this hacking cough when he woke up in the morning. Maybe it was one of the danger signals they wrote about—a persistent, hacking cough. Sometimes he wished he was healthy instead of so successful. If you really got sick, you could take the success and the money and shove it—a fat lot of good it would do you.

"Well, good night," Rosie said. "I'm sorry if I upset you, Harold. You know, I was thinking. If you're sleepy and I'm not, maybe I ought to go and sleep out in the living room on the convertible bed. I'll have to get up and feed the baby at night, anyway."

Buggsy blinked his small eyes. "Naw," he said. "You need a comfortable bed if you have to get up." He crushed out the cigarette in the ceramic ashtray on the night table. He got out of bed with his covers and pillow. "I'll sleep outside," he said. He leaned over and pecked at Rosie's forehead with his lips. Even her face was bony. And that cold cream. He put the night lamp out and rubbed the back of his hairy hand across his lips, wiping off the cold cream. *She's a walking mess of bones and cosmetics.*

Buggsy lumbered into the living room and opened the convertible bed. He tossed the pillow and covers over the mattress and rumpled them. He rolled on the convertible bed and sat there, smoking another cigarette. Presently he tiptoed back to the master bedroom and listened at the door.

Maybe Rosie said she wasn't sleepy, but she was breathing regularly.

It was the third guest room he wanted, the one down by the corner behind the kitchen, in the el of the house, near the library. The library, that was good. What the hell did they need a library for?

He opened the door of the guest room and padded inside. He shut the door behind him. The room was completely dark. He could hear Myrna breathing softly, regularly. Myrna slept like a baby. Some baby.

"Whasamatternow?" Myrna's voice, sleepy.

"Shh! It's me, Buggsy."

He wished he could see Myrna's smile. She was probably smiling from ear to ear. "You're a devil, Buggsy," she said, wide awake now. "But you know something? I like you."

"What a baby you are," Buggsy rasped.

"You shouldn't. You really shouldn't, with your wife in the same house and all."

"You care?"

"I'm only thinking how it looks."

"If I don't care, forget about it. Don't think about it."

"Buggsy, that tickles."

"You know that part of your foot I like. The instep. There. Hey, Myrna. Ahh, Myrna."

"You're nice, Buggsy. When do I get the thousand dollars?"

"Stop worrying. Tomorrow. Anytime. That's some instep you got."

"There's plenty more of me," Myrna said. "Buggsy, I told you that tickles."

The sun awoke him. He had been dreaming something about Rosie. He didn't remember what, but it was very funny. The more he tried to remember, the vaguer his memory of the dream became.

Buggsy sat up in bed and coughed. This damned cough. It was going to kill him. His grandfather had died of TB, hacking away and spitting blood until one of his lungs went and they had to deflate it and take it out or something—he didn't remember what. He pulled a handkerchief out of his pajama pocket and coughed into it. He examined the handkerchief minutely. If it was flecked with blood then he would have to worry. The handkerchief was white and clean. A lot the doctors knew. So, it wasn't flecked with blood. Did that make him healthy?

Buggsy fingered his thick-muscled neck; he massaged the Adam's apple gently. He looked down at Myrna, sleeping beside him. Her hair was a gold net on the pillow, but you could see darkness at the roots. Well, he knew she wasn't a real blonde anyway. But she was loyal. Just a casual friend, you might say, but loyal. A brief wave of tenderness engulfed him. He never felt that way about Rosie. Wives were supposed to be loyal. But Myrna. Now, Myrna. Some Myrna.

She sat up suddenly. One moment she was asleep, the next, she was up and smiling at him. Not like Rosie. Rosie took half an hour just to wake up, to turn and squirm and make little waking noises in her throat and her nose.

"Good morning," Myrna said in a loud voice.

"Shut up," Buggsy told her. "Are you crazy or something? The old lady will hear you."

Myrna cupped a manicured hand over her mouth. "I'm sorry," she whispered. "I didn't realize. I'm sorry." She giggled. "What if Rosie wakes up now?"

"I'm supposed to be sleeping in the living room, ain't that something?"

Myrna giggled again. She walked to the bathroom door and kissed her fingertips and made a throwing motion at Buggsy before she disappeared inside. Then Buggsy went back through the hall to the living room.

The sofa bed had been tidied. His covers and pillow were gone.

"Hey, Rosie!" he called.

There was no smell of breakfast in the kitchen. He walked to the kitchen in his pajamas and bare feet. It was empty. No one had eaten breakfast there.

"Hey, Rosie!"

There was a noise outside, footsteps on the flagstone walk. Running now, Buggsy reached the second spare bedroom and looked in. The portable crib was still there, strapped to the bed, but the brat wasn't in it. The other spare bedroom, the one Mrs. Fisher used, was empty. Buggsy whirled and ran for the front door.

He heard the grind of a car starter.

"Damn you, Rosie!"

She was out there in the sunlight, fifty yards down the path by Pretty Fisher's car. The ground was almost dry. Mrs. Fisher was inside the car, behind the wheel, frantically trying to start it. Buggsy ran.

The grind of the car starter became a sluggish growl, a whine. The plugs were wet.

"You weren't sleeping in the living room," Rosie said, without looking at him. "You and that woman, right in my house." She still didn't look at him. She was leaning inside the car through the rolled-down window, looking at the baby, looking at Mrs. Fisher trying to start the car.

"Get out of there!" Buggsy yelled. "Come on out."

Mrs. Fisher's shoulders slumped. She opened the door and stepped out of the car. There was a tired, hopeless look on her face. Rosie opened the door on her side of the car and reached in to get the baby.

"Hey, Myrna," Buggsy called. "Get down here in a hurry."

"I'm sorry," Rosie told Mrs. Fisher. "I tried."

"Ain't that nice?" Buggsy said, aping her voice. "'I tried.'" He turned Rosie around by her thin shoulder and slapped her face. Her head snapped back against the window frame of the car. She almost dropped the baby.

There was a change in Rosie's face, Buggsy saw. It was her eyes, mostly. There was something new he didn't like in her eyes. "You lied to me," she said. "About this girl. I know who she really is now. You've been lying to me for years, haven't you? How should I know what kind of business you had if you didn't want to talk to me about it? I read these things in the papers about you, but they say that about so many important people. Politics, I thought. That's very funny. Politics. Our whole life is a lie, from start to finish. That blonde woman in there isn't the only one, is she?"

"No, she ain't the only one."

"I want a divorce, Harold."

Just then Myrna came down the dirt path from the house. She was wearing her nurse's uniform and came gracefully toward them across the dry mud ruts of the path. When she reached them, Buggsy said, "You take the baby from Rosie."

Myrna took the baby and held him awkwardly in front of her.

"Now, you," Buggsy rasped, looking at Rosie. "My own wife. You know what this means to me, keeping Fisher's wife here? You know how important it is?"

"You never told me anything," Rosie said. "How do you expect me to feel?"

"A wife who ain't loyal is no good," Buggsy said. He jolted her chin with the heel of his palm. Her head jerked back, the thin stringy muscles of her neck going taut. Her head struck against the open fly window of the car.

Her eyes said *stop, stop, please stop.* But she didn't utter a sound. It was Mrs. Fisher who whimpered. Buggsy hit his wife again, smashing his big fist against her side as if he were holding the hilt of a knife and had plunged the blade in below her ribs. She opened her mouth and expelled a lot of air and fell down at his feet.

Mrs. Fisher walked up to Buggsy and clawed at his chest. Her face looked funny. She wasn't afraid of him. She hated him. He hadn't done anything to make her hate him, he thought. Why were people always hating him? Buggsy caught Mrs. Fisher's hands and held them. She started whimpering again.

"Lay off, Buggsy," Myrna said.

"No, I got to teach her. She ain't got no business doing a thing like that to her own husband."

Rosie was sitting at his feet. She was just looking up at him. He kicked her in the chest with the edge of his bare foot. She rolled over and lay quietly. Then she sat up again and retched emptily.

Mrs. Fisher was hiding her face in her hands and crying.

"You didn't have to do that," Myrna said.

"So now you're turning against me."

"I only said you didn't have to do that."

"Take the kid back in the house. You!" Buggsy jerked his finger toward Mrs. Fisher. "Take care of the old lady. Bring her in and make breakfast. We got to have breakfast, don't we? Make a good breakfast just like you would make it for Pretty."

Indoors, Buggsy told Myrna, "I'm going away today. I don't want them to do nothing, see? Keep them here. Knock their heads together if you have to, get me? But keep them here. There's another five C's in it for you."

"I didn't see any money yet," Myrna said.

Buggsy blinked his small eyes. This was the way it happened. They all ganged up on you. They gave you no peace. They thought you were still a punk or something. He'd remember that about Myrna, the way she wanted his money more than anything. But right now he couldn't. Right now this business with Stanley Harris had to be taken care of. He walked into the bedroom and came out wearing a bathrobe over his pajamas. He took a wallet from his pocket and gave Myrna five one-hundred-dollar bills. "Here's your down payment, baby," he said.

Myrna glanced at the money and put it in a pocket of her nurse's uniform. "They won't go anyplace," she said. "Don't worry." The baby was crying. Myrna went to fix him a bottle while Mrs. Fisher prepared breakfast. Soon Rosie joined them in the kitchen.

Buggsy sulked through the morning. He told Myrna to let Mrs. Fisher watch after the baby. Myrna had to watch after Mrs. Fisher and Rosie. Rosie didn't say a word. She just sat in the living room, or walked around the house and looked at things. Once she picked up a piece of coral they had bought in Miami Beach, and hurled it against the fireplace. She did it without any warning and without saying a word. She was going to be fine, Buggsy thought. If you had to let off a little steam, that was the best way to do it. The coral was smashed all to pieces.

At three o'clock Buggsy went into the garage. The hot car was parked near his Buick in the other slot of the double garage. That was the last place they'd look for a stolen car, out here in the garage of a seventy-five-thousand-dollar house in Syosset. Buggsy took the key from his pocket and started the motor. It kicked over at once. It was some hot car. Buggsy had had the key made by taking the doorlock out and bringing it to a locksmith.

Buggsy rolled the car out of the garage in reverse. Leaving it on the rutted path which forked over to the house just below him, he went inside and told Myrna:

"Make sure what I said."

"You don't have to worry," Myrna told him.

"If the phone rings, you answer it. If anybody but me calls, you don't know from nothing. You're the maid. Nobody's home. Maybe I'm gonna call and maybe I'm not. It depends if my friend Pretty needs some convincing. O.K.?"

"Whatever you like is O.K.," Myrna said.

"Well, so long," Buggsy said. He winked at Rosie. That usually did it. After they had an argument, all he had to do was wink.

She saw the wink and looked straight into Buggsy's eyes. It made him feel funny. It was the first time she had looked at him, right in his eyes like that, since he could remember. She said, "I never want to see you again."

"Aw, you'll get over it," Buggsy said. "I'll send you down to Asbury Park for a vacation one of these days."

Mrs. Fisher was inside taking care of the baby. Buggsy heard her making noises at it, but he didn't see her when he left.

He backed the hot car out of the driveway and headed down the lane toward Oyster Bay Road. The .357 Magnum was in the glove compartment, loaded, where he had left it.

Pretty Fisher would be waiting in Hicksville for him.

CHAPTER FIFTEEN

L ife is a funnel, Norm told himself. Little things are poured into the funnel: where you happened to be born; the small, isolated instances of your upbringing; how, in a great variety of ways, you reacted to your environment—and a fact that one night long ago you happened to be at Sunny Jim's poolroom.

You could have been elsewhere, but you were there. And that fact, too, is poured into the funnel, and the whole stream of trivia pours down toward the narrow end. It keeps getting tighter and tighter, rushing faster and faster until a point is reached. Then everything is crushed together at that point, and it's too late to do anything but watch the narrow end of the funnel. There, where all the streams of your life converge as they were converging today, was the answer to your life—and why you had lived it the way you had.

Norm was pacing back and forth in the living room of their split-level house in Hicksville. This, of course, was one of the streams which had flowed into the funnel, this house in Hicksville, and Abe and Nancy for neighbors. Nancy was also pacing and she was watching Norm. She hadn't said a word since past two o'clock and it was now almost three. Every now and then, she would go out back to see that Debby and her own children were all right. Then she would come back and match Norm's pacing. Finally, she said:

"I don't know how patient you expect me to be, Norm. You're my friend, but so is Arlene. Are you going to tell me what happened?"

"There's nothing to tell you."

"Yesterday you went to the hospital to pick up Arlene and the baby. You came back without them. Tell me what happened."

"I can't tell you anything."

"If you don't, I'm going to call the police. Believe me, Norm, I don't want to do that—unless you make me."

"Don't call them. If calling them would help, I would call them."

"They're in some kind of trouble."

Norm said nothing.

"Should I call Abe back from the store and you'll talk to him?"

"No."

"Will Arlene and the baby come back today?"

Norm didn't answer.

"First, I thought something was wrong and you left them in the hospital.

But I called up and they said the bill had been paid and Arlene was discharged."

"Please, Nancy."

"Well, what do you expect me to do? Forget they ever lived here? If they're not home by the time Abe gets here, we are going to call the police—unless you tell me why we shouldn't."

"They ought to be home tonight," Norm said. All day he had been waiting for Big Danny to contact him. He would answer the phone and say yes to everything Big Danny said. In his mind he ran through it all a dozen times. But it was only in his mind that the telephone rang. It had been ringing there last night too. He hadn't slept. He hadn't even taken off his clothes or gone to bed. He had practically chased Nancy and Abe out of the house last night. Nancy had prepared a stuffed chicken dinner, and a big "welcome home" sign had been painted on the hall mirror with cleansing powder and water.

"Listen, Nancy," Norm said. His voice caught in his throat and choked him. He went on. "Listen. You know how I feel about Arlene. I wouldn't let anything hurt her. I'd do anything for her. If telling you about it now would help, I'd tell you. You think I want something bad to happen to Arlene?"

"Is something bad going to happen to her?"

"I don't know," Norm said.

"I'm going to call the police."

Nancy headed for the kitchen and the wall phone extension there. Norm got there first and held the receiver down on the hook.

"Are you crazy?" he said. His voice was hoarse. "You want them to kill her? You want that?"

Nancy's eyes got very big. She dug her fingers into Norm's upper arm and said, "Tell me. You've got to tell me. Arlene's been... kidnapped."

Norm just stood there.

"Why, Normie? For God's sake, why? You aren't rich or anything. Who would go and do a thing like that? I'm going to call Abe and tell him to come home."

"Do whatever you want. Only don't call the police, that's all I'm asking."

The doorbell rang. Norm went out of the kitchen and up the hall to the door. He could hear Nancy following a step behind him. When he opened the door, Buggsy was standing there. He had never seen Buggsy looking like this. Buggsy's eyes shot furtive glances about the hall and the living room. Buggsy's hands were clenching and unclenching, squeezing invisible putty, the knuckles going white.

When Buggsy's eyes alighted on Nancy, he raised one hand and pointed a trembling finger at her. "You," he rasped, "get out of here."

Nancy stood still without answering.

"You better go," Norm said.

"I—"

"Take Debby with you. Please."

Nancy looked at Norm, searching his face and trying to read something there. He had nothing to tell her. His face showed nothing. He waited beside Buggsy and watched her.

After a while she turned and walked down the five steps to the playroom level of the house. She went outside and Norm could hear her voice faintly, and Debby's. Then there was silence except for the small neighborhood sounds. Kids yelled down the block. A car door slammed, an engine was started. A power mower puffed and chugged. A woman called in a high, piercing voice, "Frankie, I want to put you on your short-sleeved shirt. It's a hot day."

Buggsy said, "Is anybody else around?"

"No."

"Who was that dame?"

"A neighbor, that's all."

"O.K. I don't want to be crowded, that's why I asked. It's gonna be the same like Friday, Pretty. You remember how?"

"Yes."

"We can run through it on the way down to Brooklyn."

"It wouldn't be necessary." It didn't matter at all. He couldn't do what Buggsy wanted. Because Big Danny had Arlene and the baby, he would set Buggsy up the way Danny had asked: starting around the corner of Avenue J slowly, as soon as Stanley Harris came into sight. Buggsy wouldn't do the hitting. Buggsy would be hit.

Then Norm would give himself up to the police.

"I like to be played square with," Buggsy said suddenly. Norm nodded. "You was going to try and cross me."

Norm shook his head. If he spoke, Buggsy could tell. Buggsy was shrewd that way.

"I said you was going to cross me."

"We can get started anytime you're ready," Norm said.

"Shut up." Buggsy grabbed a fistful of Norm's shirt. Norm could feel the fabric tighten under his arms and rip. He pushed Buggsy's hands away.

"I've taken all the crap I'm gonna," Buggsy said. "From you or anybody."

"What do you want me to tell you?" Norm asked Buggsy.

"Nothing. You can relax about your old lady and the kid. Paisan ain't got them."

"I don't know any Paisan," Norm said. It didn't register at first.

"Neither has Big Danny got them. I got them."

Norm walked over to the sofa and sat down. He leaned forward and stared between his knees at the texture of the broadloom carpet. Big Danny had been with those punks who'd intercepted him on the way to the hospital. Buggsy couldn't know anything about that.

"What are you talking about?" Norm said.

"Your wife. Your kid. The dame drove them out to my place."

Norm stood up. "You're lying."

"You son of a bitch," Buggsy said, and hit him. Norm staggered back against the sofa, ramming it against the wall. "You was going to set me up for Big Danny over in Brooklyn. Where's your phone?"

"In there." Norm pointed to the kitchen. He rubbed his jaw and followed Buggsy, who picked up the receiver and dialed.

"Hello, Myrna," he said. "Everything O.K.? Put Mrs. Fisher on, will you?" He cupped his hand over the receiver and said, "I just want you should know the score." Then, into the phone: "Mrs. Fisher? You'll never guess where I'm calling from. Your place in Hicksville. Want to speak to your sweetie?" Smiling now, Buggsy handed the phone to Norm.

"Normie, is it really you? I'm so afraid."

"Take it easy, kid." But his own heart was pounding in his throat, constricting it.

"They haven't hurt us, Normie. It's you I'm scared about."

Buggsy said, "If you don't do exactly what you're supposed to, that dame is gonna get hit in the head."

"Normie, do you hear me?"

"Yes."

"Mr. Green is insane, Norm! Whatever he wants you to do, you don't have to. Don't you see? If it's some kind of trouble and you can get to the police and they get him, I'll be—" There was the sound of flesh striking flesh. A yell, Arlene's voice.

"Arlene! Hello!"

"Let me speak to Buggsy." It was a strange woman's voice.

"Put Arlene back on."

There was another slapping sound. "Buggsy," the woman's voice said.

Norm handed the receiver to Buggsy, who listened for a while, then said, "Let her run off at the mouth, I don't care. Only keep her in the house. She ain't going very far without the kid.... Yeah, sure. Another thousand bucks. You think I forgot?"

Buggsy hung up. "The bitch, all she wants is my money." He shrugged. "They're all bitches. You got to learn the hard way."

Norm buried his left fist in Buggsy's stomach. Buggsy looked very surprised as he doubled over, holding his stomach as if Norm had torn something loose from it. Norm hit him in the face with his right fist. The pain shot up to his armpit and across his chest. He wondered how many knuckles were broken.

Buggsy didn't fall down. He staggered around the kitchen, knocking the table over on its side, clutching at the sink for support. He scooped a glass off the drainboard and hurled it at Norm. In the split-second it took Norm to duck, Buggsy reached him. Buggsy used his knee in Norm's groin and the fight was over. Norm sat on the floor with the pain spreading up all over his body.

"Are you crazy?" Buggsy panted. "I ought to kill you."

Norm shook his head. He wanted to talk, but the words wouldn't come. When he tried to push himself up from the floor, he cut his hand on the broken glass. Buggsy got him a drink of water from the sink and he could barely hold it down. He would do whatever Buggsy said. He couldn't do anything else. But he had to hurt him.

"Get up off the floor," Buggsy said. "Come on, get up."

Norm staggered to his feet and began to feel better. He lurched around the kitchen and finally stood against the refrigerator and drew in deep gulps of air.

"You can't go out looking like that," Buggsy said. "You'll attract attention. I want we should be, you know, inconspicuous. You got a pair of dark glasses or something?"

Buggsy followed Norm to the bedroom. Norm found his aviator-style sunglasses in the dresser drawer. When he put them on, Buggsy nodded.

"You can't see them black eyes now," he said. Buggsy didn't miss a trick. "I want we should be friends," Buggsy told Norm. "I know you're upset on account of your old lady. If you play it smart, she'll be fine. Shake." And Buggsy offered his hand.

Norm turned and walked outside. Buggsy followed him to the stolen car, which was parked in Norm's driveway. Nancy stood down the block, in front of the Japanese maple on her lawn, watching them. Debby wasn't with her. Norm got in behind the wheel of the stolen car, waited for Buggsy to climb in back. Then he released the handbrake and backed down the slope of the driveway before he turned on the ignition. In the rearview mirror he could see Buggsy playing with the .357 Magnum, fondling it.

"There won't be no accident on that corner today," Buggsy promised.

CHAPTER SIXTEEN

More and more every day, people in the hot sticky subway would stare at him and start whispering: "That's Stanley Harris, the special prosecutor.... Sure, I've seen his picture in the papers. Some guy.... Boy, it must take guts to go after the racketeers like that.... I'll bet he gets to be D.A. himself some day or even mayor."

That was part of it, Stanley Harris thought. He couldn't deny it. He had more prestige in his neighborhood than a bank president. But there was more. He couldn't very well disappoint the runaway grand jury that was turning Brooklyn upside down. They were doing most of the work and he was getting the credit. What do people know about grand juries? They're not glamorous. People look for a man on horseback. A special prosecutor.

A man on horseback. That was good. A straphanger in the subway. Well, they liked that, too. A Brooklyn product, all the way. Madison High School in Brooklyn and enough ball playing at Marine Park to show he was a red-blooded boy, but not too much so he couldn't study. His folks had wanted him to be a lawyer ever since he remembered.

Then Brooklyn College. Twenty-five dollars a year for books. It was all he could afford. People are learning more and more about less and less, one of his teachers once said—that's education? *I want to learn more and more about less and less. I want to be a lawyer.* And after that, time out for the Army. He had managed to get a job as a clerk in the JAG corps and had even gained experience in the European Theater of Operations reviewing courts-martial of G.I.'s condemned to death for rape and murder.

The captain in charge of the section came from a small town in Maryland, where he would draw up wills for thirty dollars and sometimes less. Stanley Harris—Cpl. Stanley Harris, sir—had yet to go to law school, but already he knew more law than the captain. The captain used to tell how he had to be a bartender nights and weekends for his in-laws in Maryland so he could keep up his law practice.

Then, after the war, Brooklyn Law School. It wasn't Harvard or Columbia, but they taught you how to pass the Bar. They had a better percentage of students passing the New York State Bar than any other law school. The rest, the fine details, you could learn by yourself. You could learn them while you were a law clerk, or afterwards when you were earning a reputation as a smart young lawyer for one of the biggest legal firms in the city. You could learn them and then jump at the opportunity when the governor assigned you as a special prosecutor to assist the runaway grand jury in Kings County.

You have two jobs, Harris. Keep the runaway grand jury happy. And please, whatever you do unless you're looking for trouble and want your head examined, keep the boys from City Hall happy.

So far, he had done the first and hadn't worried about the second. At the beginning, it looked as if he might be taken off the job, but New York's newspapers, with one or two exceptions, did not like the political machine power. Stanley Harris was walking a newspaper-supported tightrope, and sometimes just thinking about it and realizing what he was doing surprised him.

My God, he thought as the express train pulled into Newkirk Avenue, *I'm a crusader.*

The doors opened. The passengers pushed and shoved their way out and walked across the cement platform to the local side.

He was lining up the cases which could send twenty or thirty hoods and assorted racketeers to the room they called the dance hall in Sing Sing. Behind it was the little chamber with the high oaken chair. He was lining them up, but not acting. A little, ulcer-producing quirk of New York State criminal law. Section 399 of the Criminal Code. Stanley Harris knew it by heart. Every prosecutor in the state of New York knew it by heart and wrestled with it.

A conviction cannot be had upon the testimony of an accomplice, unless he is corroborated by such other evidence as tends to connect the defendant with the commission of the crime.

It was almost as if the Lepkes and Lucianos and Anastasias and Moores and Fassolinos had written Section 399 into the Criminal Code. From time to time, punks sang. When the gang turned against them, they sang for protection. When the law put on a periodic squeeze, they didn't want to be the last to desert the sinking ship. There were other reasons—all sorts of reasons. But the Combination didn't publish a trade newspaper. When a punk sang, the song was about what he knew, what he witnessed, what he was a part of. That meant he was an accomplice. Unless his testimony could be corroborated, it didn't mean a thing. You compiled the lengthy, carefully worked-out, logical briefs and waited.

Like the Leo Rose killing. Twelve years ago, Rose's brother had owned a small trucking firm which delivered bread and cake for a chain of bakeries in Brooklyn. Rose's brother refused to play ball with the trucking union, which was one of Eugene Moore's enterprises. While driving along Flatbush Avenue in Brooklyn, Rose's brother got a sixty-watter for his troubles, a vial of muriatic acid thrown in his face. He was scarred for life.

Leo Rose barged into the trucking union, blood in his eye. No one knew anything about his brother. There was a fight. Rose was booked for assault, posted bail, went to borrow money from a Brooklyn shylock named Buggsy Green to pay for his defense. He had already contacted Green's friends, and word got out why he wanted the money.

On the face of what information Stanley Harris had, it could be alleged that Green asked the Brooklyn troop boss, Louis Fassolino, about it. Fassolino went upstairs and asked Eugene Moore, who owned the trucking union, among other things. Rose was getting noisy. Rose was going to tell the district attorney everything. Even if he was cleared of the assault charge, he would still make trouble. He had been a little guy, but that kind.

Hit him, Eugene Moore had said. It had come to the special prosecutor indirectly. *Hit him,* Louis Fassolino was told. *Hit him,* Fassolino told the shylock, Buggsy Green, and his cohort, Big Danny Cooper.

"You, Rudy," Big Danny had told a thug named Rudolph Seigal, "you heist a car."

Rudy was there when the orders went out to Cooper and Green, but because Rudy went for the murder vehicle he was an accomplice. He later sang his lungs out. From his information, the whole story could be pieced together. That one case would go a long way toward clearing the books for Brooklyn.

However, it was useless. Rudy Seigal was an accomplice.

Cooper and Green had murdered Leo Rose with an ice pick and a blunt instrument, then set him afire in the Canarsie dunes. According to Rudy, a punk had driven the murder car for them. No one had ever been able to find out who the punk was.

Stanley Harris sighed and lifted his heavy briefcase off the cement platform as the local train pulled in to Newkirk Avenue. Even if they did find the punk, he would be an accomplice too, his testimony interesting but useless.

Unless the punk had been *forced* to drive the murder car. Unless he had been frightened into doing it with no foreknowledge. Maybe then they had a case. But such things happened only in the movies.

Stanley Harris pushed his way into the crowded local train. He moved across the car and stood next to the outside door. The train stopped at Avenue H. A few people got off and headed for the stairs at the end of the platform. Now, in summer, big maples thrust their higher branches over the platform. It was quiet there, except for the train. Not at all like the noise and confusion downtown. It was hard to believe this was part of the same teeming borough which had witnessed so many crimes of violence.

The train pulled in at Avenue J. During the rush hour, the exit on the north side of the street would be open. Using it, he wouldn't have to cross over. He always went down that way. Habit. He had been doing it ever since he'd taken the special prosecutor's job.

The sun was still hot on the pavement downstairs. The women in sunback dresses walked by with shopping bags on their arms. Most of the men were carrying newspapers and looked uncomfortable in jackets and ties. Stanley Harris had a copy of the *World-Telegram and Sun* under his arm. He tried to read a different paper every night so he could tell which way the wind was blowing.

He crossed East Seventeenth Street and headed east on Avenue J. The stores under the El and to the west of it gave way immediately to a residential section which would continue on the other side of crowded, noisy Ocean Avenue.

The sun was hot on his back. He could feel a single drop of sweat roll down his side from his armpit. It was ten to six.

There was this punk he knew who used to love beating up the women, Big Danny thought. Hell, you never would have expected it. He was a mild-looking little guy up in Sunny Jim's poolroom all the time but probably the worst pool player in Brooklyn. He used to get excited reading in the newspapers about the queers who burned their initials in girls' thighs or on their breasts. But he used to hurt them with his hands. That was how he got his kicks. Maybe he was still doing it, Big Danny thought.

Everyone's like that. Everyone's queer in some way. You don't go around with a sandwich sign telling people about it, that's all.

Big Danny was sitting in the back seat of a four-door Mercury sedan which had been heisted on St. John's Place near Albany Avenue. A punk named Angelo D'Espirito was up front behind the wheel, patting the gas pedal every now and then so the idling engine which had overheated wouldn't conk out. The car was parked on Avenue J, seventy-five feet east of the southeast corner of Ocean Avenue and Avenue J. Angelo D'Espirito looked worried.

On Big Danny's lap was a square-butted, long-barreled Luger. He looked at his watch. Ten to six. Out of sight around the corner, Buggsy would be waiting with that Fisher punk from Long Island. Big Danny spat through the rolled-down window.

Someone was going to pay for what happened yesterday. He didn't know who. He hardly cared. He figured if he played it right, though, he could be the executioner. Maybe the big blonde dame in the nurse's get-up. Big Danny had never killed a woman, except in a double contract once, where a husband and wife got it. Maybe Li'l Paisan Ucci. Shivering fingers climbed up and down Big Danny's spine. That would be some contract, with the whole Jersey troop standing in the way. Even hitting Buggsy wouldn't be that exciting.

Big Danny tapped Angelo D'Espirito's shoulder. Angelo jumped. "Drive around the block," Big Danny said. "Drive slow." It was eight minutes to six. They would cruise around the block and approach the corner of Ocean and J from the south. Big Danny slid over to the right-hand side of the Mercury's rear seat. When they got there they would be so close he could practically lean out the window and shake hands with Buggsy. He would fire his Luger three times and there would be nothing left of Buggsy's face. If he had time, he might hit the Fisher punk, too. He wasn't sure. The Combination didn't go for uncontracted killings, but Fisher wasn't going to set Buggsy up the way he was supposed to.

Big Danny thought it was like shutting off the light and climbing into bed with the best lay in Brownsville. It was better. It was like nothing else. At times like this, Big Danny wished he understood more about science. Astronomy? Anatomy? Something like that. When the pills took Buggsy's face, they'd hit his brain too, and the injured brain would stop sending messages down to the body for breathing and heartbeat. And Buggsy would be dead. Maybe he could get a doctor to explain it to him better one of these days.

He could spot Buggsy's car a mile away. The black one, pulled up alongside the ice-cream truck. With Buggsy, filling a contract was just a business. What did Buggsy know about killing people? He'd carried out as many jobs as Big Danny, but he didn't get a charge out of them.

Buggsy didn't feel the tingling, delightful anticipation, the rapid beating of his heart, pounding inside his throat and up in his ears. He didn't smell death or taste it on a dry tongue licking drier lips. He didn't feel it in his feet, weak with excitement, or in his stomach like Big Danny, who always was hungry after a contract because he could never eat before it or sleep or do anything but wait. He could only count off the hours and the impossibly slow minutes and the seconds until everything would explode in a blinding wild surging thrill which took a man deep inside and churned him, turning him inside out and cleaning him, leaving him limp and tired but fulfilled. And if he had to do the getaway driving himself, he would just sit there and wait for the cops and say, "I did it. Yes, I did it." This was what made punks like Angelo D'Espirito, now rolling the Mercury slowly not fifty yards behind Buggsy's double-parked black sedan, necessary.

My boy, Louis Fassolino told himself, *my own boy from the old days. Buggsy. I still can't believe it. But that's him, up there in the black car, waiting. The son of a bitch, he would park near the ice-cream truck. Boy, how I could go for a few of those burnt almond ice cream pops now.*

Mr. Fats smacked his thick lips and sighed. Things sure had changed. Ten years ago, Buggsy wouldn't have gone to the men's room unless Mr. Fats gave him permission. Now he was waiting to kill someone the Combination didn't want killed.

Pacing back and forth on the Ocean Avenue sidewalk, Mr. Fats lit a cigar and stared back at the people staring at him. Sure, he was fat. Didn't they ever see a fat man before? There was a law against being fat?

His gray silk sports shirt felt damp and cold, plastered to his body with
sweat. Maybe they were staring because they could tell how he felt. He did-
n't feel so good. There was this trembling, not his hands or legs, but inside
him, in his chest, a funny kind of fluttering. If he didn't have a ticker like the
Rock of Gibraltar, it would be something to worry about. Buggsy would die
of fright if he ever felt that kind of fluttering inside his chest.

The late afternoon sun had just dipped down behind the buildings across
the street. That was better, cooler. It was a close, sticky day, though, the kind
that bothered a fat man. He shouldn't have paid off that taxi driver. He
should have waited in the cab while the sun was still hot and bright.

*Worrying like this, what's the matter with you, Fassolino? You sure have changed.
Buggsy ain't going to do anything he shouldn't, don't you know? Big Danny's around
the corner somewhere. You can't see him, but he's there.* Mr. Fats didn't even have
to come down to see the fireworks. Buggsy was good, but Danny was like
the Mounties or the Lone Ranger: he always got his man.

Mr. Fats thought he'd better find someplace he could sit down. He wasn't
so young anymore. *Only a few more minutes. It's five-fifty now. Hey, what did they
do to the air? I can hardly breathe. They're all looking at me.*

Louis Fassolino staggered across the sidewalk, the sweat dripping from
every pore of his gross body. He opened his mouth wide and tried to scream
for help, but no one heard him. He made such a tiny sound. The pain started just below the fat covering his left pectoral muscle. It was a sharp pain.
Like being jabbed with an icepick. No one withdrew the pick. The more he
tried to breathe the deeper the pick went in. Presently the pain spread across
his whole chest. He lurched toward the ice-cream truck and was going to ask
for three burnt almond pops. If he could eat the three deliciously cold pops,
everything would be fine.

He fell on his face, drumming the sidewalk feebly with his arms, ten yards
short of the ice-cream truck.

"Here he comes now," Eugene Moore told Li'l Paisan.

"Well, I still don't like it," Paisan said.

They were standing on the north side of Avenue J, between East Seventeenth and East Eighteenth Streets. A block west of them, carrying his briefcase in one hand and a newspaper under his other arm, was Stanley Harris.

"That's tough," Eugene Moore said. There was an edge of menace in his
voice. "It was your girl who didn't come through with the Fisher woman.
We're in trouble now, Paisan. You are going to help us out of it."

Li'l Paisan mopped his wet brow with a handkerchief. "You want me to fall
in step with the guy and start talking. But I know what's up there. That Buggsy Green, waiting with a cannon. You want me to commit suicide."

Eugene Moore smiled. "Hardly. I don't want Harris killed. Buggsy knows you. If he sees you with Harris, he'll be afraid to shoot. In case something goes wrong, it will give our man time to get Buggsy. You're merely the premium on an insurance policy, you might say."

"What do I talk to him about?"

"I'll leave that to you. You like publicity anyway. Meeting Harris on the street like this will probably get your name in all the newspapers."

"In the obituary column," Li'l Paisan said glumly.

"Write it any way you want," Eugene Moore said, and crossed the street briskly. He lost himself in the crowds of homeward-bound businessmen who had reached Avenue J on the same train that brought Stanley Harris. When he looked back across the street, Li'l Paisan had fallen into step with Harris. Paisan was gesturing with his small arms and speaking in an agitated manner. Harris looked angry.

"That's what I mean," Li'l Paisan said. "I wouldn't come all the way out here to Brooklyn unless it was important I talked to you. Can't I walk you home a few blocks and talk?"

"Listen, Mr. Ucci," Stanley Harris said. "I don't keep it a secret. I don't like you or any of your kind. If you were part of the Brooklyn mob, it would be different—business. I have no business with you. Someday they'll do the same thing in New Jersey we're trying to do here."

"That's what I want to talk to you about. Brooklyn."

"I don't know what you have on your mind, Mr. Ucci. I'd like to say only this: whatever it is, we ought to go at it in my office tomorrow where a stenographer can take it down."

"If that's what you want, O.K. Just let me tell you about it now." He had to stall for time, say anything. But he didn't know what to say. His palms were moist with sweat. Sweat got in his eyes and made him blink. Buggsy Green was waiting a block and a half away, he was waiting to hit Harris. Maybe Buggsy was so excited, he wouldn't recognize Li'l Paisan. But he had to take the chance. When Eugene Moore said do something, you did it. Especially when he used that tone of voice. That Myrna! He wouldn't kill her. He'd make her so ugly she'd cry just looking at herself every day of her life.

"Well?" Stanley Harris said.

"Is it all right if I talk about it now?"

"That's what you said. That's what you wanted." Harris frowned. "What kind of gag is this, Ucci?"

They crossed East Nineteenth Street, a one-way street running from south to north. Gasoline fumes gave the air a sickening smell as the cars piled up on Avenue J, idling, waiting for the light to change one block ahead on Ocean Avenue. On their left was a weed-grown lot, the only empty lot in the whole neighborhood. It was surrounded by a cyclone fence, the heavy steel wire weathered a rust-flecked gray.

"If you've got anything to say, say it now," Stanley Harris told Li'l Paisan.

They reached Ocean Avenue and waited for the light to change. Diagonally across the street, an ice-cream truck was parked. Something had happened there. A crowd of people was clustered on the sidewalk behind the truck, bending down over an object Li'l Paisan couldn't see. Double-parked alongside the ice-cream truck was a black sedan. There was one man in front and one man in back.

That would be Buggsy.

Li'l Paisan trembled. He wanted to bolt and run for it. He wanted to run down Ocean Avenue and not stop until he reached the park. But Eugene Moore was somewhere nearby, watching.

When the light changed, Li'l Paisan said in a thick voice, "It's like this, Counselor," and began to cross the street with Stanley Harris.

Any second he expected to hear the shattering roar of Buggsy's gun and maybe see a few pills spark on the pavement before one of them caught him.

"Like what?" Stanley Harris wanted to know.

"There's the bum!" Buggsy shouted.

"Look," Pretty Fisher said. "He's not alone. Someone's with him."

"Just mind your own business, Pretty. When the light turns green, go around the corner on Avenue J real slow."

Buggsy thumbed the .357 Magnum off safety. He would hit Harris as soon as he had a clear line of sight.

The prosecutor wasn't alone. Buggsy had been gawking up along Avenue J so long, with the sun glaring down the street between the buildings like a blowtorch through a tunnel, he couldn't see so good. It was his eyes. His eyes were going. One of these days he would find a good doctor who would know something was wrong with him and do something about it.

He squinted. He thought about Rosie and wondered if maybe she'd want a divorce. Screw her. Like everyone else, she was turning against him. *All my friends. I'm a loner now. A sick man, all alone. The only one who ever really loved me was my mother, but that Harris put her away. I'm gonna hit that bum Harris and then worry about the other things.*

A sob caught in his throat. They were crossing Ocean Avenue—Harris and the other bum. He could see them clearly now, with the sun no longer behind them. The other man was Rocco Ucci, the Li'l Paisan, the kingpin of Jersey. The bastards. All the no-good rotten stinking bastards in the world all against him and ganging up. After all he'd done for them, they wanted to screw him because he disagreed with them on one little thing like hitting the prosecutor.

It was all so suddenly clear, Buggsy wanted to laugh. The laughter choked him. He couldn't hold the Magnum steady at the rolled-down window. They were going to purchase a clean slate for themselves by selling out Buggsy. Li'l

Paisan was with the prosecutor now, making the deal. They had enough on
Buggsy to send him up for murder a dozen times if they sang. They were
singing now. Even now the Li'l Paisan was singing in Stanley Harris' ear.
They ought to know better. He could kill them both. He could pull the trigger and kill them both and, in that way, kill a little bit all the other people:
Rosie and the lousy doctors and all the rest, the lousy bastards who did this
to him, putting him up against a wall and making him desperate when he
was getting cancer and heart trouble and everything else. What did they care?
What the hell did they care?

"Turn the corner!" Buggsy screamed. "Turn the damned corner now!"

Norm had seen the other man with Stanley Harris. At first he didn't
remember where, but then it came back to him. Yesterday in the rain on
Horace Harding Boulevard... the little driver of the big Chrysler Imperial.

Arlene's voice on the telephone: *"Whatever he wants you to do, you don't have
to. Don't you see? If it's some kind of trouble and you can get to the police and they
get him, I'll be..."*

She'll be safe. She was going to say she'd be safe before she had been
dragged from the phone. He had waited too long. All the years. There was-
n't much he could do now. Buggsy was at the rear window of the car, waiting too, waiting in time that could be measured in seconds, not years. Seconds in which you could see the cars roll by, heading south from the city, the
drivers tensed and hunched over their wheels or nonchalant with their right
arms resting on the seat backs, driving from habit and practice and making
the right responses. Seconds in which the sun sank imperceptibly lower down
along Avenue J and touched the top of the rusty elevated line with gold.

Stanley Harris and the little man had crossed Ocean Avenue now and were
still walking. The traffic light blackened for a brief instant, then the green disc
was lit.

"Turn the corner!" Buggsy screamed. "Turn the damned corner now!"

Norm released the handbrake. The hazelnut-maple special cost fifteen
cents, a sign on the side of the ice-cream truck said. It showed a boy with
freckles spooning a mouthful of hazelnut-maple special up from the big cup.

Norm stepped on the gas. The big Olds surged forward to the corner. He
turned the wheel.

I can't, he said to himself. *I can't help kill a man. Or two men. This is different,
not like twelve years ago when I didn't know and was so scared I could hardly drive.
I can't.*

But he rounded the corner and cruised slowly at five miles an hour, the needle jiggling back and forth on the lower range of the speedometer. Across the
street, directly across from them, Stanley Harris and the other man were
walking.

From somewhere, Norm heard the faint sound of a siren, wailing and rolling, ebbing and flowing, coming closer. It must have something to do with that crowd behind the ice-cream truck. Someone must have fainted from heat prostration or something like that.

"Now!" Buggsy screamed. "Now, now, now!"

The repeated word was the rasp of a buzz saw. With it, drowning it out, came the explosion of Buggsy's .357 Magnum. Three shots in rapid succession.

I can't.

Norm jerked the wheel to the right, driving the Olds against the sidewalk, then slamming the no-shift gear lever from low to reverse and back again, stepping on the gas and rocking the car violently.

"You bastard, cut that crap out or I'll kill you!"

Across the street, one of the men was down. Not Harris. Harris was bending over him, examining him. People were running toward them. The siren was louder, right behind them.

Norm leaped over the rear seat and threw himself at Buggsy. Buggsy was cursing and trying to bring the .357 Magnum around to point it at him, but Norm fell across his body. He pushed him back against the foam rubber upholstery, held his wrist, butted his chin.

Just then there was the sound of more gunfire. A Mercury sped by, someone leaning out the rear window and firing at them. Norm didn't see the face. Because he had jumped on Buggsy and pinned him down, no one was hurt. The Mercury sped away.

The siren growled to a stop, very close. Stanley Harris was shouting and waving his arms.

Buggsy forced the gun up against Norm's cheek and fired it. Norm's head jerked back. He couldn't hear. He never even heard the sound of the Magnum going off. His cheek was on fire. He could smell the gunpowder. There was a neat hole in the ceiling fabric of the car and the metal roof above it.

Buggsy was laughing. Buggsy was drooling and hardly fighting now but waving his arms and shouting soundlessly. There were bubbles on his chin and rolling down his neck. Norm grabbed the .357 Magnum away from him and began to beat him over the head with it. Buggsy kept on laughing and laughing silently until finally he shut his eyes and just lay there with a pleasant little smile on his face.

Norm opened the rear door of the car. Two policemen were running across the street toward Stanley Harris and the man on the sidewalk. People were coming from all directions like iron filings toward a magnet. Norm crossed the street after the policemen. He was still holding Buggsy's .357 Magnum. One of the policemen turned and struck it out of his hand. It clattered in the gutter.

"That's O.K.," Norm said. "That's fine, Officer. I only want to talk to Mr. Harris." He hoped he was saying that. He couldn't hear the words. He couldn't hear anything. The policeman opened his mouth and said something.

After Norm lost consciousness, the policeman carried him to the sidewalk.

It was a large room. He was not alone in it, but at first his mind could not struggle back from its womb of not worrying, not feeling, not thinking.

He opened his eyes and watched the figures hovering near him. He could tell they were close, but they seemed somehow to be swimming through blue, blue water, far away. When his eyes cleared, he recognized Stanley Harris, the special prosecutor.

"He didn't kill you," Norm said in a hoarse voice.

"Take it easy," someone told him. "Drink this." He was given a glass. He drank what was in it, a bitter liquid which seemed to rush at once to his extremities, giving him strength.

"You did a lot of delirious talking, Fisher," Stanley Harris said. "Would you be ready to repeat it under oath in a court of law?'"

Norm sat up. Light stabbed violently in through his eyes and he shut them tight. "Arlene," he said. "Buggsy's got..."

"Yon talked about that, too. Your wife is safe now, Fisher. We contacted the Nassau County police."

"Thank God," Norm said. "God, if he had hurt them..."

"I said take it easy. They're safe now. You were talking about a lot of things. About what happened in Brownsville and out in the Canarsie dunes twelve years ago. About a man named Leo Rose."

There was a tired look on Stanley Harris' face, a look which said the years had been crowding Stanley Harris as they, had been crowding Norm. "I believe we can wrap it up if Fisher testifies," Harris said to someone behind him. "With his testimony, we'll have the corroboration we need. Fassolino's dead, but we'll have Green and Cooper—yes, and even Moore—facing a murder charge as soon as we can present the evidence to a grand jury."

The other man shook his head slowly. "Fisher drove the murder car. That makes him an accomplice. According to law, his testimony is no good without corroboration."

"You're wrong," Stanley Harris said. "I think we can show how Fisher drove the murder car without intent, twelve years ago. Now, first through his idolization of Cooper and Green, then his fear, he took part in the murder. That makes his evidence valid." Stanley Harris smiled. "About the only thing they can charge Fisher with is transporting a corpse through the streets of Brooklyn without a license." But he stopped smiling and added, "I think."

He lit a cigarette and said, "Tell me, Fisher. Are you ready to try it?"

Arlene was safe and so was Gary. Soon he would be seeing them again. And with the special prosecutor's help, perhaps he could awake from twelve years of nightmare. Through the dark squares of the windows, Norm could hear the muted noises of traffic outside. Somewhere out there, a small boy laughed, the sound fading happily into the unseen distance.

"Yes," Norm said. "I'm ready. I'm ready now."

THE END